THRESHOLD

ALSO BY JEREMY ROBINSON

The Didymus Contingency

Raising the Past

Beneath

Antarktos Rising

Kronos

Pulse

Instinct

THRESHOLD

A Jack Sigler Thriller

JEREMY ROBINSON

Thomas Dunne Books   St. Martin's Press   New York

This is a work of fiction. All of the characters, organizations, and events portrayed in this novel are either products of the author's imagination or are used fictitiously.

THOMAS DUNNE BOOKS.
An imprint of St. Martin's Press.

www.thomasdunnebooks.com
www.stmartins.com

Library of Congress Cataloging-in-Publication Data

Robinson, Jeremy, 1974–
   Threshold : a Jack Sigler thriller / Jeremy Robinson. — 1st ed.
     p. cm.
   ISBN 978-0-312-54030-2
   1. Terrorism—Prevention—Fiction.   I. Title.
   PS3618.O3268T47 2011
   813'.6—dc22

                       2010042215

First Edition: April 2011

10 9 8 7 6 5 4 3 2 1

For Norah, Solomon, and Aquila,
because you're at your best when you're together.

ACKNOWLEDGMENTS

Threshold is my seventh novel. My third hardcover. And my best book to date—I know, I know, I have to say that, but it's true! As I look back at the past few years I'm amazed and thrilled to see that the same people who supported me when I self-published my first novel, when I used three credit cards to start my own small press (Breakneck Books), and when I moved on to Thomas Dunne Books, are still in my life and as supportive as ever. So it's with great appreciation that I thank the following.

Stan Tremblay and Walter Elly, you guys get top billing this year. The time and effort you two put into helping me with web design, social marketing, and something I'm typically not prone to do: relaxing, is amazing. Some people say that it takes a village to raise a baby. Well, I say it takes a village to write a novel. You guys are my village. C'mon, group man-hug!

For consummate proofreading and story comments, I once again thank Roger Brodeur.

Thanks to my agent, Scott Miller at Trident Media Group, who discovered my first self-published book, signed me on, and has been a shrewd counselor since. Thanks also to MacKenzie at Trident Media for being fast, diligent, and fun. Go team Miller!

Now for the people at Thomas Dunne Books, who put the Jack Sigler series on the map. Thanks to Peter Wolverton, my editor. Your advice has improved my story telling immensely, a gift for which I will always be grateful. Anne Bensson, you are an amazing source of fast answers to my endless questions and an awesome support. Rafal Gibek and the production team, if not for your awesome copy-edits, people would think I was a dolt. For the incredible jacket design, thanks to art director Steve Snider and illustrator extraordinaire, Larry Rostant, whose work has always impressed and inspired me.

And always last in my acknowledgments, but never least, I thank my kick-ass wife, Hilaree, who was graced with the ability to put up with and love a moody author and artist. And to my children, Aquila, Solomon, and Norah, you remind me what it means to be a child and help keep my imagination free of the prison known as adulthood. I love you guys.

WHAT IS THIS?

Dear reader,

You may have noticed this odd looking code on the jacket of *Threshold*. For those of you who know what it is, I hope the content it revealed was an enjoyable treat. For the rest of you, keep reading to find out how you can use the code.

The official term for the graphic is QR Code, which stands for Quick Response Code. The matrix of black squares on white space encodes text, including active URLs. The code can be read by anyone with a camera equipped cell phone or smart phone, especially newer products such as the iPhone, Droid, and BlackBerry. All that's needed is a QR Code scanner app (see below to download your own). The QR Code for *Threshold* features a king chess piece, representing everyone's favorite Delta operative, Jack Sigler, call sign King.

I have always strived to be on the forefront of marketing technology, being one of the first to create viral videos, video trailers, virtual book signings, podcast novels, iPhone Apps, iPhone Games, and alternate reality games, all for the promotion of my novels. The QR Code is the next step in the evolution of book marketing and I'm thrilled to be one of the first novelists in the United States to utilize the technology.

If you would like to download a QR Code scanner for your phone or computer, visit: www.jeremyrobinsononline.com/qrcode for links to the best applications available.

Thanks for checking out the QR code, and for reading!

Sincerely,
Jeremy Robinson

Sick I am of idle words, past all reconciling,
Words that weary and perplex and pander and conceal,
Wake the sounds that cannot lie, for all their sweet beguiling;
The language one need fathom not, but only hear and feel.
—George Du Maurier (1834–1896)

5 But the Lord came down to see the city and the tower that the men were building. 6 The Lord said, "If as one people speaking the same language they have begun to do this, then nothing they plan to do will be impossible for them. 7 Come, let us go down and confuse their language so they will not understand each other."
—Genesis 11:5–7

Mathematics is the language in which God has written the universe.
—Galileo Galilei (1564–1642)

THRESHOLD

PROLOGUE
The Past

HE CONTROLLED THE world through fear—merciless fear—conjured by the memory of genocide. He had scraped the earth clean, leaving only a single bloodline alive. To remember. To fear.

But Nimrod saw through the fear, watching how it manipulated the populace like silt stirred in the Euphrates. When the rains came and the thunder boomed, the people cringed and turned to the mysterious Originator for direction. When food was scarce, they tore at their clothes and begged for mercy.

The Originator demanded nothing less, despite his promise.

Nimrod doubted that such a promise had been made, just as he doubted the validity of the mass extermination story. It had been, no doubt, conjured by his great-grandfather to control the people. And he would not fear something or someone that was not real. He would not be controlled.

As a man, he learned that fear could motivate men to do *his* work. With whip, club, and spear, he had instilled a greater fear in men than the Originator could with the story of a deluge that few living people claimed to remember. It was with this fear that Nimrod came to power and laid the foundations of his kingdom. The cities of Uruk, Akkad, and Calneh flourished under his rule, finding plentiful food and water on the shores of two mighty rivers. But it was Babylon, nestled between the Tigris and Euphrates, that had become his greatest achievement.

But even glorious Babylon would soon be outdone and the Originator's annoying voice would be reduced to a faint whisper, fading along with an age of paranoia.

As a direct descendant of his people's founding father, he had been privy to the secrets of the language supposedly taught to mankind by the Originator himself. Not only could words move the hearts and minds of men through fear, but they could also move mountains. And move mountains they did. For with them, he had constructed a tower unlike anything humanity had ever seen, rising toward the sky, higher than any thought possible. Its ominous presence instilled fear into all who saw it.

Nimrod stroked the long, gnarled hair growing from his chin. It was black with a thin streak of gray. His face, thick and leathery from long days in the sun, was just beginning to show signs of his age. But his body was healthy and fit. Combined with his formidable height and baritone voice, it wasn't hard for him to subjugate the people.

But even fear, it seemed, had its limits. For on the eve of what was to be the consummation of his greatest achievement, he had learned some distressing news.

Treachery.

It seemed his family shared some of his resistance to the compulsion of fear. But rather than use the fear, his great uncle, Shem, conspired against it.

Against *him*.

So as he sat alone in the central chamber of his newly constructed ziggurat, he considered the available options. Speaking to his uncle was out of the question. Leniency would reveal weakness, and weakness would give strength to the opposition. But without knowing the true strength of his enemies, or their numbers, he was acting blindly. A dangerous undertaking.

He needed something definitive. Something that would be feared for generations.

That's when he saw the hands. Strong and unyielding. Impervious to sword or spear, and loyal to him—the creator of gods. The statues surrounding him in the large central chamber stood fifteen feet tall, and featured the heads of wild creatures and the bodies of men—images of the heroes of old. The men of renown. The gods given shape by *his* hands and life by *his* words.

As though a block had been removed from a dam, ambition surged into his mind, filling his thoughts with images of a magnificent future. The true capabilities of the power hidden within their language were further reaching than he had ever dreamed.

The Originator, living or not, had abandoned them. And he would be replaced by someone who truly understood how to instill fear and gain loyalty all the while being praised.

He looked at one of the tall statues, whose mighty hands now stretched up to the ceiling but had just months ago laid the very stones of the ziggurat's foundation. It would begin with them.

The people had grown accustomed to their presence, but still trembled at their passing. Now they would witness their fears made real.

Nimrod stood from his chair, and walked to the nearest statue. He leaned into the marble, looked up at the large blue eyes, and spoke in the language of his forefathers, using the tones and inclinations taught to him alone.

"Versatu elid vas re'eish clom, emet."

He moved on to the next statue and repeated the phrase. He continued around the room, speaking the words into stone, ten times.

He strode back to his throne, which felt more comfortable as the growing knots in his back unwound. The assurance that normality would be restored before the rising sun cast his tower's shadow over the plains allowed him to relax again.

Even if just for a moment.

The heavy wooden door to the inner chamber swung open and clunked against the solid stone wall. Azurad, his most trusted advisor, rushed into the room speaking quickly, his long mustache twitching with each syllable.

"Slow down, Azurad. Breathe. And tell me what has you so troubled."

Azurad rested his hands on his knees, his purple tunic hanging down to the floor, which was thick with dust from a year of construction. He took a long slow breath through his nose, smelling the same earthy dust, stood straight and spoke. "My lord, Shem and his followers are approaching."

The knots returned.

"Their number?"

"In the hundreds."

Nimrod felt his chest tighten for a moment. *Hundreds* of men? It seemed an impossible number. He would be undone . . . if not for the giants now waking behind him. He couldn't see them, but the widening eyes of his advisor revealed their animation.

"You . . . you would use them . . . to kill?"

"The gods of old are not bound by—"

"You will bring down *his* wrath!"

Nimrod stood quickly. "What did you say?" He stabbed an index finger upwards. "*His* wrath is empty in comparison to mine. *His* strength is as . . ." Something was wrong. Azurad's face should have shown fear. But he was confused instead.

"Speak, what bothers you so?" Nimrod waited a moment. "Speak!"

And then he did. But Nimrod couldn't understand a word the man uttered. The sounds of his words were like nothing Nimrod had ever heard before, clearly enunciated, but sharp and fluid at the same time.

Yet he did understand the advisor's facial expressions. The fear he'd expected before came with a flush of red in the man's face. Then he screamed and ran away.

A shadow flickering in the torchlight fell around Nimrod. It moved, but not because of the wavering flame. The motion belonged to something else. Nimrod sucked in a quick breath and held it. He had yet to issue his commands to the silent giants. They should have waited for his word before moving, their minds filled only with his bidding. He turned around slowly, his eyes landing on the stomach of the closest statue.

What are they doing? he thought, and then registered the movement above the statue's head. Its clenched fists, each the size of a man's skull, rose up above its lion's head. Despite its face remaining as frozen as ever, he understood the intent behind its action.

For the first time in his life, Nimrod's eyes filled with tears. The fists dropped. The statues surrounded him, reaching for his body like wild animals, and tore him limb from limb.

Shem stood behind them, watching, arms crossed over his chest. Nimrod never knew that others in his family had learned several of the ancient language's secrets—secrets they would carry with them through the generations but never again fully entrust to a single man. Wielded by the double-edged sword that is the tongue of man, all of creation could be corrupted. Nimrod had shown him that much.

As he watched the blood of his nephew's body slide through the dust on the floor and seep into the cracks, he said a quick good-bye. "Eliam vin mortast."

Shem's heart beat hard in his chest. He understood the phrase he spoke as "Return to the Originator," but the sounds that came from his mouth were strange. He had spoken in a new tongue, one he had never heard before. He tried to remember the sounds of his native language, but only pieces remained. Most of the words, and the power they held, had been erased from his mind.

When Shem met his men outside, he found them confused and agitated. Like him, they were all speaking a new language, but they weren't all the same. The men spoke at least ten different dialects. Using hand gestures to communicate, he separated the men into groups by the sounds of their words. Out of several hundred men, Shem found only thirty-three that could understand and speak his new language.

He looked over his army, once united to protect the sanctity of their language, now separated. Could they ever work together again? *This is Nimrod's fault,* Shem thought. *He defiled the Originator's words and now the tongues of men have been confused.*

His men looked to him for guidance, but he knew only thirty-three could understand his words. Instead of speaking, he raised his hands toward the sky in a sign of supplication they all understood. As one, the men fell to their knees and, in twenty-three different languages, prayed.

LOST

ONE
2009

AS HE RAN the blood covering the man's body stiffened with coagulation. The smell of it, like dirty pennies, overpowered the pine scent of the forest around him. He staggered forward, thankful to still be alive but in tremendous pain from his still healing injuries, which burned as though held to a flame.

He clambered up a rise, slipping on the thick mat of pine needles and moist leaf litter. He had survived the impossible already, but if he were caught by his pursuers, life would not be worth living. Not for a very long time.

So he ran on despite the pain.

After topping the crest, he slid down the other side, searching for some means of escape, but saw only tree trunks, rising up to the clear blue sky above.

Suddenly, his breath returned in full. He paused, feeling better in the brief reprieve, but still unable to turn his head or inspect the wounds he'd received. The burning had faded, but was quickly being replaced by an intense itch.

A distant explosion urged him back to his feet. The battle continued without him, but it would end soon, and they would come for him.

Running down the hill, he wove through the trees until coming to a path worn into the forest floor. He followed it, pushing his way through the overgrowth.

Minutes later, a wall of white in the distance gave him hope. Upon reaching the white fence, he smiled. Beyond the fence lay a lawn of bright green grass in need of a cut and a large house with a garage nearly as big. He waited for as long as he dared, watching and listening. Detecting no life, he moved around the fence and approached the side of the house.

The driveway was empty.

He headed for the front of the home. A swing attached to the ceiling of the long farmer's porch swayed in the summer breeze. Nothing else stirred. Looking across the street, he saw the home's mailbox popped open and packed with mail.

No one had been home in a while. *On vacation*, the man thought, and then eyed the large four-car garage. He found the side door unlocked and entered. The first two spots were empty, but a tarp covered something in the third. He rushed to it, his pulse quickening. The tarp slid free easily as he pulled it, revealing a perfectly polished, black 1957 Pontiac Star Chief, its chrome sparkling in the blue light cast from the garage's overhead fluorescents. It wouldn't be fast, but no one would suspect the vehicle was a getaway car, either.

He opened the door and slid, awkwardly, into the driver's seat. Wondering for a moment if he would have to search the house for the keys, he looked down at the ignition and found them hanging there, complete with rabbit's foot.

It was turning out to be his lucky day after all.

He turned the key and the old engine roared to life. Smiling, he reached up and hit the garage-door button attached to the sun visor. The door rumbled open, filling the garage with daylight. He put the car in gear, rolled out into the driveway, and pushed the garage-door button once again.

He glanced in the rearview mirror, watching as the door closed completely. He wanted to leave no obvious trace of his being here. He looked out the driver's side window, searching the pavement for drops of blood, but his wounds had long since stopped bleeding and his clothes had dried. Unfortunately, there was not time to change from the rancid clothes, but he would find something on the road before long, when he was free of his enemies.

Not remembering if he'd closed the side door to the garage, he adjusted the rearview mirror, but moved it too far, catching the side of his face in its view. He leaned in close to inspect the bloody marks on his face and grinned as he found no wound marring the surface.

As he leaned back, an awkward pressure pushed against his back, like a clump of clothing or a wrapped-up towel had fallen between him and the seat. As he turned to look, the rearview mirror caught his attention once again. Not only could he see his face, but a second rising up behind him.

Had the man's baritone scream not been contained by the thick metal and glass of the classic car, anyone who heard it might have mistaken the cry for that of a local moose. As it was, no one heard the man, or saw him, again.

TWO
2010

"JACK SIGLER, PLEASE take the stand."

Jack Sigler, call sign King, sat down on the stand next to the Honorable Judge Samantha Heinz, who had been staring at him with distrust since he walked into the courtroom. It was an unfortunate circumstance that most military child-custody cases involved the active-duty father losing his family for one unsavory reason or another. Ultimately, King knew most of the soldiers were not to blame—combat tended to do awful things to those not wired for it. And most people weren't. He looked at the judge as she stared down at him over her thick glasses.

As the bailiff swore him in, King thought about the path that had brought him, one of the world's most elite soldiers, to a custody hearing. Six months earlier he had been summoned to the Siletz Reservation in Oregon by, he believed, his lifelong friend and the former fiancé of his deceased sister, George Pierce. But the message turned out to be phony, and when King arrived at the reservation he had found it in ruins. The town was in flames. Thousands of people were dead. And mysteriously, a little girl appeared in the backseat of his car with a note pinned to her:

King—this one is for you. I've gone after the rest.

The symbol belonged to Alexander Diotrephes, a man King believed to be the historical, and living, Hercules. His team had first encountered the man two years previous while searching for a way to stop the Hydra—one of Hercules's ancient foes reborn by modern genetics. Alexander had been aloof and mysterious, commanding a loyal following he called the Herculean Society and strange creatures they deemed wraiths. Before disappearing he had provided them with the means to stop the Hydra's ability to regenerate its body and to kill it. But he hadn't been seen since, and all efforts to track him down led to dead ends. The symbol on the note was the only proof they had that the man still existed.

Believing the girl was in grave danger, he took her to Fort Bragg where she could be under constant supervision and protection, not just by the team, but also by the thousands of Special Forces troops stationed at Bragg. Short of a nuclear missile strike, there was no safer place on earth. But that did not satisfy North Carolina's Division of Social Services office, who could not accept that a twelve-year-old orphan could be raised successfully by a team of Delta operators.

King looked around the oak courtroom, smelling the dry, dusty air. The room was essentially devoid of people, with only a child welfare representative, the bailiff, court reporter, and judge present.

The judge cleared her throat. "Mr. Sigler, as you know, this hearing is really just a formality. You have the support of some very impressive people, not the least of which is the president of the United States. That you will receive temporary custody of Fiona Lane is a foregone conclusion. However, I do not lack resources of my own, so if I feel for a moment that you are being facetious or dishonest with me, I will make such a stink that even you will beg for mercy."

She didn't know exactly who King was, but she knew his line of work, that he was close to the president, and that all other details of his professional life were classified.

"I understand," he said.

"Good." She straightened some papers on her desk and stared at them for a moment. "Then I have a few simple questions for you and you can be on your way."

King nodded.

The judge smiled. "You know, almost every single time I've said that to a soldier, the response has been 'fire away.'"

"Happy to disappoint."

"Fiona Lane. Interesting name for a Native American."

There was no question in the statement, but King thought the woman might be testing his knowledge of Fiona's past. "Many Native Americans adopted more English-sounding names. Her grandfather renamed himself George Lane. Her grandmother became Delores Lane. Her father was also named George and her mother was Elizabeth. But Fiona's middle name is more traditional. Apserkahar. It means Horse Rider."

She gave him a good squint and then asked, "Is Fiona Lane in danger?"

"Absolutely," he replied.

"From whom?"

"That's classified, ma'am."

"'Your Honor,' thank you. Is she safe?"

"As safe as she can be, Your Honor."

"Is she safe with *you*?"

"I would give my life to protect hers."

The judge's eyes widened a bit. "I'm not sure I buy that."

"It's what I do, Your Honor. I would give my life to protect yours as well."

That got a genuine smile from the judge. "Is this what you do in your line of work, Mr. Sigler? Risk your life to save others?"

"It's the duty of every enlisted soldier."

She looked back down at her desk, mumbling an affirmative but noncommittal "Mmm."

"And what about her special needs?"

This brought a confused look to King's face. The term "special needs" instantly made him think of people with developmental disabilities, but Fiona certainly didn't fit in that category. She was brilliant, funny, and because she insisted on participating in many of the team's training exercises, was more active than the average twelve-year-old girl. "Excuse me?"

The judge looked at a sheet of paper, head turned up, eyes looking down so she could read through the lower half of her bifocals. "It says here that she has type one diabetes."

King tried to show no reaction and thought, *Since when is diabetes a special need?*

"Yes, Your Honor," he said.

"Tell me about it."

"Her diabetes?"

"Yes."

"As you said, she has type one diabetes. It presented three years ago. While on the reservation she managed it with insulin shots. We now have her on an insulin pump."

The judge nodded and made a note. "Last question, Mr. Sigler."

He looked up at her, thankful that the experience was almost over. Accustomed to fatigues or T-shirt and jeans, the suit he wore—bought specifically for this occasion—was uncomfortable and hot. His black hair was neatly combed, rather than its typically slightly unkempt state. And the smooth skin of his face, usually covered in a thin layer of scruff, highlighted his strong jaw while revealing a few small scars.

She leaned over, looked him dead in the eyes, and asked, "Will you be a good father?"

King froze. It was not a question he'd been expecting. His own father had left when he was sixteen, three months after his sister, Julie, died in an air force training accident. And before he left the man had been far from a model father. As a result, King had never pictured himself having children of his own and dreaded the idea of being a father. If the rest of the team hadn't backed out of the job, if someone else had recovered Fiona from Siletz, if she had not bonded to him so quickly, or if there were anyone else he felt could protect her as well, he would not be in this courtroom.

"Yes," he replied. "Yes, I will."

The judge looked at him for another moment and then sat back. "Very well. The court finds that Mr. Sigler is fit to be the foster parent of Fiona Lane and grants him temporary custody of her, effective immediately."

"Your Honor." The child welfare representative stood up. "The state would like to request visiting rights so that we might be able to keep detailed progress notes on Ms. Lane's education, home life, and an accurate appraisal of her safety inside the confines of Fort Bragg. When the powers that be determine that Fiona is safe to live outside the protection of Fort Bragg and Mr. Sigler, we would like to find her a permanent home with a stable adoptive family."

The judge turned to King. "Is this acceptable to you?"

King nodded. "Yes."

Two knocks sounded as the judge brought her gavel down twice. "Court adjourned. You're free to go, Mr. Sigler."

"All rise," the bailiff said loudly.

As King was the only person seated, aside from the court reporter, he stood and watched the judge exit the room swiftly. When she was gone, he stepped down from the stand and walked toward the back of the courtroom, not looking anyone in the eye as he did so. If he had, they might have seen the guilt that took all his effort to hide from the judge.

He'd lied under oath.

He dreaded the idea of being a father and knew it was one job he was not qualified for. But there was no choice. Fiona had to be kept safe; not because he cared for her as a father should, but because she was the only lead they had in the investigation of an event that took thousands of American lives. Solving *that* problem *was* his job, which made Fiona his job as well.

For now, King thought.

KING HAD SEVERAL meetings after the hearing and then went out for a drink. He told himself he needed to think, but the truth was he was afraid to go home. King, leader of the most elite Special Ops team in the U.S. military, was afraid of a twelve-year-old girl. His mind was a tangle of thoughts as he tried to figure out how he would handle this new, very foreign responsibility. Could he raise a child, even for a short time? He could protect her, sure, but could he give her all the other things a kid needed? Education? Affection? Love?

As he sipped his Sam Adams he decided the first thing he'd do was have only one drink. Wanting to get his mind off his worries, he turned his attention to the TV. CNN was covering, as usual, the rants of one Senator Lance Marrs of Utah—who looked like a wrinkly Pillsbury Doughboy with slick hair and angry eyes. After losing the last election to Tom Duncan, Marrs had made a career out of spouting fear-based propaganda that blamed President Duncan for everything from 9/11 to the nation's financial woes that began two administrations ago. And the cable networks ate it up, adding a thick dose of bias and regurgitating it for the masses. *I'll stick with PBS*, King thought, before requesting the channel be changed. He nursed his beer for another hour, giving up on it when the brew reached room temperature. He left the glass half empty and headed home, knowing Rook, who was babysitting, would be eager to start his Friday night.

Good-bye Friday-night drinks, King thought, as he pulled up to his modest two-bedroom ranch home at Fort Bragg. *Hello Saturday-morning cartoons*.

King opened the front door. The air inside smelled of popcorn and spray paint, which was odd but not unexplainable. What bothered him was that all the lights were out. *Why does Rook have the lights off?*

Rook, who was a natural with Fiona thanks to his many sisters, usually had her in bed by nine and waited for King's return in front of the TV. King looked into the open concept kitchen. Not even the microwave clock was on. A quick glance outside at the lit streetlights confirmed his fear. Only *his* power was out.

He closed the front door silently and then listened. He didn't hear a thing, but he did feel a draft. In the dim light provided by the streetlamp outside he looked at the back door. It was wide open.

Something was definitely not right.

And he was unarmed. With a courtroom hearing and several meetings to attend, King hadn't thought to bring his sidearm. He moved silently through the living room and into the kitchen. He kept a locked Sig Sauer above the fridge. He took out the metal case, punched in the code, and opened the lid. His weapon was gone.

Shit, he thought.

Moving faster, King headed for his bedroom, where he had an arsenal hidden in his closet. He stopped outside his bedroom door, which was open. He stuck his head into the room, taking a quick look. The mattress was on the floor and his single dresser was in its regular place. That's when he saw a mound resting on top of the bed, silhouetted against the windows, which were lit from outside.

His mind flashed back to the horrors he had found at the Siletz Reservation. He could smell the smoke and rotting bodies. Homes destroyed.

Fires burning. Electrical wires twitching. He saw Fiona's grandmother, trampled and crushed. And everywhere, mounds of strange gray dust left like a calling card. Just like the mound he saw on his bed.

His chest began to ache as his heart pounded. "Fiona," he whispered.

He moved into the room and crouched by the bed. He reached out to the mound expecting to feel the same granular dust, but instead felt fabric. King let out a sigh of relief. The mound was his blankets.

That's when it happened.

Three rapid-fire clicks.

He was struck in the back.

Then, as he spun, something hit his neck.

The third hit his forehead and stuck.

He reached up expecting to find some kind of hypodermic dart, but clenched his fingers around something soft and rubbery. As his fingers felt the suction cup tip, a high-pitch voice shouted from within the room, "I got him, Rook!"

The lights switched on, filling every room of the home with one-hundred-watt warmth. King squinted in the light and as he searched the room for the source of the voice. He didn't see her.

"Up here," Fiona said.

King turned toward the bedroom door. Fiona, dressed in her black pajamas and black socks, stood on top of it, her back pressed into the upper corner of the room. Her black hair had been pulled back into a tight bun and she wore a black bandanna over her mouth. She held a dart gun in her hands. He recognized it as one of two bright-orange dart guns they had bought, but it had been painted black.

Stan Tremblay, call sign Rook, shouted from the living room. "Sorry, King. Couldn't stop her. I'm out!"

"Where's my gun?" King asked.

"In the closet with the rest," Rook replied.

"Bye, Rook!" Fiona shouted.

"Later, kid! Oh, and sorry about the kitchen floor, King." The front door opened and closed a moment later.

There were a thousand parental things King knew he should say at that moment. *You could have broken your neck if you'd fallen from the door. You had me worried sick. We don't aim guns at people.* And there were just as many nonstandard chew-outs. *What if I was armed? I could have shot you. I could have shot Rook.*

But he didn't say any of that. Instead he said what he really thought. "That was pretty good."

"Pretty good?" Fiona said, her voice full of mischief. "You just got taken out by a girl. And I'm not even a teenager yet. I'd say it was amazing."

He could see her smiling with pride behind the mask. It was an infectious smile, which he was grateful for because it hid his true feelings. He *had* just been taken out by a twelve-year-old girl. The very girl he'd sworn to protect. Was he so distracted by Fiona's presence in his life that he might actually fail to protect her?

She saw his distraction and brought him back to the current situation. "So, are you going to get me down or what?"

"You're the ninja," King said. "You get down on your own."

He started to leave the room. "Rook put me up here."

King gave a shrug, his smile spreading wider. "Taking out a target is useless if you haven't planned your escape." Halfway out the door, King felt a tug on his hair. A sudden weight on his back followed. Fiona had leaped from the door onto his back. She clung to him sideways with one arm and one leg wrapped over his shoulders. His protest was drowned out by her wild laughter.

King held on to her limbs and stepped back into the bedroom. He fell back onto the bed, careful to keep most of his weight off of her. He held her there, pinned and laughing. "King is awesome," he said.

"What?" she asked between laughs.

"King is awesome. Say it."

"Keep dreaming, Dad!"

That's when the laughter faded. She knew he didn't like to be called "dad," but she'd also been unable to fall asleep that night because she knew about the court hearing. She had yet to learn the results.

With her grip on King relaxed, he sat up knowing full well what she was about to ask.

"So," she said, "what's the verdict?"

He turned to her slowly, suddenly uncomfortable. He couldn't find the words. Luckily for him, Fiona was never slow at providing them for him. "Are you my foster father or not?"

He grinned. "I am."

She sat still for a moment, eyes glossing over, lips pinched tight. Seeing her like that, glowing with joy, desperate for affection, and totally vulnerable, put a crack in King's defenses. He let out a small laugh and held his arms out to her. She dove into his embrace and squeezed him tighter than he thought the little girl capable.

He lowered his head onto her small shoulder and repeated the words he knew she needed to hear. "I am."

THREE
Fort Bragg, North Carolina
2011—One Year Later

"NOTHING LIKE THE smell of a firing range on a sunny day," Rook said as he stared down the sight of his .50 caliber Desert Eagle. He pulled the trigger. The loud boom of the powerful handgun was followed by a distant ping as the fired round hit its target. He straightened, took a deep breath, and let it out with an "ahh."

Next to him, Fiona took a deep breath and coughed. "Smells like gunpowder."

King chuckled, running a hand through his messy black hair. "Gunpowder is like an aphrodisiac for Rook."

"An afro-what?"

Remembering that the girl beside him was not only thirteen, but also under his direct care and supervision, King reminded himself to watch what he said. "Never mind."

"Jack Sigler, the perfect role model," Zelda Baker, call sign Queen, said from the next station over. She was cleaning her UMP submachine gun. Her grease-stained "wife-beater" tank top stood in sharp contrast to her wavy blond hair and her face, which was feminine despite the bright red skull-in-star brand burned into her forehead.

Beyond Queen, Shin Dae-jung, call sign Knight, lay on the ground staring through the scope of a sniper rifle at an apple a half mile away. "Ears," he said.

Those not wearing protective gear covered their ears with their hands. A loud clap echoed. A fraction of a second later, the apple ceased to exist. Knight stood and offered the group a cocky grin. He looked at Fiona. "It was a bad apple."

Fiona laughed and said, "Lame."

"Lame?" Knight said. "That apple was more than a half mile away."

"Not the shot," Fiona said. "The joke."

Eric Somers, call sign Bishop, laughed quietly, his barrel chest shaking. He'd already unloaded all of his ammunition and was watching the others from the long wooden bench that stretched along the backside of the outdoor range. He rarely spoke, allowing his actions to speak for him. His quiet laugh was enough to tell Knight he was being mocked.

"Shut up, Bish," Knight said with a wave of his hand.

As King reloaded one of the assorted weapons he'd brought to the range, Fiona picked up his unloaded Sig Sauer. She aimed it downrange. King had never let her fire a real weapon, but she was eager to try. "So when do I get to shoot some bad guys?"

The team fell silent. Killing was something they did. It was their job and they were good at it. But it was not something they took lightly, especially when it came to kids killing people, which happened more than most people wanted to know. King took the gun from her hand. "Killing someone isn't something you should want to do."

"But when they're bad guys—"

"Killing is a last resort."

"But you guys joke about it."

King shared a guilty glance with the others. They were prone to raucous retellings of old missions. King was hoping someone else would join in, but they remained silent. He *was* Dad now, after all.

"Don't confuse happy to be alive with taking pleasure in someone's death." He looked her in the eyes. "Death is never fun."

For a moment King thought Fiona was going to cry. Her eyes grew wet and a slight quiver shook her lip, but she fought it down and tightened her jaw. King fought a grin. The kid was growing a thick skin.

Before the following silence grew awkward, King's cell phone rang. He walked away and flipped it open. "Jack Sigler," he said into the phone. The person on the other end spoke for ten seconds. What was said in that short time stopped King in his tracks. After five more seconds, his head hung low.

King offered a quiet, "Thanks for letting me know," and closed the phone, slipping it into his pocket. When he turned around, the others were waiting, standing around him in a silent semicircle. They knew something dire had happened when they saw a completely foreign emotion on his face: defeat.

"What happened?" Bishop asked.

King looked at each of them, knowing they wouldn't judge him for weeping. But he fought the growing wetness in his eyes, until his eyes met Fiona's. His foster daughter hadn't met her yet. Now she never would. Twin pairs of tears broke free and rolled down King's cheeks. He turned away from the team and said, "My mother is dead."

Three Days Later

"C'mon, Stan, you know this."

Rook leaned back in the yellow leather chair and pushed his legs into the floor to keep his body from sliding out. "Knight, these chairs have got to go. They're like frikken Slip 'n Slides."

"Watch the language, Rook," Queen said. "There are virgin ears in the room."

"The pip-squeak has heard everything there is to hear out of my mouth at this point," Rook said.

"Doesn't mean you should repeat it until she starts talking like a mini-Rook." Knight entered the small living room from the kitchen of his modest on-base home with an apron around his waist and flour covering his black designer shirt. He smiled, which turned his almond-shaped brown eyes, courtesy of his Korean heritage, to thin slits. "I think you're just trying to squirm your way out of the question."

Knight headed back into the kitchen. "We're a go for dinner in five."

Rook rubbed a hand through his blond hair, which was two inches shorter than his long goatee, and closed his eyes, rerunning a year's worth of history lessons through his mind. After the last two years of run-ins with creatures straight out of mankind's darkest history and wildest mythology, coupled with advanced genetics, microbiology, and linguistics, it was clear the team needed an educational upgrade. The team's handler, Tom Duncan, call sign Deep Blue, whose true identity as the president of the United States was known only to the team and a handful of others, had arranged for their highly advanced adult learning schedule.

Professors from Harvard and Yale taught history and language, while professors from MIT taught physics, astronomy, and robotics. George Pierce, lifelong friend of the team's leader, King, who'd been rescued by the team after being abducted two years previous, taught mythology. Sara Fogg, from the CDC, who also happened to be King's current girl-friend and a former Pawn (temporary team member) on the mission to Vietnam, taught genetics and microbiology. They were now the most highly educated team in the U.S. military, and as they threw themselves into learning just as readily as they threw themselves into battle, they were beginning to develop notoriety as nerds. Not that anyone dared say that to their faces. The Chess Team's battle-hardened reputation preceded them with tales of their exploits becoming as modern myths among the other Delta teams.

And their education would continue until a situation requiring their unique experience and knowledge developed. Either that or a lead in the Siletz Reservation investigation that had brought them the team's newest, shortest, and feistiest addition.

"Any day now, big guy," came the high-pitched voice again.

Bishop laughed as he sat cross-legged on the floor, which was impressive for a man of his size. Not that he was fat. Quite the opposite. He sported two hundred fifty pounds of Iranian-born, American-raised muscle. And while Queen wore her battle scars on the outside, for all to see, Bishop's were hidden. Internal. Thanks to some genetic tinkering at the hands of Richard Ridley and Manifold Genetics, Bishop's body could heal any wound, but at the expense of his sanity. Only the crystal hanging around his neck, found in the ancient Neanderthal city of Meru, kept his mind in balance. Without it he'd become a raving mad, endlessly hungry "regen" who would only stop killing when his head was removed. But with his mind kept at peace by the crystal, he could sit on a living room floor, enjoy his friends, and hold a thirteen-year-old girl in his lap.

Fiona, call sign Pip-squeak, if you asked Rook—had come to call the Chess Team her family. Over the past year she had spent every day with them, watching them spar, study, shoot at the range—absorbing every detail of their lives and attempting to apply the lessons of valor and discipline to her tutored schoolwork. But she found the Chess Team much more interesting and the subjects of their study far less boring than Algebra I. "Okay, Rook. There is a plane with a bomb on it. When it explodes, the plane will crash into a train full of pregnant women on their way to a lactation conference. The answer is the code to defuse the bomb."

Rook looked at the black-haired, brown-eyed girl and couldn't help but smile. "That's twisted."

She shrugged. "Ten seconds. The unborn lives of countless children are counting on you."

He cleared his mind and focused, playing along, but not wanting the kid, who'd become their weekly quizmaster, to gain teasing rights.

"Five seconds."

The phone rang and Rook's eyes popped open. "Djet! Djet Horus was the third pharaoh of the first Egyptian dynasty from 2970 B.C. to 2960 B.C."

Fiona formed her hands into two guns and shot them at Rook complete with gunshot sound effects. As she spun the imaginary weapons and holstered them, she said, "Way to go cowboy. You got—"

She cocked her head and looked into the kitchen.

Rook noticed her attention on Knight as he spoke on the phone. "You can't hear him can you."

Fiona nodded. "Good ears." She looked at Rook. "Something's wrong."

"What's—"

Fiona shook her hands at him, her mood growing serious. "I want to hear if it's about King!"

King had left three days ago after receiving word of his mother's death. They'd all attended the wake and funeral, but she didn't get to see him much as he greeted long-lost relatives and family friends. She knew he was supposed to be gone for another week, settling things with the estate, but she hoped he would be back sooner.

Before she could hear what was being said, Knight hung up the phone, shut off the stovetop, and returned to the living room. "Dinner's off. Keasling wants us asap."

Fiona frowned.

"Did he mention why?" Queen asked.

Knight glanced at Fiona and it was all she needed. She stood up quickly. "Is it King?" When Knight didn't answer in the affirmative, she asked, "They found something?"

Knight shook his head. "Apparently, something found us."

"Is Dad coming back?"

For a moment, no one responded. They were still getting used to King being referred to as "Dad." In fact, he'd requested several times that she *not* call him Dad. But after being raised by her grandmother and having no real father figure for most of her life, she'd quickly adopted King as her father. He'd explained that their foster placement was temporary, until the danger had passed and a good family was found. The news had been heartbreaking and she did her best to call him Jack, or King, or Siggy, like his sister, Julie, had before she died, but in moments of excitement her true feelings rose up and exited her mouth before she had a chance to rein them in.

Knight frowned for the girl. They all had come to adore her and loathed watching her endure the emotional roller coaster that had become her life. "King needs more time off."

Bishop stood, towering over Fiona. With his similarly colored brown skin, eyes, and dark black hair, he looked the most like Fiona's biological father, but his angular nose and low brow revealed his genetics as Middle Eastern rather than Native American. He plucked the girl up and put her on his shoulders. "Hey, you've still got us."

Fiona rubbed his shaved head. "I know. I just wish I could be with him." Her smile faded. "I know what it's like to bury family."

FOUR
Richmond, Virgina

KING STOOD ALONE over his mother's grave. Grass seed lay scattered over the fresh soil where she'd been put in the ground the previous day. The funeral had turned out nice—as nice as laying your last friendly family member in the ground could be. Bishop, Rook, Knight, Queen, Aleman, Keasling, and Fiona had all been in attendance. Only Deep Blue, whose presence would have been impossible to hide, was unable to attend.

The night before the funeral, George Pierce had flown in from Greece for the event. Sara Fogg had come to give moral support as well, staying with him through the night. Since she knew what it was like to fight alongside the Chess Team, their dinner together swirled with conversation about mythology, genetics, and battle-scar comparisons.

In the morning, Pierce headed back to Rome, where an excavation awaited. Sara had hoped to stay for a few days. The combination of their demanding jobs, coupled with the addition of Fiona keeping King on base, had kept them apart. But fate had pulled her away to Swaziland, where an unknown disease outbreak was under way. Since bringing home the cure to the previous year's Brugada pandemic, she had become the CDC's poster child and had been assigned to ground zero of more than a few nasty outbreaks. Finding himself alone again and without distractions, King's thoughts were once again fully with his mother.

She was the kind of woman who smiled all the time despite a deep hurt hidden within. She baked pies from scratch. Had an open-door policy for friends and family. And she always, *always,* kept a fresh pitcher of homemade lemonade ready for visitors. He'd shared the last of that lemonade with his friends the night before the funeral.

But her bright exterior was all a sugar coating. Julie's death in the fighter jet training accident was the first blow. The second blow came months later, when his father, Peter, left for a business trip and never came home. Peter had been dramatically opposed to Julie joining the air force, while Lynn Sigler had supported her children. Even when King followed in the footsteps of his dead sister.

King knew it couldn't have been easy to let him go. But she had supported him, despite the risk to not only his life but her soul. She'd gone so far as to say his father would be proud of the choice, had he been around.

After a week of rain, the day of the burial had been beautiful, refusing those gathered the stereotypical rainy-day funeral. The trees, brimming with young, bright green leaves stood tall around the St. Mary's Church graveyard. Flower beds surrounding the black wrought-iron fence bloomed with the warm colors of spring. The day was like his mother had been: alive.

But no longer—thanks to a head-on collision with another car. Apparently, his mother, weary after a day of gardening, fell asleep at the wheel and drifted into the oncoming lane. King shook his head at the thought and pushed it from his mind.

The following day's weather was much the same, but being alone at his mother's grave cast the day in a darker light. He knelt by the upturned soil of the fresh gravesite and dug into it with his fingers. After hollowing out seven shallow holes, he opened a small package and planted a single snowdrop bulb in each. He knew his work would often keep him from visiting the grave every year. This way his mother's favorite flowers would bloom every spring to mark her passing, even if he wasn't there to place them on the grave himself.

He patted the dirt down with his fingers, one bulb at a time, allowing the coolness of the earth to calm his nerves, and used the peaceful moment to remember his mother. As he finished the final bulb he sensed he was not alone.

Keeping his head down, he scanned the area and saw nothing. He turned around. No one was there.

He was alone and nerve-shot. Deep Blue was right to make him take a week away. He was off his game, sensing enemies where there were none. He placed his hand on the soil, whispered a good-bye, and stood up.

Standing, he now had a clear view beyond his mother's headstone. Thirty feet away, a man stood in the shadow of a maple tree. This alone wouldn't be enough to raise King's hackles, but when the man saw King stand, he started and took a step back. Not a casual step. It was the kind of step a man took when he was about to make a run for it. King took a step toward the man, testing the theory.

The man ran.

King was after him in a heartbeat. He had no idea who the man was. It didn't really matter. That he was running told King everything he needed to know. One, the man was guilty of something—only guilty men run. Two, he knew King was dangerous, someone to run from. And three, he was at his mother's gravesite, which meant he knew King's personal identity as well.

None of this was acceptable.

As King rounded his mother's headstone and gave chase, he took in everything about the man he could. His black hair was slicked back neat. His trench coat covered most of his body. His shoes were shiny. Fancy. Not great for running. The man hadn't planned on being chased down.

Then why is he running? King thought.

After entering a clearing lined by two rows of headstones, King broke into a sprint and cut the distance between him and the man in half. The man wasn't fast, and as King closed in he could see streaks of gray on either side of the man's head. *Must be between fifty and sixty,* King thought.

The man followed a paved path that King knew wrapped down and around a steep drop. Rather than follow the man around, King continued straight on, pounding up the rise. When he reached the top, the man passed directly below him. King jumped, landed with a roll, and grabbed a fistful of trench coat.

The coat pulled from King's hand, but the sudden jerk made the man stumble. He toppled forward, fighting to right himself, but lost his balance and fell into the grass next to the path.

In no mood for a fight or a second chase, King drew his Sig Sauer and cocked the hammer.

The man must have recognized the sound because as he got to his knees he raised his hands and said, "D-don't shoot!"

King approached the man, weapon raised, but he slowed when something about the man, the shape of his head, his ears, struck a chord. He knew this man, but couldn't place him. The distraction slowed his reflexes.

The man, who was quicker than he looked, spun around and took hold of King's gun hand, pointing the weapon to the sky. With his free hand, the man took a swing at King's face. Thick knuckles brushed across King's nose. If he hadn't jerked back, his nose would have no doubt been broken.

The momentum of the missed blow pulled the man forward. King raised an elbow to jab into the man's back, but before he could, the man charged, burying his shoulder into King's gut. King fell back under the weight.

In the second it took the pair to fall to the pavement, King completed his assessment of the man's fighting ability. He was a brawler. All heavy punches and big blows, concentrated into a single devastating attack. Old-school fighting. It worked wonders against people who didn't know how to fight, but King's abilities could be matched by very few people.

As he fell back, King dropped his weapon, took the man's trench coat in both hands, and hopped up, placing his feet against his opponent's waist. With all of his weight pulling on the man, King controlled the fall. When they struck, King rolled and pushed with his legs, sending the man sprawling into the grass.

King stood as the older man climbed up and raised his fists in front of his face like a boxer. He came in fast, taking hard swings that King easily dodged or deflected. With the element of surprise gone, the man didn't stand a chance.

After dodging a jab to his face, King caught the man's arm and, once again, used the man's own momentum to fling him to the grass. The man climbed to his feet slower than before, which gave King time to pick up his weapon and aim it at the man's back.

The man raised his hands in submission. The fight was over.

"Turn around," King said.

The man turned around, head lowered, then slowly looked up at King's gun. King blinked as recognition and a flood of memories and emotions hit him all at once. The man standing before him was his father, Peter Sigler.

"Don't shoot," his father said.

King gave his father an up-and-down glance. He wore an old gray suit beneath the trench coat. His face wasn't exactly clean-shaven, but neither was King's. His once-black hair was now peppered with gray, especially on the sides. And despite the wrinkles marking the fifty-five years on his face, his body looked well, and strong. For a moment, King felt as though he were looking through a time portal at his future self. But there was something off—the fear in his eyes.

King lowered the weapon. "I'm not going to shoot you, Dad."

Peter's eyes went wide. He hadn't got a good look at King's face while staring down the barrel of his handgun. "Jack?"

The man's hands started shaking. He took hold of one with the other and squeezed. "I didn't know who you were. I thought you might be—"

"Be what?" King asked.

"I don't know, with the church. A gardener. I thought the graveyard might be closed."

He was about to ask why he'd run from a gardener, but then thought, *Of course he ran, that's what he's best at. Running.* That didn't explain the brawling, but his father was a stranger to him now. Who knew who he'd become.

King turned his back on his father, looking toward his mother's grave, silently asking for guidance and the will to not pull the gun on his father again. "Then you weren't here to see me."

King holstered his weapon and moved to walk past his father.

"Well, I'm seeing you now, aren't I?"

For a moment King's angry resolve held out. But seeing his father again in the wake of his mother's death . . . it was a pain he didn't want to carry on his own. He motioned with his head for his father to follow him. "You hungry?"

As King walked away, he wasn't sure if his father would follow or run again. But a moment later, the sound of scuffing shoes on pavement revealed his old man was done running. At least for the moment.

FIVE
Fort Bragg—Decon

"**WHAT IS SHE** doing here?" Keasling asked about Fiona, who was sitting comfortably in the seat that was normally occupied by King.

"This has something to do with my grandmother," Fiona said to the stout but gruff brigadier general. "And who killed her."

Queen quickly cleared her throat. "Sir, everyone charged with watching Fiona and keeping her safe is either in this room or unavailable."

Keasling looked around. Sitting around the long executive table were Fiona, Queen, Knight, Bishop, Rook, and Lewis Aleman, the team's former field operator turned computer whiz and walking Wikipedia. The room itself, known as Decon, or Limbo, depending on whom you asked, was nothing to get excited about—simply a rectangle with one wall of glass looking out into the hangar bay that held the *Crescent*, the team's high-velocity, stealth transport. But the technology hidden within the table and walls was something else entirely. Concealed computers and a large viewscreen allowed the team to coordinate and plan some of the most risky, high-tech, and successful Delta operations no one ever heard about.

"I don't like it," Keasling said. "The kid shouldn't be here."

"It's all right, General." The voice, recognizable to everyone in the room, and most Americans, came from the large screen built into the front wall of the room. To the team he was Deep Blue, their handler. To everyone else, he was the president of the United States. On screen they could see the man's balding head, charming smile, and kind, gray eyes. The only thing marring his presidential image were a few small scars on his cheeks and eyebrows, reminders of his years as an Army Ranger.

Keasling turned toward the screen that offered them a view of the Oval Office and the hidden camera that allowed Deep Blue to see all of them on his laptop. He nodded. "Mr. President."

"She deserves some answers," Knight said. "It's been nearly a year."

"Agreed," Deep Blue said, "but I'm afraid all we have is more questions. And a lead." He looked at Keasling. "Show them."

Keasling opened a folder on the tabletop and took out an opened enve-
lope. It was addressed to Jack Sigler. "We've been monitoring King's e-mails
and snail mail—" He caught Rook's aghast expression. "With King's approval. This came in today. The letter was opened and red-flagged twenty
minutes ago."

He took out photocopies of the page and passed them around the
room. They all read the brief note quickly.

> King,
> Keep them safe.
>   25°21'5.17"S
>   131° 2'1.07"E
> Akala Dugabu
> Balun Ammaroo
> Warrah Ammaroo
> Elouera Kurindi
> Jerara Mundjagora
>
>   14°49'51.03"N
>   107°33'41.22"E
> Any you left alive.

"Ahh shit." Rook looked at Fiona. "Sorry."

She shrugged. "What's wrong?"

"The second set of coordinates," Bishop said, shaking his head slowly.
"We recognize them."

"Where is it?" she asked.

"The stomping ground of some of our old acquaintances," Rook replied. "Mount Meru. Vietnam."

Fiona's eyes went wide and she sucked in a quick breath. She'd spent
the last year being regaled with stories of the Chess Team's adventures

and the creatures, madmen, and amazing science they'd encountered. She knew that Mount Meru was where Bishop found the crystal that hung around his neck, where Queen received the bright red scar on her forehead, and where Rook had been made Alpha male by the last surviving Neanderthal Queen. "Red."

"That's right," Keasling said, crossing his arms, which was the general's body language for: don't bother trying to argue with what's coming next. "Rook. Queen. You'll be headed back to the Annamite Mountains. You will search for any hybrid or Neanderthal survivors. Should you find any, tranquilize them and bring them home. The Vietnamese government is still embarrassed as hell over what happened last year, so there were no issues getting you clearance to return to the site."

Rook leaned forward, elbows on the table. "And I'm going because . . ."

"Because, sweet cheeks, you're the least likely to get killed." Keasling smiled. "Being 'the Father' an' all."

"Just making sure."

"And the other location?" Bishop asked.

"Uluru, Australia."

"Ayers Rock," Knight said. "These are aboriginal names."

Keasling nodded. "Glad to see at least one of you has learned something this year. The coordinates are on the southern side of the rock. No one has lived there for ten thousand years. The site is mostly a tourist trap now, but we think these people are there now, or will be soon."

"Listen guys," Deep Blue said, "we all know what happened to the Siletz Reservation last year, so we have to assume that these people are in danger, too."

"Why not just call some government blokes in Australia and have them pick up the people?" Fiona asked Deep Blue, tinging the words "blokes in Australia" with an Australian accent.

He smiled. He hadn't had much time to see Fiona, but the regular reports he got from the team included updates on the girl. He knew she was intelligent, straightforward, and genuine. He would try to be the same for her. "Given the identity of the person sending the message—"

"Hercules," she said with a roll of her eyes. "Riiight."

Deep Blue cleared his throat. "And the unusual circumstances surrounding the destruction of the reservation, not to mention the amount of red tape and time it would take to interview the survivors, who may be in grave danger, would bring our investigation to a standstill. Good enough?"

Fiona grinned. It wasn't lost on her that the president, the man her grandmother had voted for, had just answered her question very seriously. "Quite," she said.

"Any more questions?" Keasling said.

Aleman raised his long arm. "I didn't receive any briefing on this and there seems to be no relevant tech in need of explanation."

"And . . ."

"Why, exactly, am I here?"

Keasling raised his hands toward Fiona. "Babysitting duty."

Aleman sighed. "Ahh. Right."

"It's dangerous work, I know," said Keasling. "Try not to get yourself killed."

The smiles around the room were impossible to hide. Lewis Aleman was a dangerous man in his time. But since an injury took him off field work he'd spent most of his time behind a computer. Watching Fiona was a welcome change. He turned to Fiona. "We'll bust out the Master Sergeant and kill us some aliens."

She grinned and gave him a thumbs-up.

"Adorable," Keasling grumbled, then raised his voice. "Wheels up in thirty minutes. Night is falling on the other side of the planet and we want you back in the air and on your way home by sunrise."

SIX
Richmond, Virgina

KING'S EGGS WERE cold, not to mention runny. The burnt toast chewed up as well as a slab of cardboard. The orange juice was watered down. And the sausage, cheap as it was, encased more cartilage than pork. But the breakfast, courtesy of his father's favorite hometown diner, was like heaven coated in maple syrup compared to the silence between King and his father.

What could be said to a son you deserted? To a father you'd put out of your mind? *A lot*, King knew, but he wasn't ready. Not by a long shot.

After ten minutes and one forced-down sausage, King had had enough. He'd faced down the world's most dangerous terrorists, the mythical Hydra reborn, and a horde of Neanderthal women. He could handle his father. Clearing his throat, he asked, "Did you make it to the funeral?"

His father looked up briefly, met King's eyes, and then returned his gaze to his rubbery pancakes, which still held two miniature ice cream scoops of butter. "Nope." He squished the butter with his fork, oozing the congealed paste through the tines. "I only found out two days ago and the bus was slow."

"Where were you coming from?"

"Butner."

King sat up straighter. "North Carolina?"

"Yeah, you know it?"

King chuckled and shook his head. "I'm stationed at Fort Bragg. You've been living two hours from me. Butner . . . Must have been one slow bus."

The diner door slammed shut as a patron left. Peter jumped, looking at the door and then taking a quick look around the room. He relaxed again and squinted. "What?" When King's statement registered, he took a deep breath and found the courage to ignore the subject. "How's that working out for you? The military?"

"It's a living."

"Deployed?"

"A few times."

"Anywhere interesting?"

"Haven't left the planet yet." King didn't want to talk about himself, so he quickly U-turned the conversation back to his father. "I thought you went to California."

"It didn't take."

"Couldn't find any of those California girls to take care of you?" King inwardly winced at his low blow. He had no idea what the temperament of his father was like now. As a child, the man wouldn't have stood for King's "flack," but now . . .

"You're not going to turn this into a soap opera, are you?" his father said without a hint of humor.

The man hadn't changed a bit.

But King had. He didn't have to sit and listen to his father. "Nice seeing you, Pop." He placed a twenty-dollar bill on the table and stood. He stopped briefly to admire the diner's Elvis clock and headed for the exit.

"Jack, hold on," his father said.

King hadn't had a father since his teen years and he'd long ago grown accustomed to that fact. No father was better than a bad father. He continued toward the exit. Seeing the man had only reinforced his fears about caring for Fiona. The man's blood was his own. If fatherhood was hereditary, he would eventually fail the girl. When he knew she was safe again, he'd make sure she found a good family to take care of her.

"Jack. Stop."

King paused for a moment, but not because of his father's voice. Something deep within had struck home. A pang of guilt, only a quiet whisper before, had been revealed for what it was. Without even realizing it, King was planning to do *exactly* what his father had done. He was going to give her up. He was going to leave her.

Feeling sick to his stomach, King reached for the door.

"King, wait!"

He stopped, his fist gripping the door's push-bar, the bells just starting to jingle. He turned back to his father. "What did you just say?"

His father looked stunned by the incredulous look in King's eyes and fidgeted uncomfortably as King pounded back toward him.

Waitresses, expecting a fight, stepped behind the long counter. Patrons swiveled in their chairs, turning their backs to the pair, not wanting to be involved. King stopped at the table, placed his fists on its surface, and leaned over his father. "How do you know that name?"

His father gave an awkward smile. "I named you, Jack."

King reached under his coat, pulled out his handgun, and placed it on the table. It was the second time that day he'd threatened his father with the gun, but this time it was not an accident. "You . . . called . . . me . . . King."

"Must have heard the nickname from your mother."

"Mom didn't know it."

"Well, I—"

Without raising the gun, King cocked the hammer. "Who are you?"

"I'm your father."

"Who *else* are you?"

King's father cleared his throat. He stared at the table like he was in shock, but then all his fear and worry melted away. An act. A smile crept onto his face. "You know what, you're right. The time for games is over. Why don't we go back to the house? Have a glass of your mother's lemonade."

"It's gone. I finished it."

"Don't worry, Jack. I'm sure she'll have made some more by the time we get there."

SEVEN
Annamite Mountains, Vietnam

THE SMELL OF the jungle—moist earth and organic rot—hit Rook like a childhood nightmare, bringing back memories of fear, suffering, and the stuff of monsters made real. When the Chess Team last set foot in the mountainous region of Vietnam known as the Annamite Convergence Zone, where Vietnam, Laos, and Cambodia's borders merged, they had not only come face-to-face with the last remnants of mankind's Neanderthal ancestors, but also their modern-day hybrid brood. Not to mention Vietnam's now disbanded special forces unit known as the Death Volunteers.

Rook looked at Queen, whose black face paint covered the star-and-skull brand she'd received at the hands of the Death Volunteers. To her credit, she seemed unfazed by their return to the site of her torture. Of course, she *was* Queen. He expected nothing less.

They stood in darkness at the edge of the jungle, looking at the concave remains of Mount Meru cast in shades of green through their night vision goggles. Hidden inside the mountain had been the last city of the Neanderthal people; a masterpiece of ancient construction lit by the refracting light of giant crystals, it was the inspiration for the design of Ankgor Wat in Cambodia. But now the place was a ruin.

Every entrance had been crushed. Brush and saplings had already begun to reclaim the clearing that housed the hybrid workforce, where Rook and Queen had made a half-naked dash through the rain before facing off against a hybrid and two tigers. All that remained were shards of stone spear tips flattened into the earth.

The place was dead.

"No one has walked here, let alone lived here, since we left," Queen said.

Rook knelt and pried a stone ax head from the earth. He felt its still sharp blade with his thumb. "Don't forget that these guys almost inherited the earth," he said. "Wouldn't have hesitated to kill either of us."

"I remember . . ."

"Then you might also remember that they didn't always walk on the ground." Rook motioned up with his head.

She looked up, following the trunk of the closest large tree, toward the night sky. The thick branches toward the top were marred with light-colored scratches. "They're still here."

"Not here," Rook said, lifting the night vision goggles from his eyes and looking at Queen in the moonlight. She was dressed, head to toe, in black with her blond hair tucked up inside a black skullcap. She carried an UMP submachine gun. The woman was as deadly as she was beautiful, something Rook had to remind himself about every time his eyes trailed over the curves of her face, or body. "We're looking in the wrong place. The hybrids lived here, with Weston, when he was the Father. And none of them actually lived inside Meru, not at the core at least. But now Weston is dead, and—"

"And you, being made the new Father, became a deadbeat dad and left them." Queen flashed a grin.

"They never did ask for child support," Rook said. "But the old mothers didn't live here."

She closed her eyes and nodded, remembering the stories told by Rook, Knight, and Bishop, who had seen more of the Neanderthal's underground world than she or King. "The Necropolis."

"That's the place."

"Which way?"

"South, past the river."

Queen stepped past him. "Then what are we waiting for?"

Rook watched Queen move past him and head south. They hadn't been on a mission since leaving the jungles of Vietnam a year earlier, and though they had trained continuously since then, something felt different. Queen had always been detail-oriented and focused. Driven. But now her guard was down. Not quite laid back, but indifferent to life and death.

Over the past year, she had not once mentioned the scar on her forehead, at least not to anyone on the team, and he seriously doubted she'd been to see a professional. The brand, a skull inside a star, had been burned into her forehead by Major-General Trung, commander of the Death Volunteers. It was a torture few people could endure without lasting side effects. And while Queen wasn't most people, the brutal act *had* changed her. Being trained to hide her feelings from the enemy, she would have no trouble hiding them from the team. But Rook could see it.

He realized he might be seeing something because he was looking too hard. His concern for her had grown over the past year, but he kept his thoughts to himself, afraid talking would reveal his true feelings. Was his worry for her well-being corrupting his assessment of her abilities? That seemed more likely than Queen going soft. Rook frowned. *He* was going soft. And being back in this jungle with her, where they had shared a brief kiss . . . He shook his head, trying to stay focused on the mission before his own distractions put them both in danger.

EIGHT
30,000 Feet Above Uluru, Australia

AFTER SWINGING OVER Vietnam to drop off Rook and Queen, the *Crescent* turned south and, flying at Mach 2 (1,522 mph), covered the three-thousand-two-hundred-mile distance in two hours. Bishop and Knight spent the last hour prebreathing for their impending HALO jump. They felt the stealth transport shift as its speed slowed, signaling their final approach to Ayers Rock, known as Uluru to the aboriginal Australians.

Uluru, a one-thousand-one-hundred-forty-two-foot-tall sandstone formation with a six-mile circumference stood out on the flat desert of central Australia like a crater in reverse. It had amazing views, three hundred sixty degrees of crags and fissures perfect for climbing, historical value as an ancient watering hole for desert travelers, and an ancient spiritual site of great importance since one of the sacred "Dreamtime" tracks—the paths taken by the Creator Beings as they walked the young earth—cut directly through the giant stone.

Knight and Bishop stood and walked to the hatch. Both had slept for the majority of the six-hour flight from Fort Bragg to Vietnam and had spent most of the time since then in silence—Bishop in meditation, Knight in study.

The pilot's voice filled the cabin. "Two minutes. Prep for jump."

"Copy that," Knight said, closing his binder and standing up.

With their prebreathing complete and the LZ approaching, Knight and Bishop got down to the business of prejump preparation, which for the Chess Team meant a quick refortification of their close bond.

Bishop, standing nearly a foot taller than Knight, looked down at him. "How's Grandma Dae-jung doing?"

"Could use some of that hoodoo juice from Manifold. Well, not the stuff you got. Grandma regen would not be a pretty picture."

"That bad, huh?"

"Let's just say I don't think King's mom's funeral will be the last one I go to this year."

"We go to."

Knight smiled. "Thanks."

"You ready to bag and tag some aboriginals?"

Knight's smile widened as he laughed. "Bag and tag some aboriginals? You've been spending too much time around Rook."

Bishop took the crystal hanging around his neck, gave it a kiss, and tucked it beneath his black jumpsuit. "Just finding my sense of humor again."

The light above them switched from red to green. A moment later, the back hatch opened. Both men closed their helmets over their heads, which allowed them to use their night vision as they descended at terminal velocity. Knight gave Bishop a thumbs-up. Bishop nodded. And the pair leapt, one after the other, into the whipping, frigid winds above Uluru. The *Crescent*, invisible in the night sky, banked away and disappeared.

Knight focused on the ground below. Their targets had been watched via satellite throughout the day. A group of twenty people, five of whom were on the list the team had received, had spent the night around a bonfire, reenacting the rituals, dancing, and storytelling of their ancestors. The fire, being the only source of light for three hundred miles, was easy to spot and the Delta duo aimed their bodies, now living missiles, toward the fiery target. The group of aboriginals was tucked inside a deep valley, which meant they would have to land on the nearby desert and hike in. The trek would only add a few minutes to their travel time, but with helicopters already inbound and due to arrive in twenty minutes, there was no time to delay.

As they closed in, Knight's keen eyes saw an aberration far above the target area. "What the . . ." He'd seen something moving. He squinted, searching for movement, but found nothing.

"What is it?" Bishop asked, his voice coming in clear through Knight's earphone.

"I don't know. I—" Movement streaked across Knight's vision again and he saw it for what it was. "Never mind. Condensation on my visor."

"Knight, Bishop, you read?" Deep Blue's voice filled their ears.

"Loud and clear," Bishop replied.

"Listen, there's some seismic activity in the area some of the analysts are concerned about. Shouldn't be a big deal, but the sandstone valley is crisscrossed by tiny fissures created by thousands of years of rain runoff."

"Got it," Knight said. "Watch for falling rocks."

"Exactly."

"Thanks for the heads-up, Blue, but it's time to pull!"

Bishop and Knight's parachutes deployed like gunshots, ripping open one thousand feet from the desert floor. Seconds later, they were rolling on the ground, gathering their chutes, and running toward the faint glow of the nearby valley, where large shadows danced in the firelight.

Sometimes, after completing a HALO jump, rookies stumbled on shaky legs or fell to their knees, wobbly from adrenaline. But Bishop and Knight had long ago overcome the post-jump shakes, so when both men suddenly found themselves off balance, they knew something was wrong.

They paused.

"That was a little more than a tremor," Bishop said.

Knight placed his bare hand on the ground. The sand was shaking, as though to the steady rhythm of a bass-laden hip-hop song. Either that or something—

Knight's head shot up as a distant squeal rolled over the desert. "Was that a car?"

Bishop shook his head, cautiously moving toward the valley ahead. "I don't think so. It sounded more like a—"

The scream came again, this time shrill and very human. Both men slid their weapons from their backs and ran as fast as they could to the cacophony of terrified cries pouring from the valley, praying someone would still be breathing when they arrived.

NINE
Richmond, Virgina

KING'S JAW HURT from fifteen minutes of grinding teeth. The drive back to his childhood home had been slowed by traffic and had taken ten minutes longer than usual. All the while, he worried about having to have his father, who he'd just been reunited with, committed to some kind of mental institution. And with ten years of anger and frustration yet to be expressed, let alone forgiven, King was not happy about his father getting the clean slate a mental illness would provide.

He reminded himself that when his father left, he'd been sane. That, at least, provided him with some anger to hold on to. He glanced over at his father, who watched their hometown pass in a blur as they rounded Swanson Drive, the last in a series of suburban streets that led to the house. The man's face was older, more wrinkled, but at peace.

A day after burying Mom and he doesn't have a care in the world, King thought.

"Ignorance is bliss, right?" King said under his breath.

To his surprise, his father had heard. "That's why crazy people are so happy."

"Exactly what I was thinking."

Peter grinned at him. "Except I'm not crazy."

"Mom's dead, Dad."

"Buried her yesterday."

King nodded, glancing quickly at his father. The man was certifiable. "Open casket."

"Did you look at her wedding ring?"

The rock in his mother's engagement ring had been red. A ruby. Given to Peter by his soon-to-be fiancée's father, a German jeweler. King thought about his mother's body, about her hands folded over her chest. He couldn't recall seeing the ring.

"Didn't, did you?"

"That doesn't mean anything," King said, becoming annoyed with the insanity of this conversation and the disrespect it showed his mother.

"You know, you were a smart kid. I thought you could tell the difference between your mom's body and a wax figure. Cost a pretty penny."

"Just . . . shut up until we get home."

A gentle ring sounded from his father's pocket. King shot him a curious glance. "Thought you were hard up for money."

Peter smiled. "Did I say that?" He answered the phone. "Hey." He looked at King while he listened. "We're almost there. No, not yet. He's okay. Shaken. Yup. Okay. Love you, too, Babushka."

King's eyes were wide and his foot had fallen off the gas pedal. Babushka. He hadn't heard the word in ten years and its use—a pet name for his mother—came slamming back into his mind. He grew serious, with murderous intent in his eyes. "That's not funny."

His father held out the phone. "You can ring her back if you want, but I think seeing her in person would—"

King yanked the wheel, turning onto Oak Lane, and hit the gas. Twin streaks of black rubber lanced out from the back tires as the car shot down the street. A second set of streaks squealed onto the pavement as, fifteen seconds later, King hit the brakes. He slammed the car into park in the middle of the street, flung himself from the car, and ran for the front door.

King twisted the doorknob and put his shoulder into the door like he was raiding a terrorist training camp. He scoured the living room and found it empty. Circling through the dining room, he entered the kitchen, where his mother spent most of her time either cooking or sitting in the breakfast nook, looking out at the backyard trees and her bird feeders.

The kitchen was empty. Feeling a growing anger at his father for perpetrating such a sick joke, but clinging to desperate hope, he opened the fridge. A full pitcher of lemonade, swirling with pulp, rested on the top shelf. King stared at the amber liquid and just as he started wondering if his father had come here earlier and made it himself, a gentle feminine voice broke his heart.

"Sorry to cause you so much pain, Jack—"

King turned and faced his mother, his legs weak, his mouth hanging open.

"But it had to be convincing."

A TALL GLASS of lemonade sat untouched in front of King. He sat at the small breakfast nook table with his returned father and still living mother, listening to an unbelievable tale. But what struck him more than their story was their affection. It was as though his father had never left. Their hands remained entwined the entire time. Their eyes glowed with love for each other. King had entered the Twilight Zone, and like William Shatner, wanted to throw open a door and shoot something. Instead, he picked up his perspiring glass and took a long swallow of lemonade. He placed the glass on the table and looked at his parents. They weren't decrepitly old, but their age showed, which made their story so much harder to believe.

"Spies."

His mother pursed her lips after taking a sip of lemonade and nodded. "Russian."

"He's catching on, Lynn," Peter said.

King looked at his father. "And you've been locked up for ten years, in the minimum security prison in Butner."

"Told you I'd been in Butner. Now you can see why I never came to visit you."

King rubbed his face. This was all too much. "And you went to prison—"

"I told you already, before the Cold War ended, your mother and I had fallen in love with this country. We kept our new identities and broke all ties with the Soviets in 1988."

"Did they ever come after you?" King asked.

"Just once," Peter said.

"And?"

Lynn took another drink, her eyebrows reaching up to her dark hair. When it was clear Peter wasn't going to answer, she gave a gentle cough, smiled, and said, "I shot him. You were just a baby then." She smiled at King's shocked expression. "Don't worry, he lived."

"After that," Peter added, "the Cold War ended in 1991 and we were forgotten about."

"This is why you were opposed to Julie joining the military?"

His father nodded. "I wanted you both to live different lives, and to never fear for yours. But it seems the military is part of our genetic makeup." He sighed. "If your sister had listened—"

Lynn put her hand on Peter's arm. "Not now."

His nod was nearly imperceptible. "When Julie died I thought it might not have been an accident. I started poking around. But was rusty. Asked too many questions. Was spotted poking around the base. Federal agents looked into my past and learned the truth."

"I gave them every name and contact I had and was totally honest about what secrets we had sent home in exchange for your mother's freedom and your continued belief that I had simply left. I got out of jail two weeks ago."

"Why wait this long to tell me?"

His father began to reply, but King interrupted.

"And why *fake* Mom's death?"

"There are elements in the current Russian government that are attempting to return to old Cold War policies. Shortly after my release we were contacted by an old KGB handler who assumed the dead end in our file back home meant we were sleeper agents."

Lynn looked out the window, her eyes watching the shuffle of spring leaves in the wind. "We've been reactivated."

"So you faked your death to what, escape?"

She nodded.

King chuckled.

"You think this is funny?" his father asked.

"You should have come to me from the beginning." He looked at both his parents, amused, surprised, and thrilled to have them both back. "I have friends that could help."

"You're a soldier, son. This is the spy business," Peter said. "Who do you know that could help us, chess pieces?"

King squinted at his father. "How *did* you know my call sign?"

Lynn smiled. "You let your guard down at home . . . and I'm a good spy."

King's stunned silence was interrupted by his cell phone. He ignored its ring as another question entered his mind. "What's my real last name?"

"*Our* last name *was* Machtcenko. Yours has been and will always be Sigler."

The phone chimed again.

"My maiden name," his mother added. "Your grandfather really was German."

"And a jeweler?"

She nodded.

As the phone rang a third time, King looked at the caller ID display and frowned.

"Who is it?"

"Unknown." Which on King's phone was virtually impossible. Thanks to Deep Blue, absolutely everyone who called this phone appeared in caller I.D., regardless of their personal preference. That this call showed as "unknown" meant the caller had impressive resources of their own. King stood and answered the phone. "Who is this?"

The unfamiliar voice on the other end was deep and strong. "Where are you, King?"

"You've got ten seconds to tell me who you are and then I—"

"Get back to Bragg, King. I'll do what I can, but I'm not sure it will be enough."

The line went dead.

As the pieces of the puzzle came together, King moved toward the front door.

"What's wrong?" his mother asked.

"She's in trouble."

"Who is?"

"Fiona."

His parents were on their feet, trailing him out the front door to the car, which his father had moved into the driveway. "Who is Fiona?"

Upon reaching the driver's side door, King turned to his parents. "My daughter—foster daughter."

He entered the car and started the engine. But before he could put it into reverse, the doors to the backseat opened and his parents climbed in. "What are you doing?"

His mother leaned over the backseat. "We're coming to help."

"This is going to be dangerous."

His father put a hand on King's shoulder. "Son, listen to your parents. For once in your life."

The car spun out of the driveway a moment later and shot down the street. It was a four-hour drive back to the base. King would make it in three. He just hoped it would be fast enough.

TEN
Fort Bragg, North Carolina

"GET DOWN, THEY see you."

"I can't see them."

"Above you. Flood infections!"

"Oh no . . . ahh! They're everywhere. I think I'm dead."

"Lew. Lew! They killed Lew. Ugh!" Fiona paused the game, put down the Xbox remote, and threw her hands up. "Every time, Lew."

Lewis Aleman smiled as he stood. "Sorry kiddo. If they designed joysticks as guns we'd be all set. I was great at Duck Hunt."

"Duck Hunt? Seriously? You *are* old."

"Forty-one isn't old," he said, moving from the sparsely decorated lounge to the small kitchenette. The college dorm–like space typically held a good number of off-duty soldiers playing pool, cards, or watching TV, but Lewis had made sure the space would be empty. A room full of soldiers looking to relax and have fun was not typically the right environment for a tween, boy or girl.

"If you weren't born in the nineteen-eighties or sooner, you're old." Fiona was dressed in all black pajamas and slippers—her favorite, she said, because they looked like special ops nighttime gear. The only aberration on her smooth, slender little body was a small rectangular lump on her hip. Hidden beneath her shirt, clipped to her waist, was the insulin pump that kept her blood sugar levels optimal. With a curtain of straight black hair hanging down around her head, only her brown hands and face weren't shrouded in darkness. "Popcorn time?"

The loud rattle of popcorn swirling around in an air popper answered her question. "You know how to use that?" she shouted over the loud tornado of corn kernels.

"Popcorn is my specialty!"

"You said you were good at Halo, too."

"Going to use a whole stick of butter. Can't go wrong."

"Might need to get your cholesterol checked," she mumbled.

"What?"

"Nothing! Nothing." Fiona stood by the large window that overlooked a large parking lot below and the expansive Fort Bragg that had become her new home. The nonstop movement of the base consisted of a mix of military and normal life. Men and women in uniform mixed with those in plainclothes. Jeeps shared the roads with SUVs and minivans. From her view in the barracks lounge she could also see the other barracks, their redbrick walls aglow from the setting sun.

She caught her reflection in the window and its distorted shape made her look like her grandmother, who even in old age had a youthful face. Her eyes grew wet as she remembered the woman who had raised her. Who had sung songs to her and taught her the traditions and language of a people who no longer existed. According to King, she was the last true Siletz Native American left alive. There were other descendants to be sure, but they had long ago shirked the tribe, joined the larger American society, and forgotten the ancient culture altogether. King also explained that she was the sole heir to the Siletz Reservation. And when she was old enough, she could claim the land as her own.

She lay in bed most nights daydreaming about what she would do with the reservation. She couldn't live there. Not by herself. Not without the tribe. Too many ghosts on that land. A pair of statues was her answer, one a tribute to her people, the second to her grandmother and parents, perhaps with a single road leading to them. The rest, as her grandmother had taught her, belonged to nature.

The popcorn popper fell silent.

Fiona wiped her nose and turned from the window. This was an emotional trip she made on a daily basis and she was determined to get over it. To move on. Be emotionally solid. Like Dad. King.

As she stepped away from the window, she took one last look back, expecting to see the face of her grandmother once again. Instead, she saw right through herself as a bright orange glow in the distance caught her attention. She stepped forward and placed her hand on the glass.

It was shaking.

"Lew?"

She could hear him walking into the room and could smell the buttery popcorn.

Aleman heard the concern in her voice and quickened his pace. As he approached, Fiona recognized the growing yellow orb for what it was—a distant explosion. "Lew!"

Aleman had just a second to look out the glass pane, see the fireball, register the shaking beneath his feet, catch sight of the approaching shockwave as it flattened the grass on the baseball field across the parking lot.

The popcorn fell to the floor as Aleman picked Fiona up and dove behind the thick Ikea couch.

The window blew in just as they hit the thin rug, sending shards of glass stabbing into the opposite wall, the TV, and the room's furniture. The building shook for a moment as the shock wave passed, then fell silent.

Lewis rolled off Fiona and stood, shaking the glass from his back. His handgun was already drawn and at the ready. He looked down at Fiona, his eyes more serious than she had ever seen them. "You okay?"

She nodded.

"Get up," he said, and moved to the now glassless window. A second, small explosion plumed into the air. It was followed by the distant popping of small-arms fire. Then an alarm sounded. One he thought he would never hear used. It meant the unthinkable.

Fort Bragg was under attack.

He looked back at Fiona, whose skinny body looked frail in her black pajamas. She had her eyebrows furrowed, her fists clenched, and her lips down turned. She knew what was happening just as surely as he did.

They had come for her.

ELEVEN
Mount Meru, Vietnam

AS ROOK STOOD outside the cave entrance leading to the subterranean necropolis that he, Bishop, and Knight had discovered a year ago, he listened. And heard nothing. No distinct Neanderthal hoots. No movement inside or outside the cave. Nothing. Which meant they were either being watched, or no one was home.

"This is it?" Queen asked, peering into the lightless black square cut into the mountainside. Vines had begun to grow over the opening that Rook and Bishop tore apart when they fled the cave system, but it was still easy to spot.

"Ayup. Bringing back such fond memories I can hardly stand it."

"I'm the one with a brand."

"Hey, an ape woman tried to make me her man-toy," Rook said as he pushed the vines out of the way with his M4.

"Good point," she replied before entering the cave. "That's much worse."

Rook smiled and followed her in.

The smooth grade led them down. One hundred feet in, the walls glowed. "We'll be able to remove our night vision goggles soon. The algae covering everything glows bright enough to see by."

The downward slope ended and opened up into a grand chamber, seventy feet wide, twenty tall, and longer than a football field. "What the f—"

"This isn't how you described it."

What once was a city built from the skulls and thick bones of generations upon generations of Neanderthal dead looked like a green-glowing war zone. Many of the buildings were crushed. Walls were burst. Skulls and bone fragments filled the stone streets. Statues of ancient Neanderthals had been overturned with their limbs pulled off. Rook noted that several of the skulls, which were dense and tough, had been crushed to powder, a feat he doubted even the strongest Neanderthal could accomplish.

"No bullet holes or blast craters," Queen said.

Rook nodded. "This wasn't a military j—"

A splash of dark shiny liquid caught Rook's eye. Tiptoeing through the scattered bones, he made his way to it and knelt down. He switched on his flashlight and aimed it at the fluid. The yellow light turned the black puddle red.

Blood.

And a lot of it.

He followed the trail to a pile of bones. Setting down his M4, he shoved the bones away and stepped back. The twisted face of a Neanderthal-human hybrid stared back at him. The body was tall and strong, with thick brown hair on the limbs, back, chest, and head. A male. And given its muscle mass, one of the hunters. Despite its impressive size and strength, the body was bent at an odd angle and many of the limb bones were bent where they should have been straight. This creature, who could make short work of any living human being, had been mauled and folded up like an origami puzzle. "It's a hybrid," he said. "It's been mauled something fierce."

He looked over at Queen. She had found a body buried in the remains of a small structure. "This is one of the old mothers. Same story."

Rook shook his head. For all the strength, speed, and instincts the hybrids had, the old mothers had double. "I think it's safe to assume we were beat to the punch."

Queen stood and activated her throat mic. "Deep Blue, this is Queen." She waited for a reply, but none came. "Deep Blue, do you read?"

"We're too deep," Rook said. "Go topside and warn the others. I'll poke around here and try to figure out what happened."

Queen didn't like the sound of that and said so with a look.

"This place is a ghost town, twice over," he said.

"It's a bad idea."

"If I get into trouble I'll yell."

"From a hundred feet below a mountain?"

"I'll yell real loud."

Queen shook her head, but couldn't hide her grin. She headed for the exit. "I'll be back in five minutes." She paused at the large archway leading to the tunnel. "Hey, Rook, good to be back in the field with you."

He nodded. "Likewise."

Then she was gone, running up the slope.

Rook sighed, still concerned for Queen's well-being, but also concerned over his own distraction. Queen took up too much space in his mind. As they had studied, sparred, and trained over the past year, he sometimes found his thoughts off target and on her. And in the field, that could get him killed.

Of course, they all had their distractions. Knight's grandmother's health was failing. Bishop was only sane because of a crystal around his neck. Queen had a cherry red stamp on her forehead. And King now had a foster daughter. "Course, none of the guys look as good in fatigues," he mumbled to himself.

Shuffling through a sea of green-glowing bones, Rook made his way deeper into the city. He stopped occasionally to listen as every step he made created a cacophony of noise. He would be simple to find. If anyone were looking.

After counting fifteen bodies strewn throughout the ruined city, he decided that all the Neanderthals were either dead or had fled. But he'd still found no evidence of what happened. The bodies were crushed, dismembered, or impaled with bones, but it was as though something huge and blunt had been used to kill them.

The clunk of bone on bone spun him around, M4 tight against his shoulder. "That you, Queen?"

No reply.

He waited just a moment before an off-balance bone slipped from one of the half destroyed walls and fell. He relaxed for a moment, but another clatter of bones turned him around again.

Something was making the loose bones fall.

Then he felt it. A vibration.

Something big was approaching.

Bones rattled again, but Rook didn't turn this time. He remained focused on the shaking beneath his feet, trying to determine its origin. It wasn't until the rattle of bones turned into a crunch that he turned to look. And when he did, his head craned up as his mouth fell open.

"Holy mother . . . Que—!"

Rook didn't get to finish his shout as something massive struck him in the side and sent him flying into and through the wall of one of the bone huts.

TWELVE
Uluru, Australia

AS KNIGHT AND Bishop arrived at the mouth of the valley, the sun had just begun peeking up over the horizon. The sandstone surface of Ayers Rock was well known for its ability, some believed supernatural ability, to change colors under certain conditions, most frequently at sunset and sunrise. Removing their night vision goggles, the pair saw the stone was beginning to glow red.

They paused at the valley opening, hoping to hear or see something that would give some hint about what they were about to run into. But only minutes after the attack had begun, the valley had fallen silent.

Bishop sniffed. "I smell the fire."

Knight pointed to a wisp of smoke filtering up over the red rock. "I think it's been put out."

Sudden movement brought their weapons to the ready. Both men had opted for small, light UMP submachine guns over their usual specialized weapons. Without the rest of the team in tow, Knight's sniper rifle and Bishop's machine gun made a bad combination for standard combat. With fingers on triggers, both men nearly shot the small black-flanked rock wallaby as it hopped from the valley, its eyes wide. The small marsupial paid no attention to the two men it would normally flee from, hopping between them and into the desert beyond.

Knight took a step forward, but was stopped by Deep Blue's voice. "Knight, Bishop, you read?"

"Go ahead," Knight said.

"I'm patching Queen through."

"Knight, Bish . . ." Queen was uncharacteristically out of breath. "We arrived too late. Our targets are down."

Knight and Bishop both keenly remembered the strength and ferocity of the Neanderthal hybrids and their mothers. "Seriously?" Knight said, keeping his eyes on the valley ahead.

"Looks like they didn't stand a chance. Listen, just—" A muffled boom sounded over the headset, followed by Queen's voice saying Rook's name. Then she was gone.

"I'll try to get her back," Deep Blue said. "The valley is in shadow with the sun rising so we're not seeing anything on the visual scan."

"Infrared?" Bishop asked.

"That's the thing," Deep Blue said. "I'm not seeing anything other than embers from the fire. Either everyone is gone, or . . ."

"Everyone is dead," Knight finished. "We're on it."

Knight and Bishop crept into the valley, weapons ready. They focused on every crag and shadow where someone could hide. A series of petroglyphs caught Knight's eye. He looked at the ancient pictographs. Some depicted ancient peoples and animals and others were simple swirling circles that he knew represented a watering hole. His eyes followed a streak of black algae that had grown in a water channel. Halfway up, the dry black surface became wet.

And red.

A small trickle of thick blood rolled down the stone and dripped at his feet. "Bishop!"

He followed the blood trail up and found a dark-skinned arm protruding from beneath a large boulder. It appeared the boulder had fallen on the person, but there were no cliff faces above it.

Bishop stepped farther into the valley as Knight continued looking at the crushed arm. "That stone must weigh a ton, Bishop. How—"

"Knight." Bishop's voice was quiet, but full of dread, which was an unusual inflection for a man who could not be injured or killed short of decapitation. Sensing the danger had passed, he lowered his weapon.

Knight joined him at a curve in the valley, which opened up into a large atrium. The back wall, covered in petroglyphs, rose up and hung over a large watering hole. It was fringed by adder's-tongue ferns and mulga and bloodwood trees. A small clearing held a circle of crushed, smoldering ash. But none of this held their attention. It was impossible to see the beauty of the place amid the sheer carnage.

Counting the bodies was impossible because many were torn apart and intermingled. Several were squashed, like roadkill—bodies bent, faces twisted in disgust, entrails burst from stomachs. Others lay beneath massive stones, as though they'd fallen from the sky. And one man hung upside down from a tree, twenty feet above the valley floor, his legs bent at impossible angles. Several piles of sandstone dust, now scattering in the breeze rolling down Ayers Rock, were spread among the dead.

The attack had only lasted a few minutes, but had been brutally efficient, leaving only a single wallaby as an eyewitness.

Bishop bent down to a severed head and rolled it over with the barrel of his UMP. Ignoring the look of horror frozen in the man's eyes, he focused on the Aboriginal facial features—pronounced brow, wide nose, dark skin. "These were our targets."

Knight crouched by a nearby body, possibly the one belonging to the head Bishop was inspecting. A pouch tied around the waist contained a wallet. Knight opened it and found a photo I.D. The name read: Balun Ammaroo. But the man in the photo wore a business suit and tie. "They were reenacting all this. Connecting with their heritage or something." Knight toggled on his throat mic. "Deep Blue, this is Knight."

"What's your status."

"We were too late. Everyone here is dead. Same M.O. as the Siletz Reservation."

The line was silent for a moment, then Deep Blue spoke again. "Take pictures of everything. Collect any evidence you think is important. When you're done we'll call in an anonymous tip so the bodies can be collected.

"Copy that," Knight said, "and Blue . . ."

"Yeah?"

"We've seen some crazy things in the past few years . . ." Knight looked around the clearing imagining how long it would take the Neanderthals or even the Hydra to inflict this many casualties, this brutally, and then disappear without a trace. He thought back on the large shadow he'd seen in the valley and shook his head. "And personally, I'd hoped all that was behind us, that some kind of normalcy had been restored to the world. But that's one wish that won't be coming true anytime soon. We're chest deep in it again."

THIRTEEN
Fort Bragg, North Carolina

ALEMAN RAN DOWN the staircase with Fiona over his shoulder and his handgun in his hand. Surrounded by brick and concrete, the sounds of the battle raging outside were dulled, but he could still feel the shaking of explosions in his feet. The second-floor door sprang open as three Army Rangers entered the stairwell, ready for battle. Aleman recognized them and, outranking them, commandeered their protective services.

"They're after the girl," Aleman shouted. "Do not leave my side."

The front man nodded. They had all been briefed on Fiona and knew she was under the military's protection, though they did not know why. "Where to, sir?"

Aleman had been wracking his brain on this point. They had never assumed someone would actually infiltrate Fort Bragg and hadn't come up with a fail-safe plan for such an event. They needed to be safe, but more than anything, they needed to hide. Someplace dark. Someplace secure. "Nearest fallout shelter."

The three Rangers took the lead and descended the staircase first. They entered the short hallway at the end of the stairwell and made for the lobby. At the lobby door, the last of the three Rangers held out an open hand to Aleman.

He stopped in the doorway and waited for the men to give the all clear. One man was about to, but his voice caught in his throat as his eyes grew wide. Something outside the lobby had caught his attention, and there was no time to shout a warning.

The lobby imploded as a large projectile burst through one side, plowed over the three Rangers, and exploded out the other side of the building. Fiona screamed as Aleman turned and shielded her small body with his own, taking a chunk of concrete to the back of his head. He fell to one knee, felt his mind swirl, and then forced himself back onto his feet, ignoring the warm trickle of blood dripping down the back of his neck.

He ran into the destroyed lobby, holstered his handgun, and picked up one of the dead Ranger's MP5 submachine gun.

Fiona's second scream was directed straight in his ear and caused him to drop her. She landed on her slippered feet and tugged on his shirt frantically. She pointed through the ruined lobby wall, where the large projectile had exited. "Lew!"

He turned and looked through the opening. A large gray mass, perhaps one hundred feet away, was turning around.

It heard her scream, Aleman thought.

Then it charged. In the brief moment he took to look, Aleman saw that it ran on four legs and vaguely resembled a rhino, though perhaps twice the size.

Hoisting Fiona up again, Aleman ran out the opposite side of the building and into the parking lot. A garage full of Hummers ready to go stood on the far side of the parking lot. Once mobile in one of the tough vehicles, he would make his way to the fallout shelter—after losing the behemoth, which he could hear gaining on them.

Running down a thin alley of parked cars, Aleman did his best to keep their heads low. Bullets were flying. Buildings were exploding. Bragg had become a war zone. As he exited the sea of cars Aleman turned to look for the large hunter. He saw nothing. But it was there. A car on the far side of the lot exploded into the air. Moments later a second car followed. It was charging straight through the lot, flinging cars out of its way.

Aleman took hold of the garage doorknob and turned. But it didn't budge. "Damnit!" He put Fiona down and kicked the door. Once. Twice. His head began to spin as blood seeped from the back of his skull. Knowing he wouldn't get through the door in time, he turned to face the creature.

As cars in the middle of the lot were flung skyward, he turned to Fiona. "We're going to dive out of the way at the last second, okay?"

She nodded and tried to look tough, despite her shaking lower lip.

"We'll be okay."

"Don't die, Lew," she said with a quivering voice. "Not for real."

Aleman focused on the giant gray force approaching them and refused to promise something he knew he couldn't. "Just jump when I say."

The car at the edge of the parking lot shot into the air, spinning madly as the monster burst free and charged toward them. Aleman only had time to see that the creature looked more like a bull-rhino amalgam with bull horns on top of its head and a third horn rising from its snout. But the rest of the features were dull, as though worn by time. Aleman tried to see more, to get some kind of hint about what this thing was, but his vision was blurring.

Then something amazing happened. A man, dressed head to toe in Special Ops black, charged toward the creature from the side. For a moment Aleman thought it might have been King, but the man was too tall and what he did next, well, not even King could have pulled it off.

The man took the creature by two of its horns and pushed down. The face, if that's what it could be called, dug into the pavement. The beast's forward momentum thrust its backside up and it flipped tail over head, landing on its back with a ground-shaking impact.

The man continued toward them without looking back. In his fading vision, Aleman could see the beast trying to right itself. And when it made progress he thought he saw two large shadows descend upon it. But he couldn't be sure. His attention moved back to the approaching man. Pushing Fiona behind him, he raised the MP5.

"Lew . . ." Fiona whispered.

The man raised his hands. "There's no need for that."

"Just stay back."

"I can protect the girl."

Aleman's aim faltered for just a moment, but it was all the man needed.

He stepped forward and twisted the MP5 out of his hands, tossing it to the side. Knowing he was about to fall unconscious, Aleman asked, "Who are you?"

He watched helplessly as the man scooped up Fiona, who had fallen limp, perhaps passed out, and said, "King will know." He stepped away, and then paused. "I hope he appreciates me breaking my promise."

With fading vision, Aleman watched the man retreat with Fiona in his arms. His last thought was of King and how the man would react to finding out his foster daughter had been kidnapped.

FOURTEEN
Mount Meru, Vietnam

A CHILDHOOD FEAR of drowning in a Chuck E. Cheese ball pool returned to Rook as he fought to free himself from a pile of ancient, green-glowing bones. The slippery bones rolled beneath him, making it almost impossible to move. When he felt the stone floor beneath his feet, he changed tactics—from moving forward, to moving up. He pushed up hard, shedding a shower of disassembled skeletons. He was free only for a moment when a second impact sent him soaring again.

He landed ten feet away in the middle of the street, rolling to a stop on a bed of femurs. Despite his groaning body begging him to stop moving, he climbed onto his feet and spun, looking for the . . . thing that had attacked him.

What it was he couldn't say. He'd only seen a blur of motion as it attacked. But even that revealed nothing. Whatever it was seemed to be hidden within a mass of bones, using them as cover.

Bones rattled.

Rook turned, only now realizing he'd dropped his M4.

The city was quiet. Calm. As though the thing had never been there.

Rook scanned the roofs of the buildings still standing. They weren't much taller than he was, so he should've been able to see the hulk. But there was nothing.

The building next to him shifted.

But it was thin. He could see through it and saw nothing but bones. No body. Nothing living.

He drew one of his prized .50 caliber Desert Eagles, which he referred to as "the girls." "C'mon out," he said. "Just give me a target."

A portion of the building shifted and fell. Rook franticly looked for a target within the movement, but saw nothing but bones.

Moving bones.

Some of which were moving . . . up.

Rook took a step back as he realized the truth. The building was moving. Whatever had attacked him wasn't hiding behind the bones or inside the bones. It was *under* the bones.

Rook opened fire, unleashing seven quick rounds, filling the chamber with the sound of thunder. But the moving mass showed no reaction as it rose up, shedding a layer of ancient body fragments. As the bones fell away, a ten-foot tall stone figure remained, nearly featureless except for the head, which was made from the head of a Neanderthal statue. It lunged for him.

With no time to reload, Rook did the only thing he could.

Ran.

While the Desert Eagle packed a punch big enough to put down any man or beast with a single shot, his assault rifle had a 40mm grenade launcher that could put down a whale. Maybe even a stone giant.

Bones shattered as a strike just missed him, sending an explosion of bone fragments into the chamber. The shrapnel struck Rook's back, embedding in his flak jacket and pushing him forward. He stumbled through the sea of ancient limbs, struggling back to the spot where he hoped he'd dropped his weapon. His eyes widened as he saw the barrel of his rifle protruding from the debris. He ran for it, but his foot rolled on a femur, toppling him forward.

The accidental movement saved his life as an enormous appendage swung over his prone body. While the creature recovered from its missed swing, Rook dove forward on his hands and knees. Reaching the M4, he took it up, wrapped his index finger around its second trigger—

—and held his fire.

Being only ten feet away, if he had pulled the trigger, he would have killed himself along with the monster. Crawling once again, he moved as far as he could before noticing the creature making progress. He rolled himself behind the remains of a bone wall and took aim.

The grenade launcher's cough was followed by a massive explosion. Bones and rock fragments rained down for several seconds and the air filled with the smell of explosives and the dust of the dead.

Rook leaned up and found only a bone-filled crater where the monster had stood. Before he had a chance to savor his victory he noticed his body was shaking. Were his nerves really that fragile after not being in the field for a year? But it wasn't he who was shaking. It was the chamber.

As he reloaded the grenade launcher he remembered the pulsating vibrations he'd felt before. Whatever was causing the shaking wasn't getting closer, it was—

Boom!

The cavern wall exploded as a twelve-foot giant barreled through it. Rook ducked as stone shrapnel shot through the cavern fast enough to shatter bones, toppling some of the still standing structures. Rook stood and fought to see what was happening through the dust-filled air. A large shape, its form shrouded in the foul air, surged toward him. He couldn't see the details of its body, but unlike the first, this one wasn't made from stone. It was crystal. The same kind of crystal that hung above the city of Meru. The same kind of crystal that hung around Bishop's neck. The healing stones had become a killing machine.

Rook took aim and fired. The grenade covered the hundred feet to the crystalline goliath and exploded. The force of the explosion pushed the monster to the side, but did no other damage. The crystals were strong.

Very strong.

As he turned to run, Rook once again tripped on the bony carpet and fell to his hands and knees. The ground shook with vibrations as the crystal creature pounded toward him, crushing bones beneath its tree trunk–like limbs. It had no trouble moving about the bone city.

Rook rolled over and emptied his clip at the beast. But the bullets simply ricocheted off. A cloud of dust billowed out in front of the creature as it charged through a sea of bones. With only seconds left before it trampled him, Rook prayed for Queen to show up.

But it wasn't Queen who came to his rescue.

A blur leapt from the roof of a nearby bone building. The dark shape disappeared into the cloud of dust and struck the beast. The giant stumbled from the impact, but remained upright. Dust swirled as snarling howls filled the cavern. Then the howl turned to an ear piercing yelp.

The smaller creature roared with pain before it was flung against the wall, where it lay still, a crystal impaled in its chest.

Though he still couldn't see more than a vague shape, Rook felt the monster turn its attention back to him. He slowly reached for a grenade, ready to lob it by hand. But there was no need. A sound like breaking glass rang out as the crystal giant fell, breaking into a mass of inanimate shards.

Rook regarded the pile of crystals for only a moment before running, as best he could, to the prone form of his rescuer. He recognized her immediately, and despite his nightmare experience with her kind, treated her as kindred in the wake of the unreal giants. "Red!"

He knelt beside Red's body. He was glad to see her chest still rising and falling, but immediately knew there would be no saving her. The short, but thick female Neanderthal already had a pool of blood around her, oozing from the large chest wound.

"Red," he whispered.

Her red-rimmed yellow eyes opened and what appeared to be a smile, made ghastly by her blood-covered two-inch canines, spread on her lips. "Rook. Father came back."

He nodded. "I came back."

"Red save you?"

"You did."

She grunted and coughed up blood.

"What did they want?" he asked. "Why did they come here?"

Red looked into Rook's eyes with the closest thing to kindness he'd ever seen in the species. "Bad words."

For a moment, Rook thought she was remembering some of the more colorful phrases he'd shouted at her a year ago. But then her expression turned to terror. She took Rook's arms in her hands and squeezed. Rook almost didn't hear her past the intense pain she was inflicting.

"Can't speak the bad words."

Rook grunted in pain, and Red released him, falling back. Her eyes closing. "What are the bad words?"

"Can't speak them," she whispered. "*Don't* speak them."

Her head fell to the side.

Red, last of the Neanderthals, was dead.

Queen returned moments later, weapon at the ready, but unnecessary. After working her way through the sea of bones, she stood over Rook, who was still kneeling over Red.

"You okay?"

"Thanks to her."

He moved, giving Queen a clear view.

"Red?" she asked.

With a nod, he added, "She said they wanted the 'bad words.'"

"Bad words." Queen thought back over their last year of training; training that was supposed to have prepared them for the strange and unusual events they were encountering. But the reference was too vague to even speculate about. "Could be anything."

"Yeah," Rook said. "Well, I can think of at least one bad word that's applicable after what I just experienced: we're fucked." He closed Red's eyes with his fingers, stood, and looked at Queen. "God help anyone else who tangles with these things."

FIFTEEN
Fort Bragg, North Carolina

TO THEIR CREDIT, King's mother and father didn't say a word as he pushed his car to one hundred twenty miles an hour. As they reached the highway exit for Fort Bragg, his mother's only comment was that it was miraculous they hadn't been pulled over. En route, King had put in calls to every member of the team, including Deep Blue, and finally to the office at Bragg itself. No one picked up. It could mean the team was engaged in a phones-off meeting, but Bragg not answering combined with the warning he'd received was ominous and he kept his foot pressed heavy on the gas pedal.

As they sped down the entry road to Bragg, disregarding the thirty-mile-per-hour speed limit, King saw the first security checkpoint ahead. He took his foot off the gas, intending to have the men there send word ahead. But as they drew nearer he saw that the metal gate lay broken and bent on the side of the road. The guardhouse still stood, but one of the walls had been shattered. He stopped next to the small building and saw the two guards lying dead in the grass.

"Stay here," he said to his parents before opening the door.

As soon as the door opened, the distant sounds of battle filled his ears. Despite his urge to hop back in the car and tear off into the thick of it, his training kept him rooted. First he checked the downed guards for pulses. Finding none, he collected their M4s. Before heading back to the car he stopped by the shed, kicked through the rubble, and found a handheld radio. He turned it on and shouting voices filled the air. He quickly dialed through the channels and found the same on each; soldiers shouting orders, asking for reinforcements, describing large, fast-moving objects that couldn't be stopped.

King dropped the radio. The strangeness of the attack confirmed the warning he'd received. Someone was after Fiona.

He rushed back to the car and slid into the driver's seat. He handed one of the M4s to his father. "Can you handle this?"

Peter gave a curt nod. "Been a while, but I'll manage."

King shut the door and put the car in gear.

"Hey," Lynn said from the backseat. When King looked back at her, she glanced at Peter's M4. "I'm a better shot than Davy Crockett here," she said, motioning to Peter.

King's father smiled and looked at him. "It's true. She could give Annie Oakley a run for her money."

With no time to waste wondering about his parents hidden abilities, he drew his Sig Sauer pistol and handed it back to his mother. Then they were off, speeding past the main entrance to the base, where a statue of a soldier usually stood. King gave the missing statue's base a quick glance, then veered hard to the left as a car rolled ass over teakettle past them on the right.

"Whoa!" Peter shouted as he watched the spinning car crash into the welcome center and explode.

King ignored the explosion filling his rearview mirror and focused on driving through the chaos. Soldiers ran in every direction, some firing over the car at something he couldn't see. Explosions plumed all around, some bearing the telltale signature of fragmentation grenades, but other, larger and more fiery explosions looked like fuel depots or large vehicles exploding. And others, composed primarily of brick and concrete debris, looked more like invisible wrecking balls were tearing the base apart from the inside.

Which wasn't far from the truth, King realized, as a dark blur ran up beside the car. With the car, and the object outside it, moving so fast he couldn't make out any details, but its intentions were clear. "Hold on!" King shouted, intending to hit the brakes, but never getting the chance.

A massive force struck the rear side of the car, sending it into a three-hundred-sixty-degree spin. As the tires squealed, filling the air with the scent of smoldering rubber, King caught a quick glance of a largely shapeless, but four-legged, mass still in pursuit despite the constant bombardment of rounds fired by concealed special ops soldiers.

King yanked the wheel, compensating for the spin, and setting them back on course. He gunned the engine and shouted to his parents. "Everyone okay?"

Lynn slapped him on the shoulder three times. "Just go, go, go!" She watched over her shoulder as the thing gave chase. For a moment it appeared they would outrun the monster, but a sudden shake, followed by the left rear wheel's rubber shedding off and rolling to the side of the road, slowed their progress.

King saw the creature gaining once again and made the final turn toward the barracks where he knew the highest concentration of soldiers would be—and, he hoped, Fiona.

At least one of his hopes proved true. Rounding the corner, he saw a line of Delta operators armed with a vast array of heavy-hitting weapons, from grenade launchers to antitank missile launchers laying in wait.

Knowing the speeding car with three passengers was not the enemy, the soldiers split and allowed them to pass. King stopped the car and directed his parents to the nearby barracks. "Hide in there. I'll come get you."

To his relief, his parents followed his orders, moving into the building, weapons high and ready . . . like people trained to handle weapons. Trained to kill. He forced the thought of his mother killing a man from his mind and joined the men at the line.

"Where's my team?" he shouted to Jeff Kafer, a fellow Delta team leader with a blond mop of hair and a thick mustache. He didn't know him well, but Rook and Kafer were friends. Both were loud and liked to tell jokes at the bar. Both had several sisters. And both loved their weapons like children.

"Not on base, King," Kafer replied. "And you know I don't know where."

"Have you seen Fiona?"

Kafer motioned toward the garage fifty feet behind them. "Saw Aleman back there. Looks injured, but he might know."

"Here it comes!" one of the men shouted.

Kafer raised his voice to make sure everyone heard him. "Wait on me!"

The line took aim at the charging mass of stone and waited.

King did not. He turned and ran for Aleman, who he could see slumped against one of the large garage doors, a smear of blood stretching down to the back of his head. He didn't get ten feet before Kafer yelled, "Fire!"

The air filled with the sounds of launching ordinance one moment and a rapid succession of explosions the next. King turned and saw the giant creature charging through the onslaught. Several explosions sent pavement flying into the air. Direct hits shot chunks of its body flying. A few misses shredded parked vehicles. Despite the brute force of the attack, the thing showed no response, felt no pain. It simply charged forward. When one of its legs burst free, it ran on three.

It wouldn't be stopped.

As the line of men realized this, and knew just as surely that they couldn't get out of its way in time, they raised their arms and turned their heads, as a natural reaction to being trampled. King raised his M4 and fired, just as the beast reached the line of men.

But the useless bullets King fired never hit their mark. Instead, they sailed straight through a cloud of dust that burst out and over the line of men. The giant had disintegrated. Whether from the attack or some other reason, King didn't care. It was gone, and Aleman was down.

As King rushed to Aleman's side he heard the pop of gunfire cease around the base. The battle was over.

"Lew," he said, kneeling down by Aleman's body. "Lew, wake up."

Aleman's eyes blinked open. "King . . ."

"What happened?"

Aleman tried to sit up, but a stab of pain kept him down. "Took a hit to the head. Shrapnel I think."

"Where're the others?"

"Gone," Aleman said.

"Fiona's with them?"

Aleman frowned and King knew the answer before the man said the words. "They took her."

King clenched his fists. Fiona was gone.

His daughter was gone.

At that moment all of King's fears became realized—Jack Sigler never would be, nor should be, a father. And if he were somehow able to bring her back alive, he would find a better, and safer, home for her. King picked up his friend and headed for the barracks where a makeshift triage was already being set up.

As King passed, Peter saw a flicker of something in King's eyes, an anger bordering on primal, screaming for revenge.

"What's going to happen?" Lynn asked her husband as he closed the door.

"I'm not sure," he said, meeting her eyes with a strong gaze that communicated more than words, "but whoever did this . . ." He shook his head. "I wouldn't want to be them when Jack comes calling."

"Are you sure this isn't more than he can handle?" she said, lowering her voice to a strong whisper.

Peter took her arm. "He'll handle it."

"I couldn't live with myself if something happened and we—"

Peter took hold of her other arm and pulled her close. *"He'll handle it.* We Sigler's are hard to kill."

"I hope that's true," she said. "For both of them."

SEEK

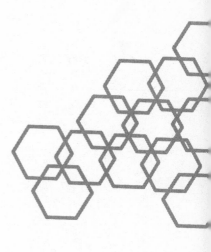

SIXTEEN
Fort Bragg, North Carolina

DESPITE AN UNCEASING urge to find out who was behind the attack and where Fiona had been taken, King was duty-bound to aid in the rescue efforts under way around Fort Bragg. Collapsed buildings buried the dead and dying. Triages treated burns, puncture wounds, and crushed limbs, some of which had to be amputated. Outside of a war zone, he'd seen nothing like it.

And neither had America.

The attack, seen and heard for miles around, was impossible to hide from the media. At first, news helicopters had hovered outside the no-fly zone, zooming in for close-up shots of the rescue operation under way, but they had since been chased away by several deadly attack helicopters now securing the aerial perimeter. Shots from visitor camera phones flooded YouTube. And a few reporters, who were already on the base when the attack occurred, took advantage of the chaos, hiding in the ruins and snapping photos of bloodied soldiers, destroyed buildings, and parking lots filled with overturned vehicles.

By the time the military launched a full-scale search to find and remove press from the base it was too late to contain the story. The world knew about the attack on Fort Bragg. The images of destroyed buildings and dead soldiers revolted each and every American who saw them.

Once they were sure the press had been cleared, the pilots of the large green and white helicopter known as Marine One were given the go ahead. The presidential helicopter swung into view above the base accompanied by two fully armed AH-64D Apache Longbow attack helicopters. A squadron of F-22 Raptor fighter jets secured the airspace above and around the base, their engines a constant roar in the sky.

The grass of the barracks' central quad bowed away from the massive helicopter as it set down, the chop of its blades slowing. As the rotors stopped spinning a small group of soldiers gathered to see if Marine One carried who they all thought it did. When the door opened and President Thomas Duncan stepped out, his face grim, each and every one of the beaten and tired men snapped sharp salutes.

All but one.

King walked past the saluting men and stomped toward the president, who he knew as Deep Blue. Two Secret Service men moved for King but Duncan stopped them with an open hand.

The Secret Service men looked uneasy as they eyed the messy-haired man dressed in jeans and a black T-shirt approaching the commander in chief. The raw anger in King's eyes set the president's guardians on edge, but they stood down. King stopped and didn't bother with a salute. "Fiona's gone."

Deep Blue's eyes opened wide. "What?" Duncan had been so inundated with presidential damage control in the wake of the incident that he had yet to read the detailed briefing from General Keasling. "How?"

"Last I checked Lewis was still unconscious, so I'm not sure."

Duncan turned and looked at the destruction, meaning to walk toward the line of approaching generals and their marine escorts. King took his arm. "Why wasn't I told about the mission?" King asked, his voice tinged with anger.

Duncan looked at King's hand then met the man's eyes.

"You put Fiona's life at risk."

"There was no way to know *this* would happen," Duncan said, motioning to the destroyed base. "We thought you needed more time to grieve your mother's—"

"My mother's not dead," King said.

Duncan looked stunned.

King pointed to his mother, who was helping pass water out to the wounded. She saw him pointing and gave a little wave. Duncan smiled sheepishly and raised his hand to her. "I don't understand."

"You don't know?"

"Know what?"

King shook his head. "We can figure out how that story fell through the cracks later. I need to find Fiona. Now."

Duncan looked around. The approaching generals, most of whom did not know the president was also Deep Blue, were almost upon them. He leaned in close to King. "I'm going to be out of commission until things settle down. Every move I make is being watched. But I want you to do whatever it takes, King. Keasling has a blank check for this. The gloves are off. Find your daughter. Find who did this. Figure out what they want and put a stop to it."

King nodded and turned to walk away, but this time Duncan took hold of him and turned him around.

"You and I may think of each other as equals, King, but when we're in public remember who you are. And who I am." He glanced at the approaching generals. "People are watching."

Despite King's frosty mood he snapped a salute. "Yes sir."

King walked away as the swarm of marines and generals overtook Duncan and moved him to a more secure location. With the team due to arrive at Pope Air Force Base in an hour, he would meet them there, put the pieces together, and then turn them loose. But first he needed Aleman for information, his parents for good-byes, an ass-load of weapons for the obvious, and a few friends to level the playing field.

SEVENTEEN
Pope Air Force Base, North Carolina

FORTY MINUTES AFTER meeting the president, King stood outside Hangar 7, Delta's personal hangar that typically housed the *Crescent*. Right now it was devoid of any aircraft but held four Delta teams made up of five soldiers each. The men, dressed in black fatigues, quickly off-loaded their gear from the two large trucks that had carried them to the airfield and stood before King. The four team leaders approached.

Jeff Kafer, call sign Mouth, thanks to his audiobook narrator's voice, said, "I hear you've got an 'ask and you shall receive' order from Keasling. Well, you asked and we're here, so mind telling us what this is about?"

King motioned to the open hangar. "Come with me. You can brief your men when we're done."

The five team leaders entered Decon, where a bandaged but conscious Lewis Aleman sat waiting behind a laptop. General Keasling stood in the corner, his short arms crossed over his chest. As the men entered the room, the tension became palpable. They'd all seen friends and comrades killed and the shock from the strange attack had not yet worn off. The team leaders, who were accustomed to sitting around this table with their own teams, sat down and turned to Keasling. He motioned their attention to King, who stood at the head of the table. "He's running the show."

"As of this moment," King said, "your teams are serving under the Chess Team. Each one of you will serve under a member of my team and will obey their orders as though each and every one of them was God himself. You will be Pawns One through Five with the team leader's designation coming first."

He pointed to Kafer. "You're Rook's Pawn One and your men are Two through Five. In the field this will be shortened to RP-One. Understood?"

Nods all around. Despite their battle-hardened experience and high rank, the men knew they were being brought, at least temporarily, into the fold of the Chess Team. Each of them felt a mix of honor and intimidation.

"We've got a connection," Aleman said before tapping a few keys on the laptop.

The wall behind King, actually a well-disguised flat-screen display, came to life. Queen, Rook, Knight, and Bishop appeared on the screen, sitting around a laptop on their end from within the *Crescent*. Their serious faces reflected that they had been briefed on the Fort Bragg attack and Fiona's kidnapping.

"Can you hear us?" Rook asked.

"We hear you," King replied and then nodded at Aleman. "Give what you have."

King had plucked Aleman from his cot, which he'd been forced to stay in, and had him working on finding answers for the past thirty minutes. It wasn't a lot of time, but Aleman tended to think faster than most men. And he didn't disappoint.

"Here's what we know. About a year ago, the Siletz Reservation was destroyed. We now have a pretty good idea how. That said, we still have no idea what actually attacked us."

"A shitload of living rock, that's what," Kafer said.

Aleman looked at the ceiling for a moment, his eyes squinted in thought.

"Lew," King said.

Aleman looked back at his screen. "Then we received tips that certain targets in Australia and Vietnam were in danger. In fact, the targets were killed before our team arrived on site. Or, in Rook's case, just after. And it was the last words of this dying victim that clued me in. She said—correct me if I'm wrong, Rook—that they were after 'bad words' that you were then told not to speak. 'Can't speak them. Don't speak them.'"

"You got it," Rook said.

"Given the ancestry of the victim, it occurred to me that her native language would be very old; perhaps one of the oldest, if not *the* oldest, spoken language on the planet. I did some research on the other victims. All of them were the last surviving speakers of nearly extinct ancient languages. The Gurdanji in Australia had five living speakers. They're all dead. The Siletz had two living speakers, Fiona's grandmother—"

"And Fiona," Queen said. "Shit."

"I compiled a list of all dying languages around the world and found a disturbing trend. Many of the last speakers of ancient languages have either gone missing or been found dead. Someone is exterminating them.

But because they're relatively few people spread out all around the world, some in obscure places, no one has noticed. I've identified the speakers of the most at-risk languages that are still living. Tinigua has two speakers. Taushiro, one. Uru, one. And Vilela, two. All four of these languages are in South America. Then there is Chulym, known as Ös to its three speakers in Siberia, down from fifteen three years ago thanks to a flu that killed thousands of people in the remote area. And Pazeh with one speaker born in the Philippines, but living in Taiwan."

"Are you assigning us to kidnap these people?" Kafer said.

"That's your mission," King replied. "Yes."

"And you've done this before?"

"Bag and tag," Bishop said, which got a smile from Rook and odd looks from the four team leaders in Decon.

"Are you questioning your orders?" King asked, his voice heavy, his eyes leveled at Kafer.

For a moment it appeared Kafer might argue the point, but he leaned back in his chair instead. "Just curious is all."

Aleman cleared his throat. "Queen and Bishop will lead two teams to South America. Knight will take one team to Taiwan. Rook will take Siberia."

"I don't need to tell you that not only do we not know *who* we're up against, but we also don't know *what*," King said. "You and your men have fought conventional wars up until now, but all that changes today. Throw out your preconceptions about human capabilities and effective tactics and do not, ever, believe a bullet can kill the enemy."

"What *do* we know?" one of the team leaders asked. "I saw the damn statue from Bragg's main entrance come to life and kill a man."

"And that about sums up our intel," Aleman said. "Someone has found a way to imbue nonliving material with, for lack of a better word, life. Statues come to life. Crude stone monsters. It doesn't seem to matter what the material is as long as it is inanimate."

"I faced off against two of them," Rook said. "One made of stone and the other of giant crystals."

"They appear to feel no pain," Aleman said, "and when their mission, again for lack of a better word, is complete they return to their inanimate state, which is why the statue you mentioned is now in a barracks lobby."

"You all need to move fast and quiet. I want you in and out of these countries with the targets without ruffling a feather, blipping a radar, or engaging the enemy." King looked up at the screen, eyeing the members of his team, and then looked at the team leaders at the table. "Because as good as you all are, you won't stand a chance." He looked back at the screen. "ETA?"

"We're incoming now," Knight said. "Wheels down and hatch open in three minutes."

King switched off the flat-screen and spoke to the team leaders. "I want you all on that bird in four minutes. Brief your men in the air. Got it?"

"Understood," Kafer said as he stood. "One last question?"

"What is it?"

"Where will *you* be going?"

King's nose twitched. "For now"—he looked at Aleman, who shrugged—"nowhere."

Kafer gave King a pat on the shoulder as he headed for the door. "You'll find her."

The men filed out of the room. Keasling followed after them, intent on ensuring that each and every man made King's four-minute schedule.

King sat down across from Aleman. He looked grim.

"Last night, did you get a chance to refill Fiona's insulin pump and move it to a new location?"

Aleman paled. He hadn't thought of that problem. "I did. The pump was on her hip. The needle just above it."

Fiona's insulin pump lasted three days when full. After that Fiona would be susceptible to hyperglycemia, which resulted in painful symptoms including coma and death, sometimes very quickly depending on circumstances such as diet and exertion. But that wasn't the most pressing concern at the moment. The girl he'd been entrusted to protect had been taken from him by a man he knew very little about.

After first hearing Aleman's description of the mystery man, King suspected his identity was none other than Alexander Diotrephes. He was sure of it. And Alexander *was* a doctor, among other things. In theory, he should be able to supply her with insulin. Hell, he could probably cure her. But what did they really know about the man? He'd helped them defeat the Hydra, but he had personal reasons for doing that. He'd saved Fiona once before, at the Siletz Reservation, but no one knew his real motives or intentions. Who's to say he wasn't behind the attacks himself? Until all of these questions were answered, King couldn't trust that Fiona's life wasn't in danger. "Let's operate under the assumption that she's not going to be cared for. There's no way to know for sure until I find her."

Aleman nodded. "You really think Hercules—Alexander—has Fiona?"

King's mind refocused on the task of finding Fiona. He couldn't do anything about her diabetes until she was safe in his care again. "Sounds insane, I know. The question is: Where did he take her? And does he have anything to do with these living statues?"

Aleman shook his head. There were so many unanswered questions he was having trouble keeping track of them all, which was frustrating because he could feel the answer to one of their questions on the tip of his tongue.

Then it came to him. *Living statues.* "Oh my God," he whispered, and then said loudly, "I know what they are."

King immediately sat up straight. "What?"

"Golem."

EIGHTEEN

"STAI BENE, TESORO?"

Fiona opened her eyes to the concerned face of a middle-aged woman with dark curly hair. She couldn't understand a word the woman said, but she recognized the language. "I can't speak Italian."

"Sorry," the woman said in English. "I should have learned to greet newcomers in English by now. Most of us here speak it well enough."

Fiona tried sitting up, but a spinning head kept her planted in what she now realized was a cot made up in white sheets. The woman saw Fiona's trouble and helped her sit. "It's the drugs. You'll feel dizzy for just a few more minutes and drowsy for another day. Maybe more because you're so small."

"Drugs?" Fiona gave her body a visual once over and saw no injuries, but her body and the woman's face were as far as she could focus. She looked up and saw brown, but the room twisted madly causing instant nausea. She turned her eyes down and saw a brown stone floor. "This isn't a hospital." She looked at the woman. "And you're not a nurse, are you?"

The woman frowned and shook her head. "I am a linguist. And no, this is not a hospital." The woman held out her hand. "Elma Rossi."

Fiona shook her hand. "Fiona Lane." She looked into Elma's eyes, wondering if she was someone she could trust. Deciding she had no choice, she asked, "Where am I?"

"Where we are in the world . . . I cannot say. There are no windows. No clues. The only thing we know is that we are underground."

Underground? Fiona focused on the floor, fought down a fresh wave of nausea, and then looked again. The wall closest to her resolved as a continuation of the stone floor, brown and featureless. The room continued to spin, but she forced herself to look, to glean what she could.

She saw people. Small groups of them gathered in huddles around the room. Some appeared to be self-segregated by race. Others lay on cots like hers, staring at the ceiling—also stone. The space was about the size of her junior high cafeteria, before the reservation was destroyed.

A persistent pain in her hip drew her attention. She lifted up her shirt and saw the insulin pump attached to her waistband. She turned it up, looking at its digital display, which showed her glucose levels, battery life, and insulin supply. All was good.

"What is that?" Elma asked.

"Insulin pump. I'm diabetic."

"That can be hard, especially on one so young. But I wouldn't worry about it," Elma said. "Those of us with medical needs have been taken care of. I'm sure you will be as well."

"I'll be fine for a few more days, anyway," Fiona said. To prove it, she stood. When she did, a fresh wave of nausea struck. She stumbled and was caught by Elma.

"Slow down, child, you'll—"

Fiona yanked her arm away. "Let me do this," she said, her little voice almost a growl. "I can do this." Driven by a deep desire to be strong like King, she did what she'd seen him do after taking a hard hit or running a long distance. Hands on knees, head between legs, and long, deep breaths. She finished with a deep grunt and stood. She felt stronger, but still dizzy. Though she didn't let Elma see that. Rook told her that when they were on a mission they had to swallow pain and discomfort to get things done. He made it sound easy.

It wasn't.

But Fiona had Elma convinced as she stood up straight and rolled her little neck. When she opened her eyes again, the woman had taken a step back with a hand to her mouth. "Child, you may be the toughest person here."

The statement helped Fiona stand still as her body threatened to buckle over and wretch. She swallowed, knowing that Rook had meant pain-swallowing as a metaphor, and forced a cocky King-style smile. "Just trying to take after my dad."

Elma's eyes were wide. "And . . . who is your father?"

"You can ask him when he—" Fiona lurched forward and vomited at the base of her cot. After three heaves and a coughing fit, she spit the remaining bile from her mouth and stood with tears in her eyes. Elma stepped forward and held her. Fiona melted into her hug. "Not as tough as you thought."

"Nonsense," Elma said, brushing a hand over Fiona's straight black hair. "Some of these people did not stop crying for days. Some still cry."

Fiona looked up at her. "How long have you been here?"

"Three months." She motioned to the groups around the room, some of whom were looking their way. "Others are new arrivals like you. The longest have been here for a year."

Fiona slumped in Elma's embrace, horrified. "A *year*."

"We are well cared for," Elma said, her voice suddenly hopeful. "Look there," she said, pointing to a door at the far end of the room that Fiona had missed during her dizzy turnabout. "We're fed three times a day. And the food isn't bad." She pointed to the other end of the room where several hanging sheets divided the space. "There is a toilet with working plumbing, and a shower with drainage there. The water is cold, but it is nice to be clean. Even the lighting was carefully chosen."

Fiona looked up at the string of lights hanging from the ceiling, spaced out every ten feet in a grid from one end to the other.

"The bulbs mimic sunlight and reduce the effect of not getting outside. It's no replacement, but it's better than regular bulbs."

"Then why are we here?"

Elma shrugged. "We do not know. But it is clear our captors mean us no harm."

"Yet . . . " Fiona added.

Elma grimaced and then nodded. "Yes. *Yet.* We are supplied with games, water, reading material, and medical supplies should the need arise."

With her emotions reined in by the conversation and her body returning to normal, Fiona stepped away and stood on her own. "Who brings the supplies? The food?"

"We do not see who brings the food," said a tall, skinny black man. "They come when it is dark. At night. When they shut off the lights. We cannot see them. But we hear them."

"Buru," Elma scolded. "Don't frighten the girl."

"She will be less frightened if she knows what to expect." He turned to Fiona. "Who do you think deposited you here during the night? None of us saw you arrive. We woke, and there you were."

Elma muttered some exasperated Italian and said, "She has only just arrived!"

When Elma threw her arms up, a black symbol could be seen on the back of her hand. It was small, about the size of a quarter, but Fiona recognized it instantly. She stepped away from Elma.

Elma's hands stopped in midair. She'd noticed Fiona's fear and followed the girl's eyes to the symbol on her hand—a circle with two vertical lines through it. "What is it, child?"

Fiona just stared, her mind putting together pieces faster than she knew how to react.

"It's a brand of a sort," Elma said, lowering her hand and holding it out.

Buru showed her his hand. Though less visible on his dark skin, the symbol was there. "All of us have one." He pointed to her right hand. "Even you."

Fiona looked at her hand, the dark symbol fresh and shining like a cancer. She tried rubbing it off, but it did not smudge or dull. *Tattoos,* she thought, and then realized their purpose. She had helped her grandmother tag goats on the reservation once. Hated every second. But the experience was etched into her mind, impossible to forget. The tags showed ownership. And she was the only one here who knew the name of their shepherd.

Alexander Diotrephes.

And the knowledge gave her strength.

Rubbing the tattoo with her thumb, she turned to Buru. "They only enter in the dark?"

He nodded, perplexed that the little girl would return to the topic. "There is a dim light from the hallway beyond the door, but that is all."

"Have you seen one?"

Buru looked at Elma, who threw her hands up, and walked away while shaking her head and muttering in Italian.

"Only shadows," Buru said. "But others have seen them."

"Dark cloaks and gray skin?"

Elma stopped and turned around slowly. Her eyes wide.

Buru was likewise stunned. "You know of these things?"

Fiona sifted through a year's worth of Chess Team education she got on top of her regular school studies. "My father called them wraiths but that's a misnomer because 'wraith' is a Scottish word for ghosts . . . and these are not Scottish. And they're not ghosts."

"What are they?" Buru asked.

She shrugged. "I dunno, but I can tell you two things for sure. First, we won't be escaping without help. Second, help is on the way."

Buru looked incredulous, like he'd just remembered he was speaking to a young girl. "How do you know this?"

She looked at Elma, trying her best to sound confident, to believe that King, her father, would scour the earth for her, and said, "I never did tell you who my father is."

NINETEEN
Pope Air Force Base, North Carolina

KING RESTED HIS elbows on the table and tried the word on for size. "Golem." He didn't like it. "As in the legendary Jewish variety?"

"You know it?" Aleman asked.

"Just the basics," King said. "That they're figures, most often created from clay and brought to life when a rabbi places a piece of paper in its mouth with the word 'Emet,' truth, written on it. Sometimes the word is inscribed on the golem's body instead. To destroy the golem the 'E' is erased, leaving the word 'Met,' death." King looked up at Aleman, who was typing away on his laptop as he listened. "You know how stupid this sounds?"

"You've seen Hydra reborn and Neanderthal women wanting to mate with Rook. This kind of thing should no longer be strange. What else do we know?"

King sat back and focused. They had covered the golem briefly during their year of study, along with a slew of other myths representing the world's cultures and religions. Visualizing what he knew of the golem, images began to fill in the missing gaps.

"The most popular golem story involved a rabbi in Prague. In the 1500s. He used a golem to defend his ghetto against anti-Semitic attacks. The golem grew violent. Killed slews of people. Non-Jews. And the persecution was stopped."

"Are they intelligent?" Aleman asked.

"No," King said. "They can't act without instructions from the rabbi who gives them life. They can't talk. I suppose they have a limited intelligence in that they can understand commands and carry them out, but maybe that's just the creator's thoughts and feelings being imprinted on the golem?"

Aleman looked up slowly.

"What?" King asked.

"Just impressed is all. I don't think you would have said that a year ago."

"That's nice, but none of it tells me who to shoot. Any idea?"

Aleman shrugged. "Beats me. But if inanimate objects really are being brought to life, maybe someone figured out how to tap into some kind of ancient creative power. God. Aliens. Intelligent capybara from another dimension. I'm leaving all the cards on the table."

King opened his hands. "Okay, fine. We'll call them golems for now, but that doesn't get us any closer to finding Fiona, which is why I'm still here. Tell me what happened again. How she was taken."

Aleman pursed his lips, looking down at the empty table. "The thing . . . the golem . . . was charging us. A man in black special ops gear, who I thought was you until he latched onto its head and drove what had to be a ton of stone into the pavement. As my vision faded I saw two things, black shapes attack the downed golem. I couldn't see the man's face, but he had a deep voice and said you would know who he was."

"And we do. But he could be anywhere in the world." King shook his head in frustration. "He didn't say anything else?"

"Something . . . maybe . . . something about a promise." Aleman looked

up as the memory returned. "Breaking a promise. He said, 'I hope he appreciates me breaking my promise.'"

"Breaking his promise?"

"Did he promise you anything?"

King's head moved slowly from side to side. "Nothing."

Aleman quickly scoured everything he could find about Hercules,
searching for the keyword "promise." He found nothing. "There's no mention about a promise anywhere in literature or online. If he was dropping
a hint, it's not something publicly known."

"Then it would have to be personal," King said. "But I never met the
man."

"Queen and Rook did," Aleman added.

"Can you search their reports?" The team kept detailed reports of all
missions including every action taken, why, and, to the best of their ability, what was said. The process was long and they often ended up with
novelettes by the time they were done, but many missions overlapped
and what was at the time a minor detail could become important in the
future.

Aleman's response was to begin typing. Thirty seconds later, "Bingo!
Queen's report has him saying, 'I long ago promised someone I loved
that I would refrain from getting directly involved in the world's problems.' The context was his refusal to get physically involved in the Hydra
mission."

"But he's getting involved now."

"And breaking that promise . . . to who . . ." King pounded the table
with his fist, but not in anger, in victory. "Acca Larentia."

Aleman wasn't used to being the one asking questions. He was typically on the delivering end of strange or pertinent information. "Who?"

"Acca Larentia. She was Hercules's mistress, said to have been won in
a game of dice and later, when he was done with her, married to an Etrus-
can man named Carutius, whose property she inherited when he died.
The property later became known as Rome."

King's thoughts shifted, knowing that history, especially when it concerned Hercules, could not be trusted. Over the past several thousand
years, his secret organization, the Herculean Society, had systematically
altered history by either erasing Hercules's influence and existence altogether, or heaping on legend to make it unbelievable. The truth that no
one knew was that Hercules was more genius than a god-man, and had

extended his life through genetic tinkering and boosted his physical prowess, when needed, by consuming adrenaline-boosting concoctions. Immortal, yes. A god, no.

He stood and paced, his energy building as the pieces began coming together. "I'm willing to bet that Hercules was also Carutius, now Alexander Diotrephes. And I think we can safely assume he's had many names in between. If he was married to Acca, then the promise he made might have been to her."

He turned to Aleman. "Are there any monuments to her?"

After working the keyboard, Aleman said, "Not a one."

King frowned, thinking of the fear that Fiona must be feeling and loathing the absolute helplessness he felt. Never before in his life had he felt so powerless. So vulnerable.

"Hold on," Aleman said. "She was supposedly buried in the Velabrum, between the Palatine and Capitoline hills in Rome. It was once a swampy area, but it's now covered by the ruins of Foro Romano—the Roman Forum."

"It fits," King said. "His last hiding place had been beneath the Rock of Gibraltar, one of the two pillars of Hercules. If the Herculean Society is dedicated to protecting the historical Hercules, it would make sense to set up shop at his most prized locations, especially one housing the body of his one, and only, love in twenty-five hundred years."

He opened his cell phone and dialed. A moment later he said, "Bring my ride around. Yes. Rome." He hung up and dialed again, waiting for the other end to pick up. When it did, he got an answering machine. "It's Jack. I'm on my way to Rome and I need your help. ETA fives hours. Thanks, George."

No one knew Rome or Hercules better than George Pierce, the man whose inquiries made him a target of the Herculean Society's cloaked thieves and, later, the mysterious wraiths. He wasn't sure if Pierce would want to help, but knew he would. King made a mental note to tell Pierce about his mother not being dead and headed for the door as the roar of a two-seat F/A-18 Hornet filled the hangar bay, signifying the arrival of his ride.

"King," Aleman said, stopping him in the doorway. "About the golems. If that's what they are, and they are mindless, keep in mind that you're not just up against dumb hulking rocks. Someone smart is behind this. And they have an agenda that is beyond us. Beyond Fiona."

"I'll take care of it," he said, but only made it one more step before Aleman stopped him again.

"I'm not sure you will, King. Not this time. Because the last three attacks happened on three different continents at the exact same time. Whoever is behind this is not alone, and has amazing resources."

King looked back. "What are you trying to say?"

"I'm saying that Hercules may not have meant us to figure out where he was. And if you're right, and find him beneath Rome, he might not be happy to see you."

"I'm going to make damn sure he's *not* happy. We might be named for chess pieces, but he's done moving us on the game board."

THE ROAR OF the F/A-18 hit him like a pressure wave as he left Decon and entered the hangar. He held an index finger up to the waiting pilot, who nodded in response as he brought the jet to a stop and killed the engines. King approached his parents, who had been sitting in metal folding chairs on the opposite side of the hangar. His mother looked worried as she sat with her hands over her ears. His father looked positively thrilled by the presence of the jet.

Peter held his hands out toward the jet and spoke to King. "You know, if this was a MiG I could fly you wherever you're going myself."

King stopped, looking at his father with a quizzical expression. He really knew nothing about his parents. In many ways they were strangers to him, and small things, like the creases around his father's eyes that had once given away his jests, now said nothing.

Peter waved at him. "I'm kidding, Jack."

"Right," King said, but he still wasn't sure if the man was joking or not. His parents had been spies. His mother shot a man. That one, or both of them, could pilot a jet at this point wouldn't be too shocking.

Lynn placed her hand on King's back and rubbed hard, the way he had liked as a child when sitting through a boring event. "Honey," she said, standing in front of him. She took his cheek and pulled his face down, while glancing at the jet. "Are you someone important?"

King couldn't help but smile. For all the secrets his parents had, he had just as many. Whatever documents his mother had seen, most likely an I.D. or message from one of the team, wouldn't have given away exactly what it was he did. They knew as little about him as he did about them.

But they were family.

King hugged his mother. "The things I do . . . no one will ever know about them. I'm no one, Mom."

"You're a father," she said.

"Foster parent," he corrected, leaving his mother's embrace and standing up straight. "And not a very good one."

"Bullshit," Peter said. "Where you're going, is it dangerous?"

"Yes," King said, not wanting to lie to his parents and realizing his father wasn't asking for important details.

"You could get killed?"

"Yes, Dad."

King could see worry creeping into his mother's eyes and didn't want her to break down in tears.

"And you're doing this for your daughter?"

King thought about the question. It was his job to put his life on the line for all Americans. He did it all the time. But this was different. This was personal. It was for Fiona. "Yes."

"Son, there is no greater love than a father who is willing to lay down his life for his children." He took King's shoulders in his hands. "Do you understand?"

The words resonated with King. He wasn't a good father. He knew that. How could a single man on the world's most mysterious and elite Delta team attend to a thirteen-year-old girl? But that wasn't his father's point. The point was, he would die to save Fiona.

Strange, that a man who spent the last ten years in prison could make so much sense, King thought, and then held his breath. Peter had gone to jail and suffered the loathing of his son so that he could have a normal childhood. He had given up his life to protect King from the realities of their past. The tough old ex-con, ex-spy, without realizing it, had just told King he loved him.

"I understand, Dad. Thanks." King headed toward the jet and looked back with a grin. His mother grew weepy as he climbed the ladder. He turned back toward Decon where Aleman stood in the doorway. "Find them someplace to stay."

Aleman saluted in reply.

He climbed into the jet's rear section, sat down, and strapped in. He tapped the pilot's head and they began moving back out of the hangar where an empty runway awaited.

As the jet taxied out of the hangar and Aleman walked toward them, Peter looked down at Lynn's teary face. "All set?"

She nodded and said, "I don't like this."

Peter squeezed her arm. "He'll be fine."

Aleman arrived and said, "How do you feel about Best Western?"

"As long as they have a continental breakfast, I'm good," Peter said.

The three exited the hangar together and watched King's F/A-18 roar into the air, headed east. A loud boom washed over them as the jet broke the sound barrier, becoming a distant speck in the sky.

TWENTY

HE SAT TWO hundred feet beneath the surface of the earth surrounded by darkness, and yet able to see. The large circular space had once served as a kind of sitting room, a bath perhaps, but had, for the past year and a half, been used as a laboratory, though some might call it a torture chamber. His test subjects included insects and animals from the desert above, humans from surrounding villages, and even the earth itself. They were like clay in the hands of an artist, malleable, but his skills needed honing and his manipulations often cost the living their lives while the inanimate found life—at least temporarily.

Those brought to life had vastly different roles. The quickly animated stone subjects were large, strong, and doltish. But they followed orders without pause or moral hindrance. Unfortunately, they didn't last long. If he didn't repeat the words that granted life within fifteen minutes, they would return to their prior state. Clay held together best, enduring without need for a repeated imbuement, and with it, his finest creations came to being.

But there was more to accomplish. Much more. He had a firm grasp of manipulating the inanimate, but the animate still eluded him. And that was key. A computer programmer couldn't rewrite software code if he didn't know the language in which it was written. But if that language was learned, the code could be hacked and rewritten. The same was true of the human mind, the world's most sophisticated, organic computer. And he was close to deciphering the original coded language. Once he knew the language, he could rewrite the code of the human mind. Only a few fragments of knowledge still eluded him and they were nearly lost to time.

Sometime, far in the past, the human race spoke one, unifying language. But suddenly, as though erased from the minds of its speakers, the language was lost—though not completely. Fragments of the ancient language remained hidden in the new dialects, passed down orally through generations. Even fewer fragments had been etched into stone by those wise enough to realize the knowledge would die with them. Identifying the lost written fragments had taken time, but the tracks of the ancients were easy to follow once you knew what to look for. With the last stone fragments still being tracked down, there was time to perfect a few more tricks.

He read through his notes one last time as he would soon attempt something he knew could have disastrous results. Even the smallest mispronunciation could undo him. He might survive, in fact he didn't doubt it, but even a small explosion could reveal his position to his enemies stationed above.

He sipped from his teacup and noticed the time. The others would be checking in soon.

A blue glow lit the space around the man as he turned on his laptop. It revealed lab tables covered with cages, some containing rodents or reptiles. Several different types of rock, sand, clay, and crystal filled a collection of bowls. Lines of metal bars came next—an assemblage of earth elements.

The laptop chimed a moment later. *Seth.* The man answered it, looking at a reflection of his own face. "All went well, Alpha," Seth said. "All living specimens have been eradicated and all traces of the written language have been destroyed. No interruptions this time."

A second chime indicated a second call. *Enos.* Opening the second call and networking the three, Alpha said, "And how is Australia?"

"No problems," Enos said. "Have you heard from Cainan yet?"

They were all nervous about Cainan. Their successes around the globe couldn't dull their apprehension about facing the mass of special Forces stationed at Fort Bragg. At the same time, it was an excellent test of their true capabilities.

He glanced at his watch, seeing Seth and Enos do likewise on the screen. How alike they all were.

The computer chimed.

Cainan.

Alpha took the call and patched it in, allowing the five of them to talk as though each were in the room despite being worlds apart. "Cainan." The tone of his voice was loaded with questions that didn't need to be voiced.

"Bragg is in ruins. The U.S. special forces took large casualties and were unable to mount a successful counterattack."

Alpha knew well enough that Cainan was delaying the meat of his report. He cleared his throat. "And the girl, Fiona?"

"*He* was there."

"King?"

"No, the other one," Cainan said. "The thorn in our side. He took her."

Alpha grimaced. The man, whose identity and location were still unknown, but were being tirelessly researched, had first made his presence known at the Siletz Reservation in Oregon. In the confusion, the girl had escaped into the arms of Delta, behind the fortified walls of Fort Bragg. And since then he had thwarted many of their attempts to eliminate those that, know it or not, had the knowledge to undo what had taken half his life to achieve. They had succeeded in as many attempts, but the cumulative knowledge of those now protected in secrecy . . .

He pushed his fears aside, focusing on the problem at hand. "King will go after her. Wherever he goes, follow him."

Enos nodded. "He's resourceful. He'll find her."

"He's being tracked?" Alpha asked.

Cainan's head bobbed up and down. "The assets did their job. He's on a jet over the Atlantic."

"Alone?"

"The other chess pieces left earlier, each leading an individual team. I don't know where."

Alpha's eyes widened momentarily and then he chuckled. "They've gone looking for others. Identify which at-risk languages are the most likely targets."

"You don't want us to intercept?" Cainan said.

Alpha was grinning. "Not at all. But I think letting several countries know that U.S. special forces intend to invade their territory and abduct their citizens will create a hostile atmosphere that might do the work for us. If any of them are headed for Russia, our friends there will be most welcoming, I'm sure. That would leave only King as a concern for the future."

"And what if King finds us?" Enos asked.

Alpha smiled and stood, taking a small lizard by the sides and picking it up. "I am leaving for Pontus shortly. And should he track us here . . ." He held the lizard up and spoke the ancient words he had recited so many times in his mind. The lizard began thrashing in his hand, changing before their eyes. "He will find only death."

Seth, Enos, and Cainan watched with wide eyes as the video appeared on their laptops in Vietnam, Australia, and the United States. Identical grins stretched on their faces.

After placing the still changing lizard into a large cage, Alpha returned to his seat and paused. Something about killing King was unsatisfactory. The man had taken everything from him except the one thing no man could take: his life. King deserved worse. He deserved to know the same pain. "On second thought, Cainan, take the girl. Bring her to me. If King survives the journey, we will welcome him here."

He disconnected the call and powered off the computer. When the screen went black, he caught his hideous reflection in the glossy laptop display and frowned. "I'll take care of you soon enough," he said before closing the laptop.

He sat back and looked at a clipboard. A long list of communications gear—satellite dishes, servers, routers, miles of cable, and enough computing power to handle a worldwide network—ran down the page and onto two more following it. The writing was in Russian, but after forming an alliance with factions of the Russian military, he had taken the time to learn the language. They were supplying him with the means to change the world, while he supplied them with technological advances. The least he could do was learn the language. It would soon be extinct.

Once he had the missing pieces of the ancient language and the equipment from the Russians was connected, he would access the world's media—TV, Internet, radio, everything—and undo the damage done to mankind so many millennia ago. The world had been fractured. The original code had been rewritten.

It *could* be rewritten.

He would remake mankind.

In *his* image.

He turned to the collection of insects caged on the table behind him and leaned down to them. "But first, let's see what can be done with you."

TWENTY-ONE
Rome, Italy

AFTER A FIVE-HOUR flight that ended on the USS *Enterprise* aircraft carrier deployed to the Mediterranean Sea, a two-hour boat trip, undercover, to Porto Cesareo, followed by a six-hour drive to Rome, King found himself exhausted. To wake himself up and help him fit in with the nighttime tourists, he helped himself to a large cioccolato fondente gelato that Rook had raved about since Queen made him try it during their second trip to Gibraltar. The dark chocolate snack not only tasted good, but was packed with caffeine and sugar that King could already feel opening his eyes.

Working his way through the crowds of locals and tourists mingling by the shops and cafés of the Piazza d'Aracoeli, he paused to watch a family snap photos in front of a Renaissance fountain. The mother and son stood in front of the father, who held a second son on his shoulders. They smiled as a college student used their camera to snap a photo. The flash lit the street and snapped King out of his thoughts. He turned away and quickened his pace.

The street rose up and merged with the Piazzo Venezia, which he crossed and then stopped, looking up. Before him was a staggered ramp of short and deep stairs that led up the Capitoline Hill. Two statues of caped men standing with horses known collectively as the Dioscuri—Castor and Pollux, the sons of Zeus—stood at the top of the hill. Behind them was a large, open plaza designed by Michelangelo with a bronze statue of Marcus Aurelius on horseback. The plaza was surrounded by large buildings built during the thirteenth and fourteenth centuries, but the one that interested King lay straight ahead—the Palazzo Senatorio, or Senatorial Palace, now used as city hall. He headed up the steps of the bell tower–topped building, past a fountain featuring several river guards, and approached the front door.

Despite being closed for business and to visitors, it was the building through which he would gain access to the Roman Forum's ruins. The door inched open at his approach. After making sure no one was watching, he slipped inside and closed the door behind him.

The main hall inside the palace was dark, lit only by a single flashlight, but King could see the face of George Pierce smiling at him. They had connected by phone during King's long drive to Rome and he had explained everything as best he could and, hopefully, got Pierce's mind working on solving the problem of locating a second Herculean Society getaway.

Having seen each other at Lynn's funeral, which Pierce now knew was bunk, and after speaking for an hour on the phone, the two had no pleasantries to exchange. Pierce motioned down the hall with his head and said, "Follow me."

They wound their way through the hallways, heading for the back door that led directly into the ruins of the Roman Forum.

"So how did you manage to get an all-access, after-hours pass to the ruins?" King asked as they descended a staircase.

"Actually, it wasn't me. Mayor Alemanno owed Augustina a favor." Augustina Gallo, a friend and colleague of Pierce, had been central to uncovering the location of the Herculean Society hideout beneath Gibraltar. In doing so she had saved the team's lives and provided the means to restore Pierce back to his fully human self after Manifold Genetics had modified his genetic code using the legendary Hydra's DNA. "So the doors were left unlocked while the guards looked the other way. In fifteen minutes we wouldn't be able to get in."

"How are we going to get out?"

Pierce paused at the exit and looked back at King. "I have no idea, but if we get arrested your bosses can pull a few strings, yes?"

"A few," King said.

The door swung open revealing the darkness of night beyond. The warm air outside carried the smells of the city, but the streetlights ringing the acres of land did little to light the ruins. With the moon covered by clouds, Pierce's flashlight shone like a beacon. It would make them easy to spot, but Pierce didn't seem to notice as he took out a second flashlight, clicked it on, and handed it to King. He didn't like being exposed, but had little choice. Time, as usual, was not on his side, and a daylight search in the midst of tourist throngs would draw unwanted attention.

As he stepped out into the ruins and moved his flashlight side to side he realized what an impossible task this could be. The ancient site included several temples, basilicas, and atriums, some built on top of one another, forming layers of history. On the far side of the space was the Coliseum, which was brightly lit in the distance. That seemed as fitting a place as any for Hercules and his wraiths to hide out, but impossible to search in solitude. King sighed, not knowing where to begin.

Pierce clapped him on the shoulder. "Have no fear, George is here. This way. I have an idea."

King followed Pierce into the ruins, descending a path of large flat stones spaced out just enough for tufts of grass to grow—the remains of an ancient roadway. The path was fenced in on both sides by short black metal fences that seemed more like a reminder to stay off the ruins than an actual deterrent. During the day the site might inspire awe, at night King felt the ruins looked more like some eerie underworld that housed creatures of the night. The truth, he knew, might not be far from that. But despite what he thought might be waiting for them under the earth, it was their exposure to onlookers that had him on edge. He couldn't help but feel they were being watched. There was no evidence of it. Just his instincts.

Instincts he had come to rely on.

He drew his Sig Sauer pistol and held it in line with his flashlight. It wasn't always effective against regenerating capybara, Hydras, Neanderthals, or giant rock monsters, but it almost always gave him a head start, and that could save his life, and Pierce's.

TWENTY-TWO
Washington, D.C.

PRESIDENT DUNCAN SAT in the backseat of The Beast, a black stretched Cadillac with five-inch-thick military armor, run-flat tires, and bulletproof glass. The car could protect him from almost any enemy, except one: the press.

The assassination attempt on his life a year earlier, which almost led to a global pandemic, coupled with the fourth major attack on U.S. soil in the nation's history, had the press swirling like vultures. This wasn't a terrorist attack on civilians like the World Trade Center or Siletz Reservation, which rallied the nation together. It was an assault on the country's most elite military facility. An act of war. Worse, it was a successful attack.

Thanks to the earlier successes of his presidential career, stamping out terrorist organizations around the world, the press saw this as retribution. To the world it looked like he'd picked fights with the world's terrorist organizations and grossly underestimated their resources. Speaking volumes to this were the number of American dead and injured, not to mention the complete lack of enemy casualties.

Duncan and many of the soldiers at Bragg knew that was because the enemy had simply fallen to pieces, but he couldn't very well say that on television. The American public would think him insane and incompetent.

Instead, he would do something he loathed. Something he had done only once before as president.

He would lie.

When the attack on the Siletz Reservation had gone public it was declared a terrorist attack. But with no one claiming responsibility and their investigations turning up no leads, the country's anger had been swallowed and contained, but not forgotten. The country's rage simply lay in wait for a target.

Once again, without an enemy to point his finger at, without a clear target of the nation's wrath, not to mention the military's, the American people would have no outlet for their anger. Unfortunately, there was always someone who would attempt to turn that anger toward his office. Presidents were blamed for scores of the world's problems, especially when someone was gunning for the job. With an election year coming up, the political wolves smelled blood. Lance Marrs, a senator from Utah and the man who ran against Duncan in the last election (and lost), had come out with guns blazing. The man hit every media outlet that would have him, blasting Duncan for not only failing to prevent the attacks, but inviting them. It was the same old shtick from Marrs, but people were buying into it this time.

A small flat-screen TV that swung down from the car's ceiling played his latest news conference. The man was doing his best to look presidential. Hair slicked back. Trophy wife waiting off to the side with a candy smile. Flag pin prominently on his chest. "Tom Duncan has failed the

American people, not once, not twice, but three times now. When the good people of this nation elected him president, I accepted the decision. The people had spoken, and as one of the people, I accepted my defeat."

"Horseshit," Duncan murmured. The man had accused Duncan of fixing the election, called for recounts, and had even talked of a lawsuit. But with Duncan claiming nearly sixty percent of the vote, no one believed the results could have changed enough for Marrs to win.

"When Duncan put his hand on that Bible and was sworn in, he became the landlord for our nation. When something breaks, he's supposed to fix it. And if our house is broken into, not once, but twice, installing a little security seems like an obvious step to take!" The statement was followed by cheers. "But he clearly neglected his duties to the people of this country. I used to think highly of President Duncan. I thought he was a good man. A man of character. But now I realize he is nothing more than a slum landlord!"

More cheers. Duncan was sure the crowd was stacked with former "Marrs for President" supporters, but it was still disturbing to see. In a time of crisis, when people are afraid, they tend to listen to the loudest voice. And right now that was Marrs.

And the results showed in the latest polls. A growing percentage of the population now thought Duncan was at least partially to blame for the attacks. Duncan turned off the TV and reminded himself that he'd suffered through worse, both in combat as an Army Ranger and on the campaign trail. Putting Marrs out of his mind, he took one last look at the speech in his hands and exited the vehicle.

The path from the car to the podium was clear of people save for his Secret Service escorts. Four of them waited, faces grim, hands ready to draw weapons if need be. They received or uncovered more than two hundred threats on his life in the last twenty-four hours and no one was taking chances. He scanned the roofs of the Fort Bragg barracks surrounding the quad and counted ten snipers. His eyes fell to the base of the buildings where a hurried reconstruction effort was under way. There would be no delay like at the World Trade Center. The military was in charge of the cleanup and repair and expected the base to not just be fully functional within the month, but also much more heavily fortified.

Duncan's practiced confident stride didn't falter when he saw the press, who had been allowed back on base for this press conference, turn and face him. Photographers snapped photos and Duncan met them with his handsome face held high. His eyes were set and serious. His shaved head and rigid posture letting the watching world know that this former man of action would take action. But while his body language spoke of a man ready to wage a war, his mind fought with the fact that the words he would offer were ultimately hollow.

General Keasling and Dominick Boucher, head of the CIA, waited for him at the podium that had been erected at the center of the quad. Construction vehicles were hard at work in the background, a strategic view to let the people know that recovery was already under way. The two men were his closest advisors on the subject of war. He nodded to them as he passed and ascended the podium steps.

The seated press suddenly stood, no longer able to control their brewing barrage of questions. A sea of voices flooded over him. He raised his hands for quiet, ignoring the individual voices.

When the press realized he wouldn't be answering any questions yet, they quieted down and let him speak. He delivered his speech, offering contrived words and phony facial expressions. He asked for patience while they hunted down the identities of those responsible for the attack. He promised swift and just action. And he pleaded for calm and logic, reporting anything strange to the authorities instead of taking action into their own hands.

Much of this was the truth, but just as much was misdirection. Duncan knew the best deceptions were ninety-nine percent truth, so as he crafted his story, he worked in the truth about the number of dead, the monetary costs to rebuild, and the timing of events. But he added a layer of deceit when he placed blame on the Arab world. He mentioned Iran, Saudi Arabia, and Yemen by name. He dropped the names of known terrorist organizations and played the Osama bin Laden card. At the same time, he couldn't blame any one of them specifically and no one was taking credit.

What made the deception worse was that his words fueled tensions around the world. Hate crimes against Arab-Americans would increase. Violence in the Middle East and Israel would continue. And actual terrorists, bolstered by the belief that some of their own had wounded the heart of the American military, would find their ranks replenished.

As Duncan took a breath, a daring reporter used the momentary silence to shout a question. "Senator Marrs has laid the blame for the deaths of several thousand United States citizens on your shoulders. How do you—"

Duncan's frustration got the better of him. "Senator Marrs is a self-serving vulture," he said, then immediately regretted it. His own anger was eating him up. He had no desire to be here. To be lying to these people. He needed to take action, not manage his reelection PR. Screw the upcoming election, he needed to get things done.

But his hands were tied. He knew that. Every action the president made during a crisis was scrutinized. Too much time fulfilling the duties of Deep Blue would garner unwanted attention for the team for whom secrecy was tantamount. When the Chess Team, when the world, needed Deep Blue the most, his duty as the president always got in the way.

As the sea of stunned reporters wrote down the quote that was sure to be the next morning's headline, he said, "Thank you. That's all for now."

Duncan took the stairs down from the podium two at a time, catching the press off guard. Silence lingered for a moment before the din of questions came. Leaving the loud voices behind, he approached Keasling and Boucher. "This is a waste of time," he grumbled.

Boucher matched the president's stride as he walked back to The Beast. "It's your job, sir."

A Secret Service agent opened the rear door. Duncan paused before entering. He looked back over at the press who were being held at bay by a line of military security. It all seemed a ridiculous circus to him. He met Boucher's eyes. "I know, Dom. I'm just starting to see things a little differently."

Duncan climbed into the dark interior of the car and slid into the shadows. Before the Secret Service agent could close the door, Boucher climbed in next to him.

Duncan sighed. "What?"

As The Beast pulled away, Boucher smoothed his mustache and said, "Tom, this will all blow over."

"I'm not so sure."

"He's a hot-air bag. People are going to realize that when the dust clears. They always do."

"You're assuming the dust will clear." Duncan looked out the tinted, bulletproof window. The ruins of Fort Bragg passed by as they headed for Pope Air Force Base. "We don't even know what we're up against."

"We will," Boucher said, filling his voice with confidence. "You've got the best team—"

"An incomplete team."

Boucher nodded. When Deep Blue was unavailable it took a team of CIA analysts and strategists to replace him. But the team could never operate at full efficiency without Deep Blue directly involved. When the CIA team handled ops they still needed executive approval on the big calls—decisions that could not be made from a press conference podium—the delay could cost lives. Having Deep Blue in the game gave the team real-time executive power. Fleets could be diverted, air support called in, or political pressure applied with a phone call.

"Even without you, they're still the best. They'll get the job done."

"And if they don't? If Marrs continues to control the airwaves?"

"He won't."

"You going to make him disappear?" Duncan said, a grin showing on his face.

"Don't need to," Boucher said before switching on the TV. It wasn't Marrs on the screen. It was Duncan. "Senator Marrs is a self-serving vulture."

"You came out swinging. The American people will remember you're a fighter. And so will Marrs. He's not going to want a second round."

"I hope you're right, Dom."

"I'm a spook. I'm always right."

TWENTY-THREE
Rome, Italy

"**THE TEMPLE OF** Saturn," Pierce said as they rounded the ruins of an ancient temple that had been reduced to a foundation and eight columns supporting a worn but still impressive pediment. "The Senate and people of Rome restored what fire had consumed."

"What?" King asked as he looked up at the impressive columns.

"The inscription," Pierce said, panning his flashlight beam across the text etched into the pediment. "The original temple, which was the oldest structure in Rome, built in 498 B.C., was dear to the city. And when it burned down they rushed to rebuild it. In fact, they were in such a rush that one of the columns was placed upside down."

"That's unfortunate."

"For the builders more than the temple," Pierce said. "It's rumored those responsible were killed in the Coliseum."

"The wrath of Saturn," King said.

Pierce shook his head. "The wrath of Rome. Saturn was the god of agriculture."

Pierce narrated the history of Rome in hushed tones like a conspiratorial tour guide. They continued onward from the temple, following the serpentine path as it twisted past what little remained of the Milliarium Aureum. It was once a statue of Augustus Caesar where all roads in the Roman Empire were said to begin, but had long since been reduced to a marble base.

Next came the Arch of Tiberius, which was little more than a foundation for an arch, whose history and significance had been long forgotten. Beyond the arch, they walked along the side of the Basilica Julia, which stretched out on their right. A long line of marble steps led up to a large rectangular area filled with rows of foundation pylons and a mash of scattered stones and blocks. The building, which housed shops, courts, and banks had once been a favorite gathering place for Romans. So much so that checkerboards had been found carved into some of the steps. But the building held no interest to Pierce, whose narrative ended as soon as they were past that stretch of ancient city.

He paused at the corner of the Basilica Julia and raised his hands toward three, tall, fluted columns glowing orange in the nighttime lighting. The columns, which looked like they could fall apart in a stiff wind, still held a piece of entablature on top. "I give you the temple of Castor and Pollux."

"Castor and Pollux," King repeated, recalling his Greek history. "They were twins who helped defeat the Tarquins." His eyebrows rose. "Also the sons of Jupiter, aka, Zeus, aka the legendary half father of Hercules. This could be it."

Wasting no time, King hopped the fence, climbed the shambled staircase, and entered the ruins, which were raised up several feet atop what remained of the foundation. As Pierce debated following—this was a major breach of archaeological protocol—he noticed that King had his weapon drawn. Knowing King would not do so without reason, he climbed over the fence and followed his friend into the remains of the ancient temple.

Entering a clearing at the center of the temple ruins, Pierce found King quickly moving from one feature to the next. Foundation stones, step fragments, wall remains—nothing escaped his scrutiny. "Any particularly interesting history I should know about?" he asked.

"Nothing outstanding. The location of the temple is supposed to be where Castor and Pollux came to water their horses after their successful battle. The Senate gathered here for a time and later housed a few different Roman offices, but nothing extraordinary."

"And nothing related to Hercules."

"Just the lineage."

"Then what should I be looking for?"

"Honestly, I was kind of hoping there would be an engraving like we found beneath Gibraltar."

"The Herculean Society's symbol." King frowned. He'd hoped Pierce's lead would be more substantial, but they were searching for a location that had been kept secret in the heart of Rome for thousands of years. It wouldn't be found that easily.

Slowed by the loud revelry of nearby late-night Roman parties and the rumble of vehicles, both of which kept King on edge for intruders, they spent an hour searching every nook and cranny of the site.

And found nothing.

Sweating from the humid Roman heat and discouraged by the apparent dead end, King sat on a stone and looked up at the cloudy sky. Silhouetting the temple's three columns, the moon's glow had just begun to pierce the thinning cloud cover.

Pierce sat next to him. "Sorry. This was the best I could come up with."

"Don't beat yourself up. I asked you on a hunch to find something that might not even be here. This was my idea."

"Your hunches typically save a lot of lives."

"Not always the ones that matter."

Pierce stood. "Well, we've looked everywhere at this site. I think we should check out the temple of Jupiter. We've got a few hours of darkness left."

After walking a few steps, Pierce turned around and found King still sitting. His eyes were fixated on the three columns. "What?"

"We haven't looked *everywhere*," King said before standing and heading for the columns.

Pierce realized what King was about to do and attempted to voice a protest. "King, wait. You can't—"

But King was already scaling one of the outside columns like a champion logger. Pierce flinched as he heard crumbs of column falling onto the marble base. *If Augustina finds out about this,* he thought, *she might turn me in herself.*

After reaching the top of the column, King inspected the exposed top and then climbed on top of the entablature, scouring it with his flashlight.

Pierce waited below like a nervous teenage vandal, bouncing his foot and scanning for onlookers. He could hear King above, moving about. The scrape of plastic on stone preceded a clunk as something fell from above. Pierce cursed in his mind as he began to wonder if bringing King here had been a mistake. His thoughts stopped when he realized that King had fallen silent. He looked up expecting to see King inspecting something with his flashlight, but saw nothing.

King's flashlight was off.

For a moment, all he could hear was his own shaky breath, but then a loud scrape sounded from above and a rain of debris sprinkled onto his hand. As he pointed his flashlight up he saw King descend in a blur. King landed next to him, grabbed Pierce's flashlight, and switched it off.

"What's wrong?" Pierce asked, his heartbeat pulsating hard in his throat.

"Guards. Four of them coming this way. Two from the north. Two from the east."

"What are we going to do?"

"Keep looking."

Pierce looked astonished. "What?"

"I saw something."

"Up there?"

"To the northeast. It looks like a pit beneath a modern covering, across from the Basilica Julia."

Pierce took a sharp breath and whispered, "The Lacus Curtius."

"You know what it is?"

"No one really knows for sure. It's been covered over with ancient stones and it has yet to be excavated. Probably never will be."

"Why's that?"

"Politics. Some in Rome believe archaeology does more harm than good. Every request I know of involving an excavation of the Lacus Curtius has been declined. But it's said to be the entrance to a chasm. There are several stories about the site's origin and name. One has Mettius Curtius falling into the pit during a battle with Romulus. Another has a horseman, Marcus Curtius, throwing himself, horse and all, into the pit because an oracle deemed it would save Rome. And another—"

Pierce took another quick breath, which King knew signified a revelation. "What?"

"It's said that Gaius Curtius supposedly dedicated the site in 445 B.C. after . . ." He looked at King, barely seeing him in the darkness. "A lightning strike split the earth, forming the pit."

"Lightning . . ."

"The favored weapon of Zeus," Pierce said. "At the time, Zeus would have been seen as the source. That it's not mentioned in the historical record—"

"Means it was erased." A soft scuffing hit King's ears. He put a hand on Pierce's shoulder and pushed him down to a crouch.

"What is it?" Pierce asked with a rushed whisper.

"I must have missed two of them."

Pierce listened, willing his ears to open wider. Then he heard them. Two sets of footsteps climbing over the pebble-covered ruins. But the sound wasn't from outside the temple of Castor and Pollux, it was from within.

And close.

King leaned in to Pierce. "If one of them gets off a shot or shouts a warning, the others out there"—he motioned to the forum with his head—"are going to have an army of police descend on us. And even if we do escape, security will be beefed up for a long time to come. When was the last time you were in a fight?"

Pierce felt like he might vomit. "You fought all my fights for me."

"Not this time," King said. "I can't be in two places at once. All I need is a few seconds."

The shuffling shoes came closer, this time complimented by a pair of equally hushed voices speaking Italian. "When I tap you, count to three Mississippi, then go. Don't hold back."

"Okay."

The tap came thirty seconds later, when the sound of footfalls was only a few feet away, just on the other side of the foundation they were hiding behind. Pierce counted.

One Mississippi . . .

Two Mississippi . . .

TWENTY-FOUR
Chaco Province, Argentina

THE SHOULDER-DEEP WATER of the Negro River slowed Bishop and his team, but also helped quiet their approach. It didn't, however, help the nerves of the team following his leadership. Designated Bishop's Pawns One through Five, they followed his orders without question. But that didn't stop them assigning two men to watch the water for crocodiles. Not that their night vision goggles could penetrate the river, which really was as black as its name implied.

During the daylight hours Bishop and his team, dressed as tourists, split into three teams of two, casually seeking out a sixty-seven-year-old man named Miguel Franco and his forty-five-year-old son, Nahuel. The pair lived together in downtown Resistencia with the single son supporting his out-of-work father.

Casual interviews with neighbors, local bars, shops, and churches revealed that the pair often spent nights camped out on the Negro River where the father would make up for his unemployment by catching a haul of fish, sometimes enough to sell at the local market.

Bishop could feel several of those large fish swimming circles around his legs. He pushed through them, closing on the campfire that revealed the team's two targets sitting on a small sandy beach, lines cast and fishing rod handles buried in the sand. A half-finished twelve-pack of beer sat between them, which complicated the fact that a shotgun, presumably for warding off crocs, lay in the younger man's lap. He had no doubt that anything bigger than a fish emerging from the water would be greeted by an explosion of lead pellets.

Making a mental note to wait for the men to move away from the firearm, Bishop paused by a log as the team gathered behind him. He turned to whisper the game plan when a snapping branch somewhere in the jungle cut through the cacophony of nighttime calls.

His first thought was that a jaguar or croc might be stalking the group, but they were hidden from the shoreline by thick vegetation. It could just as easily be a wild boar . . . or a person.

The team fell silent as one, all listening for another sound. For thirty seconds there was nothing but silence. Then it was broken by the elder Franco's loud, drunken laugh. As Miguel's amusement dulled to a chuckle Bishop again heard movement.

This time he brought his handgun up and aimed it at the jungle. Timing an approach to coincide with surrounding noise was a hunting technique used by only one predator on the planet.

Man.

TWENTY-FIVE
Taipei, Taiwan

KNIGHT LOOKED GOOD dressed in black slacks and a dark blue button-down silk shirt. As he approached Mackay Memorial Hospital, flanked by two of the five Delta operators assigned to him, he wore a large grin required by his cover. As a wealthy benefactor looking to donate money to the hospital and to the Presbyterian church that ran it, the plan was to tour the facility where he would meet an exceptional ninety-five-year-old man, Walis Palalin, who for the past twenty-five years had spent three days a week volunteering in the children's ward. Apparently, the man had lost his son in this very hospital twenty-five years ago and had been paying tribute to him ever since.

Upon meeting the man, Knight would offer a million-dollar donation—if Mr. Palalin would accompany him to a dinner. Right then and there. No delays. Just the two of them and Knight's two security guards.

Once in their vehicle, getting the man onto a ship and back to America would be a simple thing . . . if the man's health didn't become a factor. He had a clean bill of health and could very well live another ten years—perhaps longer—but the emotional jolt of being kidnapped could undo the man's well-being fairly quickly, especially if he was on any medication, which is why the missing three members of Knight's team were rummaging through Palalin's apartment looking for any medications or supplements that the man needed.

The industrial hospital wasn't exactly inviting-looking. Surrounded by the neon glitz of Taipei, it had a depressing facade. But the smiles Knight got from the women he passed on the sidewalk as he approached the front entrance were enough to lift any male hospital visitor's spirits. Of course, in Taiwan they could be working women, but it was still mid-afternoon, so he doubted it. Ten feet from the concrete staircase leading up to the double-door entrance, he saw a stunning woman. She turned, met his eyes and smiled.

As he returned the woman's smile, he noted that hers had frozen and become forced. The woman, dressed in a dark gray power suit, turned fully toward him. He noted her open jacket and the two items attached to her belt.

A badge.

And a gun.

With one hand the woman drew her sidearm.

With the other she spoke into a radio Knight hadn't noticed before.

TWENTY-SIX
Asino, Siberia

THE DISTINCT SMELL of a cow pasture rolled over the open hill and wafted past Rook. Despite being a distasteful odor to many people, it reminded Rook of his home in New Hampshire, where he grew up down the road from a cow farm. He couldn't see the farm itself, but the smell and distant cattle calls placed the farm somewhere on the other side of the green grassy rise to his left. To the right was a forest of pine and birch trees that was home to bears, reindeer, and, judging from the continuous buzz of chain saws, a thriving forestry business. The odors, combined with the cool mid-morning air, felt invigorating.

As Rook, dressed as a local in dirty work pants and a thick gray wool sweater, walked down the road toward town, his team followed along in the forest, wading through a sea of bright green ferns. Fortunately, the three targets lived on the outskirts of town, in a home that backed up to the forest. Rook would approach from the road, posing as a local in need of car assistance. When he was invited in to use the phone, he would drug the group and his team would abscond with them, each pair carrying one of the two women and one man—all that remained of the Chulym people. A truck hidden two miles away in the forest would transport the group to an airfield where a small plane, operated by a local CIA operative, waited to whisk them (with two landings to refuel) to neighboring Georgia, where a much faster transport would take them to the United States.

It was one of the more complicated and slower extraction plans Rook had seen, but that was to be expected when kidnapping three people from a country that wasn't exactly on hugging terms with the United States. Quiet and careful was preferred to loud and fast in this case.

A sign ahead, written in Russian, read, "Thank you for visiting Asino. Population 28,000." Rook quickened his pace, knowing the turn onto his targets' street was only a mile ahead. He wanted to get this over with and the long trek home started.

The trees on the side of the road shifted under a breeze. A fallen tree caught in the grip of a second squeaked loudly as entwined limbs rubbed against each other. The sudden foreign noise returned Rook's attention to what he could hear and he noticed something had changed. The cows had fallen silent. Perhaps feeding? But the distant whine of chain saws had quieted as well.

Kafer's voice filled his ear. "Rook, RP-One here. Do you he—"

Rook muted his earbud as the sound for which Kafer had broken radio silence for struck his ears. Still distant, the deep bass staccato was easily identifiable as not one but several approaching helicopters.

Big ones.

TWENTY-SEVEN
El Calvario, Colombia

UNDER THE COVER of darkness, Queen and her team of operators watched the small mountainside town of El Calvario through night vision goggles. Few lights remained on and many of those bore the telltale flicker of television sets. The town was at rest. And when they woke in the morning, two of them would be missing. But despite the town's quiet demeanor, it bore the scars of a violent past, most recently as the epicenter for a magnitude 5.9 earthquake in 2008. Six people had died. Hundreds more were injured. But the buildings in town took the brunt of the damage. Those that had collapsed remained so and many others, including the tall yellow church, had cracked walls or bent frames.

The two men—the last speakers of Tinigua—had been citizens of El Calvario since they were born. The first, Edmundo Forero, was born sixty-nine years previous and was the oldest resident in town. The second man, Tavio Cortes, born sixty-four years ago, had been a neighbor of Edmundo's, and as a result picked up the language that he and his mother spoke. The language that now only the two of them knew.

The challenge for Queen and her team was that despite being close friends, Edmundo and Tavio now lived on opposite sides of town, which wasn't just a matter of horizontal distance, but also vertical. El Calvario's main drag rose straight up the mountainside at an amazingly steep angle. The obvious choice was to split the team in two, taking both men at the same time. But Queen had seen more than a few bullet holes in buildings and knew the area had seen some violent unrest. Despite the gross exaggerations about Colombia being a haven for terrorists and drug runners, these elements *did* exist in the fringes of civilization, and the town had clearly seen some firefights in its past. What made this a challenge for the team was that people who experienced violent events tended to prepare for the next encounter.

Queen's team moved as one. Like a black-clad anaconda stalking its prey in the darkness, they moved in a fast single-file line, weaving through the tight alleys between the turquoise and white homes. They gathered beneath the tall stilts supporting their target's back porch. While three men kept watch below the porch, two more followed Queen up the stairs.

Queen, along with QP-One and -Two, huddled by the back door for a moment while she picked the lock. Once inside, she drew a tranquilizer gun and moved through the home, heading for the living room where the TV flickered. Just as she hoped, Edmundo lay asleep in a reclined chair, a beer in one hand, a cigarette burned to the nub in the other.

"Bastard is lucky to still be alive," QP-Two said.

Queen took aim and shot him in the chest. The old man's eyes launched open, wrinkling the flat, leathery brown skin of his forehead. He stood, saw their black masks and night vision goggles, and before he had time to fully register what he'd seen, fell face forward into Queen's arms. She handed him to QP-One and -Two, who carried him outside and down the steps to where the others still waited.

As Queen walked down the steps, she activated her throat microphone and spoke. "Queen here. Edmundo Forero is ours. En route to second target."

"Copy that, Queen," came the voice of Dominick Boucher, who was sitting in for Deep Blue until he was able to free himself from the media shit storm.

"Out," she said before disconnecting. With a quick hand signal she motioned for the team to move and they were off again, working their way through the town with Edmundo in tow. As hoped, the old man's light frame combined with the downward climb allowed them to move just as quickly.

Reaching the bottom of the hill, they stopped at the edge of the main street. Tavio's home, and their LZ, lay on the other side. But before they could make a move, a loud car engine roared at the top of the street. It was followed by the squeal of braking tires and the shouts of men. While the team fell back, Queen chanced a look up the mountain road and saw three jeeps, large machine guns mounted on each, and fifteen armed men flooding into Edmundo's home.

Ducking into the shadows, she activated her throat mic again. "Mission has been compromised. Local authorities were tipped off."

She didn't wait for a reply before switching off and prepping her UMP submachine gun. She suspected they wouldn't escape without a fight. A second set of engines, coming from below, confirmed her fears. She turned to the Delta team behind her and pointed to Edmundo. "Leave him and be ready to haul ass."

The old man was placed on the ground were he would sleep peacefully through the chaos that would soon add more scars to the town.

TWENTY-EIGHT
Rome, Italy

THREE MISSISSIPPI!

Pierce stood, bolted out and around the debris they'd been hiding behind, raised his fist, aimed, and threw the only punch he was sure he'd get to make. Aiming was difficult in the darkness, but he saw the silhouette of a head and tried to direct his fist just below. Strike the throat . . . strike the throat . . . strike the—contact.

The impact was solid, knuckles on bone.

Not a soft throat.

And it took all of Pierce's self-control to not shout out in pain. His fist ached and his arm tingled. But he had made contact.

A dull thud sounded as the attackee collapsed at his feet.

Pierce's adrenaline surged as he realized he'd taken the guard out with a single punch to the head. For a moment he understood the rush King must feel when on a mission. Then King's flashlight clicked on revealing the man he had attacked.

He was young and unconscious, dressed in a pink dress shirt, holding a black dress coat in his flaccid arms.

Not a guard.

The light drifted toward the body at Pierce's feet. When he saw the face, he stepped back with a hand to his mouth. "Oh God."

King moved to the pretty young woman and checked her pulse. She was alive, which was good for her and his friend's psyche. "She's alive," he said, then took her by the arms. "Get the guy."

They dragged the couple who'd simply been in the wrong place at the wrong time behind the remains of the temple's interior walls. King could see Pierce was distracted over hitting the woman. "It had to be done," King said. "If you didn't do it, I would have."

"So this was a 'can't make an omelette without breaking a few eggs' situation?"

King nodded. "Sometimes you have to be a bad parent to be a good parent."

Pierce let out a quiet "Huh" as a memory of King's sister returned. "Julie used to say that."

With a grin, King said, "So did my dad."

Pierce looked at his fist with a grin. "It was a good punch."

King clapped him on the shoulder. "Would have made Jules proud."

They both fought against laughing. They both knew that Julie had been a strident feminist who believed men and women should be treated equally in every way, including combat. Which is why she worked so hard to defy the system and become a fighter pilot. She really would have been proud.

King led him back to the northwest corner of the temple. To the north and east they could see the security guards closing in on their location—flashlights giving away their positions. King knelt down and motioned to where they'd hid the bodies. "They're here for them."

"You're sure?"

"Well, maybe not exactly them, but they're probably expecting to find drunk socialites pissing on a column, not . . ." King held up his weapon, letting it finish the sentence for him. "Let's go."

The series of foundation stones remaining within the long rectangular ruins of the Basilica Julia hid the pair as they snuck around the guards. They stopped directly across from the Lacus Curtius and looked to the right. The two guards, walking away from them toward the temple of Castor and Pollux were oblivious to their presence. But the guards approaching from the other side were now facing them, albeit from more than one hundred feet away. King quickly judged the distance and the intensity of the flashlight beams and decided it was too risky.

Then he saw all four flashlights turn toward the temple of Castor and Pollux. He grabbed Pierce's shirt and pulled him up. "Let's go!"

They hopped the small black fence and crouch-ran across the footpath. The ruins on the other side, along with a short, low-hanging tree, provided ample cover. Concealed again, they headed for the ancient pit long since covered. King was surprised to find the structure built over

the pit to be constructed of metal poles and beams. The thing was solid
and held a large flat roof at an angle to divert rainfall. They crawled beneath the low roof and inspected the site.

Aged rectangular blocks of white marble were laid out in grids on either side of a circular, layered pit. Two layers led down, like steps, to a
flat, stone base. A stone on the top of the pit's far side had been moved out
of alignment with the rest, ruining the circle.

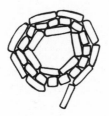

It was, in every way, unremarkable. Despite its mysterious origins,
King could see nothing that made this site worthwhile . . . or worthy of a
rain guard when the rest of the far more extravagant forum was left to
brave the elements. "Why is this covered?" he asked.

Pierce scratched his head. "I've heard that before it was covered rain
would collect there—" He pointed to the small basin. "And would leak
through to whatever is beyond. They feared erosion would undermine
the stability of the site and possibly the surrounding sites as well, so they
covered it up. Why do you ask?"

"Just seems odd. What do you think is down there?"

"Aside from a chasm created by Zeus's lightning bolt? The entire area
surrounding this hill was a swamp before Rome was built. Today it would
have been a protected wetland. They drained the swamps and built the
city. Best guess is it's an underground lake. This whole area of the city is
probably full of underground rivers, too. Without the swamps, the whole
system might be dry now, but really, who knows."

King sighed. None of this was helpful. He stood to get a better look at
the pit and hit his head on the low-hanging ceiling. The metal sheet
sounded out like a gong. "Shit," he whispered, knowing the guards would
soon be upon them.

Ignoring the panicked whispers of Pierce and the distant voices of the
guards, King focused his attention on the pit. Once again, there were no
markers of any kind. Then he looked up at the ceiling. Its plain surface

held no clues, either, but the two I-beams supporting the ceiling did. They were separated by five feet, each crossing over the circle of stones. He mentally stripped the ceiling away and pictured the I-beams over the circular pit.

King jumped into the pit, scouring every surface for something more.

"Did you find something?" Pierce asked, joining him at the bottom of the two-foot-deep depression. "The guards will be here any second!"

"The I-beams," King said. "From above, they cross over the circle."

Pierce saw the image in his mind. The symbol of the Herculean Society. But not quite. The circle was broken. "Help me move this," Pierce said, taking hold of the misaligned stone. "Pull it back into the circle!"

The guards' voices grew louder. Commanding. They'd found the bodies and discovered they hadn't passed out, but had been knocked out. The squeal of distant sirens—police and medical—converged on the forum, which would soon be an inescapable quagmire of men in uniform.

And the stone wasn't budging.

"We're trying to force it," Pierce said. "Maybe it's a more complicated lever." He placed his hands on top of the stone like he was about to do CPR chest compressions. "You pull. I'll push."

As the legs and feet of the approaching guards came into view, King nodded.

Pierce put his weight onto the stone and felt it drop a fraction of an inch. King pulled and the stone shifted easily, completing the circle and the Herculean Society's symbol. They let go and moved back. The stone began shifting back into its previously unaligned position. It clicked into place as a flashlight cast it in yellow light.

The first guard to arrive drew his weapon and pointed it beneath the low ceiling where he thought he'd seen moving shadows. But the pit was empty and looked untouched. He stood and scanned the area, finding no one but his partner. If someone had been there, they were gone now.

TWENTY-NINE
Washington, D.C.

DOMINICK BOUCHER HAD been wrong.

Not only had Marrs not backed down, but he'd responded to the vulture comment like something out of a Tazmanian Devil cartoon, spinning madly from rally to news station to rally again. With a beet-red face, he shouted at the media. At crowds. At the television audience. And despite the flying spittle and shaking jowls, people were listening.

He turned the self-serving vulture comment around on Duncan. "If one senator keeping the president accountable is enough to make him crack, how is he going to lead the nation?" he had said.

When the media picked up on the fact that Marrs was also responding in anger, he spun the story. "I'm responding to a man who has failed this nation several times. A man who's inaction has led to the deaths of our children. I should be angry. Every good citizen of this nation should be angry. At Duncan for not preventing the attacks and at the people who perpetrated them. But who is our president angry at? Me! The office needs transparency. It needs accountability. If he can't handle it, well . . ." With that he threw up his hands.

The man provided enough sound bites and accusations to keep the media and the public focused on Marrs and, as a result, on Duncan. His hands were bound more than ever now. The media requests didn't stop coming. There were protesters surrounding the White House grounds and more arrived every hour.

Alone in the Oval Office for a few minutes before meeting with a slew of advisors on a range of issues arising because of the current crisis, Duncan looked out the row of windows. The south lawn, trim and neat like a marine's head, stretched out before him. The trim grass annoyed him. Nothing was that clear cut anymore. In the Rangers there were good guys and bad guys. Black and white. Right and wrong. He had successfully carried on that tradition through the Chess Team. But now . . .

now there were other battles, unnecessary battles that had to be fought. With Marrs. With the media. With public opinion.

And given the sensitivity of the Chess Team's mission, he couldn't fight back. He couldn't say he had teams spread out around the world, infiltrating the territories of sovereign nations in order to kidnap the sole survivors of ancient languages. If that got out it might start a war. And it would certainly ruin his presidency and provide a lifetime of fuel to Marrs's smear campaign. Hell, it might make Marrs look enough like a hero that he could be the next president.

Let him try, Duncan thought. After learning the truth behind the threats against the country—mythical monsters, gene-splicing madmen, Neanderthal viruses, and stone golems—the man would resign with his tail tucked between his legs.

But right now Marrs had freedom to act. Freedom to say what he wanted to whomever he chose. Freedom to disappear if he chose. And for those reasons, Duncan envied him.

There was a knock at the door.

"Come in."

He heard the door open, but he didn't turn around. A woman's voice said, "They're ready for you, sir."

"I'll just be a minute," he replied.

After the door shut, Duncan looked down at his right hand. He held his M9 Beretta; the same one he had used as an Army Ranger. The weapon had saved his life a few times, but it couldn't help now. As much as he might like to have Marrs stare down the barrel of this gun, a different solution had to be found; one that would not only put an end to the recent attacks and catch those responsible, but also free the team up so they could really function as a cohesive unit. Only then would the American people be safer.

Duncan opened a drawer on the Resolute Desk, placed the handgun inside, and locked it. Before heading toward the door, he looked around the Oval Office, and for the first time during his presidency, the space felt cramped.

THIRTY
Rome, Italy

THE LAST THING King saw before descending into total darkness was a shrinking crescent of light above him. He realized that they'd fallen through a triggered hatch that was now quickly, and quietly, closing. All thoughts of the hatch left his mind as his body impacted against a cold stone floor. He landed at an odd angle, which compressed his ribs near to breaking and knocked the wind out of him.

Unable to speak, he listened as Pierce whispered his name. "Jack . . . Jack, where are you?"

A bright light struck his face a moment later as Pierce switched on his flashlight.

Seeing King squint from the light and in pain, Pierce said, "Sorry," and moved the light away, revealing a nondescript stone tunnel. After King caught his breath and was helped to his feet, he looked at Pierce, who seemed unfazed by the fall.

Pierce noticed King's attention and questioning gaze. He smiled. "I landed on my feet."

King shook his head. The bookworm archaeologist was becoming a catlike Tomb Raider while he, an elite soldier, became a potato sack.

When Pierce's grin turned cocky, King said, "At least I didn't hit a girl."

Pierce had opened his mouth to issue a retort, but stopped short and then deflated. "Hey, what happened to 'you have to be a bad parent to be a good parent'?"

King shrugged. "I was trying to make you feel better."

Pierce forced an unsure smile as King used his conscience against him. "B.S. You've hit girls."

"Not like that," King said. "You coldcocked the kid."

"Kid!" With a laugh and a raised fist, Pierce said, "Better watch it, or you're next."

"Don't make me tell Queen you hit a girl," King said as he found his flashlight on the floor, picked it up, and switched it on.

The light cast a now serious George Pierce in bright, white light. "That's not even funny."

King gave him a firm pat on the back. "C'mon, let's find out which layer of hell we've dropped ourselves into."

King led the way, flashlight out, gun at the ready. The tunnel, a simple brown tube tall enough to stand in and just wide enough for the pair to stand side by side, led down at a steady angle.

"We must be under the Lacus Juturnae by now," Pierce whispered.

But King wasn't interested in what lay above. He wanted to know what waited below. The color of the tunnel ahead shifted from dark brown to a dirty, mottled white with splashes of color. Pierce's eyes went wide with recognition and he rushed past King.

The walls of the tunnel were covered in mosaic tiles, many chipped or fallen away, but enough remained so that the pictures could be pieced together. Blocky shapes slightly more detailed than a sixteen-bit Nintendo game formed pictograph story lines. King couldn't make them out, but Pierce deciphered it aloud.

"Look here, at this swamp," Pierce said. "This must be the land Rome was founded on." He counted the hills in the image, whispering the numbers to himself. "The seven hills of Rome. The original settlers had villages on each hill, but they eventually drained the swamp and formed the city."

He moved on, looking at a large image of a woman, whose beauty was impossible to hide, despite the rough condition of the wall.

"Who is she?" King asked.

Only fragments of the name spelled out in ancient Greek above the woman's head remained, but it was enough. "Acca Larentia. We found her."

They moved faster, all but ignoring the images of Rome's early development and battles. The tunnel ended in an arched doorway that led to a T junction. They passed through and found a second arch to the left, leading into a small chamber, and a second hallway to the right. Not wanting to proceed too quickly, King entered the small room and cast his light side to side, stopping at the room's only feature—a marble tomb. They approached the tomb and found a relief of a woman on its lid. Acca Larentia.

"She's been here the whole time," Pierce said, his voice full of the same kind of wonder that Rook displayed when assembling a new weapon.

Pierce reached out to touch the woman's face, but was stopped by a guttural clicking growl. The sound was organic, but inhuman.

King spun and fell to one knee, aiming both flashlight and handgun toward the entrance.

A cloaked figure in the doorway flinched away from the light and blocked its face with the loose fabric of its black sleeve. Clearly uncomfortable in the light, the creature stepped back but made no move to retreat or advance. It simply stood there, crouched and swaying slowly side to side.

Waiting.

King recognized the creature. The cloak and bits of gray face and arm he could see were exactly what Rook and Queen had described. A wraith. One of Hercules's mysterious gofers. Despite the wraith having an aura of evil, King knew it meant them no harm. He lowered his weapon and aimed his flashlight to the floor.

Free of the intense white beam, the wraith stood taller and lowered its arm. In the dim light reflected off the room's brown walls, King could make out the lower half of the creature's face. There was no nose to speak of, simply a horizontal slit in its skin. And its mouth, well, there wasn't one—just a patch of wrinkled gray flesh.

For a moment, King felt pity for the wraith. It had clearly once been a human being, but now . . . it was a monster. Then it turned, motioned for them to follow with its hooded head, and hopped up onto the hallway wall. It crawled away like a four-legged spider. *Or,* King thought, *like a gecko.*

Keeping his weapon ready, King and Pierce followed the wraith, which paused when they fell behind. It led them through a confusing maze of tunnels through which neither man could retrace his steps. Some tunnels were plain stone bearing no markings of any kind. Others housed portions of ancient columns, ruined busts, and half-buried arches.

"These are the ancient layers of the city," Pierce said. "We've been so afraid to hurt what was on top we never thought to look beneath. But cities this old are always built on layers. This is the stuff of legend." He looked at King. "This was the Rome that Hercules would have known. Before the Caesars. Before the Coliseum. Before the vast empire."

King was about to respond when he heard a voice. A woman. He stopped at a crossroad and listened. The sound distinctly came from the right-side tunnel. He cocked his ear toward it, as did Pierce.

"Sounds like an Italian accent," Pierce said.

A second voice, also feminine, but higher pitched and American replied. King's heart pounded. Fiona! He took one step down the hallway when a darkness swept above them and descended before them like a wall of shadow. King raised his pistol at the wraith's head and slowly brought his light up toward its face.

As the light grew closer to the skin of its face, the creature let out a low shriek. King could see its slit of a nose vibrating as the call slipped out.

Sensing a violent conclusion to the stand-off, Pierce backed away.

As King continued to bring the light up, the wraith did something unexpected. Instead of shying away from it, it leaned into the light, fully exposing its face and revealing its large, oval eyes with black, quarter-sized pupils. The light caused it immense pain, which could be seen in its deeply furrowed brow, but it refused to back away. Its actions told King that despite being hurt by the light, it would not be intimidated by it. He also noted that it was not at all concerned about the handgun.

Pierce took another step back and was suddenly in the grasp of a pair of large hands. He let out a shout that spun King around. A man he had never seen in person stood behind Pierce, holding him in place. He was tall and burly, but well dressed in a black casual suit. His face was chiseled and hadn't been shaven in perhaps a week. He had a barrel chest and a confident gleam in his eyes that either came from always being in control of a situation, or from being an expert at pretending to be.

King lowered his weapon. It would do him no good. "Hercules."

"Please," the man said. "Call me Alexander."

THIRTY-ONE
Chaco Province, Argentina

BISHOP WAITED FOR the sound to come again, but the jungle had gone silent—tense—like every living creature knew something bad was about to happen. They sensed it, just as Bishop and the five Delta operators with him sensed it. But what was going to happen, he had no idea.

Closing his eyes, Bishop relaxed in the dark water, focusing all his attention on his hearing.

He listened to the jungle. The large palm leaves of the trees overhead scraped against each other. The river bubbled as it rolled over rocks on the shoreline.

He listened to his men. Silent. Waiting.

He listened to the targets, Miguel and Nahuel Franco. Bishop opened his eyes. The Francos had gone silent, too.

Bishop peeked up over the log that hid him from their line of sight and saw both men still sitting on the sandy beach. But Nahuel was holding the shotgun and Miguel had produced a revolver. At first glance, Bishop thought the men had heard the same sounds in the jungle, but when he took a closer look he realized the awful truth.

They were looking toward him.

Not the jungle.

Bishop turned to his men and spoke quickly. "Ditch your weapons and night vision. Do not engage. Do not speak. I will come for you."

He ducked under the water and disappeared into the darkness.

BP-One blinked twice in surprise. Then he nodded and passed on the orders. The team quickly put their weapons and night vision goggles into the water and let them sink to the muddy bottom. They'd all been warned that the Chess Team did things a little differently, but had yet to experience it firsthand. It seemed Bishop's Pawns were about to get their first taste in truly unconventional warfare.

After a minute passed and Bishop had not yet surfaced, BP-One thought, *suicidal warfare.* Then he became distracted by the row of rifle muzzles sliding out of the jungle. Following orders, the team silently raised their hands.

Ten darkly clad Argentine National Gendarmerie soldiers exited the jungle, keeping their weapons trained on the intruders. Bright lamps from within the jungle and from the sandy beach filled the river with daylight luminosity. "Mantenga sus manos hacia arriba y salir del agua. Ahora," one of the men commanded, his voice firm and in control.

Only BP-Three could speak fluent Spanish, but he remained silent, following Bishop's orders to the T. Instead, he translated through his actions, stepping out of the water and entering the jungle, motioning for the others to follow. As BP-One stepped out of the river, he glanced back one more time, wondering how Bishop had remained submerged for so long. He could have swum away, but the river was wide and long. Anywhere he surfaced would have been seen.

While the Delta team was restrained in plastic zip-tie handcuffs, three of the ANG soldiers scanned the river, looking for signs of movement. They scanned with flashlights, highlighting every inch of the water's surface and the far shoreline.

When five minutes had past, BP-Two shot BP-One a nervous glance. They were all wondering the same things: *Where is Bishop? And is he dead?*

WHEN BISHOP DUCKED beneath the water he released all the air in his lungs and sank to the bottom. Finding a tree trunk, he slid underneath it, wrapped his arms around it in a great bear hug, and squeezed for all he was worth. Just as his body began to crave more oxygen, the ANG soldiers had made their move. Bishop watched as lights lit the scene above, but failed to pierce the ten-foot-deep black water. When the flashlights began panning across the river, his body shook with the need to breath.

That was five minutes ago.

He'd been in the water for seven.

At the four-minute mark he had been unable to fight his body's natural urges any longer. His mouth snapped open and his lungs filled with water. But no bubbles rose to the surface. With no air in his lungs, Bishop's drowning went completely unnoticed. As his body convulsed he focused on one thing—hanging on. For three more minutes he continued to drown, his body dying and regenerating over and over again. It was a torture unlike anything he'd ever endured before. Having a limb torn off, even nearly losing his head, had been less agonizing than this. Because no matter how well he *knew* he would survive, his body *believed* it was dying.

The lights moved away from the river a minute later and then faded as the group moved off. After waiting another full minute, until the light had fully extinguished, he let go of the tree trunk and rose to the surface. It took all of his mental energy to rise slowly out of the water, to allow the water to drain fully from his lungs before taking a breath, but he managed the task. His resurrection from the watery grave was silent and unnoticed. He crawled onto the shore, mentally and physically exhausted. Ten seconds later, thanks to his regenerative abilities, Bishop stood, full of energy and feeling fine—as though nothing had happened.

Despite that, his psyche had taken a beating. He hadn't just tasted death, he'd shared a meal with the Grim Reaper himself. Bishop rolled his neck, took a deep breath, and pushed the memory of drowning out of his mind. A fear of death would not help him retrieve his men, especially when it was likely he would survive his death several more times before the night was through.

He shed the majority of his wet clothes, improving his mobility without losing any stealth thanks to his dark skin. He also left behind his night vision goggles, which were not appropriate for running. The only weapons he kept were his silenced sidearm and KA-BAR knife.

The jungle tore at him as he ran through the darkness, but he gave the momentary pain no heed as his body quickly healed every superficial wound. He didn't slow until he heard angry voices speaking Spanish. Seven of the ANG soldiers had stopped to perform an impromptu interrogation before bringing the men in officially. When he peeked through some brush and saw his men bound and on their knees, he wondered if they would be brought in at all. When the man questioning brought his handgun up and shot BP-One in the leg, it was all the motivation Bishop needed to act.

Over the shout of pain from BP-One, no one heard the whistle of Bishop's KA-BAR knife sailing though the air. But they saw the end result as the seven-inch blade buried itself into the interrogator's leg. The man shouted and fell, clutching the knife.

Bishop followed the knife's path, charging from the jungle with his silenced Sig Sauer raised. Aiming for the soldier's body armor, he squeezed off two shots, dropping a second man. The rounds didn't kill the soldier, but the impact, like punches from a young Mike Tyson, took away his breath and will to fight. The five remaining men opened fire, riddling his body with bullets.

Flesh flew.

Blood sprayed.

But still he charged.

As he fired four more shots, aiming through blood-coated eyes, Bishop saw abject fear enter the eyes of the remaining ANG soldiers. Suddenly, three of the four men fell to the ground, where Bishop's Pawns One through Five, who had easily freed themselves from the plastic cuffs, made short work of them, each following Bishop's lead in subduing but not killing the soldiers.

The last standing ANG soldier unloaded at Bishop's chest. As Bishop felt the bullets enter his chest and exit his back he worried that one might strike the crystal that kept him sane. He leapt forward with a yell, fearing insanity more than death, and struck out with his fist. Despite his arm taking three rounds, it regenerated by the time it struck the man's helmeted head. Despite the helmet dulling the blow, the man crumpled to the jungle floor, unconscious.

Bishop grunted as the intense pain from being shot innumerable times overpowered his adrenaline. He fell to one knee, clenched his eyes shut, and waited for the wounds to heal. The pain was replaced by a fiery itch and then faded completely. He stood up, a bloody, but hale, mess of a soldier and looked at his team, who were staring at him.

BP-One looked at the unconcious ANG soldiers, then back to Bishop. He grinned. "You do realize how entirely fucked up that was?"

Bishop nodded. "Tip of the iceberg." He pointed to BP-One's injured leg. "Can you make it to the LZ?"

"It's not going to heal on its own, but I can make it."

Bishop headed out. His team had survived, but the mission was a failure. And he'd nearly lost everything. Had the crystal been destroyed . . . He made a mental note to find a way to keep the crystal better protected and started the long trek home.

THIRTY-TWO
Taipei, Taiwan

THE WOMAN IN the power suit leveled her weapon at Knight's head. When he dove to the side, she fired. The round whistled past his ear—he could feel its heat—and struck a passing taxi.

As he hit the sidewalk and rolled, Knight heard the taxi's tires squeal over the screams of fleeing pedestrians. The vehicle's driver lost control, possibly hit by the round meant for him. The woman shouted something in Chinese that he couldn't make out as he got his feet under him again. He spun toward the woman, drawing a weapon of his own, and when her body lined up in his sight, he pulled the trigger without hesitation. The silent round sailed out of the gun, striking the woman in the throat. The dart, meant for Walis Palalin, dropped her to her knees as she held her throat in surprise. She slid down the stairs on her back, stopping on the sidewalk.

He opened her suit and inspected the badge. National Police Agency. *How did the Taiwanese police force know we were coming?* Knight thought.

But there was no time to figure that out. A loud engine announced the presence of a large gray van, its side stenciled with the Chinese text that translated to: SWAT.

The Taiwanese SWAT were elite fighters who were not just brutally efficient, but also masters in hand-to-hand kung fu combat. Knowing that a full squad of heavily armed and highly skilled men would burst from the back of the van at any second, Knight scoured the street for some hope of escape.

The taxi that had been shot sat empty and running. The owner had stopped on the curb and limped quickly into the hospital, a trail of blood marking his passage. He had taken a round and, being at a hospital, wasted no time in seeking help. In doing so, he'd left Knight the perfect getaway car.

He turned to his two teammates. "Get to the taxi!"

Shrieking tires followed by hard metal bangs and angry shouting voices filled the air behind Knight. The SWAT van had stopped and expelled the men inside, who were now shouting at him to stop. But stopping was impossible, both because he couldn't afford to get caught, but also because he was airborne, leaping over the hood of the taxi.

He landed on the driver's side and hopped into the front seat of the still-running vehicle. As his teammates opened the back doors and jumped in, a sound like thunder erupted behind them. But there were no storm clouds, only twenty men opening fire with automatic weapons.

One of the Delta operators in the backseat shouted in pain, struck by a round. As the cloud of bullets ate up the back of the vehicle, Knight knew it wouldn't be long before all three men were reduced to tenderized, indistinguishable meat. He slammed the car into drive and hit the gas.

Bullets pursued them as they shot out into the road, turned left, and merged with traffic. Sirens could be heard converging on their location. Escape in the taxi, which was easy to spot with its shot-up back, would be impossible. As the rubber of the left rear tire sheared off and rolled away, Knight stopped the vehicle in the middle of the road and ran to the black sedan parked to the side.

He opened the driver's side, sat down, and started the engine of the team's car. He looked back as his teammates entered the vehicle. One man was bleeding from the shoulder. Nothing serious. But what he saw rounding the corner behind them was very serious. The SWAT team had run on foot, entering the street fifty feet back. Knight rolled down his window and tossed a small object into the ruined taxi.

He hit the gas, drawing the attention of the SWAT team, who had been focused on the taxi. They adjusted their aim, but before a round could be fired, the taxi exploded, sending metal fragments and a ball of fire into the air. The SWAT team ducked for cover and missed Knight's quick left-hand turn.

Knight slowed his pace, took several turns, and merged with the busy city traffic. Of course, their car had been seen and would have to be abandoned shortly. But as police vehicles swarmed past them, headed toward the explosion, the team took comfort in the fact that their car's tinted windows hid their identities. Driving toward the team's rendez-vous point at one of the city's many ports, Knight activated his throat mic and contacted the other members of his team. "This is Knight. Abort mission. Meet at the port in thirty. We're bugging out."

"Copy that, Knight. We had no— oh shit!" Knight recognized the sound of bullets striking metal and glass. He could hear shouts. Angry at first. Then desperate. The return fire was loud in his ear. Then everything went quiet. And he knew what that meant.

The rest of his team was dead.

THIRTY-THREE
Rome, Italy

"I'M AFRAID THAT'S impossible," Alexander said, leading King and Pierce into a nearby storage room. He sat on a tarp-covered crate while Pierce inspected the remnants of an old worn statue and King paced. The wraith had gone, but they knew it lurked nearby.

"Nothing's impossible," King replied.

Alexander laughed. "Now that you have encountered some of the strangeness our world has to offer, you fancy yourself an expert on what is, and what is not, impossible?"

"Just let me see her," King said, his voice less demanding than the first time he'd asked to see Fiona. "She's diabetic and needs insulin."

"I noticed the insulin pump and have taken steps to see that she is provided with refills when required. If I allowed you to see her it would brew hope of rescue among the others. Hope would lead to discontentment, unruliness, and anger. Right now they are content prisoners. Right now, they are safe." Alexander crossed his arms. "So it is as I said before, impossible."

"The others?" Pierce asked, turning from the statue. "How many people have you kidnapped?"

"Fifty-seven. But kidnapping implies a negative intent," Alexander said. "I am saving their lives."

"By keeping them in a subterranean tomb?" King asked.

"You were charged with keeping just one of them safe," Alexander said. "And we know how that turned out. Until the matter is cleared up, they must remain under my guard. They will be safe in the secret places that only my people and I know about."

"The Herculean Society?" Pierce asked.

Alexander gave a nod and a grin. "Your old friends, yes."

King hated to admit it, but he agreed with Alexander. His methods were shady, as they had been in the past, but what he was doing wasn't any different from the mission the rest of the team had undertaken; to protect the last speakers of ancient languages, they had to be stealed away and hidden. The difference was that Alexander employed inhuman helpers and kept the prisoners in the dark, both figuratively and literally.

Alexander leaned back, his large elbows resting on another crate. "Of course, your presence here debunks my claims of safe refuge." His eyes, brimming with a mixture of cockiness and annoyance, glared at King. "How did you find me?"

"You didn't mean for us to find you?" King asked.

"Not at all."

King explained how they pieced together Alexander's two separate mentions of a promise to someone—a promise he was now breaking by getting involved with the problems of the world. He related the logical jump to Acca Larentia and the hints about her burial place not in what history said, but in what it was missing. When he was done, Alexander looked stunned.

King noticed the ancient man's flabbergasted expression. "What?"

"I'm . . . impressed." Alexander sat up straight. "I thought you were simply a man who knew how to kill people."

"I'm that, too," King said.

"Dare I ask if you could have been followed?"

King thought about his unease while in the ruins of the Roman Forum. He'd felt a presence watching them, but he was sure it was the guard's they had encountered that his instincts had detected. "We weren't followed."

Alexander didn't look convinced. "These are strange times. The rocks themselves can have eyes."

"Only Lewis knew exactly where I was headed," King said. "We *weren't* followed."

"Mmm," Alexander said, still not entirely convinced, but moving on. "You say you entered through the Lacus Curtius?" Alexander asked.

Pierce nodded. "A ladder might be a good idea, though."

Alexander smiled. "It's a favored entrance of the Forgotten. They don't need ladders."

"The who?" Pierce asked.

"The cloaked men you have encountered. They are as ancient as I am, but lost their voices and souls long ago."

"Who were they?"

"Test subjects," Alexander said. When he saw the angry stares of both King and Pierce, he added, "Unending life has slowly peeled away my curtain of immorality. I do not see things the way I used to when I was young. When I was mortal. I wasn't all that dissimilar from Richard Ridley."

King pictured Ridely, the head of Manifold Genetics, who had tried to unlock the secrets of immortality. The man's pursuit of godhood had been ruthless. Human experimentation left victims insane and nearly impervious to harm. Thousands more had come close to death when Ridley's actions resulted in the mythical Hydra being reborn. No price was too steep, and in the end he achieved his goal of immortality, but lost his company, his men, and his fortune. But he was free, and had all the time in the world to make a comeback. He pictured Alexander in a similar role and the image frightened him. *Thank God he's on our side.*

Alexander continued. "The Forgotten are proof of this. I keep them to remind me of what I could be. What I have been. And what the cost of my failures can lead to."

King waited for the account to continue, but Pierce had already put the pieces together. "They killed Acca. The Forgotten?"

A sudden sadness swept over Alexander. He stared at the floor. "Could you believe it still stings after all this time?" He looked up at them. "They are prone to madness on their own. Desperate with thirst. Hundreds died at their hands in the early years, before Acca was killed. Since then I have kept them sated with a supplement that replaces their craving for blood."

"You're not saying they're vampires," King said.

Alexander shook his head. "Not in the traditional sense, but it's possible they're responsible for the legend."

"My God . . ." Pierce said.

"Their hands are covered in pores, each containing a small, strong, and hollow tendril. Thousands of them. This is how they walk on walls. It's also how they drain blood through their victim's skin." He demonstrated by grabbing his own arm with his hand. "May you never end up in their embrace. It is an awful thing."

For a moment, King wondered if that was a veiled threat, but the distant look of heartbreak had returned to the man's face. He'd *witnessed* Acca's death.

"How did it happen?" King asked. "With Acca?"

"She stumbled across my lab. She was always curious. Always searching for answers. It's part of what I loved about her. But it also got her into trouble. When she found them, locked behind bars, they hadn't eaten in weeks. They were starved and pitiful-looking. Assuming they needed water, she held out a cup. Her act of mercy resulted in her death. The water spilled to the floor. They drank her dry."

Alexander sniffed a deep breath through his nose and stood, his body thick, towering, and strong. All thoughts of the past were gone. "Enough of this. I'll have one of the Forgotten escort you out at a secure location."

King raised an eyebrow. "To quote you: 'impossible.'" To punctuate his statement, King placed his hand on the handgun tucked into the front of his pants.

"You realize that's useless in here, yes?" Alexander said, showing no fear of the weapon.

"But it will hurt," King said with a grin. "A lot."

Alexander chuckled and relaxed. "What do you want?"

"The same thing everyone locked away in your dungeon wants," King said. "Hope. And if you have them, answers."

Alexander walked past King and Pierce, entering the dark hallway. "I don't know everything. But I can point you in the right direction."

King fell in step behind Alexander. "That's all I need."

THIRTY-FOUR
Asino, Siberia

ROOK RAN DOWN the street, headed for the turn onto his targets' road. He had no intention of giving up the mission because the Russian military happened to be flying overhead. The choppers had yet to arrive, but they would soon. The chop of their rotor blades pulsed through the forest as they grew closer. With his earbud back in place, Rook contacted his team again. "Give me a sitrep."

"Rook, this is fubar," RP-Two came back. "These helos aren't flying by. They're circling."

What the fuck? Rook thought. It explained why he'd been hearing them for so long, but had yet to actually see one of the helicopters. But had the team? "What are we dealing with?"

"Unknown. We've seen shadows through the trees, but haven't got a clear look. Best guess is that there are three of them, though."

Rook's earbud crackled to life again, but the voice didn't belong to the five men on his Delta team. "Rook, this is Dominick Boucher. Queen reported mission compromised. Bishop has gone silent. We have reports of shots fired and men down in Taipei. Abort mission. Abort mi—"

Boucher's voice was drowned out by the sound of an explosion. A pressure wave shot out of the forest carrying a cloud of pine needles. The shouts of his men followed the boom. "Rook, they're Werewolves! Fully armed. Shit, they're right on top of us!"

Gunfire ripped through the forest as the five-man Delta team returned fire. But Rook knew it was hopeless. Werewolf was the nickname for Russia's Ka-50 Black Shark attack helicopter, so named because it seemed only a silver bullet could knock it out of the sky. They were heavily armored tank- and jet-killing weapons of war. With an armament that included antitank missiles, aerial rockets, air-to-air missiles, and an array of machine guns, three of which was severe overkill for taking out a five-man team.

Unless they knew who they were up against, Rook thought.

"Abort mission!" Rook shouted. "Lose them in the trees and—"

The buzz of two miniguns ripped through the forest.

Rook held his breath.

A loud *cracking* filled the air as a tree fell. It *swished* to the ground and struck with a *boom*.

Labored breath came through his earbud, followed by a voice. "RP-Two through Five are down! Two of the helos are on me. One is headed your way!"

Rook had been so stunned by the battle being waged in the forest that he still remained rooted in the middle of the country road. But there was nowhere to hide. Running toward the choppers was suicide and they clearly had thermal sensors to help locate warm human bodies in the cool forest. The road stretched on endlessly in either direction. And across from the forest was the open hilly pasture of the cow farm. Armed with only a handgun and three grenades, hidden beneath his thick sweater, he would last only as long as it took for the gunner to line him up and pull the trigger.

Knowing he didn't have time to find cover, Rook decided to hide in plain sight. He leaped a short barb-wire fence into the pasture and ran up the hill. As he pounded up the soft loamed hillside, a second explosion blasted apart the forest. The missiles being fired, meant for tanks, had no doubt reduced Jeff Kafer, his friend, to slurry. Rook's rage carried him up and over the hill just as a lone helicopter rose up over the forest and bore down on him.

He quickly turned his run into a walk, joining the fringe of a large, spooked cattle herd. He looked over his shoulder. The obsidian helicopter looked absolutely evil, its two wings carrying enough firepower to fight a war. But he just watched it approach; hoping his lack of fear and his clothing would make the gunner think twice. As the helicopter banked sharply and circled the hilltop, he knew his plan had worked. At least for the moment.

The helicopter swiveled around and returned, facing him head on. As it descended, the herd panicked and broke into several stampeding groups. Confused, the cows ran over each other, making a mess, their anxious moos drowned out by the coaxial rotor chop.

Rook could see the pilot and gunner giving him the once over so he used his very real anger over the death of his team and channeled it as the fictitious owner of a panicked herd of cattle. With a beet-red face he let loose with a string of Russian curses, violently gesticulating at the helicopter and the scattering cows. When the helicopter remained rooted in place he got bold, picking up a small stone and lobbing it at the chopper. It struck the windshield and made the men inside laugh.

The helicopter rose up and flew just over his head, reuniting with the others still circling the forest. Rook watched them for a moment, but when two military trucks full of soldiers rumbled down the road, he retreated toward the farmhouse, where he hoped to find some kind of vehicle. As he neared the home, a vehicle wasn't waiting for him. Instead it was a man speaking on a mobile phone and raising a double-barrel shotgun at him.

Rook stopped when he saw the weapon. He tried to hear what the man was saying, but became distracted by the chop of rotor blades growing louder. Not just one, but all three choppers were returning. Before Rook could speak, think, or move, the rising sound of approaching war machines was drowned out by the blast of two shotgun shells.

THIRTY-FIVE
El Calvario, Colombia

HIDDEN IN THE shadows, Queen and her team watched as four more vehicles entered the town from the low side road. They stopped near the bottom of town, fifteen feet below the team's position. But something was different about these vehicles. They were SUVs, perhaps 1990s models, black and mud-covered from off-roading in the jungle—not military. The twenty men who exited the vehicles were armed with a variety of semi-automatic and automatic weapons, but nothing the Colombian military was known to use. Most were dressed in olive green, like the fifteen men at the top of the rise, but the hodgepodge of uniforms smacked of militia. The anger in the men's faces revealed who they truly were: drug runners.

And the military was not welcome. Whether or not the military knew the runners had set up shop nearby wasn't clear, but they were about to find out. Queen was about to make sure of that.

While the drug runners had no idea the team was there, the military was certainly seeking them out. And more might be on the way. They needed a distraction, and a big one, first to get across the street without being seen, and second to make it through the jungle to the LZ where a UH-100S stealth Blackhawk transport helicopter waited to whisk them back to friendly territory. It would be a dangerous flight over hostile terrain, but the still classified chopper was invisible to all but the naked eye and piloted by a "Nightstalker" from the 160th Special Operations Aviation Regiment. They were the most highly trained pilots in the world and Delta had first dibs.

But even the best pilot in the world is no good when your body is full of bullets.

Queen relayed her plan to the team. After being greeted with wide eyes and dropped mouths, the team glanced at each other and then nodded to her. For the first time in her life, Queen could clearly read a man's mind. They thought she was nuts. That the chick Delta operator with the skull brand on her forehead no longer feared death and was going to get them all killed.

In part, they were right. She didn't fear death. The problem with their assessment was that her fear of death was conquered long before the events of the previous year.

She left the team where they were and snuck into a neighboring home. The two-story house was old and the floors bent at odd angles. If another earthquake struck the area she had no doubt the building would collapse. But it would serve her needs, barring any earthquakes.

After inspecting the first floor and finding an older couple asleep in a bedroom at the back of the house—where they should be safe—she headed upstairs. Stepping on the outside edge of the staircase, she quietly made her way up. A quick check of the two upstairs rooms revealed no other occupants.

A second-floor window faced up the hill, giving her a clear view of the military jeeps. The men were now exiting the Forero residence, guns raised and heading straight toward them. She had no idea if the military was working with the drug runners, or if the groups simply tolerated each other, but neither side had fired a shot, despite now being in clear view of each other. Fearing that one side might back down from a fight, Queen raised her UMP, aimed it at one of the jeeps and squeezed off two separate three-round bursts. The six bullets pinged off the jeep, sending military men diving to the ground. Moments later they responded as predicted, by opening fire on her position.

She ran.

The window behind her exploded, sending rounds and glass shards into the far wall.

The barrage was followed by a second, much closer demonstration of firepower. The drug runners, fearing an attack, opened fire. Both sides were now fully engaged.

As Queen entered the upstairs hallway, a little voice came out of the darkness in the back bedroom. "Papa?"

Queen's eyes went wide as she saw a little boy, no older then seven, standing in the bedroom doorway, rubbing his eyes and looking nervous. How she had missed him she had no idea, but she couldn't leave him here. If he were to walk in front of the window from where she'd fired, the military would cut him down.

With two fast strides, she reached the boy, threw him over her shoulder, and leaped the banister. She landed on the stairway with a hard thump, and jumped the rest of the way down. At the base of the stairs, the boy's papa stood ready with a shotgun.

Their eyes met for a moment and came to an agreement. He could see she was helping the boy, and given her professional gear, and perhaps the fact that she was a woman, decided to trust her. The man lowered his shotgun and took a step back. Queen put the boy in his arms and said, "Permanecer abajo hasta que la batalla ha terminado."

She paused at the door way and added, "Gracias."

The man tilted his head forward as he headed to the back room with the boy. "Y a usted."

As Queen rounded the back of the house she came nose to barrel with one of her men's submachine guns. He drew it back without pause and met the other four, whose weapons were trained on the street side of the alley. Anyone who entered would be torn apart. She tapped the men on the shoulder, getting their attention, and then led them around the building to their right. The alley on the other side emerged five feet behind the last of the drug runner's vehicles. The men were using the car doors and rear ends as shelter when reloading.

Queen paused at the front corner of the house. "Stay low, move fast, and try not to get shot." She finished the statement with a fiendish grin that intimidated her teammates but also brought smiles to their faces. Queen *was* nuts, but she was so good at it. And it gave the team a supernatural confidence.

They struck out into the road, ducking low. With the drug runners' attention on the top of town and their bodies hidden by both darkness and the black vehicles, they moved without being seen.

That is, until one of the runners ducked and turned around, intending to reload his weapon. Instead he took a silenced bullet to the center of his forehead courtesy of Queen's sidearm. Before his body had slumped to the pavement, the team had entered the other side of town. Two minutes later Queen lead her team into the jungle. Another fifteen and they were airborne, heading north over the jungle and wondering what kind of hell the rest of the Chess Team had been dropped into.

THIRTY-SIX
Rome, Italy

"**WHY DON'T WE** start with what you know," Alexander said as he led King and Pierce into a large circular chamber. The fifty-foot-diameter room had three arched exits, was lit by rows of recessed lights, and its tan walls and floor were polished to a shine.

But it wasn't the finished sheen of the room that held King's and Pierce's attention, it was the gallery of objects held within.

Like a museum, the space was filled with glass display cases, glass-domed pedestals, and even a few finely preserved statues. King also noted that the room held several security measures similar to the most high-tech museums—ceiling-mounted cameras, infrared sensors, ultrasonic sensors, and motion detectors. He glanced back at the entrance they'd come through and saw several circular bars hidden in the floor and in the top of the arch. Should something be taken from its place, the room, which was really more of a vault, could be locked down.

King focused on Alexander's questions while Pierce quickly wove through the displays, looking at the contents with wide-eyed fascination. "We know they're some kind of golem," King said, feeling stupid as he did. That they were fighting golems still seemed ridiculous, despite who he was talking to.

Alexander sat in what looked to be a very old chair, its frame built from thick wood. Its leather back and seat cushion were faded and cracked. "Go on."

"They're part of Jewish folklore and are created by speaking the word 'Emet' and destroyed by the word 'met.' Any inanimate objects can be animated, but clay is preferable."

Alexander waited for more, but when King didn't speak, his eyebrows slowly rose. "That's it?"

Pierce's voice interrupted. "Are these apple seeds?" He was leaning over a pedestal, peering through its glass top.

"They are," Alexander replied.

Pierce stood up straight, like he'd just been struck by something. He looked at Alexander. "Not from the Garden of the Hesperides?"

"The same. And before you ask, they have great healing properties, but do not grant immortality."

Pierce mumbled excitedly to himself and continued his journey around the room.

"How much more is there?" King asked. "What don't we know?"

"A great deal," Alexander said. "The tales of rabbis using the ability of words to bring golems to life is simply one of the more modern documented usages of a very ancient power. It is something long forgotten by most of the world and buried in many of our ancient languages. Despite being only a fragment of something much larger, the ability to bring the nonliving to life, it is the most commonly used application of the ancient power and can be easily traced through history.

"In the sixteenth century, Judah Loew ben Bezalel, a rabbi in Prague, is said to have brought a golem to life to protect his community from the Holy Roman Empire, which had decreed that all Jews should be cast out or killed. You know the story, yes?"

King nodded.

"It was a skill either taught to him by his predecessors, but used infrequently, or documented in a text the rabbi found. Either way, the knowledge was passed down to the rabbi through a line of Jewish ancestors going back to ancient Israel, where a well-known Jew could manipulate the elements with his words. But the knowledge is older than Israel. The Jews who had fled Egypt took the knowledge with them, led by a man who seemed to have mastered many elements of this ancient power."

"You're talking about Moses?"

Alexander gave a nod.

"And the 'well-known Jew' who could manipulate the elements?"

"Jesus. Who could walk on water, turn away storms, and, if you believe it, rise from the dead."

"I'll believe *that* when I see it," King said.

Alexander chuckled. "He would have liked you, King. You have a lot in common with Thomas."

King looked incredulous. "You *knew* Jesus?"

"I met him."

"And you heard him speak this language?"

"No, but others did. Some claimed to understand it, hearing his words as simple commands. Others were dumbfounded by it."

"So, what, Christianity is founded on a magical charlatan?"

"Jesus spent his childhood in Egypt, as did Moses, so it's possible both men found some ancient source of knowledge and used what they learned to perform amazing miracles. But their mastery of the ancient language and its powers went far beyond the creation of golems. It could just as easily be argued that they had supernatural instruction."

"Hey!" Pierce shouted from the other side of the gallery, where he stood in front of a lion skin that hung on the wall. He gripped its curly black hair in his hands, close to pulling it out from excitement. "Is . . . is this?"

"I wore it in Nazca," Alexander said. "But it was one of many I wore in my early life. When I was still a hunter."

King cleared his throat. "So the source of this power is in Egypt?" King asked, hoping to keep the conversation on track.

"The trail leads to Egypt, where golems were used as slaves, along with the Jews, to help build the pyramids. Once you understand that golems were fairly common in the ancient world, you can trace their history and involvement in ancient cultures around the world. The pyramids in Central America, Stonehenge, Easter Island—"

"The ziggurats of Sumer." King could finally see where Alexander was going. The ziggurats of Sumer were mankind's first truly amazing construction projects. It was also the cradle of modern civilization, giving us our first written human language, cities, and code of laws.

"And it is there, in Babylon—the capital city of Sumer—that we discover how this ancient language was lost to humanity, hidden within the scores of languages developed shortly after that period of history."

The answer came to King before Alexander could speak it. "The Tower of Babel." King knew the biblical account well enough. God, upset that the people had built a tower to reach Heaven, had confused the population's language and scattered them around the planet. And he didn't buy a word of it.

"You don't sound convinced."

"It's another Jewish myth given a few verses in the Bible."

"Not just the Bible, or more accurately, the Pentateuch. It is also mentioned in the Book of Jubiless, Josephus's *Antiquities of the Jews*, the Greek *Third Apocalypse of the Baruch*, the Midrash, Kabbalah, and the Qur'an. The Sumerians tell the story as Enmerkar and the Lord of Aratta. But perhaps most interesting are the Central American traditions. In one, a tower is built that will allow Xelhua, a survivor of a great flood, to storm Heaven. But the tower is destroyed and those who built the tower had their language confused. Then again from the Toltecs; a tower known as a *zacuali*, is built by the survivors of a deluge, but once more their language was confused and they were scattered around the planet. The ancient history of the world is recorded very similarly in most cultures, including a great flood, the Tower of Babel, and, most importantly, a protolanguage that every human being had been speaking since the dawn of Homo sapiens."

THE DIM LIGHT wasn't exactly easy to read by, but it was better than nothing. The same could be said for Fiona's reading material—a three-week-old copy of the *New York Times*. After reading the movie and book reviews she searched for a comics section, but found none. *What a rip-off!* She had hoped a little humor might distract her from the growing tension of those around her.

The revelation that she knew about the wraiths before being imprisoned made her a pariah. Her confidence about being rescued by her father, whose identity she refused to divulge, only made the others more skeptical of her presence. Some thought she was a spy. Only Elma continued to speak to her.

A hand bearing the mark of the Herculean Society took hold of the open newspaper and pulled it down. Elma's head poked over the top. "Any interesting news?"

Fiona lowered the paper to her lap. She sat cross-legged on her cot, wrapped in a blanket. Still dressed in her black pajamas, she looked like a typical girl about to be tucked in by her mother. But she was not a typical girl, and Elma, as nice as she was, could never be her mother. Though kind, she lacked patience, a sense of humor, and an imagination. King had her beat, hands down. "If you consider movie reviews news, then yes."

Elma blew air through her lips, a noncommittal sound that was neither laugh nor disapproval. She sat on the bed, bending the mattress toward her weight, which seemed heavier than usual. "The others have been talking," she said.

Fiona had been observing the group since her arrival, watching their movements and listening to conversations with her keen ears. There was a subtle pecking order that kept things orderly, but also created a kind of caste system. Certain prisoners ate first, bathed first, and made decisions for the group. With so many different cultures represented, it seemed the one with the most dominant social structure had been adopted. They had become an underground society with rings of social position. Elma was on the outer ring, mostly for the kindness she'd shown Fiona. Buru, who was speaking to a group of men, had pulled away from Fiona and maintained his position at the society's core.

But Buru had not forsaken Fiona. The information Elma occasionally delivered came straight from Buru. Which is what made Elma's next words so worrisome. "They want to get rid of you."

Fiona sat up straight. "What? Why?"

"You frighten them."

"I'm just a kid."

"Since your arrival, you have shown greater strength, knowledge, and resilience than any of them. They believe you are either here to watch us or are the cause of all this."

"What are they going to do? It's not like you can have me transferred to another cell."

Elma just looked at her gravely.

They're going to kill me, Fiona thought. Her face filled with fear, but it was momentary. Anger came next. "You just let them try it," she whispered through gritted teeth.

Elma's hands shot up in frustration. "You see! Even as these people plot to kill you, you show them to be cowards." She sat quietly for a moment, then asked, "Where does this strength come from?"

Fiona had never thought of herself as strong. She just got by. She adapted. Life on the reservation hadn't been easy, starting with: "My parents died when I was little. I was raised by my grandmother. But I think I took care of her just as much as she took care of me."

"Life without parents can be tough," Elma said, "but you—"

"A year ago, my reservation was attacked. More than three thousand people were killed, including my grandmother."

Elma's hand went to her mouth. The Siletz Reservation attack was well known around the world as the worst terrorism attack since the World Trade Center. "The news said there was a survivor, but never gave an identity. It was *you*?"

As Fiona nodded, Elma reached out and touched her face, then her hair, as though to confirm that this little girl was in fact a Native American. "It's no wonder you're tough . . ." She stood up. "This will change everything. You don't have to wo—"

The chamber shook. The lights hanging from the ceiling swayed.

As the pounding of giant feet grew louder, Fiona shuffled back against the wall. She knew the sound. "They're coming for me," she said.

Elma looked at her, eyes wide. "Who is coming for you?"

Fiona pointed in the direction of the noise, toward the back of the chamber. "They're coming for us all."

The back wall of the chamber broke apart, falling into rubble. A tunnel was revealed. A whispering voice came from the tunnel. The crumbled wall shifted into two piles and began taking shape. As two hulking bodies of stone emerged, Elma filled her lungs to scream.

ALEXANDER CONTINUED HIS explanation. "Which takes us back to the very beginning and the very first recorded mention of a golem, 'The Lord God formed the man from the dust of the ground and breathed into his nostrils the breath of life, and the man became a living being.'"

"Adam?" King did nothing to hide his continued skepticism.

"Adam is represented in the ancient stories of many cultures. Try not to get hung up on the Judeo-Christian baggage and try to see the truth. The Bible, *and other sources,* say that God *spoke* the universe into being. Light, earth, water, life, all came from His *words*. And man was formed from dust. We are all golems, but have retained the life imbued to us.

"So this is what, the language of God?"

"Call it what you want," Alexander said. "But it is the protohuman language, and with the right speaker, it is capable of amazing, and terrible, things."

"Is that why you broke your promise," King pointed to the entryway they'd come through, "to her?"

"What humanity does to itself is of no concern of mine," Alexander said, his voice suddenly harsh. "I, unlike some"—he glanced at Pierce—"am a protector of history."

Pierce had moved closer, his attention captured by the new twist in the conversation. "You're an eraser of history."

"To preserve it, sometimes it must be forgotten. The past does not belong to the present. Should your grave be exhumed in a thousand years, would you want your body dissected, put on display, or any number of other crimes committed against the dead done to you?"

King thought about how he felt standing over his mother's grave. He understood Alexander's point. Life was sacred and our bodies, in death, were as well. He also understood the man's motivation. "You knew them," he said.

Alexander looked at King and then to the shining floor. "There are men I knew on display in museums. Men who would find the treatment of their bodies scandalous."

"But what about what we can learn from the past?"

"What man learns, he soon uses to destroy. The fascination with uncovering secrets is simply a craving for power. And this situation is no different. The protolanguage was disseminated for a good reason. It should not be in the control of modern man. It is a rape of history that cannot stand."

"That's it?" Pierce said. "That's why you've been running around the planet collecting people? To keep someone from learning this ancient language?"

"And to protect their lives," Alexander said. "They are the last speakers of ancient languages. Their knowledge—their lives—are precious to me. Whoever is doing this is desecrating everything I have sworn to protect."

"Then you don't know who's behind the killings?"

"No," Alexander said. "Nor do I know how this language truly works.

But I have identified a man—a genius physicist and former rabbi, who dabbles in genetics and biology as well, who might be able to—"

Pierce suddenly stepped closer. He looked nervous. "Do you two feel that?"

King trained his senses on the physical world around him. He could feel a gentle vibration tickling his body. He'd been so caught up in the conversation that he'd missed it. "Is there a subway nearby?"

Alexander shook his head no, and stood to his feet. "The land is protected above and below."

"Protected from construction," Pierce said. "But from attack?"

"Every entrance is watched by heat sensors and motion detectors," Alexander said. "There is no way in without my knowing."

"What if someone created a *new* way in?" Pierce asked.

A flash of concern appeared on Alexander's face.

"Fiona," King whispered.

Alexander burst into motion, running out of the gallery, back the way they had come. King followed close at his heals, knowing the immortal man was going to protect the people he'd worked so hard to hide away. Pierce lingered a moment, not wanting to leave the room of archaeological treasures behind, but then followed.

As they entered the maze of hallways the vibrations became intense enough that they had to stop moving to remain standing. When the shaking dissipated and the rumbling of stone quieted, a new sound filled the tunnels—a woman screaming.

THIRTY-SEVEN
Washington, D.C.

PRESIDENT TOM DUNCAN sat at the head of an executive table in a West Wing conference room. Seated with him were twenty-seven advisors on everything from the school system to the space program—apparently every sector of the country was feeling the pinch. But none greater than the economy.

"People are staying home," Claire Roberts said. She was one of five top financial advisors. Her expertise lay in foreign investments and lending, but she was rarely ever wrong. "People are choosing to watch movies online rather than go to the theater. They're driving less. Buying less. And if it keeps up, they'll all start losing their jobs."

"C'mon," said a firecracker of a man. Larry Hussey, Duncan's domestic economic advisor, was eternally optimistic and, without fail, disagreed with Roberts. "Internet sales are up. Way up. The market will self-correct when the crisis is over. The American people are still consuming, just in the privacy, and safety, of their own homes."

Roberts sighed and looked at Duncan. "He's right about Internet sales. The economy is hanging on, but it's by a thread. Here's the difference. When the average American goes out to buy a book, they don't just spend eight dollars on a paperback. They spend between three and five dollars on gas unless they're driving a hybrid. They buy a chai latte or frappachino. A large percentage of those people end up eating at restaurants afterward and another chunk of people will go see a movie as well. To buy a book online requires no gas, shipping is often free, and there are no opportunities for residual spending."

"It might solve the country's credit card debt," Hussey grumbled.

Roberts raised her voice. "The vast majority of online sales are made with credit cards."

Hussey slouched a little. Though the man would never verbalize defeat, Duncan recognized the body language.

"That leaves us with the question of 'why' and the potential solutions," Roberts continued. "The why is simple. In normal times of crisis, war for instance, people spend less money on nonessentials. Movies, books, music. Luxury items. All the entertainment industries take hits to the pocketbook. People feel unsure about the future and instinctively hoard a little bit. But what we're experiencing here is something a little different. People are afraid to go out. They're afraid to congregate in large groups because that might make them targets. After all, if Fort Bragg can be hit hard, what's to stop the bad guys from striking a concert, or football game, or a packed movie theater? Even church attendance is down, and that normally goes up during wartime."

"Solutions?" Duncan asked. He hated the question because he had his own answer: to personally hunt down and catch whoever was behind the attacks. Instead he was stuck deciding what to do about the population's spending habits. There might be ways to ease the problem, but he knew damn well that the only real solution was to rain down a healthy dose of Deep Blue justice.

"People are afraid," Roberts said. "We have to make them feel safe. Encourage cities to increase patrols. Address the nation. Talk about the progress being made in tracking down the 'evil doers.'"

"What progress?" Hussey said.

Roberts rolled her eyes. "Exaggerate if you need to. The point is people won't go out. They won't congregate in places with other people if they feel like it puts them in the crosshairs."

"You'll need to appeal to their wallets as well," Hussey said. "Making them feel safe is one thing, giving them incentive to spend will pull people off their couches and out of their homes."

"Larry . . ." Roberts said. She apparently knew where Hussey was headed and wasn't comfortable with it.

He waved her off. "It's a good idea, Claire." Then continued. "Suspend sales and meal taxes for a week. Maybe two. Some people won't be able to resist. And when nothing bad happens to them, the rest will follow."

"That would require a lot of state cooperation," Duncan said.

"Mm-hmm," Hussey said. "We'd likely have to reimburse their losses. But it could prevent a financial meltdown."

"Sir," Roberts said, trying to interject.

But Duncan liked the idea. "Get it done."

Roberts sighed. It was her turn to deflate. "Why don't you tell him whose idea that was, Larry."

Hussey's face went pale.

The door to the conference room opened. Duncan's secretary entered and fought her way through the packed space. Duncan knew by the serious look on her face that she had an important message to deliver, but he needed an answer from Hussey, too. "Spill it, Larry."

"I thought you would have known," Hussey said. "It was on the news."

"I've been a little distracted," Duncan said. The secretary was almost there.

"The idea was Marrs's."

Fuck. Marrs was going to eat this up. Not only had he already committed to the idea in front of all his advisors, it was also a good idea. He couldn't back out on it just because it came from Marrs first.

His secretary whispered in his ear. He flinched, having forgotten she was incoming. "Dominick Boucher called. Wants you to make contact asap."

The nation's economic woes took an instantaneous backseat. "Make contact. Those were his words exactly?"

The secretary nodded.

It was a key phrase they had established. It meant that Boucher needed to have a chat with Deep Blue. And that meant it was mission related, and, he looked at his watch, it was far too soon for the teams to have reported in. And that meant something was wrong.

Duncan stood.

A sea of voices rose up with him.

Documents had to be signed. Approval given. The nation managed. And Marrs's plan had to be put in motion. None of it could happen without his John Hancock.

He stood rooted for a moment, torn between his conflicting duties. Manager and warrior fought a battle for his attention. His pulse quickened. He could feel it in his neck. The voices of his advisors were like needles in his eardrums. He had to take action. Every cell in his body cried out for it.

But that wasn't what he signed up for.

He held out a hand, silencing group. "One at a time. Quickly."

As the first form was handed to him by Larry Hussey, the form that would set Marrs's plan in motion, Duncan turned to the secretary and said, "Call Boucher. Tell him I'm digging a trench and will call him when I'm done."

"Digging a trench" wasn't code for anything, but he knew Boucher would understand. No one liked digging trenches, but they could save your life when the mortars started flying. And if the crisis wasn't ended soon, the skies would be clouded with rounds.

DUNCAN ENTERED THE empty situation room, hidden in a basement of the White House, and sat down at the head of the empty executive table. Using a small remote control, he dimmed the room's lights and sat in darkness. After rubbing his eyes, he leaned forward on his hands, rubbing his temples. It had taken him forty-five minutes to sign all the required paperwork.

In that time, the news networks had already caught wind of Marrs's seeming ability to dictate presidential policy. And the press along with Marrs had brewed a firestorm. Marrs called the decision to use his suggested tax pause a smoke screen, an attempt to distract people from his failings. The man could turn anything, even his own ideas, into an attack.

The loudest pundits called him a traitor. A warmonger whose policies on terror endangered the nation. Comparisons to Hitler and Stalin were casually hurled by men seeking higher ratings. Marrs led a rally in Washington, D.C., shouting for justice and shaking his fist.

Duncan wanted nothing more than for Marrs to come to his office and try shaking that fist face-to-face. But instead he had to remain measured and calm. "Defuse the powder keg," his advisors said. Settle. Appease.

It was all bullshit.

The man was brewing fear, contaminating the people with it and making sure Duncan's assurances of safety were ignored. He would probably derail his own tax pause idea, too, but would not be held accountable for it.

But every time the American public's focus turned away, Marrs brought them back with wild allegations or bolder calls to action. The most recent one being impeachment. He'd heard the same call to action a year previous when the nation faced a killer pandemic thanks to a weaponized strain of the Brugada syndrome used in an assassination attempt on his life. He had taken drastic measures—quarantining the White House staff and hundreds of U.S. citizens against their will. The rumbles died down when a cure had been provided, but the whispers never faded. With new ammunition, the guns of impeachment fired again.

He didn't fear impeachment. It was a ridiculous notion championed by the minority. But they were loud and persistent. They kept the national attention focused on him, binding his actions. The fools were unknowingly crippling his efforts to find the people responsible for the attacks.

He hit a second button on the remote. A blue screen lowered from the ceiling, stopping behind him. Once lowered, a bright light backlit the screen, making it glow and casting him in a silhouette that disguised his identity. He switched on the laptop in front of him and established a secure video feed with Dominick Boucher, who had been overseeing the team's latest batch of rescue missions. He stood in Delta's tactical HQ and was surrounded by an array of stations with men and women watching satellite feeds, monitoring endless flows of information from news, police, and military sources around the world. It was the intelligence heart of every Delta operation. One that he normally commanded.

Boucher's white mustache twitched when he faced the screen. It was a telltale sign that things were not well. "Dom, what's the score?"

There was no "What took you so long?" No annoyance in Boucher's eyes. The man knew the score: Deep Blue was the president of the United States and he sometimes had shit to do. Instead, he simply cut to the chase. "Bad guys four. Us, zip. We've been played. The authorities in Taiwan, Russia, Colombia, and Argentina knew we were coming."

Duncan's mind spun, trying to figure out who knew enough to reveal their hand. The list was short.

"I don't think we have a snitch," Boucher said, as though able to read Duncan's thoughts. "We tracked down calls to several other countries that resulted in troop mobilization. All were on our list to hit next. Whoever did this only knew we *would* be looking, but not where we were going first. They were shooting scattershot, hoping to hit us."

"Which they did."

Boucher's mustache twitched again.

"How bad is it?"

"Bishop's team was captured, but escaped without being identified as U.S. military."

Duncan felt some of his tension slip away.

Boucher quickly added, "But not before wounding seven Argentine National Gendarmerie soldiers."

His tension returned with a vengeance, squeezing the small of his back.

"Queen and her team escaped after instigating a gunfight between the Colombian military and a bunch of drug runners. Both sides received casualties, but there were no reports of our team's involvement."

None of this was good, but so far it was manageable. Any claims of U.S. involvement from these countries could easily be denied. But Boucher's face grew grim. He had worse news to report.

"Knight's team took three casualties when Taiwanese SWAT struck their position. The bodies aren't identifiable, but the Taiwanese are claiming they're ours. The tipster apparently told them as much."

"And Rook?"

The mention of Rook's name turned Boucher's face to the floor. "They were attacked by three Ka-50 Black Sharks. His team is dead. Same story as Taiwan. Can't be I.D.'d, but they're claiming the men are ours."

"What about Rook? Is he—"

"Unknown." Duncan tapped his keyboard. "Satellite imagery was intermittent at the time, as satellites passed in and out of range. But we have a few shots of him."

Duncan's screen filled up with satellite images. He combed through them, looking at the three black helicopters from above. There were images of explosions in the forest, Rook running up a hill, and then facing off against one of the Black Sharks. But in the five minutes following, there was nothing. The next image showed a mass of troops running north, through the cow pasture. Using his remote connection, Boucher circled a small area on the last image.

Duncan zoomed in on the circle, seeing a splash of red on a patch of yellow grass. "Is that blood?"

"Looks like it," Boucher said. "We believe Rook was shot. Here, listen for yourself. This was his last message before we lost communication."

Rook's voice came through the computer. He sounded shaken and out of breath. "They're all dead. My team is KIA. And I'm bleeding out. So don't come looking for me. Tell Queen—"

The connection cut off.

"We're not sure what happened," Boucher said. "But he's gone without a trace."

Duncan sat back in his chair. Allegations from Russia, Taiwan, and Argentina would soon become public. And though he could deny the citizenship of the men killed in action, it wouldn't convince the Russians, who might very well see the incursion as an act of war. And it didn't feel right.

No matter how it played out, the allegations would add fuel to the media firestorm. Despite all that, he couldn't keep his mind far from the safety of his team. Three were safe. Rook was MIA. But there was still one unaccounted for.

"What about King?"

THIRTY-EIGHT
Rome, Italy

WHAT ROME WOULD later deem a small, localized magnitude-four earthquake shook the underground tunnels. Dust fell from the ceiling, stinging King's eyes and further obscuring his view of the dim hallways lit by the occasional electric bulb.

Following Alexander proved to be difficult. The man was faster than he looked, and his intimate knowledge of the tunnels made every footfall well placed. He also seemed to be unaffected by the dirty air, which congested King's and Pierce's lungs.

The three emerged into a larger hallway, free of dust, and picked up speed. Shrieks of the Forgotten suddenly drowned out the screams of dying people. Somewhere ahead, Alexander's guardians were fighting back. But King knew it wouldn't be enough.

He also knew there was very little the three of them could do against the golems he'd seen. But he would rather die than not try.

Alexander stopped in front of a door that had been torn off its hinges. A body, cloaked in black flew out and struck him in the chest. They both fell back hard against the tunnel wall. The Forgotten shook off the impact, spun to its feet, and dove back into the room with a shriek.

As a wound on his shoulder quickly healed, Alexander stood and took a small bottle from his pocket. It looked like the small liquor bottles they served on airplanes. He drank the contents down and turned toward King. "Stay here. It's not safe for you."

Then his body shook with a strange kind of energy that made his eyes gleam with intensity. With a battle cry, he charged into the room.

King approached the door, his weapon drawn and ready. The tunnel shook with a massive impact, causing him to catch himself. He looked back at Pierce, who shook his head. The message was clear: don't go in. But he had to. This was where Fiona and many other people had been held, and not one of them was screaming now.

Thinking of Fiona, King spun around the doorframe and pointed his weapon inside the room. His eyes took everything in, but his mind took several seconds to process what he was seeing. The floors, walls, and ceilings oozed with overturned cots, human body parts, smeared flesh, and a thick coat of crimson blood.

Fighting in the center of it all were two Forgotten, Alexander, and one very large stone monster constructed of ancient marble columns, bits of arches, tiled wall, and a worn bust for a head. The golem was more refined than the one King had seen before. It wasn't just humanoid, with arms, legs, and a head, it also had fingers for gripping. The giant was hunched over, a Forgotten clinging to its back. It swung its arms side to side, trying to grasp the dark cloaked creature, but couldn't reach.

Alexander dove at the golem's leg, sweeping it out and knocking it off-balance. The second Forgotten descended from the ceiling, adding weight to the golem's back and knocking it to the floor. The chamber shook as the several-ton giant fell. But when it did, King was allowed a clear view of the back of the room.

Two more golems walked toward the rear of the chamber, where a large tunnel awaited. They flanked a man, dressed in black. He was tall, bald, and white. But other than that, distance and violent vibrations made any details impossible to glean.

There was his enemy, the man who had killed fifty innocents and countless others around the world. King burned with rage. *The man who had killed Fiona and everyone else held captive by Alexander.*

King took aim. Despite the distance and shaky footing, he knew he could make the shot. "Hey!" he shouted, wanting to see the man's face before he put a bullet in it.

As the golem on the floor struggled to stand under the strong hold of the Forgotten and Alexander, the man slowed his pace and stopped. The golems to his sides did as well.

"Turn around!" King instructed.

As the man complied, King's eyes were drawn away from his face by what he held in his hands. A small limp body with long black hair.

Fiona.

King was instantly unsure of his aim. Hitting the man somewhere wouldn't be an issue, but he couldn't guarantee a clean headshot. And he wouldn't take the risk.

The gun lowered in his hands.

The man raised a hand, giving King a wave. The gesture brought

King's attention back to his face. As the man backed into the darkness of the freshly made tunnel behind him, King caught a quick glimpse of his face. "No . . ."

Pierce looked over King's shoulder and saw him, too. "Oh God."

Both men recognized him.

Richard Ridley.

Ridley grinned at them as the two golems with him sealed off the tunnel with their bodies and returned to their former, solid, lifeless stone forms. The madman whose genetic tinkering turned Bishop into a regen, who tortured Pierce, and killed scores of people in the name of scientific progress, available to the highest bidder, had returned.

King's mind whirled. Ridley must have know about Fiona. Why else would he take her? His foster daughter had just become a human shield for the vilest man on the planet. He fought against the twisting in his gut. He couldn't let himself be consumed by worry. Ridley knew King, knew what he was capable of and the force he commanded. He would keep her alive, at least long enough to complete whatever it was he was doing.

A shout pulled him back to the situation at hand, which was far from over. The golem on the floor regained its footing and tossed one of the Forgotten into a wall. There was a loud crack as it hit. Though King doubted it was dead, it would clearly not be rejoining the fight any time soon.

Alexander flew through the air next, landing at King's feet. "Run!" He shouted at King. "To the gallery."

King saw the golem stand, gripping the Forgotten in its stone hands. The ancient dark specter shrieked as it was pulled in two directions. As he turned and ran, following Pierce, King heard the shriek rise in pitch and volume before it was cut off by a wet tear.

"Go!" Alexander shouted from behind as he fled the room behind King.

A pulsing vibration filled the tunnel, growing in intensity. A sickening impact followed as the golem crashed through the wall behind them. King allowed Alexander to pass him in the tunnel, knowing Pierce was likely to get lost. He looked over his shoulder as the golem righted itself and gave chase.

King fired his weapon over his shoulder. He knew the bullets would have no effect on the creature, so he aimed for the lightbulbs, darkening the tunnel behind them as they moved. He wasn't sure if the monster had eyes to see with, but it was all he could think to do.

Besides run.

Thirty seconds later he was out of ammo. Despite the darkness, the tight confines of the tunnel and its eight-foot height, the golem closed the distance. It lunged at King, reaching out for him with its heavy hands.

King rounded a sharp corner and was knocked forward by the impact of the golem striking the wall. Had he not reached the corner, he would have been crushed like a frog under a steamroller. He gave a quick look back at the golem, which he now noted was dark red in color, smeared with the dead Forgotten's blood, and bolted for the archway entrance to the gallery.

Pierce, with wide, panicked eyes, waved him on. "He's going to lock it down!"

King ran for the arch, remembering the metal beams hidden at the base and top of the entryway. The ground shook at his heels as the golem gave chase once more. With a glance over his shoulder, King saw a large hand reaching out for his head.

Then he was through the door.

Alarms sounded. Metal screeched. The room shook.

King fell to his stomach, rolled over, and scrambled to his feet, ready to keep running. But it wasn't necessary. The golem's stone arm had been sheared off. It lay on the floor as inanimate rubble.

The one-armed golem slammed into the thick bars twice, but had no luck. It wouldn't be getting through.

Alexander appeared at his side raging with anger. He shouted and punched a marble statue of himself, breaking it in two.

King marveled at the man's power. Whatever he had drunk before joining the battle had boosted his strength amazingly. But it hadn't made him impervious to harm. The hand he'd just punched with was a crumpled bloody mess.

"It seems we share a common nemesis," Alexander grumbled as his hand stitched itself back together.

King nodded. "Ridley." He looked at Alexander. "You mentioned a physicist-ex-rabbi who might be able to help. Still think so?"

Alexander looked at his fully healed hand, his nerves calming. "He's in Haifa. Israel. At Technion Institute of Technology. He shouldn't be hard to find."

Alexander led the way out of the gallery, explaining that they would exit into one of his Roman homes, where they could rest and coordinate. As they left the gallery amid the chaos of sounding alarms, flashing lights, and the occasional slam of stone golem against steel bars, King and Alexander failed to notice Pierce pause at one of the gallery displays, taking the ancient contents and hiding them in his pocket.

THIRTY-NINE
20,000 feet

KING LOOKED OUT the window of Alexander's Gulfstream G550. The Mediterranean sparkled like an azure crystal, twenty thousand feet below. Alexander sat next to him, his eyes covered by a blindfold. The man was sound asleep, looking like nothing more than a tired businessman on his private jet. Pierce had insisted on coming, but King wouldn't place him in harm's way again, so he remained behind in Rome.

King leaned back in his seat, closing his eyes. Despite the freakish things he'd witnessed in the past few days, his thoughts were on family. He'd been trained in combat, survival, and intelligence gathering, but none of that prepared him for the emotional upheaval he'd been going through. His dead mother had been resurrected while his deadbeat father was redeemed and returned from jail. Add to that the revelation that his parents were in fact Russian spies, and then the kidnapping of a girl who called him Dad despite him not wanting the title and doing a piss poor job of protecting her.

Giant killer golems had some fierce competition for his attention.

Thoughts of Fiona came to him as vivid images. She'd been wary of him at first, waking up in the backseat of his rental car. She remembered flashes of the attack, of a man who had saved her from the wreckage, and then King. He did his best to smile at her, to put her at ease, but he'd never been good with kids. Then, his awkward first words to her—"You're a girl"—had made her laugh. He still didn't know why he said that. It had just come out, as though she'd just been born to him.

In the following months their relationship grew fast as Fiona lived on base, under their protection. She brought smiles to a team that faced horrors on a regular basis. Her presence was a blessing, especially when their reeducation began.

But an injection of stress came into the mix thanks to the child welfare office. The job of foster father fell on him like a piano dropped from twenty stories above. His studies suffered as he became distracted by his new, parental duties. Sparring matches became a painful reminder of his inadequacies. And though he didn't feel up to the task, Fiona took to the idea and ran with it. It was a responsibility King never wanted, but was duty bound to take on.

What surprised him the most was that now that she had been taken from him, he was terrified he might lose her for good. Because despite all his fears, discomfort, and doubts, he'd become smitten by her. He wanted his parents to meet her. He wanted to finish reading *The Hunger Games* with her. His career-oriented five-year forecast was in disarray because it now involved a girl he had no right raising. And he knew child services would agree.

King checked his watch. The others should have completed their missions by now. He powered up his cell phone, which he'd shut off during his and Pierce's nighttime search of the Roman Forum, and found eight messages, which was an unusual amount since only seven people in the world had his number. He ignored the messages and dialed the number he knew would get him answers.

The line clicked as the connection was established. After a single ring, a familiar feminine recording asked him to leave a message. He gave his name, "King."

The feminine voice followed with, "Voice print confirmed," and the phone began ringing again.

The ringing was quickly replaced by the voice of Tom Duncan, Deep Blue. "Where have you been?"

King immediately heard the tension in Duncan's normally relaxed voice. Things were not going well on the home front. "Rome. I'm on my way to Haifa now, with Alexander Diotrephes."

Duncan's voice brightened. "You found her?"

"She was here, but . . . I lost her. Alexander had fifty people, all speakers of dying languages, hidden beneath the Roman Forum. They're all dead now."

King heard a whispered curse on the other end before Duncan's voice returned in full. "What's in Haifa?"

"A physicist slash rabbi Alexander thinks can help."

"What do you think?"

"I'm rolling with the punches," King said. "How about you? Are the others back yet?"

"Knight, Queen, and Bishop are en route as we speak. They should be ready to deploy wherever you need them within four hours."

King could hear the man had more to say, but was having a hard time spitting it out. He'd noted Rook hadn't been included in the last sentence and followed the lead. "What happened to Rook?"

Duncan sighed. "The foreign countries we deployed to were tipped off. They knew we were coming."

King winced. Rook had gone to Russia.

"Queen's and Bishop's teams made it out intact. Knight took three casualties. And Rook . . . his team is down and he is MIA, possibly KIA."

Killed. In. Action. They were words King dreaded hearing, especially about members of the Chess Team. His chaotic emotions began to swirl again, threatening to overpower his soldier's mask.

Then he realized a connection. "He was able to follow me, too. He took Fiona and killed the others. Controls the golems."

"You know who's doing this?" Duncan asked.

"Richard Ridley."

"Son of a bitch . . ." Duncan was silent for a moment. "I'll have every law enforcement agency in the country on the lookout for him in case he returns to the U.S., and I'll have Boucher coordinate with any foreign agencies still willing to talk to us."

King was about to ask what had happened, but came to his own conclusions. If several countries had been tipped off that U.S. soldiers were kidnapping their citizens, provable or not, an international drama would be unfolding. That, combined with the post-attack-on-U.S.-soil madness that must be consuming the country, Duncan had his presidential hands full. He decided not to press the issue. "If I find anything in Haifa, I'll let you know."

"Ditto on Ridley," Duncan said. The statement was followed by a click and a dial tone. The man was busy.

King hung up the phone and dialed a second number. Aleman answered it almost immediately. "Aleman here."

"Lew, it's King. I just wanted to check in on my parents."

"Dropped them off at the hotel. Your father seemed pretty excited about the continental breakfast. They asked a lot of questions about you. *Lots* of questions. If they weren't your parents I'd think they were digging for intel."

For a moment, King worried that it could be true, and then decided it was. His parents now knew his job was a lot more interesting than they had previously believed. They probably wanted to know everything about him. "So what did you tell them?"

"The truth. That you're on the Special Ops Galley Team—and let's face it, that's about as threatening sounding as 'the Chess Team'—and your current mission has you scouring the globe for truffles."

King grinned. The humor felt good. "Uh huh."

"But once we got to the hotel they wanted nothing to do with me. Asked me not to come back. Said they'd be fine."

"That's odd," King said.

"What's odd about it? They've been apart for what, ten years? And now they have a few days in a hotel. I'm telling you, they're going to get a lot of use of the 'Do not disturb' sign."

King let out a laugh. "Thank you, Lew. You have just managed to overshadow all the awful things I've seen with something worse."

"Any leads on Fiona?"

"We just missed her in Rome."

"You'll get her back."

King had no reply. His confidence waned with every new discovery.

"Take care, King."

"Copy that."

King hung up the phone and thought about his family. He was eager to see his parents again. To catch up. To re-form lost bonds and heal old wounds. More than anything, he wanted his parents to meet Fiona. Together again, they could use a grandchild to dote on, and Fiona, missing her grandmother deeply, could use a pair of caring grandparents in her life. It would do them all good, even King.

But first he had to find Fiona and bring her home.

He turned toward the window. The blue waves below grew larger as the plane descended for a landing at Ben Gurion International Airport.

FORTY
Haifa, Israel

THE HOUR AND a half drive from the Tel Aviv airport to Technion was quiet and uneventful. Views of the Mediterranean were spectacular during the long coastal trip. And Haifa turned out to be the kind of quiet, café-filled town that college students adored. The only hiccup was that King had to leave his weapon behind; even the mighty Hercules had to submit to customs when leaving the ultra-secure airport. Alexander drove a black Mercedes that had been waiting for him in an airport garage. He maneuvered through the streets and highways like a local. King remembered the ancient man's tale of meeting Jesus and realized he had likely made this trip several times in the past, perhaps on horseback, or even in sandals. The man might be just as comfortable anywhere in the world.

As King began to think about what he would do with twenty-five hundred years of life, they pulled into a campus parking spot and stopped. The campus was a sea of white buildings and green trees. But there wasn't a student in sight. Like zombies to a shopping mall, most of the student body had been drawn to a science symposium being hosted on the other side of campus.

King noted Alexander's familiarity with the campus and commented, "You've been here before?"

"I've taken classes actually," he replied.

"With Davidson?"

"He would have been a child when I attended." He opened the front door of the tall white building that had five long windows stretching the full length of its facade. He held the door for King, allowing him to enter first. A receptionist greeted the pair as they entered.

Alexander approached her with a smile, showing her a faculty I.D. card that had been waiting for him in the Mercedes's glove compartment. She read the card, which identified him as a professor from the medical department. "I'm looking for Professor Davidson," he said in Hebrew.

She returned his smile and pointed him toward the elevator. "Fifth floor. Turn right off the elevator. Second door on the left."

"Thank you," he replied.

Thirty seconds later they exited onto the fifth floor and headed for Davidson's open door. The man's voice filtered out as he spoke on the phone, his back to the door. King knocked twice and then entered, followed by Alexander, who closed the door behind him.

Amzi Davidson, who wore a bright yellow button-down shirt rolled to his elbows, held up a finger indicating he'd be right with them. The office was sparse. A small desk, a bookcase on either side of the door, and two metal-framed chairs were the only furniture. A large window looked out over the campus and provided a clear view of a modern art sculpture that looked like a metallic obelisk. The two other walls in the room held giant whiteboards. Multicolored notes in Hebrew, equations, and drawings filled both boards, which were stained gray from being erased over and over without actually being washed.

Davidson hung up the phone and spun around with a smile. His gray eyes, shrunk by the thick, black-rimmed glasses he wore, were excited. But the genuine smile on his face fell when he saw them. He squinted at them. "You're not from the medical department," he said in Hebrew.

"No, we're not," Alexander replied, also in Hebrew. "May we continue in English for my friend?"

Davidson glanced at King. "Sure," he said in perfect English, his face brightening. "Are you with the press?"

"Afraid not," King said.

The man soured. "Then what's this about?"

Alexander took a seat and cut right to the heart of the matter. "Golems."

Davidson leaned back slowly. A pen appeared in his hand and went to his mouth. "What's the application? Is this for a theory?"

"Real-world application," Alexander replied.

Davidson plucked the pen from his mouth. "Well, I'm afraid that while the written word is powerful, it is not that powerful. It cannot grant life."

"What about the spoken word?" King asked.

A grin came to Davidson's face. "So you are seeking the opinion of a physicist *and* an ex-rabbi?"

King's and Alexander's silence answered the question. Davidson looked at his watch. "Very well. I have a few minutes. I must warn you, however, to not expect two diverging theories. My research in religion and science have come to the same conclusion."

"That's why we're here," Alexander said.

"Then let's start at the beginning. The big-bang theory attempts to answer *how* the universe was first formed, but it doesn't answer the bigger question: *Why* does the universe exist? Because of this, it's a hollow mathematical model. It assumes everything came from nothing, ex nihilo, and states that the universe had a beginning. But there is another option: the universe has *always* existed."

He stood and erased a portion of the whiteboard, marring his yellow sleeve. He wrote out an equation: $0 = 0 + 0 + 0 + 0 + 0 \ldots$

"This is the mathematical statement that shows the big bang is impossible. The sum of nothing, is nothing!"

He erased some of the plus signs and added minus: $0 = 0 - 0 + 0 - 0 + 0 - 0$. "This is the Null Axiom, developed by Terence Witt, which states that the difference of nothing is nothing, meaning everything is made of nothing. Thus, the universe never had a beginning because it is nothing, which is also limitless and timeless."

Davidson checked his watch. "Limitless also describes my thoughts on the matter and I need to speak at the symposium in an hour, so rather than blather on about nonexpansion, cosmic microwaves, decaying photons, or eternal equilibrium, I'll cut right to the theological meat of the matter.

"Null physics mathematically describes the *speaking* of the reality into existence. In the same way the press spins a story by changing the context of facts, the nonreal is made real by the words of a creator spinning the context of limitless nothingness and telling a story."

King rolled his head from side to side. "So . . . if God"—he made air quotations with his fingers—"spoke existence into being, what language did He speak?"

Davidson burst into laughter. When he saw neither of his guests sharing in the moment, he stopped. "You're serious? The language of God?"

"Quite," Alexander said.

The pen reentered Davidson's mouth. "Some have speculated that DNA is the language of God. It has a coding system—an alphabet if you will—rules of spelling and grammar as well as meaning and purpose. In many ways it resembles computer code. And ninety-seven percent of it is considered junk, meaning we have yet to figure out what it says. It also obeys Zipf's law, which simply shows that when words from a document, say a novel, are graphed by the number of times they appear in a book, from most popular to least popular, you get a straight line. DNA broken up into words and listed by popularity align perfectly with Zipf's law. Shazam, it's a language!"

"But we can't speak the language of DNA," King said. "We can't verbalize it."

"In your case, you don't have to. It's already present, but if your speech spins the context . . ." His eyes brightened. "Researchers at the Hado Institute Australia have shown how words can affect the physical world. Spoken words create vibrations. Each word has its own unique resonance—its own pattern of vibration. They spoke different words, both positive and negative, to water before freezing it, transforming it into its crystalline state. Water exposed to the words 'angel,' 'beautiful,' and 'life' formed dazzling, symmetrical crystals. Water exposed to words such as 'dirty,' 'devil,' and 'death' became malformed, cracked, and burst, almost like something had exploded from within.

"A sound wave is, in essence, a disturbance moving through a medium, shifting energy from a starting point to an ending point. And where there is energy, there is information. We detect sound waves through our ears, which transfers the information to our brain, where it is translated into sound. But there is more information in sound than our brains can decipher."

"If sounds are affecting the physical world around us, why are we not noticing?" King asked.

"We are limited by what we can sense. In the same way that our ears cannot hear the information conveyed in every sound, our other senses might miss the results. Take steganography for instance."

King nodded. He was familiar with the use of steganography in military applications. World War II microdots, Morse code in fabric patterns, and sign language hidden in photographs had all been used in military history. In more modern applications, terrorists had used the technology to communicate through coded message board avatars.

Davidson opened his laptop, tapped the keys, and brought up a Web site. He showed them a photo on the screen.

"Though this looks like an ordinary photo of an oceanside park, it is much more. By adjusting the pixels minutely, you can encode text or other photos within an image and it is imperceptible to the human eye. Decoded, this picture reads . . ."

He clicked on the image, which opened a page of text:

> *Science! true daughter of Old Time thou art!*
> *Who alterest all things with thy peering eyes.*
> *Why preyest thou thus upon the poet's heart,*
> *Vulture, whose wings are dull realities?*

"Poe," Alexander said. "Part of his sonnet to science. Cute."

Davidson waggled his finger. "Perhaps even more applicable to your query is the spectrogram."

King sat up straighter. Much of what the professor had said either sounded like bunk, or he already knew. But spectrograms were new to him and he suspected the man was about to uncover a nugget of truth.

"As I mentioned before, sound carries more information than the human ear can perceive. A spectrograph is a visual representation of a sound wave. Most times it's innocuous, but images, and messages, can be coded into sounds and, in theory, into words. There is a video online . . ." Davidson spun the laptop around, showing them a YouTube video titled "Alien Abduction Caught Live on Ustream."

King winced, fearing Davidson was a crackpot.

The facial expression didn't go unnoticed. "Have no fear, this is just an example of clever marketing." He played the video, which showed two men talking about aliens and abductions before one of them moved to the kitchen where a star chart, and an alien in the window, awaited. What followed was a creatively made abduction scene featuring bright lights and a wavering, high-pitched sound.

"That sound you hear is much more than a simple noise. It is an image." Davidson quickly located a file online, downloaded it, and opened up a small software package. He ran the sound through the software and an image of several vertical and horizontal lines was shown. He zoomed in on a portion so the lines could be more easily seen.

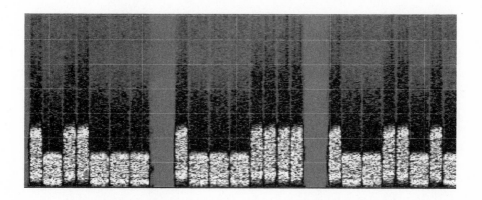

The lines meant nothing to King, but Alexander figured it out. "Binary. Tall lines represent the number one. Short lines . . . zero. Or vice versa."

"Exactly right," Davidson said. "Within the sound is a binary code, which translates into English. A Web site I believe, which leads to another site. All part of an alternate-reality game."

Davidson stood and erased the equations he'd written on the whiteboard. He picked up a red pen and wrote as he spoke. "So we have deduced that, one, there is much more information in sound that we can perceive. Two, sound is capable of altering the physical world, implying that said extra information exists. And three, ninety-seven percent of DNA is a mystery to us. Who's to say the right DNA, carried as information in a sound wave and applied to the physical world, couldn't affect life in the nonliving? Of course, if this were used to create a golem there would be other concerns."

"Such as?" King asked, trying not to sound over interested.

"Traditionally, a golem created for less than noble purposes will become more and more evil each time it kills. But the dark energy that consumes the golem remains with its creator, even after its destruction. Any subsequent golems created will be corrupted as well. It's said that golem masters often die with black hearts, their bodies and souls corrupted. It's all hearsay of course; you know how it is with history."

Alexander wore a funny grin. "I do."

"Perhaps the stories are a warning," Davidson said, "to not use the life imbuing language?"

King and Alexander glanced at each other. Given what they knew, it seemed a likely scenario.

Davidson saw the look they shared. He sat up straight. "You've discovered this language, haven't you?"

"No," King said.

"We're just researching the idea," Alexander added quickly.

"For a movie."

This last statement totally deflated Davidson's excitement. He was about to ask them to leave when King's phone rang. He answered the phone, "I'm here."

"We found Ridley," Duncan said on the other end.

"Where?"

"London. Security camera caught a glimpse of him at Heathrow Airport."

"Was Fiona with him?"

"She's not in the shot, but that doesn't mean—"

"I know. And it doesn't matter. We're going to London."

"I have every available resource tracking him. Call me when you land."

"Will do." King hung up the phone and looked at Alexander. "He's in London."

Both men stood. Alexander opened the door to leave. Davidson stopped them with a clearing of his throat. "Who's in London?"

"Brad Pitt. Thanks for your help," King said, then exited the room.

The professor, who now wore a broad smile, said, "If you see the press on your way down, send them up."

King stopped and leaned back into the office. Something about Davidson expecting press coverage put him on edge. "You never did mention why the press was coming to see you today."

"I published my theory. Null physics and the Spoken Creation. Technion put out a press release yesterday. I'm giving a speech on the topic in"—he looked at his watch, his eyes widening—"forty-five minutes."

King tensed. If Davidson had made his theory public and Ridley discovered it, he would instantly see where the research would eventually lead. He had already wiped out every ancient language that might be used to reproduce the so-called language of God. But if modern science were to uncover the language again by studying the effects of sound on the environment, then . . .

Davidson saw King's sour expression. "What? What's wrong?"

"I'm afraid you may have painted a very large target on your—"

Movement outside the large office window caught King's attention. The metal obelisk that had been standing outside was hurtling toward the office like a spear.

"Get down!" King shouted, diving for the professor.

A second later the obelisk crashed through the window with the force of a wrecking ball.

FORTY-ONE
Washington, D.C.

TOM DUNCAN SAT behind the Resolute Desk in the Oval Office. His suit coat hung over the back of his chair, his sleeves were rolled up, and his tie dangled loosely. He looked like any other hardworking president, except for the fact that he was leaning back in the chair, staring blankly at the ceiling. For all the power his office granted him, he found himself momentarily immobilized. As the eyes of the world watched his every act outside the rounded walls of the Oval Office, scrutinized every word, every inflection of his voice, every facial expression—looking for a flaw—inaction became the safest course of conduct. With the wolves circling and out for blood, anything he did might make them attack.

What made this hard for Duncan was that he was also a wolf. As a former Army Ranger he excelled when in the movement. As president he applied his energy to the challenges faced by the country, and as Deep Blue, he focused his military mind on the Chess Team's missions. But now he could only monitor and advise. A deeper involvement could expose and endanger the team. The Chess Team was hidden but not buried, not black. There had been no reason to hide their existence from the government he ran. But now . . .

The time for a new direction, a new plan, was upon him.

Hard choices and big changes needed to be made.

So he retreated to his office, cleared his mind of the media, of Marrs, and searched for solutions.

Before he could focus his thoughts, the phone on his desk rang. Its digital chime didn't get a chance to finish as Duncan sat up and hit the speakerphone button. The White House switchboard had been given strict instructions to allow calls from a very short list of people through, each with a unique ring. This one belonged to Dominick Boucher.

"What've you got?"

"I'm faxing it over now."

The full-color fax machine behind the desk blinked as the incoming file transferred.

"Is this about Ridley?"

"Yes sir," Boucher said. "Two major developments. He rented a gold Peugeot 307 Cabriolet from Europcar at Heathrow. Europcar GPS chips all their cars and we tracked it to Wiltshire County."

Duncan recognized the name. He'd been there once, in college, as a backpacking tourist. "Stonehenge?"

"We believe so, yes."

"But why?"

"I couldn't tell you that for sure, but if he's interested in ancient languages, perhaps there is more to Stonehenge than we know. Something that hasn't been uncovered yet. The site is incredibly old and we know very little about the people who built it. Whatever it is must be important because he's taking bold risks to get it."

"Are Queen, Bishop, and Knight ready to go?" Duncan asked. Keasling was on the task of debriefing and briefing the team, getting them geared up and ready to drop wherever King needed them.

"Well, that's why I'm sending the fax. Development number two. I'm not sure we should send them to King."

Duncan's forehead scrunched. He looked at the fax machine. *What is Boucher sending?*

The gears of the fax machine finally kicked in, sending a single piece of paper through and coating it with hot toner. An eight-by-ten photo rolled out. Duncan snatched it up. A couple dressed in tank top vests and cargo shorts appropriate for warm weather archaeology smiled for the camera. Behind them were groups of people—locals, interns, and other science types—milling about. And in the background was what looked like a very large, very old staircase partially covered by vegetation and snaking tree roots.

"What am I looking at?"

"The photo was uploaded to Flickr an hour ago, and you can see in the bottom right the date stamp is today. So this is fresh. The structure in the background is la Danta Pyramid in El Mirador, Guatemala—the largest ever built by the Maya, and even bigger than the great Cheops pyramid at Giza."

"That's all well and good, Dom, but what's the significance."

"I don't want to tell you what to see, in case we're wrong. I want you to—"

"What the hell," Duncan whispered as he saw a familiar face in the image. The man was walking behind the couple, carrying a backpack. No one paid him any attention. He wore the same comfortable smile he did in the brochures his company had published. But his presence in the image made no sense. How could Richard Ridley be in England *and* Guatemala at the same time?

"I take it you found him?"

"How's this possible, Dom?"

"I'm afraid that's a question your team is best suited to answer, but his presence at both locations, as impossible as it seems, solidifies his apparent interest in ancient sites around the world. Shall I divert Queen, Bishop, and Knight to Guatemala?"

"Do it," Duncan said. "I'll inform King."

FORTY-TWO
Haifa, Israel

A STREAM OF Hebrew curses flew from Davidson's mouth as he lay beneath King on the floor of his office. Their bodies were coated in glass and plaster from the ruined ceiling. But it wasn't the destroyed office that held either man's attention, it was the glistening metal lance tip that had stabbed through the window and far wall. Twenty feet of stainless steel separated into vertical ribs that normally made the structure appear to be rotating, had impaled the building.

On his back, staring up at the glistening structure, Davidson recognized what it was. "It's the obelisk."

Alexander reached a hand beneath Davidson's desk. "Take my hand."

Davidson reached out and was snagged by Alexander, who easily pulled the physicist out of harm's way and into the hallway. King crawled out behind him and stood in what little remained of the office. He instinctually reached for his weapon before remembering he was unarmed.

Shuffling forward through the sea of glass, he chanced a peek out of the window. While twenty feet of the obelisk had impaled the building, its remaining sixty-two feet were jutting out the side, like a giant spear. A large chunk of concrete clung to the end, where it had been ripped out of the ground. Gravity began to work on the protruding end, pulling it down. The force both bent the obelisk and caused the tip to tear into the ceiling. Flakes of plaster crumbled down on King's head.

"I don't understand," Davidson said with a shaky voice. "Why would someone want to destroy the obelisk?"

"They weren't trying to destroy the tower," Alexander said.

Davidson fell silent, wondering what he meant.

"I didn't see anything outside," King said.

Alexander twisted his lips. "They've most likely assumed he's dead."

King agreed, but he knew they were far from safe. "They'll check to be sure."

"What are you talking about?" Davidson shouted. "Who are 'they' and who will they assume is dead?"

King reached down and pulled Davidson to his feet. "I was trying to tell you before, Professor. You're a target now."

The man's eyes went wide behind his thick glasses, but not from King's statement. He was looking beyond King, down the hallway. King spun and saw what appeared to be a large reptile. Something about it seemed familiar, but he couldn't place it. The creature was built similarly to a komodo dragon, but its back was tan with brown stripes and its underbelly was white. Aside from its eight-foot length, sharp teeth, and clawed toes, what bothered King the most was the look of menace mixed with intelligence in its eyes.

A long forked tongue flicked out of its mouth—tasting them from a distance. Knowing it was here for Davidson, King looked for an escape route. The only door between them and the lizard was another office. The hallway behind them was blocked by the obelisk.

As a breeze tickled King's cheek he turned toward the broken window. The ribbed obelisk continued its slow bend toward the ground five stories below. It was the only way out.

He turned to Alexander. "Take him through the window."

"I'll fight the beast," Alexander replied, rolling up his sleeves.

"Sorry, Herc," King replied. "I'm not strong enough to carry him."

Davidson blanched. "Carry me?"

Alexander grunted in defeat, then took Davidson and slung him over his shoulder. "See you in Elysian Fields, King." Then he was moving. He ran through the destroyed office and leaped out of the window. Davidson screamed the entire way until Alexander took hold of one of the stainless-steel ribs and swung them atop the structure.

King turned back to the lizard and shouted. It had already charged, moving silently over the linoleum floor. As it reared up to strike, King saw its claws, retracted for silent movement, reemerge and swipe toward his neck.

King ducked the blow and sidestepped, allowing the creature's momentum to carry it past him and into the obelisk. It struck with a force that reverberated through the entire structure.

Alexander stumbled, still holding Davidson over his shoulder. He managed to remain upright and continued moving toward the slowly lowering base.

Unsure of how to fight the giant reptile, King struck out with a hard kick to its back, hoping to break its spine. But the string of vertebrae simply flexed with the impact and then pushed back. King fell to the hallway floor. As he righted himself, the lizard hissed at him and then bolted into the office. Despite King's attack, the lizard only had eyes for its target.

Davidson.

King scrambled to his feet and gave chase. As the creature climbed onto the obelisk, King dove out, snagging its tail. The lizard lurched back, unable to pull King along with it. With one arm wrapped around the thick, but stubby tail, King reached out with his free hand and picked up a shard of glass. He swung it high and stabbed it into the beast's lower back, slicing open his hand in the process.

The creature wailed and violently shook its back end. King thought the lizard was trying to shake him free, but as he fell to the floor, still holding the tail, he realized it had shed its tail. The open wound where the creature's tail used to be oozed a few drops of blood and then dried. Like many lizards in the world, this one could shed its tail to distract predators while it escaped. But King wanted nothing to do with the still wriggling tail in his hands.

As the lizard ran out the window, he climbed on to the obelisk and gave chase.

Davidson let out a shout when the monster appeared behind them, its legs flailing out to each side as it charged down the obelisk. His shout was cut off as Alexander's shoulder rammed his gut. Had there been any air left in him, he would have screamed again as he and Alexander went airborne.

Alexander leaped into the air, landing on the concrete base of the obelisk, sixty-two feet from the physics building. The sudden weight sped the obelisk's descent. But not fast enough. The lizard was nearly upon them.

King shouted at the beast as he pursued from behind, but his hurled words did little to slow it down. He wouldn't reach them in time. Alexander was on his own.

Turning to face the creature, Alexander showed no fear for his life, but without knowing the creature's capabilities he wasn't sure if he could protect Davidson. But he didn't have to. Gravity provided a temporary solution as, fifteen feet from the ground, the obelisk finally gave way and bent quickly. Just before the base struck the cobbled walkway that stretched up the center of the Technion campus, Alexander jumped away with Davidson. The pair fell five feet and rolled away from the concrete base as it crashed into the hard ground.

The obelisk's impact shook the structure, bouncing the lizard into the air. It landed on its side, and then slid off the edge, falling ten feet to the ground.

When the obelisk dropped away beneath King, he fell forward. Pain pulsed through his body when he landed on his stomach. Now lying on the obelisk, his descent didn't slow. The steep incline pulled him over the smooth metal ribs like it was a giant slide. Using his hands to keep himself centered, King left a smear of red behind him—blood from his wounded hand.

He saw Alexander take off running with Davidson still over his shoulder. He was headed to a nearby construction site where piles of sand and stacks of cement bags waited to form the foundation of a new building. A moment later, the giant lizard lunged after them. It moved swiftly, but seemed slightly off balance, perhaps from the fall or because of its missing tail.

King rolled onto the cobbled walkway and onto his feet, giving chase. He could see Alexander and Davidson in front of the lizard, and the construction site beyond. Seeing the sand triggered his memory. He'd seen something like this before, only small enough to hold in his hand. It was a sandfish, a species of skink native to Iraq. While on a stakeout in Iraq, before being assigned to the Chess Team, he had watched the small creatures and marveled at their abilities.

That's why he knew, without a doubt, that sand was the wrong place to be with a killer sandfish.

THE CONSTRUCTION SITE was a labyrinth of building materials and equipment. Alexander ran through the maze, not just searching for a way through, but also for the perfect place to stop. He found it between two stacks of cement bags. The bottleneck would allow him to confront the lizard head on, and hopefully give Davidson enough time to make his escape.

He skidded to a stop, his feet sliding through the deep sand covering the construction site. He put Davidson down. The man was panicked and clung to Alexander's back like a child not wanting to be separated from its mother. He'd seen the beast behind them and feeling his legs go wobbly beneath him, knew he couldn't outrun it.

"Why are you putting me down? Keep running!"

Alexander pushed him away. "You go. I'll stop it."

"But—"

"Go!"

The look in Alexander's eyes and the boom of his voice triggered Davidson's feet. He bolted deeper into the construction site. Though he quickly disappeared from view, his high-pitched squeaking breaths could be easily tracked, and Alexander had no doubt the creature would be able to follow his scent as well. The man was oozing fear pheromones.

Then the creature appeared. Thirty feet away. It paused on the sand, flicking out its tongue.

When it charged, the lizard didn't focus on Alexander's head, or torso, or any other vital location a predator might strike. Instead, it was looking down, at his feet.

Not at my feet, Alexander thought. *In front of them.*

Before he could figure out the meaning of the charging lizard's strange attack, it leaped into the air. Alexander raised a fist to strike the beast's head, but never got a chance to swing. The lizard arched its back and began a face-first descent toward the sandy ground. Its body began wriggling back and forth, slowly at first, then building in speed until almost a blur.

It struck the sand like an Olympic diver, and just as gracefully disappeared into the sand as though it were liquid. Alexander felt a slight undulation beneath his feet.

The lizard had passed beneath him!

He spun around and saw the creature emerge from the sand twenty feet away. Without pause, it continued in its relentless pursuit of Davidson. Alexander gave chase, fueled by his anger at being outsmarted by an oversized reptile.

DAVIDSON STUMBLED AS he ran—if you could call it running. His legs felt useless, as though in a dream. His hand landed on a stack of metal beams, but the weakness in his legs had moved to his arms and he fell forward, striking his head. Still on his feet, but dazed, he struggled forward. His vision narrowed. His head spun from a mixture of pain and fear.

Then a voice cut through his body's fear-induced stupor. "Davidson, it got by me!"

Though he'd only just met the man, he recognized the voice as belonging to the inhumanly strong Alexander.

He felt a thump inside his chest. Then another.

His vision suddenly returned. His head cleared. And his muscles not only lost their gelatinous weakness, but they itched with energy. The knowledge that the creature was almost upon him had triggered an adrenaline rush. But it was too little, too late.

The lizard had found him.

It rounded the corner at top speed, its short legs flinging out in wide circles as it ran.

Two things saved Davidson's life. First, he ran. Second, the creature's missing tail removed its ability to stabilize its body. A combination of speed and not enough room to make a wide turn sent the lizard rolling into a large pile of sand. A layer of sand sheared away with the creature's impact, creating an avalanche that quickly buried the upended beast.

Davidson saw this and paused, a smile creeping onto his face.

The smile disappeared when the large sandfish launched from the sand pile, once again moving at top speed. Realizing he wouldn't escape this attack, Davidson let out a scream of horror.

Then he was struck hard.

Davidson fell to the ground. Alive. He looked up and saw King standing in his place as the lizard lunged.

The monster struck King in a blur and both fell, landing on Davidson's feet. Pinned beneath the weight of King and the lizard, he shouted and clawed at the ground, pulling himself out from the tangle of bodies. Once free, he quickly stood.

Expecting to see the lizard tearing King apart, he glanced back as he began to run again. But the creature lay motionless. Davidson stopped. A long metal pole entered the lizard's mouth and exited out its sheared-off tail. A giant lizard shish kabob!

A grunt emerged from beneath it. King was alive. "Think you could get this thing off of me?"

Davidson took hold of the pole protruding from the creature's mouth and lifted. But he only managed to wiggle the heavy reptile.

Alexander arrived a moment later, quickly understood what had happened, and lifted the lizard away with little effort. Davidson just stared at him in awe. He felt like he'd met David and Goliath, but they were on the same team.

Alexander helped King to his feet. "I'm impressed," he said with a smile.

King grunted. Unlike Alexander, his body couldn't heal quickly, and he knew the pain he felt now would only intensify over the next few days. He looked at Davidson. "Unless you know a fancy physics trick for becoming invisible, we're going to have to take care of you the old-fashioned way."

FORTY-THREE
Again, 20,000 feet

AFTER GIVING DAVIDSON a wad of cash, putting him up in a random hotel under a false name, and telling him to stay put until told otherwise, King and Alexander had returned to the airport and took off for England.

King hung up his cell phone and paced in the small open space at the front of Alexander's Gulfstream jet. He was trying to wrap his mind around the idea that Ridley was in two places at once, which meant that one of them was an impersonator. Either that or they were—he hated thinking it—clones. That there could be more than one Ridley was bad on its own. But it also meant they had no idea where Fiona had gone. If there were two Ridleys, there could be three. There could be fifty.

And Fiona could still be in Rome. The entire trip to England could be a massive waste of time. But it was all they had. And even though *this* Ridley might not have Fiona, he might know where she was being held.

But what was the point? Try as he might, King couldn't pin down Ridley's endgame. He decided to review what he knew. Ridley was creating and using golems to do his dirty work, yet they were tools, not the goal. *But they hint at the goal,* he thought. The sandfish was nothing new. Ridley had created genetic monsters before. But had the sandfish been created in a lab or manipulated by the strange protolanguage? These were all symptoms of something larger, but he couldn't think of what that might be.

He focused his attention on what he knew about Ridley. He was a genius, ruthless beyond comparison, and considered no person his equal. The man had a god-complex to the point of successfully achieving immortality through science. Likewise he had now learned to grant life, at least temporarily, to inanimate objects. While Davidson had given them some insight into the science that gave the ancient language world-altering capabilities, he had yet to—

King's thoughts froze on the words "world altering." In a sense, that's what Ridley was doing. Living statues, giant lizards, copies of himself. He was manipulating reality. But how far could it go? How much could he manipulate and to what extent? Could he become a god? As soon as the question formed in King's mind he knew the answer.

Yes.

Ridley would be immortal and hold the keys to life, death, and to some extent, creation. He would be a god and much of the world would bow down and worship him. But that couldn't be the end. Not for a man like Ridley. He was interested in power. In domination. But he was just one man. It might take him centuries to build a large following and he wasn't a patient man. There had to be something else.

With his mind spinning with theories, King headed back to his seat. His body ached and he needed to rest. Alexander sat at the rear of the plane, his seat tilted back, and his eyes closed. King marveled how the man was able to fall asleep so quickly when there was so much to think about.

He sat down across from Alexander and sighed.

"Unforeseen complications?" Alexander asked.

King jumped at the man's voice. It seemed he wasn't sleeping at all. "You could say that."

Alexander opened his eyes and sat up. After pushing a button on his armrest, a stewardess entered from the front of the plane. "Yes sir?"

He held up two fingers. She nodded and disappeared.

"In your . . . experiments with Hydra's blood. When you created the Forgotten and made yourself immortal, did you ever . . ." King searched for the right words. They all sounded ridiculous. Then again, so did immortality. "Duplicate yourself?"

As usual, Alexander took the question earnestly, without laughing or even cracking a smile. For him, nothing was out of the realm of possibility. "No. Never. Removing the head, in Ridley's case, and in mine, would simply render the body dead. Regeneration would begin at the neck. Splitting into two unique selves is not an attribute of Hydra's genes."

"So he couldn't just hack off a body part and grow a new self?"

"He is limited by the DNA of Hydra, and if he did his job correctly, regeneration is the only gene he transplanted into himself."

"So it's not possible?"

"I didn't say that. There are species that have the ability to split in two, creating two separate entities, which can later split again. Earthworms for instance. If he continued to modify his genetic code, well, anything is possible. What resources were available to him after the Hydra incident?"

"Manifold was shut down," King said. "His funds were frozen. But he likely had secret accounts. Facilities no one knew about. It's possible that Manifold Genetics is operating under the radar."

King adjusted his body in the seat. Despite the plush cushion, he couldn't find a pain-free position. "Like you said, anything is possible."

The stewardess returned with a tray. Two glasses and a dark brown, one-ounce bottle, sat atop it. She placed the tray on the foldout tabletop in front of Alexander. "Anything else, sir?"

"No, thank you. How long until we land?"

"Fifteen minutes."

He tilted his head in thanks and she left without looking back. Once the cabin door was closed again, Alexander continued. "Where is the second Ridley?"

"Danta Pyramid in Guatemala."

"Interesting," Alexander said, rubbing his chin.

"You know the place?" King asked, and then thought, *Of course he does.*

"It's a Mayan city stretching over ten square miles that was consumed by the jungle. I've been meaning to visit, but haven't had the chance."

King felt a mild surprise at the ancient man not having been everywhere in the world.

"What's interesting is that like the ancient pyramids in Egypt and the Tower of Babel before it, the construction techniques that allowed the Mayans to build a pyramid of such magnitude remains a mystery. Of course, you and I know that golems were used as laborers in the old world. And that several other ancient architects used the same method for building wonders all around the world."

King saw where he was going with this. There was a connection. "Including Stonehenge."

Alexander opened the brown bottle and extracted a dropper. A tan liquid with tiny swirling flakes filled the glass vial. He dropped five drops into each glass. "It would appear he is visiting the ancient sites for some purpose, perhaps in search of information or relics that might add to his knowledge of the protolanguage."

Both men sat in silence for a moment. Alexander focused on the steps they would take upon landing. King's mind drifted back to Fiona. He looked at Alexander, the oldest man on the planet and asked, "Do you have any children?"

The question took Alexander by surprise. He turned to King, with a lopsided smirk. "Children?"

King waited for more.

"There was a time, before I was immortal, that I wanted children. Acca and I tried to conceive, but she was barren. I never did get an heir. As it turns out, I didn't need one. But there hasn't been anyone worthy of bearing my children since."

"You . . . haven't been celibate all this time?" King asked.

Alexander gave a gentle laugh, which escaped his nose as a sniff. "For fifteen hundred years, yes."

King couldn't believe what he was hearing. Alexander was wealthy beyond belief, handsome, could speak a number of languages, live anywhere and do anything. And he'd chosen to live underground and alone for fifteen hundred years? It didn't add up. It didn't seem . . . human.

Alexander could see what King was thinking and ended the line of question with a preemptive statement. "I have seen and done everything imaginable with the opposite sex. After nearly a millennium of indulging, some things lost their novelty, starting with the primal act of procreation."

"You *are* an old man," King said with a grin.

Alexander smiled. "Very old." He looked out the window for a moment, and then turned back to King. "While I may not be able to answer the questions of a new father, I can tell you this with confidence: for men like us, nothing is impossible."

King's smile widened, but wasn't fully genuine. Despite being flattered that the immortal Hercules was starting to think of King as an equal, he still felt unsure about being a father. The problem wasn't whether or not he *could* be a father, but whether or not he *should* be a father.

Alexander picked up both glasses and swirled them around until the tan liquid dispersed in the water. He offered one to King.

"What's this?" King asked.

"You look tired."

"You didn't answer my question."

Alexander smiled. "You don't trust me yet?"

"I don't think I ever will," King said, and he meant it. Alexander, unlike Ridley, *was* a patient man. He'd already lived more lifetimes than Ridley could imagine. And though he had no concrete evidence, he suspected Alexander's involvement in tracking down Ridley was more than altruism or one immortal protecting the world from another. The man had an endgame, he was sure of it. But finding out what that was would have to wait. For now, Alexander was an essential asset in stopping Ridley. After all, Alexander had coexisted with mortals for thousands of years without enslaving the human race. But that could change, King knew, and for that reason, Alexander needed to be watched closely.

Alexander gave a chuckle and made a face that said, "I'll drink first." He swigged the water down and grinned. He also looked much more rested and energetic.

"If you weren't immortal," King said, "that gesture might mean something. What's in it?"

"It's a homeopathic mix. My own. I cannot say what it contains. In the wrong hands it could be very dangerous." Alexander looked out the large round window next to him. The rocky shore of England wasn't far off. "When we land we will be moving fast. And since I have yet to see you sleep or rest that mind of yours, you will need some help to keep up."

King wanted to argue, but couldn't. As well trained and physically fit as he was, without rest his body would start to work against him. He already felt fatigued, and if things got rough in England, he might become a liability. He took the drink and swallowed it in two gulps. It tasted like mildly sweet water with a touch of—

A burst of energy hit him and brought an involuntary smile to his face. He felt rejuvenated and awake. And his mind was clear and focused. It wasn't the adrenaline boost he'd seen Alexander give himself in Rome, but it was amazing. He could see how this tonic in the hands of the military could cause trouble. An army that didn't require sleep to be at its peak would be a very dangerous thing.

"Feeling better?" Alexander asked.

"Much," King answered.

"Good," Alexander said, "because from now until we finish this fight, we won't slow down."

FORTY-FOUR
El Mirador, Guatemala

THE HELICOPTER LURCHED downward. Wind and rain beat against its black shell. Dark clouds blocked the rising sun while lightning coursed through the sky, illuminating the jungle beneath in a continuous strobe. A streak of lightning flashed past, striking a tree below with a burst of sparks. The immediate boom generated by the bolt as the super-heated air around it expanded into a shock wave pushed the chopper to the side.

Hell had temporarily taken up residence in the airspace above northern Guatemala.

The chopper's three passengers weren't fazed by the inclement weather, but the pilot, Luis Azurdia, was terrified. However, the bonus offered to him by his three wealthy clients was too generous to pass up. During the rainy season, travel to El Mirador was nearly impossible by land, and the site was mired with mud, flash floods, and few options for overnight stays. Tourists were few and far between as a result. The money Luis stood to make from this flight would cover the rest of the rainy season.

A second flash of lightning filled the cockpit with blinding light a fraction of a second before a resounding crash filled the air. Luis's heart pounded. He'd never flown in a storm like this. Hell, if it was raining most tourists would cancel their trip.

He looked back at his passengers, hoping to see them fidgeting nervously, praying for fear in their eyes. If they called off the flight he might still be able to get that bonus. But the big Arabian man appeared to be meditating with his eyes closed. The skinny Asian man bobbed his head to music supplied by iPod earbuds. And the woman, her striking blond hair and forehead covered by a blue bandanna, simply looked out the window with a scowl. She, at least, looked like she wanted to be someplace else, but the storm was not on her mind.

Queen focused on the jungle below, watching an endless sea of trees.

El Mirador was one of the most remote locations in Guatemala, which allowed the ancient Mayan city to remain fairly unexplored until 2003, when a team of archaeologists set up camp and began excavating the overgrown city. Despite the area's natural beauty, the mysterious location they would soon explore, or the potential danger that awaited them there, her thoughts were half a world away.

In Russia.

With Rook.

News of his team's extermination had been a blow to all of them. The men were comrades and friends. But Rook's M.I.A. status was especially disturbing. He was more than a friend. She had worked hard denying her feelings, fighting against them as hard as any mythical creature they had faced, but with Rook missing, possibly dead, she couldn't bury how she felt. And right now, she felt pissed.

She had petitioned to be freed from the mission in order to track down Rook, and if possible, rescue him. But she had been denied by Deep Blue himself. The mission came first. She knew Rook would agree, but it didn't loosen the knot twisting in her stomach. To lose him now . . .

She shook her head, willing herself to not think it. She *would* find him when this was over.

What bothered her most was that despite being brave in almost any scenario, neither of them had the guts to talk about their feelings for each other. Ever since their kiss a year previous she had sensed his quiet discomfort around her. But they never spoke of it. Like the hardships of battle, they swallowed it. Buried it. Because they both knew that love on the battlefield could get people killed.

She realized now that soldiers died on the battlefield either way. And now Rook may have as well; a fact that would not have changed if their relationship had become romantic. *At least then he would have died knowing*, she thought, and then forced a new thought: *I'll tell him when I find him.*

A flash of light made her squint and look away from the window. As thunder rolled over and through the helicopter she glanced toward the cockpit and made eye contact with Luis. He looked desperate and pale.

"I— Is the storm too much?" he asked, sounding hopeful.

She grinned. "Not at all."

As a frown came to his face, Queen added, "We are more than halfway there, yes?"

"Sí," he said with a nod. "We are almost there."

"Then we will be on the ground shortly and the storm will most likely have passed or dulled by the time we leave."

Luis thought for a moment before smiling and nodding again. "You are right."

As Luis turned his eyes forward again, Knight plucked his earbuds free. "Almost there?"

"Yup," Queen replied.

"You okay?"

"Fine."

"She's worried about Rook," Bishop said, eyes still shut.

"We're all worried about him," Knight said. "But—"

Bishop opened his eyes and glanced at Knight. "Seriously?"

Knight opened his hands with a shrug. "What?"

Bishop responded by raising his eyebrows.

After a moment of thought, Knight realized what was being communicated. "Really?" He leaned forward and looked at Queen. "*Really?* Rook?"

The slightest of grins showed on Queen's face. She slugged Bishop's shoulder and turned to Knight. "I don't want to break that pretty jaw of yours, Fancy Nancy, but I will."

Knight was all smiles until Luis's voice came over the headset. "El Mirador at three o'clock," he said as he spoke his next words. "We made it."

Queen, Bishop, and Knight leaned over and looked out of Queen's window. For endless miles in the distance the jungle grew in a flat sheet of green, but here it rose up high into the sky, as though mountains had sprung up in the middle of a plain. But they weren't mountains. They were ancient temples and pyramids built by the ancient Mayans. Near the peak of the tallest rise, the jungle cleared enough to see the dirty white stone hidden beneath. To most, the site felt both ominous and wondrous.

To Queen, Bishop, and Knight, it was something else entirely. For each knew that if they found the man they were looking for, it would become a place of violence and death not seen since the ancient Mayans soaked the forest floor with the blood of human sacrifice.

FORTY-FIVE
Amesbury, England

A GRAY HAZE hung over the late-afternoon sky, threatening to descend and cover the landscape in fog. If not for the patchwork of green and yellow fields on either side of the road, the day would have been depressing. Despite the gloom, the drive from Heathrow International Airport in London had gone smoothly, once again thanks to the plush black Mercedes awaiting King and Alexander.

King found himself riding shotgun as usual. Alexander knew the way and enjoyed driving his cars fast, which didn't normally bother King, but a driver that can't be killed may not take as much care as a mere mortal.

To distract himself from the breakneck driving, King opened his cell phone and placed a call he'd been avoiding. Not because he didn't want to speak to his parents, but because he didn't know what to say. There was no time for a conversation and calling just to check in seemed wildly inappropriate given the fact that his mother was supposed to be dead and his father had been recently freed from jail.

"Hi honey!" his mother answered on the second ring.

"Hey Mom."

"Have you found them yet? The men behind the attack?"

King grinned. It was business as usual with Lynn. "You know I can't tell you anything."

Alexander took a right turn at a fork in the road. Stonehenge loomed to the left. After driving through the city and now the country, the megalithic monument seemed out of place, like it had been transported from someplace far away. Then his phone rang. After looking at the caller ID screen, Alexander answered the call with a hushed voice.

King strained to hear what he was saying, but Peter's voice shouted from the background in his own phone. "Is he in Iraq? That's still a hot spot for these kinds of things."

"Are you in Iraq, dear?" his mother asked.

King sighed. There was no harm in telling them he wasn't in Iraq and it would stop them from worrying. "No, I'm not in Iraq."

"Will you be?"

"No, Mom, Iraq is not on my radar."

"Oh good. Good."

With the monotony of the conversation already getting to him, and a desire to eavesdrop on Alexander's conversation, King spoke quickly. "Listen, Mom. I was just calling to make sure you were both okay, that you're both safe."

"Oh, we have nothing to fear here," Lynn said. "We're safe."

They entered the parking lot across the street from the monument and pulled into an empty space. A large red, double-decker tour bus pulled up behind them. Eager to get out of the car and not thinking about what might be outside, King exited the Mercedes and was greeted by an amplified voice.

"Welcome to Stonehenge, ladies and gentlemen, and thank you for choosing London Hills Tours."

King closed his eyes and sighed. Maybe she hadn't heard. She certainly hadn't reacted. "Mom, I have to go now."

"Okay, hun. You'll call back when you can?" she asked. "Don't make us worry."

"I won't. I will. I have to go. Love you." King ended the call as Alexander finished his own.

"Just the two of us," King heard him say. "A few days, and make sure it's dry. Good."

Alexander hung up the phone, slid it inside his pocket, and exited the car.

"Dinner date?" King asked as he exited as well.

"Reservations of a sort, but not for food." Alexander closed his door. "Nothing to concern yourself with."

But King was concerned. Everything Alexander said and did raised more questions, and with each unanswered question, his trust of Alexander ebbed. Who was he talking to? Who were the two people he mentioned? And what were these secret reservations? The only reason Alexander had to keep secrets from King—who wasn't interested in money, power, fame, or immortality—was that he wouldn't like what he heard.

"Throwing me a surprise party?" King asked, searching for information without an outright confrontation.

But Alexander acted as though he hadn't even heard the question. "I can hardly remember my parents," he said. "But I know I'm glad I didn't have a cell phone when they were alive." He shook his head with a grin.

King saw through the phony smile and understood the meaning behind Alexander's deflection: back off. Not one to back down from anyone, including immortals, he was about to push the subject when a mob of tourists exited the tour bus. Some went to the visitor's center for pamphlets, restrooms, and drinks while the rest made a beeline for the subterranean passage that led to the other side of the road and a spectacular view of the stones. Other than the new arrivals, the parking lot was largely empty, save for a few cars. By Stonehenge standards, they had the place to themselves.

The air smelled of wet grass and car exhaust—a strange mix of nature and civilization that reminded King of more than a couple battle zones. But it was mildly cool and comfortable, despite the dreary weather.

"Sorry if I blasted you," the tour guide said as she exited the bus. She was tall, all smiles, and had a tangy British accent. Her short brown hair was partially tied back in a ponytail. When she smiled, her thin eyes became squints and her lips became slivers of pink. "Saw you gabbin' on your cell."

"Ah, no worries luv," Alexander said.

King flinched and glanced at Alexander. While his accent was spot on, they hadn't discussed any kind of cover.

"Locals are ya?" she asked.

"Born an raised in Amesbury," Alexander replied. "But my friend here's a highlander fresh out of the mountains. Never seen the stones before."

"Ohh," she said flirtatiously, sidling up next to King. "A Scotsman, eh?"

King did his best not to roll his eyes and said, "Aye."

"Well if you have any questions about Stonehenge, I'm the one to talk to. Never mind the guides in there," she said, motioning to the visitor's center. "They're dead from the neck up."

King couldn't help but smile at the woman. Making sure to keep his accent, he said, "Are all the lassies in London this highfalutin?"

She gave King a funny look and laughed. He knew he was laying on the Highlander role-play a little thick, but he intended to come off as flirtatious. Given the broad smile on the woman's face, he was succeeding.

"I just know my shit is all," she said and then motioned to her bus. "Been top banana on this crimson cruiser for five years now. And no one knows more about the wonders of Wiltshire County than me. It's why I get top whack for my tours." She nudged King in the ribs. "But I'll give you handsome gents a first-rate tour on the house."

King extended his hand. "The name's Calum. And my counterpart here is Humphrey."

The woman giggled. "Bit of an old-fashioned name, eh?"

"He's older than he looks," King said.

She shook his hand. "Lauren Henderson. Owner and operator of London Hills Tours."

"You know," King said. "There is something I've been wondering about."

Lauren cocked her head to the side. "Oh? And what might that be?"

"I've asked Humph a few times, but when it comes to history, he's something of a dolt."

Alexander chuckled and began wandering toward the tunnel entrance, scanning the parking lot, the visitors, and the site across the street. While listening to the conversation, he was also watching for anything unusual. King and Lauren followed him.

"Are there any examples of words, umm, spoken language being used to manipulate the elements?"

She stared at him for a moment, then cracked a big grin. "You highlanders are into some cheeky stuff." She elbowed him again. "Ahh, I'm just winding you up."

They stopped in front a tall green sign at the tunnel entrance. "So, just to be clear, you're asking about magic, right? Casting spells?"

He hadn't considered magic as a term to describe what Ridley was able to do, but the more he thought about it, the more he realized that's exactly what it was. And with the realization came the epiphany that the mythology of magic most likely developed as a result of this ancient language. And there may have been genuine magicians who had learned certain phrases that allowed them to do amazing things.

"Aye," King said. "But specifically spoken magic. Is there any association with Stonehenge?"

"In fact, there is," she said, excitement in her eyes. "It's said that the bluestones were quarried in a remote region of Africa and were brought first to Ireland by giants."

"Giants?" King asked. "Stone giants?"

Lauren's smile disappeared for a moment, her train of thought ruined. "I dunno. Giants are giants." Her smile returned and she continued. "But the man responsible for bringing the stones from Ireland to Britain was none other than the grand wizard Merlin himself. If you've got the time, you can read about it in Geoffrey of Monmouth's *Prophetiae Merlini*, the Prophecies of Merlin. Stonehenge was referred to as 'the giant's circle' back then, on account of being built by the giants."

Lauren had just confirmed a slew of suspicions: Merlin's spoken magic and giants that smacked of golems. It all made surreal sense. What King didn't understand was that when he spoke again, his voice shook like he was being rattled around in the back of a bus.

Then he realized what was happening.

The ground was shaking.

FORTY-SIX
El Mirador, Guatemala

QUEEN, KNIGHT, AND Bishop exited the tour helicopter and entered a hellish nightmare. Blinding flashes of lightning pulsed in the sky. Rain whipped by high winds stung their exposed skin. A loud hiss created by rustling palm leaves and rain filled the air, broken by the occasional boom of thunder. But the storm had its bonuses. With no other tourists on-site and the science team weathering out the storm in their tents, they could explore the site without interference. Or so they hoped.

After taking their cases, which contained equipment no tourist should have access to, they left Luis behind and headed into the jungle. The pilot was happy to remain safe and dry inside the chopper.

A clearing full of large sturdy blue tents sat just inside the jungle, buffeted by the elements. Rainwater, diverted by tarps, flowed away as small streams that had already eroded the topsoil. Muffled conversations could be heard as the science team took cover from the storm. A large tent, this one built on top of a wooden platform four feet off the ground, lay at the center of the site. Given its size and the effort taken to protect it from flooding, Queen pegged it for the site's laboratory and headed for it. If Jon

Hudson, the archaeologist behind the excavation, was anything like the scientists they'd collaborated with in the past, he'd be hard at work despite the inclement weather.

The wooden steps creaked under the weight of Queen, Bishop, and Knight as they entered the tent, but the man inside showed no reaction to their approach. He sat with his back to the door, hunched over a worktable. He suddenly reached out his hand, snapped twice, and pointed. "Get me a clean brush, will you?"

Queen saw the brush in question, picked it up, and handed it to the man. He immediately went back to work, brushing dust from a shattered Mayan relief.

"Thank you," he said. "It's nice to see not everyone is hiding away because of a little storm."

"You're welcome," Queen said.

The man stopped working at the sound of Queen's voice. He turned around and with widening eyes looked Queen up and down. Dressed as a tourist in cargo shorts, green poncho, and blue bandanna, much of her finer qualities were disguised. But that didn't seem to matter as the man beamed at her. When he saw Bishop and Knight all signs of pleasant surprise faded. Whether she was available or not he would never know. The two men with her were too intimidating to even risk asking the question.

"Tourists?" he asked.

"Of a sort," Queen answered.

"Are you Jon Hudson?" Knight asked, reaching under his poncho.

Fear crept into Hudson's eyes. "You're not looters?"

Knight removed his hand from under his poncho. He held a photo of Richard Ridley. "Hardly," he said. "We're looking for a friend."

Hudson took the offered photo and looked at it. He showed no reaction, so little reaction in fact, that it was clear he did recognize Ridley. "A lot of people come and go here. Tourists, interns, too many faces to remember. And I spend most of my days looking at faces carved into stone. Speaking of which, I'm sorry to disappoint, but I really do have a lot of work to do and thanks to the weather, no one brave enough to help out."

Queen flashed a phony grin. "We'll let you get back to it, then. If the weather improves, would it be possible to get another look at the site? A tour perhaps?"

"Of course, of course." He turned and went back to work.

Queen stood there long enough for the moment to become uncomfortable. She turned and rolled her eyes at Bishop and Knight, who grinned in reply. All three left the hut, worked their way back out of the camp, and entered the jungle. Hidden from view, they climbed a short hill, lay down on top, and waited for the inevitable.

HUDSON CONTINUED BRUSHING away at the piece, its visage both beautiful and haunting, but his thoughts were not on work. They were on the three strangers looking for the man who had become his friend over the past few months, Marc Kaufman. He was also keenly aware that they had made the journey to El Mirador in the midst of one of the worst storms the rainy season had brought that year. He had no idea what Kaufman's relationship to the three visitors was, but they oozed bad intentions.

I'm a good judge of character, Hudson thought, *and those three are up to no good. I need to warn Kaufman.*

After waiting long enough for the strangers to leave camp, he left his workspace and stood in the doorway. A loud static hiss, created by rain beating down on the black tarps, filled the air. But visibility was good and he couldn't see anyone in camp or in the jungle surrounding the site. Crouching, he skulked through the camp. As his booted feet squished through mud, water rose up over them, soaking his feet.

He arrived at Kaufman's tent and squatted by the entrance. "Kaufman," he whispered. "Are you in there?"

After getting no reply, he whispered again. "Are you asleep, man? Wake up!"

Impatience got the better of him and he unzipped the tent. He flung open the blue flap and looked inside. Kaufman wasn't there.

Hudson stood up, scratching his head. He turned to head back to the science hut and came face-to-face with Queen. With a shout, he fell back into Kaufman's tent. As Queen, Bishop, and Knight crouched down around him, he moved deeper into the tent.

"Who's Kaufman?" Bishop asked, his statement punctuated by a boom of thunder that shook the forest floor.

"I don't—"

Queen cleared her throat. She had a handgun leveled at Hudson.

Hudson's face twisted in fear. "The man in the photo. He's a . . . a journalist. He's doing a piece on El Mirador for *National Geographic*. What . . . what do you want with him?"

"Where does he spend his time?" Knight asked.

Hudson looked at him dumbly.

"Is there a specific location he's shown interest in?"

Hudson thought for a moment. "He toured the whole site, but has spent most of his time at the biggest pyramid."

"La Danta?" Queen asked.

"Yes. In fact, that's probably where he is now." He nodded. "I'm certain of it. Since discovering the entrance he's been—"

"Where's the entrance?" Queen asked forcefully.

"On top. A tree had put its roots down in it. A storm knocked it over a few days ago. You . . . you don't need me to take you there . . . do you?"

"No, boss," Queen said, tightening her grip on her weapon. "We don't." She pulled the trigger, firing a dart into his neck. Thanks to a powerful sedative, he lost consciousness immediately. After shoving his feet inside and zipping up the entrance, Queen stood and joined Bishop and Knight, who were looking at a map of the site.

"Which way, boys?"

"East," Bishop said. "Mile and a half."

Anyone who saw them running out of the camp, dressed in dark green ponchos, concealed by sheets of rain, and accompanied by earthshaking thunder might have mistaken them for one of Alexander's Forgotten. As a result their exit from the camp went unhindered.

FORTY-SEVEN
Wiltshire, England

THE SHAKING SUBSIDED as quickly as it had begun, leaving King and Alexander on edge. It felt like a simple tremor, but they knew the source was much more likely to be Ridley.

Lauren flashed a nervous smile. "Now *that* doesn't happen much round here."

Eager to get a better view of Stonehenge, King headed for the tunnel, but was stopped by Lauren's next words. "Now what do you suppose that is?"

King looked to where she was pointing. A black plume rose into the sky in the distance. It spread, dissipated, and was carried off by the wind. "What's over there?"

Lauren glanced around and looked up at the sun, getting her bearings. The dark cloud had risen from the northeast. Her eyebrows arched. "Durrington Walls and Woodhenge."

"I've never heard of them," King said.

"Not surprising for a Scotsman."

"Woodhenge is a circle of timber," Alexander said. "Similar to Stonehenge, but built of wood, which rotted long ago. The postholes have recently been filled in with modern beams."

Lauren looked at Alexander, impressed with his knowledge. "You'd be surprised how many of our kinsmen don't even know that much about the site. Durrington Walls is only five hundred meters beyond Woodhenge, but is more significant because it not only held a wooden henge, but a village as well. Several homes have been uncovered. The sites might have been used for burials, with cremated bodies being carried from one site to the other before being discarded in the river. But that would've just been the peasants. Some think that religious leaders or cultural champions, like the designer of the circles, would have been buried beneath Stonehenge. It's one of the reasons a planned highway tunnel project, which would have burrowed through the earth under the henge, was scrapped. Seems like no one will see what's buried under there at this rate—archaeologists or contractors."

The ground shook again.

They all looked northeast, expecting to see a second dark cloud rise up. But nothing happened. Still, King thought they were connected. Whatever was causing the ground to shake had begun at the Durrington Walls.

"How far is it?" he asked.

"Two miles straight shot from here to there, but a little more if you don't have wings." Her face brightened. "I can get you there in three minutes if you don't mind getting your hair mussed." She looked at King, his hair slightly askew as usual. "Which I can see won't be a problem for you."

She cheerfully walked to the bus, though her walk was now closer to a skip. She hopped in the big red double-decker, turned on the engine, and gunned the gas twice. A thick cloud of gray coughed from the muffler. She leaned out the window. "C'mon, mates. I have forty-five minutes before I have to take these Yanks to the next stop."

Alexander motioned to the bus. "After you."

They entered and took seats behind Lauren. Then they were off, speeding back onto the road. She glanced at them in the large rearview mirror. "It's always boggled my mind why people are so much more interested in Stonehenge than the Durrington settlement. Granted, the stones are something to look at, but when it comes to history, the village is far more informative. What they ate, how they cooked, what they slept on, what weapons they had. It's all boring details to some, but it reveals who lived there. Who knows, maybe Merlin's magic wand is buried in that field's dirt?"

King thought her statement might not be far from the truth, then held on tight as she made a hard left turn.

"What's really interesting is that both sites were constructed at the same time as the pyramid of Cheops in Egypt."

"That *is* interesting," King said.

"The sites are thousands of miles away from each other and somehow, around 2500 B.C., people simultaneously developed the technology to move giant stones over long distances? Bollocks, I say. And we still can't figure out *how* they did it."

Alexander pointed beyond her. "We're here."

Lauren hit the brakes hard, bringing them to a stop across the street from a green field, which was now scarred by a dark hole at its center.

They left the bus and entered the field. The hole opened up before them, thirty feet across, burrowing into the soil at a forty-five-degree angle. Darkness filled the void, but echoing from deep within was a constant droning rumble.

King took a step in and turned to Lauren. "Best if you notify the authorities. Get the Stonehenge parking lot cleared out."

"What? Why?"

"Because this tunnel heads southeast and we're not feeling the rumbling here like we did there. Whoever made this hole is beneath Stonehenge by now."

Lauren's eyes widened and then squinted. "Hey, what happened to your accent? You sound like a Yankee."

Alexander entered the tunnel. "He *is* a Yankee."

King took her by the shoulders and glared into her eyes. "Never mind who I am or where I'm from. You go do what you need to do to clear out that parking lot."

"But I don't understand. Why?"

"Because if you don't it's likely they'll all die."

A look of horror came over Lauren as she realized that King and Alexander knew a lot more about what was happening then they let on. She broke out in a run back to the bus, hoping that King and Alexander were crackpots, but somehow knowing they weren't. And that terrified her. Because it meant there was something big, something evil, beneath Stonehenge that wanted to kill people.

And she was heading straight for it.

FORTY-EIGHT
Location Unknown

FIONA AWOKE, HER head throbbing. Though the dizziness that accompanied her last wake-up was missing, the pain she felt more than made up for the lack of disorientation. In fact, after a cursory glance around her new cell, she wished for some way to escape reality.

The cell was an eight-foot cube hollowed out of wet gray stone. There were no seams where floor met wall or wall met ceiling, though there were a few cracks. There was no entrance to speak of, only a four-foot-long, six-inch-tall horizontal slit that allowed fresh air and a small amount of light into the otherwise sealed space.

She lay on her back, the stone floor cold beneath her. They air itself was chilly, but bearable, even in her black pajamas, which were now covered in layers of dirt.

As she focused beyond the pulsing headache she became aware of the pain filling the rest of her body—stretched limbs and tight pressure. She looked down at her body and found her hands bound and tied to her feet. She'd been hog-tied and left.

As pain flooded her head again she lay back on the stone floor. Staring up at the vacant stone ceiling, she recalled the horrors she'd seen before being knocked unconscious. The walls came to life. With no place to go, the prisoners couldn't hide. She saw some trampled underfoot, some crushed by stone fists, and others, like poor Elma, torn apart.

But for some reason, she'd been spared. One of the golems even moved to avoid her. Tears broke free and rolled down the sides of her face, dripping into her ears. The tickling of liquid striking earlobe annoyed her and turned her sadness to rage. She let out a scream, pulling on her bonds. Her scream ended quickly as a rush of pain struck. She was bound physically and emotionally.

Why, she thought. *Why spare me? What made me different from all the people that were killed?*

King.

I'm either bait, or insurance. A hostage.

Before losing consciousness she thought she had seen King in the cell's entrance. He had come for her. He would again. And that was the only reason she still lived. Though she wasn't sure how much longer she would remain alive.

The headache meant she either had a serious injury she couldn't yet inspect or was seriously dehydrated. Or both.

She tensed again in frustration, this time just pulling with her arms. Her hands came up almost all the way to her face, pulling her bound feet with them. She could clearly see the old rope that had been used to bind her. It was thin and flexible, but frayed. Pushing with her hands and pulling with her legs, she rocked herself forward into a sitting position, legs open, hands bound to feet.

She groaned as the blood draining from her head caused a new throb of pain. With eyes squeezed shut, she rode out the pain. With each beat of her heart, the headache dissipated. When she could finally think straight she looked down at her bonds. Had she not been kidnapped twice, drugged, knocked unconscious, and left for dead, she might have smiled. Her bonds could have held an adult, but she was a thirteen-year-old girl. She lowered her knees nearly to the floor and leaned forward. With her face at her hands she began gnawing at the rope, putting her flexibility and sharp teeth to good work.

Desperate for freedom, she ignored the oily flavor of the rope, chewing it like a rat. She spat out some fibers, allowing herself to feel a measure of hope. *Hope isn't just something given,* King told her once, when they spoke about why it was important for people the team helped to sometimes continue the fight after they'd left, *it's something you have to believe in.* The words rang clear in her thoughts.

She would break free of her bonds.

And then what? She didn't know. But she was hopeful. Not for her escape, but for her rescue. Her hope was in her father. He'd come for her once. He would come again.

Her hope was shattered by a grinding of rock. She looked up and saw the stone wall parting. A man stood on the other side, silhouetted by a light source behind him. He wasn't looking at her, so she quickly laid down and closed her eyes, pretending to be unconscious. A prick in her arm popped her eyes back open, but only for a moment. As the drug took effect, her eyes closed again, this time against her will. She heard a man's voice as consciousness faded.

"Time to go, child. Babel awaits."

FORTY-NINE
El Mirador, Guatemala

THE BACK SIDE OF the la Danta pyramid looked like it could crumble apart and bury them in an avalanche. The latticework of wooden planks, platforms, and ladders rising up the massive slope looked wholly inadequate for containing the structure's bulk. Queen, Bishop, and Knight stood at the base, looking up. Several thin, pale trees still clung to the pyramid, most likely left in place because the roots helped hold the wall together.

As they neared the temple, the three fell silent. Finding no footprints in the mud at the base of the pyramid, they circled around slowly, using the jungle for cover.

The continuing thunderstorm made hearing anything impossible, but the rising sun had brightened the cloud cover, improving visibility. As they reached the front of the pyramid and found no one present, they hid and observed the site.

The front side of the pyramid was much more impressive than the back. Its slate gray stone surface was covered in several levels of staircases that led all the way to the top. Trees covered much of the building, but the most impressive and well-preserved staircases were clear. Climbing to the top would be easy for all but the out-of-shape.

As Bishop looked at the top of the pyramid he imagined what the site would have looked like two thousand years previous. A high priest adorned with bright-colored feathers and paints. Slaves and animals lined up for sacrifice, ready to appease Chac, the god of rain. Given the raging storm overhead, it seemed Chac was in a very bad mood; perhaps from being denied a sacrifice for two thousand years, perhaps because his temple had been recently violated. Bishop didn't really care. Chac would not help him catch Richard Ridley, no matter how many lives were sacrificed. If that were true, Ridley would have been caught long ago.

"No one's here," Bishop said.

"Let's do it," Queen said, drawing her hidden UMP submachine gun from beneath her poncho.

They moved as one, crossing the clearing between jungle and pyramid quickly. Scouring the steep grade for movement as they climbed, they ascended the ancient temple. They reached the summit without incident. Above the jungle, they could see the Guatemalan countryside in all its glory. Trees shifted in waves as great gusts of wind rolled past. Lightning split in fractals across the sky. It was an untamed landscape.

A green tarp, torn free by strong winds flapped madly from the tree it was still tied to. Beneath it was a rectangular opening. A stone staircase, covered in pools of water, descended into the pyramid.

After donning night vision goggles, Queen led the team inside. The tunnel, lit in shades of green, was unremarkable at first. The occasional spider was their only company. The staircase turned one hundred eighty degrees, like a mountain trail switchback. The walls on the next flight down bore huge relief murals carved into massive stones. Fluid scenes of human sacrifice, executioners, and angry gods covered the walls.

As the stairs continued deeper, the images became more violent, taking the viewer through a story line that involved ritual preparation, ceremony, bloodletting, and death. Several different acts of killing were displayed—decapitation, organ removal, burning.

As her nerves tensed Queen realized that those being led down this staircase would understand the images as the horrors they would soon endure. It must have been enough to paralyze them with fear. Queen, on the other hand, had the opposite reaction. Anger filled her veins, pumping adrenaline into her system and boosting her senses.

The staircase ended at a gently sloping, curved tunnel that Queen guessed lined up with the base of the pyramid. Everything from here on would take them underground.

As she took a step forward into the curved tunnel she felt the stone beneath her foot drop almost imperceptibly. She froze.

She held her hand up, stopping the others. She pointed at her foot and they understood at once.

A trap.

She listened for the telltale signs of a trap, shifting weights, grinding gears, but heard nothing. She chanced a whisper. "Maybe it's too old? Rotted?"

A clunk overhead proved her wrong.

Queen looked up in time to see a shower of long, sharp darts fall from the ceiling, falling at her like a hundred miniature spears.

FIFTY
Wiltshire, England

THE SMALL FLASHLIGHTS they carried did little to light the deep craggy tunnel, but King and Alexander moved quickly despite the low light. If Richard Ridley was at the end of the tunnel, they wanted to catch him by surprise. If they didn't it might mean battling one of his golems or oversized sandfish.

Or several.

Their best bet was to knock him unconscious and shut his mouth before he knew they were there. Not knowing what waited for them at the end of the tunnel made King apprehensive, but he fought against the feeling with the knowledge that he had beat Ridley before, and the man beside him had killed the legendary Hydra on his own—a creature that took the entire Chess Team and Alexander's aid to defeat in the present day. Having his handgun at the ready eased his nerves, too. Upon seeing Ridley, who could not die, he didn't need to sneak up and knock the man unconscious; shooting him in the head until his mouth was bound would work just as well and provide some catharsis.

The tunnel walls were rough at first, loose soil had been dug away and pushed out through the entrance. Stone had been crushed. It was a giant burrow. But just fifty feet in the scene changed. The tunnel became square and gray. Man-made. Old.

"Merlin was a busy man," Alexander said.

"You buy that story?" King asked.

Alexander paused and gave King a lopsided smile that said: *Remember who you're talking to.*

"Right," King said. "If it's possible Stonehenge was created by Merlin, what would he have buried beneath it?"

"Given Ridley's interest, I would assume some form of ancient knowledge regarding the mother tongue. In what form, I can only guess."

King didn't like guessing, or the perpetual feeling of being two steps behind, which he felt in regard to Ridley and Alexander. He lacked a complete picture of both men's motivations, and that disturbed him.

They paused at the change in tunnel structure.

King moved his light over the wall, which was made from lines of giant rectangular blue-tinged stones. "Its bluestone," King said. "Same as many of the henge stones. You think this runs all the way to Stonehenge? Two miles?"

"It seems likely. Perhaps a symbolic journey to the underworld."

"Or literal," King said as he started moving forward.

"Let's hope not," Alexander replied, breaking out into a quick jog.

King wasn't sure if Alexander's reply was serious or an attempt at humor, but followed without a word. He wasn't about to look like a fool by asking. The two ran in the near darkness, dimming their flashlights with their hands as much as possible to conceal their approach.

They ran blindly, unable to see or hear anything ahead. When King judged they'd run almost the entire two miles, he slowed. "Were almost under Stonehenge," he whispered.

They walked a short distance more with their flashlights off and then stopped to listen. All was quiet. They continued forward in darkness, hands on the tunnel walls for balance and direction. Then the walls fell away on both sides.

After what felt like a lifetime of quiet breathing and listening, King flicked on his flashlight. He scanned it back and forth, handgun in hand, looking for a target. He found nothing to shoot. The circular space was devoid of living or animated targets, but it held plenty of fascinating finds. The floor was covered in two-foot-tall vertical stone poles that looked like the stumps of a petrified forest. They were arranged in a classic glyph pattern with some rings of pillars being larger than others. The room was constructed entirely of bluestone. A large sarcophagus sat at the middle of the room, encircled by rings of stone.

King and Alexander slowly made their way through the circles, panning their lights around the room. Closer to the sarcophagus, King could see that the lid had been slid away. It sat shattered on the floor on the far side. Their flashlights revealed a body within.

The body was wrapped in tight linens from head to toe. Gathered around it were gold objects and sealed vessels. Its face, partially exposed by time's rot still held remnants of a white beard.

King shook his head. "It looks—"

"Egyptian," Alexander finished.

"Is that possible?"

"Anything is possible. It's likely this man fled Egypt with knowledge of the mother tongue. Seeking to start his own empire, he used golems to create this monument, just as the people he left behind in Eygpt were doing to create the pyramids."

King looked closely at the man's face, the bone structure and hair. "He doesn't look Egyptian. Or Arabian for that matter."

"That's because he's not."

King looked at Alexander, who looked extremely unhappy.

"He's Jewish."

"You don't think this is . . ."

"Moses? No. But possibly a member of the exodus. Someone close enough to Moses to pick up some of the mother tongue. And someone who would have heard about the pyramids, but never saw them."

"Why's that?" King asked.

"The original generation that fled into the desert is said to have all died out during their forty-year migration. Even Moses didn't enter the Promised Land. He only saw it from a distance before dying. Whoever this man was, he knew about the great monuments constructed by the golems, but knew nothing of their architecture." Alexander took the man's hands, which were bent open, as though in prayer, and turned them inward. They moved with ease until one overlapped the other.

"And though I cannot tell you who this man was, I can tell you who he likely became."

King came to the same conclusion before Alexander could voice it. "Merlin."

"Which is a shame," Alexander said. He saw King's confusion and explained. "There will be no way to hide this discovery. Within hours, the site will be swarming with British authorities. Within months, everything that can be carted away will be. And the body of this man, buried in peace for thousands of years, will be carted off to a museum. He will be tested, dissected, and eventually put on display. Millions will flock to see the body of the great Merlin, whose dying wish had been to be buried in the tomb he created, with his most cherished possessions . . . including the one that was stolen."

"Stolen?" King said. "Something is missing."

Alexander removed his hands from the body's hands. They hovered in the air, clutching an invisible object. "His hands were pried open. Whatever he was holding is gone. And the thieves with it."

"Damnit," King said. Ridley seemed to be one step ahead of them at all times, like he knew where they were. King's eyes widened at the revelation. "He knows we're here."

A series of rumbles from above shook the chamber. Dust fell through the cracks of the bluestone ceiling. If it collapsed they would be crushed to paste. But it wasn't the ceiling of the chamber that collapsed. It was the tunnel. King turned toward the tunnel, aiming his flashlight down its throat. In the distance he saw a wave of debris falling from the roof and filling the void beneath. The tunnel was being packed tight from above.

Tons of bluestone, bedrock, and soil filled the tunnel and spilled into the burial chamber, stopping at their feet as though held at bay by the ancient powers of Merlin. King scanned the tunnel entrance. It was packed tight. He turned around the room, searching the walls for some sign of an exit. He found none.

They were trapped. Buried alive one hundred feet beneath Stonehenge.

FIFTY-ONE
El Mirador, Guatemala

A CRUSHING WEIGHT fell on top of Queen, knocking her to her knees. But there were no pinpricks of pain that she'd expected to feel from the shower of trap-triggered needles falling from the ceiling. She rolled away and stood. When she turned around she saw Bishop, hunched over in pain. Close to a hundred needles stuck out of his back like porcupine quills.

Bishop grunted and fell to one knee. "Poison," he said through gritted teeth. With the number they were doing to Bishop's body, Queen had no doubt she'd already be dead on the floor. He'd saved her life.

Quickly and carefully, Knight and Queen plucked the darts from Bishop's back. As the last dart came out, Bishop stood tall and shook his head; other than a poncho full of pencil eraser–sized holes, he was no worse for wear.

"I don't understand why this trap hadn't been marked," Knight said, looking over one of the poison-tipped needles that now held a thin coat of Bishop's blood on its black tip. "Hudson doesn't seem like the kind of guy to wait on exploring a find like this."

Queen saw the answer lying on the floor in an alcove obscured by loose stones—a bright orange "danger" sign featuring a decal of a man bending forward, arms up, and a shower of needles falling from above. She pointed to it. "I think someone down here was covering their back."

She knelt down by the stone that triggered the trap and turned on a small pocket flashlight. A faint yellow residue, invisible to anyone wearing night vision goggles rimmed the stone. "A chalk outline was wiped away. We're going to have to be more careful."

"Or I can go first," Bishop said, stepping over the marked stone.

"Or that," Queen said, extinguishing her flashlight and following a few steps behind.

They successfully passed another trap without incident, descending the downward spiraling tunnel for another two minutes. Bishop stopped when his view of the tunnel brightened. There was an artificial light source ahead.

After removing their goggles, the team inched forward silently. The tunnel exit ahead was bright with light. They would be exposed if they got too close. Being the stealthiest, Knight went first, sliding forward on his stomach. With his eyes scouring the floor for signs of wiped away chalk it took him a few minutes to cover the distance in silence, but when he reached the tunnel exit his patience and gentle movements were rewarded.

The tunnel exited to a large circular chamber, fifty feet in diameter. The space was lit by a bright electric lantern, which rested atop a flat, stone altar top. Vertical stripes of black char rose up along the walls above a circle of small holes that would have held torches. A stone staircase decorated with the carved faces of the damned descended to a stone platform that encircled a pit at the center of the chamber. Four sections of the light gray stone surrounding the pit were stained dark brown with ancient blood. Funnels carved into the stone would have directed the flow into the pit, which looked like an ancient throat.

Here, like the tunnels above, the walls were covered in carvings, but between several murals was what looked like writing. In some ways it was similar to Sumerian cuneiform, but more stylized.

Seeing nobody present in the chamber, Knight waved the others to join him. When they arrived he pointed to the one thing that revealed where their quarry had gone—a rope. Tied to the five-foot-tall altar that held the lantern, a rope hung over the edge of the pit. Glowing from deep within the pit was a second light source, and a voice.

The words were hard to make out, but the deep, bass-filled voice was unmistakable. Ridley was at the bottom of the pit.

Queen grinned. He was right where they wanted him. Trapped, helpless, and at their mercy. One cut of the rope would leave him stranded for an eternity, like the Hydra from whom he stole his regenerative abilities.

They descended the steps and peeked over the edge. Were it lit solely from above it would have appeared bottomless, but Ridley's light below revealed the bottom some two hundred feet down. Despite the distance, the sea of bones at the bottom was easy to make out. Ridley stood nearly waist deep in them, searching through them like a kid with an overfull toybox. In one hand he held a small digital recorder.

They watched as he picked up a small chunk of tablet and read off the words, which sounded strangely foreign, but felt familiar. When he was done he smashed the tablet against the stone wall.

Knight remembered that along with human and animal victims sacrificed to the gods, the Mayan also sacrificed their prized possessions including gold, silver, jewels, and codices. *He's collecting the ancient language written on the codices and then destroying them,* Knight thought. He drew his knife, held it against the rope, and nodded to the others.

"Ridley!" Queen shouted, standing in clear view.

The man's head snapped up in surprise. Then a smile crept onto his face. "The Chess Team arrives. I must admit I'm surprised to see you here. How did you find me?"

"You've got thirty seconds to tell us where Fiona is before we cut the line and leave you to rot," Queen said.

"You seem to be missing a member," Ridley said. "I know King was in Rome, but where is Rook? Did something go wrong?" His smile grew wider.

Queen's UMP came up fast. She took aim and fired a three-round burst. Two of the rounds missed, shattering ancient bones, but one struck Ridley square in the forehead. He flinched as it struck, turning his head down. When he looked back up there was no injury, just his perpetually smiling face and gleaming bald head. There wasn't even a splotch of blood.

"Afraid I'm not intimidated," he said.

"He's not going to talk," Bishop whispered.

Queen looked at Knight. "Do it. He might be immortal, but we'll see how cooperative he is after starving for a few weeks."

Knight cut through the rope and let it fall.

Expecting some sort of protest or angry retort, the team flinched when Ridley began laughing. They looked down at him.

"All you've done is leave me with an army," Ridley said, and then began speaking in hushed tones. The sea of bones around him began to rattle and shake.

Knight realized what was happening and said, "He's about to go Ray Harryhausen on our asses."

"What?" Queen asked.

Knight pointed down at the shifting bones. "Golems are the inanimate made animate. And he's got a whole lot of inanimate buddies down there. An army of skeletons."

"But they're at the bottom of a—" Queen's words were cut short by a deep rumbling from below. The pit floor was rising as a horde of living Mayan skeletons fused together and turned their empty eye sockets up at the stunned team.

FIFTY-TWO
Wiltshire, England

DUST CHOKED THE air, making it hard to breathe and nearly impossible to see. And with tons of earth between them and the surface, a rescue would not soon be coming.

King couldn't see Alexander through the soupy brown air, but he saw his light move to the far wall of the chamber. He moved the light up and down on the wall, slowly making his way around the space. "What are you looking for?" After speaking, King took a breath and coughed hard. If the air didn't clear soon he might lose consciousness.

Alexander didn't pause his search as he replied. "The man in that tomb might not have had knowledge of pyramid architecture, but he was certainly familiar with the burial rites of the Pharaohs, which he must have fancied himself as. He's mummified his body, been buried with sacred possessions, and encased in an elaborately grand tomb. Maybe his father aided in the construction of the Cheops tomb itself, I don't know."

"You're looking for a hidden exit," King said, making his way to the wall opposite Alexander so he could start his own search.

"It was a common practice by ancient Egyptian tomb builders, who sealed the tombs from the inside, and then exited via a secret shaft. It was also convenient for builders turned grave robbers."

They quickly finished searching the tomb walls and found nothing. The ceiling came next, but its massive stones looked immovable. In fact, there was nothing in the room that looked small enough to move but big enough to hide a tunnel.

Then King's attention locked on the sarcophagus. *That would work*, he thought. Coughing as he moved, King rushed through the maze of bluestone pillars and crouched by the sarcophagus. It stood on a raised circular platform, which was covered in dust. King blew the dust away, further fouling the air. He covered his mouth with one arm and wiped the surface of the floor with the other.

Alexander joined him. "What are you looking for?"

King stopped wiping. "That." He pointed to the corner of the sarcophagus where an ancient scratch still marred the floor. "The sarcophagus swivels."

Alexander immediately moved to the other side of the sarcophagus and pushed. It didn't budge. King joined him and they pushed together. But it was no use. The stone wouldn't move.

"Can we destroy it?" King asked.

Alexander grew angry. "We will *not* desecrate this tomb any further. I would sooner die."

"Says the guy who can't die." King shook his head in frustration. It might be an offense to history, but if any other member of the Chess Team had been by his side, rather than Alexander, they would find a way to tear down the sarcophagus and escape. Of course, brains often achieved the same results as brawn. King smiled as an idea came to him. He stood and climbed atop one of the nearby pillars. When nothing happened he moved to the next.

"What are you doing?" Alexander asked, his voice still tinged with annoyance.

"Just be ready to push," King said, continuing his circuit around the room, hopping on one pillar after another. His hope was that one of the pillars would trigger some kind of release for the sarcophagus. His fear was that it was one of the pillars buried beneath the stone and dirt that filled half the room.

He hopped up on the last of the large pillars and felt it give a little beneath his weight. A loud clunk sounded beneath the stone floor. "Push!"

Alexander pushed hard. Stone scraped against stone. A hiss of escaping air filled the chamber. The ancient seal was broken. The sarcophagus slid open revealing a smooth tunnel that spiraled out of view. But it wasn't tall enough for a man to walk or even crawl into—it had to be slid into.

When the sarcophagus had shifted ninety degrees, it could no longer move. A second clunk sounded immediately and Alexander grunted. "It's moving back! It may not reopen!"

King hoped off the pillar and rushed to his side. He looked at the small, downward sloped tunnel and shook his head. *Time to find out if I'm claustrophobic,* he thought.

"Hurry!" Alexander urged. "It's going to move faster when I let go."

King put his flashlight in his mouth and dove into the tunnel head-first. Contrary to how it looked, he didn't slide down. The rough stone clung to his body like Velcro. Dragging himself forward, he moved down and around into the tunnel. A moment later, he felt Alexander's hands on his feet, pushing him forward. He scrambled as fast as he could, feeling his elbows and knees already becoming raw.

"Despite being able to grow back limbs," Alexander shouted as the sarcophagus began squeezing his feet, "I don't enjoy the experience of losing them."

King felt Alexander lunge forward, bringing his body up on top of King's legs, pinning them to the floor.

With a thud, the sarcophagus sealed over them. They were in a downward spiraling tunnel barely tall enough for King to raise his head. And with Alexander's weight crushing his legs to the sharply rough floor, he could no longer move forward.

King took a deep breath, steadying himself before claustrophobic panic could set in. He pictured the situation behind him and quickly came up with the solution. "Exhale as much as you can and press yourself against the ceiling."

The pressure on King's legs lessened as Alexander complied, but not by much. They were packed tighter than he thought. Gritting his teeth against the flashlight, King reached out and pulled as hard as he could. Pain stabbed his knees as the rough floor tore into them. He grunted and stopped. "One more time."

As the pressure lessened again, King gave a mighty pull. He slid forward, but his knees were torn apart. He shouted in pain. The flashlight fell from his mouth and rolled free, following the spiral around and down. King watched the light fade.

But then it stopped with a *thunk.*

That's either good news, or bad news, King thought. His torn-up knees ached with every slide forward, but with more room to move, he was able to position his legs so his wounds were off the floor. He moved steadily downward, following the spiral. As he descended, the light from his lost flashlight grew brighter.

"You're bleeding," Alexander said. He couldn't see King's wounds, but the smell of blood was filling the tight tunnel.

"I'll be fine," King replied. "We're almost at the bottom."

"What do you see?"

King stopped as he saw the flashlight ahead. The tunnel leveled out and continued in a straight line. He pushed forward, not knowing how far the tunnel stretched. When it grew smaller he could no longer lift his head up. Still he pushed forward, not knowing what lay ahead. It could be an exit, a trap, or a squeeze too tight to fit through. As it was he could feel his back scraping against the ceiling with each pull forward. Pulling with his arms and pushing with his toes, he continued forward for ten minutes. Then his flashlight, aimed toward the side wall, showed an open space. He picked up his head and found a small chamber. He quickly pulled himself free of the small tunnel and checked out the space, which was about the size of an economy car interior. While the extra space was nice, the light gray wall blocking his path crushed his hopes. Crouching, King moved to the wall. As Alexander exited the tunnel behind him he placed his hand on the smooth surfaced wall. Modern concrete.

They were trapped.

Again.

FIFTY-THREE
Washington, D.C.

"**YOU WANT TO** what!" Boucher said, as he stomped back and forth in the Oval Office.

Duncan had spent every waking minute working through his options. The world needed defending. The Chess Team lacked a handler. His skill set—brilliant strategist, resistant to pressure, extreme determination—fit his role as president. But it was all for nothing when political chest thumping and loud-mouth pundits could tie his hands. He had come to a decision and just dropped the bomb on Boucher, who would be one of few people to ever know the truth.

"I can't do it, Tom," Boucher said.

Duncan could see Boucher working through the proposal despite his vocal opposition. He waited, leaning back on the couch. Boucher's pacing slowed, which meant he was coming to his final decision; everything said before then was just blown-off steam.

Boucher stopped pacing.

He sat down on the couch across from Duncan.

His mustache twitched a few times. "Damnit, Tom."

The irritated CIA chief looked at the folder in Duncan's hands. "You have this all worked out, don't you?"

Duncan handed him the folder. "Every detail."

"Of course," Boucher said, laying the folder open on the coffee table between the two men. He sifted through the pages. Each page represented a separate step in the president's plan. E-mails to be faked. Documents to be forged. Databases to be altered. CIA stuff. All of it damning evidence that Duncan had knowingly ignored credible threats against the Siletz Reservation and Fort Bragg, that he had grossly underestimated the reach of their enemies, and that he had purposely provoked their wrath with the hopes of expanding the war on terror via the invasion of the countries responsible. Essentially, everything Marrs claimed to be true but wasn't. The documents would reveal that Duncan did all of it despite strong opposition from Boucher, who had saved e-mails, recorded phone calls, and kept tabs on the president's poor choices. The world would blame Duncan for more than three thousand five hundred American lives lost.

Boucher was integral to this plan. Duncan couldn't do it without him.

The last few pages interested Boucher the most. He picked them up, reading each page in detail. Duncan saw him nod a few times. He was beginning to see the big picture.

Boucher finished reading and put the pages back into the folder. He sat back, crossing his legs. "This might work."

"It will work."

"It's a huge sacrifice."

Duncan nodded.

"Everyone will believe the things Marrs has been saying."

Duncan shrugged. "It wouldn't be possible without Marrs."

"It could land him in this office in the next election."

"We'll worry about that later. What's important is that we bury the truth deeper than any future president would think to dig."

Boucher smiled. "I'll break out my shovel."

FIFTY-FOUR
El Mirador, Guatemala

BEFORE THE BASE of the sacrificial pit reached the top, two things happened. The mismatched living skeletons began scaling the rough walls, eager to attack. And Ridley disappeared within the writhing mass of white spindly limbs. While many climbed the walls, scores more were still forming below.

Not wanting any of the undead golems to reach the top of the pit, Queen, Bishop, and Knight opened fire. Sparks filled the air as bullets pierced brittle bones and struck stone. As limbs shattered and fell away, several of the skeletons toppled down, but whatever remained intact merged with loose bones below and rejoined the fight. All the while, the stone floor brought the horde closer.

"We can't stop them," Knight said as he reloaded.

"If we can subdue Ridley, maybe we can—"

A rattling wave filled the air as the platform neared the top, allowing the bone golems access to it. In clear view, their patchwork bodies became more evident. Limbs of children mixed with adult heads. Mismatched arms and legs. Missing parts. They packed a lot of power when it came to inducing fear, but their physical prowess—hindered by age and handicap—dulled their effectiveness in combat. What they lacked in speed and toughness they made up for in numbers and an inability to feel pain.

They arrived as a wave of death, flowing out of the pit and heading straight for Bishop, Knight, and Queen. The first to arrive were shredded by bursts of bullets, but with only thirty rounds per magazine, ammo ran dry quickly.

Three skeletons dove at Queen, knocking her back. She tore the head from one, but its body continued to fight. They stabbed at her eyes with bony fingers, used their limbs like clubs, and congested the air with the foul-smelling dust of their long since decayed flesh. She struck back with balled fists, sweeping kicks, and bone-crushing head butts.

She remembered the last time she'd delivered a head butt. It was to the man who had branded her forehead. Now it seemed he had returned from the dead with an army to exact his revenge. As she fell back under a surge of weight, it seemed like it might happen.

Bishop, with his large size and resistance to injury and tiring, had more luck against the bone golems. Swinging his massive arms, the bodies before him simply fell apart. As a result he had a clear view of Queen going down and Richard Ridley making his escape.

He looked for Knight and found him climbing up a large wall relief. Once on top he was free to move quickly, which was one of the things Knight did best. "Help Queen, I'll go after Ridley!" he shouted, then ran above the skeletons, leaping for the exit. He ascended the stairs and disappeared into the dark hallway a moment later, leaving a slew of confused bone golems in his wake.

Bishop waded his way through the golems, trying to reduce them to powder. But the ancient bodies crowded over him. He stumbled on a broken limb and fell to his hands. While his back was pummeled he felt a rumble beneath his palms. Something was shaking. The pit, he realized; without Ridley it was returning to its original state!

"Queen don't move!" he shouted. One false move could send them falling two hundred feet. The drop would kill Queen and leave him trapped at the bottom.

Bishop pushed up hard and felt the bone golems clinging to his back fall away. He struck out to his right, sweeping his thick arm in a wide arc. The impact drove the skeletons back, tripping them up. Then a group of them fell away, disappearing into the pit. With his fear confirmed he shouted, "The pit is open again!"

Making no effort to fight the reanimated dead, Bishop chose to simply charge through them. He hunched his shoulder forward and ran to where he'd last seen Queen. Like an NFL linebacker playing against a Pee Wee League team, he barreled through the mass of bodies and dove forward. The effect was immediate. Bodies fell away or fell to pieces under his weight. He stopped above Queen, tossed aside the golem on top of her, and pulled her to her feet.

In a blur of movement Queen lobbed something over his head. He tried to track and identify it, but it disappeared into the sea of golems on the other side of the chamber. Her next words told him exactly what it was.

"Fire in the hole!" she shouted.

A grenade.

Bishop turned away and saw Queen laying on the floor, curled into a ball, her back toward the impending blast. She had her hands over her ears, her eyes clenched shut, and her mouth open, ready for the contained blast. But with all the stone and bones filling the room, shrapnel could tear her apart. He moved to cover her with his body, but was too slow.

A deafening explosion filled the ceremonial chamber before Bishop could take cover. He was thrown into the air and smashed against the stone wall. He growled in pain, but before the dust had even begun to settle, the ringing and pain in his ears faded. The shrapnel in his flesh popped out and the wounds healed. He looked for Queen.

She was on her knees, shaking her head with a stunned look on her face, but she appeared to be unharmed. Still, she could have been shredded to bits.

"You should have let me cover you," he said.

Queen stood, looking slightly offended. "You might be Superman, Bish, but I sure as shit am not Lois Lane."

Bishop grinned and said, "Copy that." Queen might not be able to heal, but she knew her limits, and how to survive. She did not want, or need, a protector.

She coughed from the foul air, removed her bandanna, and tied it around her mouth. "Where's Knight?"

"Went after Ridley."

That's when the chamber ceiling, buried beneath hundreds of feet of jungle and the world's largest pyramid, shook. Something massive had struck the surface above. Queen and Bishop charged up the stairs and into the tunnel, knowing that Ridley had most likely conjured something much stronger than golem skeletons. And whatever it was, Knight would be facing it alone.

FIFTY-FIVE
Wiltshire, England

"WELL, THIS IS unfortunate," Alexander said as he exited the tiny spiraling tunnel and looked at the dead end.

"Unfortunate is an understatement," King said.

Alexander squatted next to King, cramped in the small space. "I suppose it is."

King leaned back against the exposed concrete wall, hiding it with his body. Time was short, but he wanted some answers. "Now that we have some time to kill, why don't you answer a few questions."

"I don't think that—"

"Who were you talking to on the phone?"

"An associate."

"A member of the Herculean Society?"

Alexander turned his palms up with a shrug. "They would not have my number otherwise. But this—"

"Who were you talking about? The two people, who are they?"

The combination of King's questions and his constant interruptions were causing Alexander's face to turn red with anger. He was pushing it, he knew, but answers flowed more easily from angry lips. "Why are you really here?"

But Alexander was either too smart or too experienced to fall for King's bait. Just as he was about to shout something, he stopped, grinned, and leaned back. With a calm voice, he said, "I could ask the same question of you, King. The death of your sister made you a fighting man. And now a little girl, who you've taken as your own—which was never my intention, by the way—has replaced that missing relationship and you're desperate to get her back. You're doing this just as much for yourself as you are for the 'greater good.'"

King felt his own anger rising. Alexander knew too much about him and had turned the conversation around. The problem was, King's personal motivations didn't conflict with the mission. He had no idea what

Alexander's endgame was, and it was clear he would get no closer to finding out.

"You would do well to remember that you are here because I allowed it."

King was about to argue, but it was true. Alexander had led King to the Siletz Reservation and Fiona. And since being found beneath the Roman Forum, Alexander probably could have left King behind at any point. The question was, why? Why did Alexander, a man with extraordinary resources, intelligence, physical power, and a clandestine organization, allow King to tag along. So he asked, "Why?"

Alexander grinned. "I've always enjoyed a good game of chess."

The implication of the statement was obvious. To Alexander, King was a pawn. *We'll see about that*, King thought, but simply forced a grin. He'd pushed the subject enough. Trapped in a tiny cave with a man who could tear him apart started to make him feel like a frog in a blender. It was time to leave. He pointed to a trickle of water behind Alexander's head. "With a steady supply of water, how long would you be able to regenerate your body?"

"Indefinitely," Alexander answered. "Why?"

"If we're stuck in here for a long time, or forever, I can eat you to stay alive for as long as it takes."

Alexander sneered at the thought, looking at King like he was a madman. "You would—" Then he paused, seeing the slight smile on King's face. "You're joking? You— What do you know?"

King moved to the side, giving Alexander space to approach the concrete wall. "Put your ear against it."

Alexander leaned down and placed his ear against the cold, rough wall. Being close to the wall he could see a subtle curve to its shape. And within, he heard something . . . water!

"It's a drainage pipe," King said. "Not built by Merlin, which means—"

"I have no qualms about destroying it," Alexander finished. "Move aside."

Alexander reached into his pocket and took out a small vial of black liquid. Before he drank it, King asked, "Would that work on me?"

"The adrenaline rush alone might be enough to destroy your heart," Alexander said. "And if you survived that and managed to employ your newfound strength, it's likely you would break most of the bones in your body, which get no added strength from this brew. It's only my ability to heal that allows me to use it."

Alexander poured a few drops of the liquid under his tongue. "You may envy my strength, but you shouldn't. I don't enjoy it. The pain is"—Alexander's body shook as the adrenaline took hold—"excruciating."

King stepped aside as Alexander's eyes went wide, his pupils dilating. Leaning back on his hands and one leg, Alexander struck out with his right leg, smashing the concrete. He grunted in pain, paused, then struck again. His fourth strike resulted in a loud crack. On the fifth, his foot shot through the wall into the void beyond. With the hole begun, it wasn't long before he had kicked away an opening big enough for them to fit through.

When he was done, he moved aside, his face twisted in pain. "The adrenaline is wearing off. I'll just need a moment to heal."

Being eager to leave the tight confines of what was almost their tomb, King nodded and slid through the hole. After his waist passed through, he fell and landed in a stream of water. The drainage pipe was large enough to crouch in and the air fresher than the tomb's, though tinged with mold. A ring of sunlight from a vertical tunnel farther down the pipe provided enough refracted light to see by. "I see an exit," he said.

But the joy of their impending escape was short-lived as he heard what sounded like a sporting event—loud shouts merging with the excited ebb and flow of a game. But there was no excitement in this cacophony of voices. Only terror. He suspected they were underneath the Stonehenge parking lot, which meant . . .

King turned toward the tomb from which he'd just escaped. "Alexander! The car park is under attack!"

Alexander quickly joined King in the tunnel and they rushed toward the circle of sunlight. When they reached it they found a metal rung ladder leading up to a drainage grate. King moved to the side.

"You go first," he said. "In case it needs persuading."

Alexander climbed the ladder and after two swift strikes pushed the grate aside with a scrape of metal on pavement. He poked his head outside and paused. After grunting with displeasure, he pulled himself out of the exit. King launched up the ladder and climbed topside.

His first breath of fresh air was welcome. His second was out of a nightmare.

FIFTY-SIX
El Mirador, Guatemala

THE CLOUDS OVERHEAD had thickened, blocking out more of the rising sun's light. Combined with the thick jungle canopy, it was like a permanent twilight. Lightning occasionally lit the scene, allowing Knight a clearer view of his fleeing target. But his eyes were keen. Dim light or not, he could see Ridley ahead, weaving in and out of the tall, thin trees that filled the jungle. Ridley was a bigger man and a slower runner, but he also didn't tire. Catching him would have to be done quickly, especially given the direction in which he was headed—straight back to the campsite where he would have plenty of hostages.

Though the jungle canopy was thick with giant leaves, the ground was virtually vegetation free. Knight poured on the speed. While Ridley still ran in a haphazard line, most likely fearing a bullet shot, Knight only shifted if a tree or some other immovable object crossed his path.

He closed to within twenty feet and drew his sidearm. He couldn't kill Ridley, but a few shots to the head should put him down long enough to subdue. He took aim and saw something disturbing.

Ridley was smiling.

Why would he be—

The forest floor exploded as something massive struck with the force of a bomb.

Knight slid to a stop, landing on his backside in a puddle of mud. In front of him, a long stone lay half buried in the dirt. A loud slurping sound came from the object as it began rising out of the muck. Knight followed the movement and saw a large silhouette standing above him.

The stone is an arm!

With a flash of lightning he saw the golem. It was a twenty-foot-tall statue of Chac, the Mayan god of rain. His eyes, carved thousands of years ago, were angry. His mouth was down-turned. Its body was covered in the horrified faces of those sacrificed to him. The frightening Mayan style only accentuated the menace emanating from the now-living stone.

As though sensing Knight's rising fear, the golem raised its giant hand to strike again.

Knight scrambled in the mud, his feet slipping out from under him. Grasping a thin tree, he yanked his body out of reach just as the golem struck. The force of the impact knocked him forward. Rather than fall into the mud again he leaped, curled his body, and landed in a roll that flung him back to his feet. He continued the pursuit without pause.

Though now he wasn't just chasing Ridley, he was also running for his life. Lightning flashed again and he caught a glimpse of Ridley in the distance, still making for the camp. He gave chase. When the ground began to shake, he knew the golem had done likewise.

Ridley rounded a mound that hid a smaller, not yet excavated temple inside, and disappeared from view. Rather than take the circuitous route around, Knight headed straight for it. He tore up the side and quickly realized his mistake. The ground was saturated and slippery. Each step slid out from under him, cutting his speed in half and giving the golem time to catch up.

He looked back and saw a huge, perpetually clenched fist flying toward his body. With the mud working against an ascending escape, he allowed gravity and the slick ground to save his life. He slid down the slope as the golem's fist punched into the mound, impaling several feet of dirt and buried temple. Knight came to a stop at the golem's feet.

He looked up and saw it looking down at him. It tried to yank free, but its arm was held tight.

Trapped.

But not immobile. The golem picked its foot off the ground and tried to step on Knight. But he saw it coming and ran between its legs, stopping safely behind it.

Just as he was feeling the fight was over, the golem put its whole body into pulling the arm free. But it didn't come free of the temple mound. Stonelike sinews stretched out where the shoulder met torso. With a grinding crunch the arm tore free.

Showing no signs of pain, the golem turned on him, its ghastly expression still frozen on its face. But all it saw of Knight was his back, quickly shrinking as he ran around the temple, hoping to make up the distance between him and Ridley before he reached the camp.

With a healthy head start on the golem, Knight couldn't feel its thunderous footfalls, but he could hear the trees in its path snapping. He gave a quick glance over his shoulder and saw the one-armed golem fifty feet back, running straight for him. Trees shattered and fell as the giant cleared a path.

Knight had no such luxury. As the jungle grew dense, he had to weave his way through trees and over large root systems that spread out like Medusa's mane of snakes.

But he could see Ridley ahead once more.

And the camp beyond, glowing with artificial light.

Suddenly he was through the trees and in a clearing. Willing his body to move faster despite the burning in his lungs and the ache in his legs, Knight closed to within shooting distance once again.

A grove of trees separated the clearing from the camp where an unknown number of researchers hid from the weather. He needed to stop Ridley *now*.

Taking aim, Knight ignored the loud crack of trees behind him as the golem entered the clearing. He ignored Ridley's phony shouts for help. The rain. The lightning. The thunder. All his attention was on his aim. In the fraction of a second when his running body reached the top of a step he pulled the trigger. The bullet spun out of the gun barrel, cut through the rain, and covered the distance to Ridley.

A large chunk of flesh exploded from Ridley's kneecap. He stumbled, lurching forward. It was the pause Knight was hoping for. He stopped running and took careful aim.

The golem charged across the clearing. Geysers of mud burst into the air around its heavy, stumplike feet. It reached out.

Knight unloaded a full clip of ammo into Ridley, striking his legs and head several times.

Ridley fell in a heap, landing in a patch of grass.

The golem fell with him.

It landed facedown with a boom that rivaled the thunder. Carried forward by its momentum, it slid through the grass and mud, pushing up a mound in front of it. It stopped only feet from Knight's position with a pile of earth half covering its head.

Knight looked back at the golem, letting out the breath he'd been holding.

Lightning lit the scene.

The golem was immobile and in pieces.

And Ridley was . . .

Knight ran to the flattened grass that marked Ridley's fall. Something was there, but it wasn't Ridley's body. He knelt down, turning on his flashlight. A gray mass in the shape of a man's body rest atop the grass.

"What the . . ."

Knight put his fingers in the material. It was cold and wet. He scooped some up and rubbed it between his fingers. Then he smelled it. The scent brought back memories of digging the stuff out of river bottoms as a child. He knew what it was, and what it meant.

Hearing Bishop and Queen arrive behind him, he turned to them.

"Did you get him?" Queen asked, catching her breath.

Knight stepped aside, showing them the mass of wet, gray material. "It's clay," he said. "This wasn't Ridley. It was a golem."

FIFTY-SEVEN
Wiltshire, England

THE STINK HIT King first—a mixture of copper, feces, and something unidentifiable but equally grotesque. Before he saw the disemboweled corpse, he knew it was there. A man wearing a baseball hat and a camera around his neck lay ten feet away. His body had been folded backward—head resting on heels—and his gut had split open. King drew his weapon and surveyed the parking lot.

Bodies were everywhere, torn apart and crushed. King had seen a similar scene before and recognized the work of a merciless golem. Several cars burned. Screams rolled over the hills from the distance. People were still alive, but given the high pitch of their screams they were either being killed or expected to be at any moment. "Let's go!" King said, running into the lot and heading for their car.

Before reaching the vehicle he could see something was wrong. The driver's side tire was bent at an odd angle. When he reached it, he found the whole front end imploded. Something huge had crushed the car.

The ground shook.

Something was still out there.

King closed his eyes in dread. "He wouldn't . . ."

"What is it?"

King didn't answer, he just ran for the tunnel that led beneath the road. He entered the tunnel at full speed, made his way through, and rounded the ramp on the far side. At the top he saw his fears realized.

Stonehenge was missing.

Circles of large pits were all that remained of the ancient monument. Knowing a golem constructed from the bluestones of Stonehenge wouldn't be hard to find, King spun around and found the giant much closer than he expected. Standing thirty feet tall, the gray giant was as large as it was featureless. But even without a face of any kind, it glowed with malice. And right then, the target of its rage was a ruby red, double-decker tour bus.

Lauren.

Not only was the bus in mortal danger, but it was also their best chance of escape. Realizing this at the same time, both men hopped the chain-link fence and waved down the bus. It screeched to a halt next to them and the doors opened.

"Get in!" Lauren shouted.

As Alexander leaped up the steps into the bus, King said, "Let me drive."

Lauren complied immediately, closing the doors as King took the driver's seat, threw the bus into drive, and gunned the gas. Looking in the rearview he could see the golem nearly upon them and gaining. His only chance of escape was to outmaneuver the behemoth.

Right, King thought, *I'm going to outmaneuver this thing in a double-decker bus.*

The bus gained speed quickly as they headed downhill, and maintained it at the bottom, but King saw a new problem ahead. The tunnel they had followed from the Durrington Walls to the tomb hidden beneath Stonehenge had collapsed, creating an impassable sinkhole that stretched the distance.

"Hang on!" King shouted, yanking the wheel and sending them into a sharp left turn. The driver's side tires lifted off the ground for a moment, but King turned the wheel the other way and righted them. The bus crashed through the fence that lined the road.

King saw the large golem pass by behind them, unable to turn as quickly. But it reached out with its long arm and struck the back of the bus. The back half of the upper deck was torn away with a shriek of metal.

Lauren screamed, ducking with her hands over her head. "What the hell is that thing!"

King looked back, his view clear thanks to the missing back half of the bus. They had gained ground on the golem, but it hadn't given up the chase. "You know the story about Merlin using giants to carry the stones to Stonehenge?"

Lauren looked incredulous. "Yeah?"

"It's not a story." He looked back again. The golem was gaining as the bus fought against the slick soil of the field they were speeding through. "Though I suppose no one needed to carry the stones if they could carry themselves."

Lauren let out a nervous laugh. "Please just drive."

King steered the bus through a second fence and onto a straight dirt road that was part of a large grid crisscrossing through the fields. With a road beneath them, they began distancing themselves from the golem again, taking the large vehicle up to eighty miles per hour. The copious amount of potholes made the drive rough, but it wouldn't be catching them any time—

"Incoming!" Alexander shouted.

King whipped around and saw a large rectangular stone hurtling through the air toward them.

"It's throwing parts of itself!" Lauren shouted.

King watched the stone sail overhead. It crashed into the road, twenty feet ahead. He turned away, plowing into the field. A second stone slammed into the field to their right. King veered back on the road and shouted at the bus as he pushed the gas pedal all the way down. "C'mon you piece of shit! Move!"

A loud crash rang out as the bus shook violently. King looked back and found one of the small Stonehenge stones hanging impaled in the ceiling. Had it been one of the larger stones, they would all be dead.

"Something's happening," Lauren shouted.

Looking back, King saw the golem fall to its knees, still reaching out for them but unable to move. Then it fell to pieces, reducing Stonehenge to an unceremonious pile of giant stones. King had no doubt the stones could be returned to their proper place, but the destruction of a national treasure such as this would draw unwanted attention. "We need to get out of the country," he said to Alexander.

Alexander opened his cell phone and dialed a number. "Ready the plane," he said, and then hung up.

Lauren looked back and forth at the two men. "Who the bloody hell are you two?"

King drove the bus onto a main road and pulled over. "It's better if you don't know who we are," King said. "And it's better if you never remember seeing us . . . for your sake."

Lauren gave a quick nod. "Just be glad I'm insured or I would have killed you both myself."

As a car drove up and stopped, King and Alexander both exited the bus. King drew his weapon. "Out of the car!"

The man inside went wide-eyed. He turned the car off and exited, the keys held in a raised shaking hand. King took the man's keys and said, "I'll make sure you get the car back."

The man bobbed his head to acknowledge that King had addressed him and stepped away.

King slid into the driver's seat as Alexander climbed into the passenger's side.

Inside the car, King asked, "Where to?"

Alexander held up a chunk of the Stonehenge bluestone that had impaled the bus. "Back to Israel."

"You think Davidson can figure out how to resurrect a golem?"

"If he can, we might learn how to kill it."

The plan made sense to King. When it came to the unknown, research and understanding usually won over brute force. Though he doubted Davidson would be happy to see them again. He steered the car around the bus and gave Lauren a subtle nod of thanks as he passed.

The stunned driver of the car approached Lauren and looked over her ruined bus. "Who the hell were they?"

Lauren shrugged. "I have no idea."

FIFTY-EIGHT
Siberia, Russia

ROOK'S EYES BLINKED open to the sound of a creaking door. Disoriented from the cold, lack of sleep, and loss of blood, Rook almost called out to the visitor, but came to his senses in time. He drew his .50 caliber Desert Eagle handgun and inched toward the door. He would defend this refuge if need be, but prayed the visitor wasn't aggressive. He barely had the energy to pull the trigger, let alone find a new place to hide.

He had run north for days. And the farther north Rook ran, the colder it got. The patrols searching for him had dropped away along with the temperature, but the chill threatened to drain what was left of his strength. After fleeing through woods, across rivers, and over mountains, he had finally evaded the Russian military. Not that the Russians needed to put a bullet into him to kill him. His failing health would do him in on its own. His body shook from cold and fever. His mind spun with each step. If not for the cabin he had found, deep in the pine forest, he would have died from exposure the previous night.

The cabin, which consisted of three rooms—a living room that also served as a kitchen and dining room, a bathroom, and a small bedroom—was quaint and casually decorated with quilts, a few cracking landscape paintings, and a reindeer head mounted on the wall. White lace curtains hung in the windows. Dried wildflowers sat in a small vase atop a table big enough for two. It smelled of pine, mildew, and animal furs, which covered two chairs in the corner next to a small bookcase.

He paused at the bedroom door, leaning one hand against the wall for support. With several shotgun pellets still lodged in his side he had to fight to not grunt in pain. He focused on the sounds coming from the living room. He heard the thumping footfalls of a single person walking over the cabin's wood floor. Then came a dragging noise.

A body, Rook thought.

He tensed, sensing the person's approach. He took a step back from the door, raising his weapon. A floorboard creaked beneath his foot.

Holding his breath, Rook waited for some sign that he'd been heard. When it came, it wasn't what he expected.

"Hello?" said a feminine voice speaking Russian. Given the tone and pitch of the woman's voice, Rook thought she sounded like his mother, who was sixty-two. Harmless. He quickly tucked his weapon into the back of his pants and speaking Russian, said, "I thought the cabin was abandoned."

The door opened slowly. A woman with gray hair tied back in a braid stood on the other side. She held a hunting rifle in her hands, aimed at Rook's chest. A dead reindeer, drained of blood, lay on the floor behind her.

Not so harmless, Rook thought. *But not yet a threat.*

She looked him up and down, her eyes freezing on his torn-up sweater and the deep, blood-red stains surrounding the wound.

"You've been shot?"

"Hunting accident."

"You did this to yourself?"

Rook wondered what the best story would be. He needed this woman's cooperation, but she was clearly a self-sufficient old hermit who might not take kindly to visitors, especially visitors stupid enough to shoot themselves. "No," he said. "I was hiking in the woods. They must have mistaken me for a deer. After they shot me, I was unconscious. I woke in the back of their truck and overheard them talking about killing me."

Rook paused, searching her eyes for some sign that she was buying his story. He saw that her anger had softened and continued. "I jumped from the truck and fled. I came across your cabin last night and took shelter from the cold."

She squinted at him and then glanced at the fireplace. "You didn't make a fire."

"I thought they might be looking for me."

She pondered this for a moment and then lowered the rifle. "You still have some buckshot in you?"

Rook nodded, and then lifted up the front of his shirt. His skin was covered in small red wounds that were surrounded by deep purple bruises.

She inspected the wounds, counting ten. "Could have been worse. Had the shooter been closer or a better shot, you might be dead."

Though he hated to admit it, the woman was right. Not only had the

Russian military got the jump on him, killing his entire team, but a simple farmer had as well. For him, it was an unforgivable failure.

As the woman moved to the kitchen area and rummaged through some drawers, she said, "I'm Galya, by the way."

Rook came out of his thoughts and replied, "Stanislav. You can call me Stan."

Galya returned with a tray, which held a sharp knife, a pair of tweezers, needle and thread, vodka, and a glass. "Now then, Stan, lets take those pellets out of you before they get infected."

FIFTY-NINE
Location Unknown

THOUGH HE WAS never truly alone, Alpha longed for contact from the outside world. He had spent so much time underground that he was beginning to feel like a creature of the underworld. More to the point, he still looked like one. And Adam, who was always present, was just as eager to be freed from their subterranean existence. They both awaited the arrival of the others with great anticipation—for their company, but also for the new puzzle pieces they had uncovered.

Cainan was the first to arrive. He walked into the stone chamber, eyes wide and a smile on his face. Though his head was as bald as both Alpha's and Adam's, it held a tan the other two envied. He looked with awe at the circle of glowing, golf ball–sized orbs that floated around the room like miniature suns. They revealed the ancient circular space that stretched two hundred feet in diameter around them. Like their other dens, Alpha had filled the center of the chamber with lab equipment, ancient resources he'd collected over the years, and specimens of every sort. But this space also contained all the communication equipment they needed to reach the ears of every man, woman, and child on the planet.

A laptop on the tabletop in the middle of the space, networked to a row of computers hidden on the side of the chamber, would manage the feed, processing the audio and relaying it to every media outlet on earth—from the largest networks to the smallest podcast. Cables snaked out of the room, some descending into the earth where they stretched for miles before connecting with phone and cable landlines. Others rose up into the ceiling, attached to an array of hidden satellite dishes that would only be revealed when the transmission had begun. Once the audio playback was complete they would no longer need to fear discovery. They would emerge from the darkness, reborn into a remade world.

The room was split into a central atrium. The ceiling looked like a hollowed-out step pyramid, rising one hundred feet at its core. This was surrounded by a ring of ten decorative columns where the ceiling was lowest, though to call them columns was a disservice. They were statues, each with hands raised to the ceiling, as though in supplication; a posture that didn't quite fit their hulking, grim forms. The outer wall beyond the statues was covered in a combination of hieroglyphs and carvings.

Cainan's attention remained on the bright orbs. He pointed to one. "Are these . . . ?"

"And God said, 'Let there be light,' and there was light," Alpha said.

"God saw that the light was good," Adam, whose voice was similar to Alpha's but distorted, as though gargled, continued, "and He *separated* the light from the darkness."

"Soon, Adam," Alpha said. "Soon."

Cainan held out a dirty white sheet laden with the weight of a small body. He placed it on the floor before Alpha and Adam. As he let go of one side it fell open revealing the sleeping face of a thirteen-year-old girl.

Alpha knelt down to Fiona and brushed her hair off her face. "She is the last?"

Cainan gave a slight nod. "And probably not cause for concern on her own. In fact, the danger she poses now is in bringing our enemies to us. Perhaps it would have been wise to kill her with the others?"

"I find live bait works best," Alpha said. "And having one more test subject on hand never hurts."

"You really want King to find us?"

"I want to take everything away from him. I want him to see it slip away." Alpha rolled his neck to one side. "I am simply returning the favor he extended me."

"There is nothing to fear from King," Adam said. "With her here, he will approach with caution rather than overwhelming brute force."

"She gives us the advantage," Alpha finished. "Bring her."

Alpha led Cainan down a short tunnel, stopping in front of a small, carved-out alcove that had once been used to store building supplies. "Put her in."

With Fiona placed inside the space, Alpha crouched next to her.

Cainan leaned against the wall. "Even if King can find us, how do you know he'll get here in time? If he's out there"—he motioned to the cave ceiling but referred to the world beyond—"when the time comes he'll change with the rest of them."

"He'll make it on time," Alpha said before tugging something loose from Fiona. "He's the kind of man who doesn't miss a deadline, and the clock is ticking."

Alpha held up Fiona's insulin pump, stood, and smashed it against the wall. He picked up the ruined device and handed it to Cainan. "Put this someplace King will find it."

Cainan smiled. "Tick tock."

Alpha matched the smile. "He'll waste no time tracking her down."

After the pair left the cell, Alpha whispered to the walls. The stone shook and stretched out. Soon, all but a small slit merged into solid stone. A noise from the central chamber caught their attention. They hurried back to find Mahaleel studying the inscriptions on the walls.

"This is fascinating," Mahaleel said as the others entered.

"Do you have it?" Alpha asked, his impatience oozing from every syllable.

Mahaleel was unfazed. He waggled his finger toward one of the research tables. "There."

Alpha found a padded satchel on the table, opened it, and began unwrapping the object contained within.

"Have you deciphered all of this?" Mahaleel asked.

"Of course," Adam said, also sounding annoyed, but not being preoccupied with opening the package, he turned and faced Mahaleel, who had been joined by Cainan in his inspection of the walls. "But there was nothing to be learned. It is a warning, carved into the stones after the language fracture." Adam waved his small arm in the air dramatically quoting: "'The language of the ancients has been diluted. May each tongue carry its knowledge with wisdom lest the wrath of the Originator'—capital O—'whose will can protect or destroy all things, return to this world. Do not be corrupted by temptation. For if his words are used for evil again, the guardians shall descend from on high and lay waste to the tainted.' It carries on like that all around the room. Fire and brimstone."

"Who is the Originator?" Mahaleel asked.

"God," Adam replied.

Cainan turned away from his close inspection of the hieroglyphs. "Have we considered that the Originator spoken of on these walls might not be God?" The others, even Alpha, looked at him. "What if the Originator was a man? After all, what we're attempting is nothing less."

Alpha nodded and held out the stone tablet that Mahaleel had brought. It contained an inscription readable only to those whose understanding of the ancient language was comprehensive. And right now, only Alpha and Adam could claim such understanding. The key to unlock the human mind was in their grasp. "Thanks to Merlin, we are one step closer." He turned his head to Adam's. "Our time is near."

FOUND

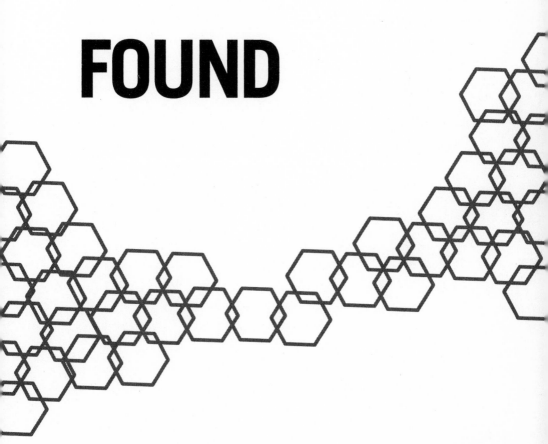

SIXTY
Haifa, Israel

STANDING NEAR THE top of Mount Carmel, the Crown Plaza Hotel looked like a stark white modern-art waffle. At road level it stood five stories tall, much of it used up by the lobby. Five more floors were hidden in the rear as the building descended the mountain's slope.

King and Alexander had parked several blocks away and walked to the hotel, winding their way through a confusing maze of streets and alleys surrounding the hotel, just in case they had a tail. As they walked the final block, the hotel clearly in view, King decided to broach yet another topic he'd been wondering about.

He ran a hand through his hair and asked, "You've been alive for what, twenty-five hundred years?"

"Give or take a few decades," Alexander replied with a grin, a lit cigar clenched between his teeth.

"And in that time, you've done what? Other than the myths you're known for, have you been anyone else in history?" A straight answer might not help him figure out exactly what Alexander was up to now, but it might give him some indication about the kind of man he was, or had been.

"You mean, have I been anyone important? A king. A general."

King just waited for an answer.

"George Washington."

As King whipped his head toward Alexander the man burst out laughing.

"I was being serious," King said, realizing a straight answer out of Alexander might be more impossible than cracking the secret of immortality, which to his knowledge had been accomplished twice already. He stepped ahead of Alexander and opened the hotel's front door. "After you, Mr. President." Alexander snubbed out the cigar in the hotel's outdoor ashtray and entered the hotel. King gave the street and parking lot a quick glance. No one had followed them. Not that he could see, anyway.

The hotel lobby was four stories tall capped by a grand arched ceiling. Tall windows and an array of sconces flooded the gaping space with light. Four palm trees, covered in white lights, stood in the center. It looked one part Hollywood at Christmas and one part opulent Arabian palace. King was fond of neither look, but still could not take his eyes off the surreal lobby. He had waited outside when they dropped Davidson off and had yet to see the hotel's interior.

"You haven't answered my question," King said. But Alexander just kept on walking, heading straight for the elevator.

Alexander entered the elevator and hit the button for the fifth floor, which was directly over the lobby. He didn't even acknowledge that King had spoken.

Growing impatient, King said, "Have you done *anything* meaningful with your life? Cured a disease? Freed an oppressed people? Anything at all?"

Alexander remained stoic.

"You haven't, have you?" King grew angry at the thought. Alexander had infinite resources, a devout following of Herculean Society members, immortality, and a genius intellect; nothing should have been out of reach for him. "In twenty-five hundred years you haven't done a damn thing."

Alexander looked at him with a smile. "I can tell you one thing I've done," he said. "I've learned to not let angry men with no concept of time ruffle my feathers. One hundred years from now, I will have all but forgotten this conversation. I live outside your understanding of time. Like a chess player, I can set things in motion and not see the resulting goal until several moves later, which for me could be hundreds of years. Sometimes longer."

"Then why do you give a damn about what's happening now?"

"Because my opponent is cheating."

At least it was an answer, King thought, though he knew it was only a half-truth, if that.

A digital chime rang out and the doors opened. Alexander exited the elevator and headed down the hall. King followed behind him, thinking about what he'd said. Could his endgame be hundreds of years off? If so, did it really even matter? King would be long dead and the human race was likely to nuke itself into oblivion by then. Or was it all a smoke screen? Was the endgame just around the corner and Ridley's actions putting it in jeopardy? Alexander might be working toward something begun during the time of Jesus. King shook his head. Ignorance *was* bliss, which was why he was starting to feel so unhappy.

Alexander knocked on the door of suite 907. They could hear movement behind the door. Davidson was no doubt peering at them through the peephole. The deadbolt slid away and the door opened a crack. The chain lock kept it from opening all the way.

Davidson peeked out at them, his eyes nervous.

"It's us," King assured him.

"Right. Sorry." The door shut and the chain was pulled away. Davidson opened the door again and let them in.

It was a large hotel room, standard in most every way—queen-sized bed, a TV, a single lounge chair, and a small desk. What made it different from other hotel rooms was the glossy hardwood floor, the large window split into large waffle squares, and the amazing view of the Mediterranean it provided. The desk was covered in hotel stationery. Notes in Hebrew and mathematical equations covered the pages. Several room service trays holding half-eaten food sat on the still-made checkered bedspread.

Davidson closed the door behind them, locked both locks, and headed to the desk. He sat down, looking disheveled. His face, which had been smooth the previous day, was rough with stubble, and his yellow dress shirt was wrinkled and covered in a big red stain. King took note of the stain.

"You okay?"

Davidson looked down at his shirt. "Oh, yes. It's marinara."

Alexander glanced at the large number of room service trays. "I see you've been taking advantage of my hospitality."

"I, well, yes." Davidson looked to the floor. "But I was up all night and have some new thoughts on the golem."

Alexander sat down in the room's lounge chair and opened his arms as though to say, "Let's hear it."

King sat down on the bed beside the trays. He eyed a plate of french fries. He hadn't eaten anything substantial in days. Not that french fries would provide much in the way of nourishment, but they would fill his belly.

Davidson noted his attention. "They're only an hour old."

Alexander cleared his throat as King dug into the food.

"Sorry. Ahh. What's important to realize about a golem is that they are not actually living. I suppose you could say they were quasi-living, but they don't possess true life. Now, somehow, which I have yet to fully understand, inanimate objects are being animated in a way that mimics life, but these golems lack intelligence. I suspect they have a very primitive knowledge imbued into the atomic structure by their creator—the ability to walk, the desire to kill a certain target—but they can't communicate. They can't reproduce. They don't consume or digest. Based on the files Alexander faxed over—"

"What files?" King asked. He had no idea Alexander had been in touch with the professor. He shot Alexander an annoyed glance as Davidson handed him a folder. He opened it and found several newspaper clippings about the attacks on Fort Bragg, a handwritten detailed account about their experience at Stonehenge. But what really held King's attention were the several classified documents from the U.S. military, including surveillance-camera still shots from Bragg. He wanted to ask Alexander where he got the documents, but already knew the answer. The Herculean Society was in every nation and in every government.

That's what Alexander had done in twenty-five hundred years. He might very well control the whole world without a single person knowing. And his direct involvement now might only be because Ridley threatened to upset the balance.

The thought filled King with anger and he wondered if Alexander was so deeply entrenched that he could feed missions to the Chess Team? Just how far did the man's influence reach? *Questions for later,* he decided. "Go on," he said, placing the files on the bed beside him.

"Based on the reports in those files, the golems seem to contain enough energy for a short duration. In every case, the golems simply return to their inanimate state after about fifteen minutes. Without a continued utterance from its creator a golem cannot continue living, err, existing."

"Like someone chanting?" King asked.

"No, more like a recharge. Something that keeps it energized and on task. It could be as simple as repeating the phrase that animated it in the first place. I'm not really sure. But this is an apparent weakness, time. And brains, or lack thereof. I would compare them to ancient missiles. Their force can be spurred into action and directed, but they cannot be sustained indefinitely and then can be outsmarted."

King had to admit the professor's assessment seemed accurate, and useful to a point. But he had hoped for more. Given the anxious glances Davidson shot Alexander, he had, too.

"You mentioned a sample," Davidson said to Alexander.

Alexander reached into his suit coat and pulled out a small chunk of bluestone. King's distrust of Alexander continued to grow as his role in the mission became secondary to Alexander's whims. And that threatened King's personal goal of finding Fiona. If Alexander's objective shifted, King might be left high and dry. He would continue, of course, but with time short for Fiona, the delay could be deadly.

Davidson took the stone and looked it over. "This is actually a piece of a golem animated from the stones of Stonehenge?"

"It is," Alexander said.

Holding it up close to his eyes, Davidson stared at the stone as the bright sunlight glimmered off the blue specks. "We need a lab."

Alexander stood. "I have one waiting." He stood, leading the way out of the room.

Davidson eagerly followed.

King hesitated for a moment. Could he trust Alexander? If he turned bad, could he be stopped? Deciding the answer to both questions was an unquestionable "no," King took a handful of fries and followed after them.

THE LAB WAS both impressive and sketchy. The equipment looked new, or at least rarely used, and the small warehouse that held it was in a seedy part of town. In fact, everything looked like it had been brought in and rigged to be used specifically for this occasion and would likely disappear when they were done.

King didn't like that everything he had done since heading to Rome was outside the reach of U.S. resources, but he couldn't deny the results. Though those results were slow in coming this afternoon. The hot Mediterranean sun beat down on the metal building, heating its insides like an oven. Even the mighty Hercules had shed his suit coat and unbuttoned the first few buttons on his shirt.

"It's too bad your people didn't think to bring in an air conditioner," King said.

"I'll be sure to have them take care of it next time," Alexander replied.

As King wondered whether or not Alexander was joking he realized that the man had just confirmed his suspicions. This *was* a temporary lab.

Tension had King's body in a tight grip. Unless they found some kind of lead soon, their investigation will have run dry. King checked the date and time on his watch. Day four was well under way and Fiona was now out of insulin. He gripped the edge of the lab table he was leaning on, feeling his anger rise.

"I've got something," Davidson said, backing away from a microscope he'd been standing over for the past ten minutes.

King stood straight and headed for Davidson, eager for news.

"At first glance, the sample looks like any other stone, and to the human eye acts the way we all expect a stone to act—like nothing at all. But at the microscopic level, well, take a look." Davidson switched out the slides. "This is a normal stone."

King arrived before Alexander and took a look. He saw a patchwork of stone crystals mashed together.

"Stones are composed of varying sizes of mineral grains. Differing amounts of minerals give us limestone, granite, basalt, et cetera. In this case we have Preseli spotted dolerite containing chunks of plagioclase feldspar, which adds to its bluish tint, especially when wet. The point is, the minerals contained in stone are compressed in a random formation that does not shift unless the stone is broken." Davidson switched out the slide when King stood back. "This is a sample of the bluestone."

King looked again. The stone crystals were now an orderly formation of overlapping minerals. Their placement throughout was still random, but it was as though they had been snapped into an organized grid. "It looks like chain mail," he said.

"Exactly, which would give the stone flexibility, and the ability to merge, at least temporarily with similarly affected stones. Like Velcro. Or a zipper."

Alexander quickly looked at both slides. "Anything else?"

"It has no traces of DNA, if that's what you're wondering," Davidson said. "As I mentioned before, they're not living. Simply animated by some kind of energy."

The statement struck a chord in King's memory. His family had taken a southwestern summer trip in an RV. The strange site had been one of their stops, at the insistence of his father. "This isn't totally unheard of in the natural world. The sailing stones in Death Valley move on their own. Some are as heavy as eighty pounds but travel across the flat desert appearing to move under their own power. They leave grooves in the ground hundreds of feet long, make ninety-degree turns, and sometimes travel in pairs before breaking off in different directions."

"Amazing," Davidson said. "Are there theories about how they move?"

"Heavy rain coupled with high winds is the best I've heard of," King said.

"Perhaps wind alone is enough?" Davidson said. "If stone can be affected by sound, such as with a golem, perhaps there is a rock formation that produces a certain tone at the right frequency, something that sends a simple command: move! Has anyone looked at the stone's microscopic structure?"

"They didn't talk about that on our family vacation," King said.

Alexander began switching off the lab equipment. "If there's nothing else, I think we should be go—"

"We're not going anywhere yet," King said, wondering how much more Alexander had planned without his knowledge. "You may think the world is your playground, that you have the right to go anywhere, do anything, and treat the human race like game pieces, but you don't. I, on the other hand, represent the wishes of the president of the United States, a man with real power and authority in this world. And I am in charge of this mission. Not you."

A darkness consumed Alexander's face. He turned to King, staring him down with eyes that showed a desire to kill. King had no doubt it had been a long time since someone spoke down to him, and he did not take it well. But King didn't falter. Instead, he turned his eyes away from Alexander's glare and looked at Davidson. "Is there anything more to glean from these stones?"

"I . . . I would need more samples. Different samples."

"Like this?" came a deep voice from the darkness at the end of the warehouse. A figure emerged holding a glass jar. Inside it was a lump of gray material. The man holding it was Bishop. Queen and Knight followed him.

King greeted the others with a nod. He had made a call to Deep Blue shortly after leaving the hotel, requesting the team's deployment to Israel. He knew they would arrive quickly thanks to the *Crescent* and had left his cell phone on so they could track his location. With the majority of his team present, he felt a renewed calm and measure of control return to the situation. This King was a pawn to no man, even one who couldn't be killed.

Alexander glared at King and with a raised voice said, "You had no right to bring them here without my knowledge."

"You seemed to have access to privileged U.S. intelligence. I thought you would know."

Alexander lost his patience and stomped toward King. Davidson ducked out of the way.

King didn't flinch as Alexander stopped inches from his face. "Do I detect a hint of megalomania?" King poked him in the chest, purposely instigating a reaction. He had a point to make. "Don't like not being in control, do you . . . little man." He punctuated the statement with one last poke to the chest.

When the punch came, King was expecting it. He ducked to the side, feeling the breeze of Alexander's fist pass his face. The fist smashed into a metal support beam behind King. A loud clang accompanied by the crack of breaking fingers rang in King's ear. The missed blow would have normally been enough for King to take the upper hand in any fight, but Alexander didn't react. Nor did he react to the perfectly placed punch King delivered to his side. Instead he took King's arm, spun him around and pinned him against the support beam. The impact split King's lip and the pressure on his arm would soon snap it. He fought against the pain.

"Don't be stupid. You can't win this fight alone," King said.

The pressure increased.

"And your secrecy is compromising my mission."

"Your mission? You're a fool to think yourself my equal," Alexander said between clenched teeth.

"I don't consider myself your equal," King said. "But unlike you, I'm not alone."

The barrel of a handgun tapped against the back of Alexander's skull. "Hey," Queen said. "Remember me? We met a few years ago. I never did get a chance to thank you for the help, but if you mess with my boy here, I'm going to thank you by putting a bullet in the back of your skull. And please don't fool yourself into thinking I'm incapable of hacking off that handsome head of yours and burying it in the sand."

Alexander tensed for a moment before releasing King. He stepped back and eyed Queen. "I do remember you. You're as charming as Rook."

King saw Queen tense. The confrontation between him and Alexander had been brewing and needed to be worked out. But Alexander would regret lighting this fuse with Queen. "Any word on him?" King asked, stepping in.

Queen looked at him. "Not a peep."

King turned back to Alexander. "You're welcome to stay on with us, but you need to toe the line. If I sense you working another angle from this point on, I'll drop you from the team."

Alexander stared at King for several seconds before smiling. "You're lucky I like you, King. I agree to your terms."

The look in the man's eyes revealed the agreement would last only as long as it continued to serve his needs, but King was okay with that. The reverse was true as well. He needed Alexander's knowledge and resources to track down and stop Ridley, but when they'd accomplished that, he would leave the man behind.

Seeing the confrontation ebb, Davidson stepped forward. "Um, excuse me, but did you say you had a new sample?"

Bishop handed him the jar full of gray material.

"Is this from a golem?" Davidson asked.

"Formerly known as Richard Ridley," Knight said. "Now known as Richard Hunk-of-clay."

Davidson's eyes grew wide. "This had a name? It was a . . . a human golem? Made of clay?"

Knight gave a nod.

"Fully human?"

"Until he turned to clay," Bishop said. "Before that he seemed to have all the intellect, memories, and personality of the actual Richard Ridley. He lived among people who had no idea he wasn't fully human."

"Lived with people?" Davidson asked with wide eyes. "For how long?"

Knight shrugged. "Days, maybe weeks. We're not sure yet."

"There goes your fifteen-minute continued-utterance theory," King said.

With a nodding head, Davidson said, "I should say so." He turned to King. "But this was a clay golem in the form of a man. What applies to the crude stone giants may not apply to something this . . . sophisticated."

Davidson untwisted the cover from the sample and smelled the clay. His face was pale, but excited.

"What is it?" King asked.

Davidson held the sample aloft like it was some kind of ancient treasure. "We shouldn't call this man Richard." He looked King in the eyes. "We should call him *Adam*."

SIXTY-ONE
Location Unknown

FIONA WOKE IN a new cell, similar in size and shape to the last, but the stone was now brown and flat. A small slit on one side was the only feature. It allowed air and a small amount of light into the space. But where she was didn't matter. She still needed to free herself from her bonds and set to work upon waking up.

Fiona spit a bloody clump of rope fibers onto the floor next to her. She had been working on the rope for what felt like several hours, chewing feverishly and taking breaks. Her gums had become raw and bloody, but the injury was minor and fairly painless in comparison to the pain she felt in her body. Bound tight and struggling for so long, her muscles had begun to cramp. Waves of dizziness struck. Her headache persisted and accompanied a dire thirst. She tried to ignore her discomfort and focused on her bindings, which were now held together by only a few strands of twine.

Fiona's arms shook as she pulled them apart. The fibers grew taut and tore slowly as one strand after another snapped. When the chewed rope reached its breaking point, it broke in two. Her arms flew out to her sides and then fell limp.

She was exhausted from her efforts, but her hands were free. Fighting against the tiredness gripping her body, she reached down to her feet and began untying the rope binding her ankles. What normally would have been a quick job took ten minutes as the severe tingle of full blood flow returning to her fingers made every movement agonizing.

With her feet free, Fiona stood slowly, using the wall for support. As she did, a wave of nausea struck and threatened to return her to the floor. She placed her face against the cold stone wall. She took a moment to breathe and let her body figure itself out. Once she felt a measure of balance return, she slowly bent down and touched her fingers to her toes. The stretch felt good. She stood tall again and breathed deeply. She felt better, but still quite dizzy and the headache and thirst had yet to diminish.

Moving as quietly as she could, she walked to the cell's only light source, the long slit in the stone wall. She peered through the slit, expecting to see a guard. But there was no one there.

Why would they guard a cell with no doors? Fiona thought.

The space directly outside the cell was just another stone wall. She moved to the left, angling her view so she could see down the hallway. It opened up ten feet beyond. The light was brightest there.

And there were shadows.

Moving.

And a voice. She listened, but couldn't understand the quiet words being spoken like a chant. A moment later she heard something she did understand.

"Damnit!" The shout was masculine, deep, and held a supernatural menace—as though the word hadn't just been spoken by a single man, but by two, out of sync by a fraction of a second.

The chanting started up again. The language was again unknown to her, but bits and pieces struck a chord. Portions of words sounded familiar. Tones. Inflections. Not enough to figure out what was being said, but some part of what the man said was familiar to her. She realized she was hearing fragments of Siletz, a dead language to all but her.

The chant ended in frustration once again with the pound of a fist. She jumped at the sharp noise, but remained quiet. She was intent on hearing anything and everything going on outside her cell.

What she heard next, shook her to the core. "Please, sir," a man said in a weak, heavily accented voice. "No more. I know nothing. I do not know what you are asking."

"I'm not *asking* anything," the deep voice said. This was followed by an angry shout and the smack of flesh on flesh.

Without seeing what was happening, Fiona could imagine what was going on. There was a man, bound, maybe sitting in a chair. He thought he was being interrogated, but the other man, the one with the deep voice, wasn't asking questions. Then what was he doing?

She heard one of them spit. She wasn't sure which one until the captive said, "If I knew what you wanted I would tell you nothing! American pig!" And then he spat again.

There were two shouts. One of anger. One of fear. The smack of wood striking stone came next. The chair had hit the floor. Hard breathing. Wet clicks. A shifting scuff of feet on the floor.

Her eyes widened as her imagination created the most likely image. The captive had been knocked over and was being strangled. The killer stood, cleared his throat, and then spoke the strange language again, this time with practiced ease. "Versatu elid vas re'eish clom, emet."

She repeated the words in her head, not knowing the meaning, but determined to remember them if they turned out to be important. King had always stressed the importance of collecting intelligence before taking action. And she had nothing better to do in her featureless cell.

A new shadow shifted in the room, this one mobile. Each step the figure took was marked by a loud grinding of stone.

"Get me some water," the deep voice said.

The rough footsteps faded into the distance, then returned a moment later. She heard the man sip some water. Her mouth salivated. She wondered if she should ask for some, but decided against it. If the man knew she was awake and free of her bonds she would never learn anything.

"Tisioh fesh met," the man said.

The second shadow stopped shifting.

As she realized she had just heard the creation and undoing of one of the stone monsters she had seen at Fort Bragg and her previous prison, fear consumed her, chasing the words from her memory. The fear was then replaced by chills. She couldn't remember a time in her life when she felt more ill.

Oh no, she thought as the reality of her situation finally sank in.

She lifted up her shirt, looking for her insulin pump. It was gone. Nausea surged with her emotions, threatening to send her to the floor. She breathed deeply, willing it to pass, and cleared her mind.

It must have fallen off when they took me, she thought.

And now she understood why she felt so awful. The dizziness. The headache. The dehydration.

Hyperglycemia.

That normally meant she'd have a week or two before things got bad, before she slipped into a coma, or worse, died. But those numbers were for people with a regular diet and food. Drinking a lot of water would help keep her system clean, but she had none. Some people lived five to six days without water, but most died in three. Already dehydrated and feeling the first effects of hyperglycemia, she doubted she'd last another day.

She tried once again to focus on the man's words. To her frustration, she no longer remembered precisely what he'd said. Nausea coursed through her again. She fought against the urge to vomit. The effort caused her body to shake.

She moved back to her post at the slit in the wall, praying the man would say something important, hoping her father would arrive in time to put her intelligence gathering to good use. As a new voice rolled down the tunnel, rescue seemed less likely.

"We have only one more test subject," the new, gargled voice said. "Should we send for more?"

"Not yet," the deep voice replied. "We don't want to draw unnecessary attention. Not until we're ready." There was a shifting of feet and then, "If the next one doesn't survive we'll use the girl."

Fiona prayed they weren't talking about her, but knew in her core she would soon be sitting in the dead man's chair. What the men said next, solidified her fear.

"How will we know if she's truly changed?"

The man fell silent for a moment and then let out a quick laugh. "This . . . this is perfection. What better way to punctuate King's failure than to have his little girl put a knife through his heart. That's our final test. She's going to kill King."

SIXTY-TWO
Siberia, Russia

THE FUR-COVERED CORNER seat held Rook's weight without any trouble. And the fire burning in the nearby fireplace warmed the outside of his body as much as the vodka warmed him from within. But the creature comforts and alcohol did little to stifle the pain in his gut.

Galya was a ruthless surgeon. She had dug and cut into him without mercy, plucking the shotgun pellets from his flesh one at a time. After a grueling hour without anesthetic, she had finished and sewed him up. In the day since, he had tried to move as little as possible, lying in bed or sitting still while sipping vodka and watching Galya hustle around the cabin.

Despite her age, which she would not disclose, she was fit and energetic. She moved with efficiency and assuredness, tidying up the cabin and putting on a stew of potatoes, carrots, and meat from the reindeer she had shot and butchered.

She entered the cabin with fresh firewood, blowing on her hands to warm them. "Going to be another cold night."

Feeling a little tipsy from all the vodka, Rook flashed her a lopsided grin and, still speaking Russian, said, "I bet I can find a way to keep you warm."

She paused and looked at him. Her face serious and crossed with wrinkles from years of hard work. A smile spread on her face, revealing a mouth with several teeth missing. She laughed hard and sat down by the fire. "I'm more woman than you could handle, boy."

Rook chuckled. "A real Russian bear, eh?"

Galya pulled a stool, which was nothing more than a chunk of a tree, over to the fireplace and sat down. She stretched her hands out, warming them. She grew solemn. "There was a time, when this cabin wasn't occupied by myself alone, that that might have been true. But this bear is beyond her wild years. Now I'm just trying to live." She looked at Rook, forcing a grin. "Not that you can really call this living. It's closer to surviving."

"You don't like it here?"

"This is my home. It has been for twenty years." She returned her gaze to the fire. "But it has been tainted since Kolya's death two years ago. In the time since, I have kept up my duties and taken on his, simply waiting for death to rejoin us. Unfortunately for me, my mother and grandmother each lived to nearly one hundred."

"That gives you what, another fifty years left to live?" Rook said.

She gave him a wry smile. "Still trying to get me in bed?"

Rook laughed and then winced. Even a subtle flexing of his stomach sent waves of pain through his body.

Seeing his pain, Galya stood. "We best get you back into bed." She offered her hand to Rook and helped him stand.

Towering more than a foot over the old woman, Rook looked down at her with a wide grin. "I knew you couldn't resist getting me in your bed."

She swatted his chest. "Do you ever stop?"

"Not with people I like," Rook said, though he knew the truth was far more complicated. The good company, humor, and alcohol were dulling more than just a physical pain. The memories of his teammates' deaths were still fresh in his mind and he hoped to forget them, if only for a night.

With one arm around Rook's back she helped him toward the bedroom. But before they reached the door, she paused. Rook noticed her attention turn swiftly toward the front windows. "Someone's here," she said.

The rumble of an engine grew louder and slowed with a squeak of brakes.

Adrenaline spiked inside Rook. They were here for him. "I'll go out the back window."

"You think it's the men who shot you?" she asked.

"Do you get any visitors out here? Ever?"

Her frown answered the question. No.

Leaving Rook by the bedroom door, she moved to the front window and peeked out. Two men in camouflage uniforms stepped out of a black SUV. At first glance they appeared to be the very hunters Rook had spoken of, but the weapons they held—AK-74M assault rifles—identified them as Russian military. She swung around toward Rook. "You were shot by the military?"

Rook wasn't sure if Galya would turn him in, but there was no sense in lying to her. "Yes."

"Will they kill you now?"

Rook reached behind his back and drew his handgun. "They'll try."

Galya froze as indecision gripped her. The two men outside approached the cabin, weapons raised. "Don't leave the cabin," she told him, then reached for her rifle.

"Wait, what are you—"

"Stanislav, I'm tired of waiting." She approached the door and stopped. Rook winced as he tried to cross the room to her. But the pain was too great. "I have a brother, Maksim Dashkov. He's on the northern coast, in Severodvinsk. He can get you out of the country."

Rook's concern over Galya's intentions diminished as it appeared she intended for him to flee out the back, as he had suggested. "You're sure he'll help?"

"Tell him it was my dying wish."

As the statement sunk in, Galya opened the door, stepped outside with a friendly greeting, then raised her rifle and fired. Rook saw a puff of pink outside the window as the single shot found its mark in one of the soldier's heads. But Galya never got off another shot. The second soldier unleashed a barrage. Many of his rounds missed and tore into the cabin, forcing Rook to duck. But five found Galya's body. As she fell, her rifle dropped inside the cabin.

The remaining soldier, unaware of Rook's presence, approached Galya's body. He kept his weapon aimed at her, pushing her body with his foot. She was clearly dead, but the soldier, angered by the death of his comrade, raised his rifle and took aim at Galya's head.

"Hey, buddy," Rook said.

The soldier whipped toward Rook, but didn't get a chance to fire. Rook pulled the trigger of Galya's rifle and shot the man in the chest. He dropped his weapon and fell to his knees. He looked at Rook with a mixture of surprise and loathing before tipping forward and crashing to the pine needle–laden ground.

Rook checked Galya for signs of life despite knowing he'd find none. He placed her rifle back in her hand, closed her eyes, and kissed her cheek. "You *were* a bear. Thanks."

He hated doing what followed, but Galya was a survivor. She would understand. He took what supplies he could from the cabin, including a map, a little money, food, matches and candles, and then headed out on foot. The only way his presence could remain undetected was to leave the scene of death as it was, which meant he couldn't bury Galya's body. The authorities had to be convinced this was a tragic misunderstanding between two soldiers and an old hermit with a rifle. Otherwise they would be fresh on his trail.

It also meant he couldn't take the SUV. Feeling a little bit like David Banner at the end of every *Incredible Hulk* episode, Rook struck out walking. He headed north, toward colder weather and the possibility of freedom. He knew he could call for help and get an expedited route out of the country, but he wasn't sure he wanted to return to that life. Like Galya, he needed to be alone, to search his soul, and if necessary, find a meaningful way to join the dead he'd sent to Valhalla ahead of him.

SIXTY-THREE
Washington, D.C.

BOUCHER SAT BEHIND a large antique desk, leaning back in a brown leather chair that had conformed to its owner's thick body over time. As a result, the chair was uncomfortable. It didn't belong to him.

Nor did the office.

And no one knew he was there. Not the secretary sitting at the desk outside the closed doors. Not a single subordinate at the CIA. Not a single security guard. He was a ghost. But that was easy to do when your security clearance granted you access to most of Washington, including security feeds, keys, and schedules.

He'd waited for fifteen minutes now, but expected company soon. If Marrs stuck to his regular morning schedule, he'd swing through these doors, no doubt feeling light on his feet, in about thirty seconds.

Boucher passed the time by scanning the office and gleaning what he could about the man. There was a painting of Arches National Park. It was decent, but plain. There were photos of family on the desk, all smiling. All posed. A map of Utah hung opposite the painting. Diplomas. Awards. Certificates. An American flag stood behind the chair. Several framed photos with world leaders and former presidents hung between the windows.

Everything in the room screamed, *I care about Utah and the United States.*

But it was all for show. No one who really cared about public service and the good of the people worked so hard to show it. Marrs put on a convincing show and ran his mouth like a good politician, but when it came to actions, to really doing what had to be done for the good of the people, the man was impotent.

Boucher almost got up and left. Helping Marrs in any way, even if it was the right thing to do, made him queasy. But before he could think on it, the door opened. Marrs's silhouette filled the door.

"Maggie, why in the hell are the shades drawn?" he said.

Boucher heard an "I dunno" from the outer office. Marrs shook his head, entered, and closed the door behind him.

With a quick tug, Boucher sent the shade shooting up. It struck the top of the window frame and spun with a force that nearly launched it free. Marrs shrieked and jumped back, dropping his briefcase.

Marrs was squinting in the fresh light. "Who's there?"

Boucher didn't answer. He enjoyed the terrified expression on Marrs's face. But his eyes must have adjusted to the light because he suddenly recognized his visitor. "Boucher?" Marrs circled the desk. "Don't you have grunts to bug offices?"

"I do."

"Then what are you doing here?"

"Deciding."

Marrs picked up the phone and dialed a three-digit extension that Boucher recognized as the number for security. But he didn't react. Didn't need to. The phone was unplugged.

"Deciding what?" Marrs asked before putting the phone to his ear. When he heard no ringing or dial tone he knew the phone had been disconnected.

"If you're the right person."

Marrs had taken a step back toward the door. A bit of fear had crept back into his face.

"How about this," Marrs said. "You can tell me what you decided from the inside of a cell. CIA chief or not, this is illegal."

When he took another step toward the door, Boucher launched up, slid over the desk, and reached Marrs just as he was turning around to run. He took hold of the senator's pinky and twisted it back. The man yelped as the digit neared the breaking point. Boucher pulled him back, leading him by the finger, and sat him down in a chair opposite the desk.

"Did Duncan send you to bully me? Is that it?" Marrs rubbed his finger. "I'm not going to back down."

"I don't want you to back down," Boucher said, turning to the window so Marrs couldn't see how hard these words were to say. "There's a folder on your desk. Open it."

Marrs looked at the desk. A folder sat at its center. He stared at it for a moment. Distrustful. But curiosity got the better of him. He leaned forward, snagged the folder, and opened it.

He froze on the first page, reading every word. When he finished, he asked, "Is this real?"

"All of it, yes."

Marrs quickly scanned the rest of the documents.

"As you can see, I've been keeping a record of all the poor choices President Duncan has made. I can't sit and watch things continue to unfold like this. I've . . . admired your passion and thought you might be the right man to take it to. The man who can do what needs to be done."

Marrs slowly closed the folder. He looked horrified. For a moment, Boucher thought Marrs might back down. Was this too much? Did he lack the guts to really put his words into action?

"This will destroy him," Marrs said. He wasn't gloating. Just stunned.

But then a smile began to show. He was up to it all right. "You'll testify in support of this?"

Boucher knelt down, picked up the phone line, and reconnected it to the wall jack. "I will."

Marrs picked up the phone and dialed a three-digit number. A phone on the other side of the office door rang once before being answered. "Call a press conference," Marrs said. "Get me everyone. Tell them I have proof."

Boucher heard the secretary's voice through the door. "About what?"

"About everything."

SIXTY-FOUR
Haifa, Israel

"WE DON'T HAVE time for this," King said in frustration. His concern for Fiona coupled with the soaring temperature in the makeshift warehouse lab made him impatient.

"We'll find her," Queen assured him, her confidence unwavering, but her own thoughts half a world away with Rook.

"Tell me again what we have," King said.

Knight looked over several photos that had been spread out on the table. He had taken them before leaving El Mirador. They showed the cuneiform scrawled on the walls beneath la Danta pyramid. "Cuneiform. We can't read it, but we know its origin is in Sumer. That coupled with the oversized sandfish you bagged points to Iraq."

"Which is a big country with plenty of places to hide," King said.

"And with all the troops still stationed there, one of the last places we would think to find someone hiding from us," Bishop added.

King looked at Davidson, who was waiting for test results at a laptop. "How long, Professor?"

"A few more minutes." He turned to King. "I've been thinking. The level of violence you have described is beyond anything attributed to golems before. They've been killers, to be sure, but the wholesale killing of thousands is unheard of."

"What's your point?" Alexander said. His voice had been tinged with impatience since the confrontation with King.

"A warning I suppose. Back in my office—which no longer exists, thank you—I mentioned the cycle of, what's the right word? Evil. The cycle of evil is said to be transferred from master to golem upon creation and from the golem to master after it has killed."

"Black hearts," Alexander said. "I remember."

"From what I've heard, this Ridley character was dark to begin with."

"The darkest," Knight said. "He's willing to kill anyone and do anything to achieve his goals."

King eyed Alexander. Was he any different? Had he committed unforgivable crimes in the past? There was no way to know. The man had spent a lifetime covering his tracks and erasing himself from history.

"Then the first golems made would have contained that lack of regard for human life. And they've killed thousands over the past year?"

King nodded. He could see where Davidson's line of thought led. "And all of that death, all of that evil, has been transferred back to Ridley."

"Exactly," Davidson said. "However evil your man started out, I assure you he is now much worse."

"He is nothing," Alexander mumbled.

King wasn't sure what to make of the statement, but Queen had already shifted gears.

"When you said we should call Ridley Adam," Queen said to Davidson. "Were you referring to the biblical Adam?"

"Who was molded from clay and given life through the breath, some would say the words, of God. To breathe something into being is to speak it into being. Yes, that Adam." Davidson adjusted his glasses. "Which I find quite disturbing. Animating a golem is one thing. It's simply animating a nonliving thing. We do it all the time with vehicles, robotics. Along with artificial intelligence we can create animated creations that are far more lifelike than an actual golem, though they are far less durable and coordinated.

"But what you described with this Richard Ridley fellow goes beyond that. Using clay, his creator imbued him with what appeared to be genuine life. He was intelligent. He could speak. He emoted and coexisted with a population of people for days without raising suspicions. As amazing as this is, it is also an abomination. That Ridley is using the protolanguage to create nearly human copies of himself is narcissistic in the extreme."

"We already knew he had a god complex," Knight said.

"No," King said. "A man who can give and take life, who can cure nations or destroy them, who can perform the very act of creation, doesn't have a god complex. He wants to *be* God."

"I don't understand how clay can become human," Knight said. "It doesn't sound possible."

"Even the science world acknowledges that clay had a likely hand in the creation of life," Davidson said. "Though I disagree with the concept of accidental, random creation, there are many who believe clay catalyzed the formation of organic molecules. Take hydrothermal vents for example, life is supported there, not just by the heat provided by the vents but also the vast amount of clay surrounding them and expelled by them. I agree it's a stretch, but clay seems to be at the center of both religious and scientific theories on the creation of life."

"And so we end up with golems that can create golems?" Queen asked.

"I think you might need to consider a new term for the Ridley duplicates. While they return to clay after being . . . killed, they are not simply inanimate objects given the illusion of life. They are *alive*. And capable of speech. Thus capable of using the same protolanguage to create more golems."

King's phone rang. He answered it quickly and listened to the voice on the other end. "So we'll know if he enters any other countries?" King asked. "Good. Thanks for letting me know."

He hung up the phone and looked at the others. "That was Boucher. Ridley—both of them—were traveling under aliases using fake passports." He looked at Knight. "Your man at El Mirador was Enoch Richardson." He turned to Alexander. "Our man from Stonhenge was Mahaleel Richardson."

"They used the same last name?" Knight asked.

"Richardson," Bishop said. "Son of Richard."

"He's naming them after himself," Queen said. "Like they're his children."

Davidson stepped closer to the group, his expression grim. "I'm afraid their names reveal much more than the paternal feelings Ridley may have for his creations. Enoch and Mahaleel are both descendants of Adam—the biblical Adam—in a very specific genealogy leading up to Abraham and eventually to King David."

"And if you believe in it," Alexander said, "to Jesus Christ."

Davidson conceded the point with a nod. "But what is important to note is that he is naming these golems using a very specific bloodline that leads back to the creator." He turned to King. "Your earlier assessment was correct, he believes himself a god. And if he is naming them using this genealogy, you can assume there are at *least* six more of these Ridley golems."

"*Six* more?" King asked.

"Enoch is the seventh in line," Davidson said. "Before him are Jared, Mahaleel, Cainan, Enos, Seth, and Adam."

Something nagged at King. Ridley wouldn't put in so much time and effort, and risk exposing himself, without something significant to be gained. He could already live forever. Like Alexander, with time he could do anything and become anyone. The world was his eternal playground. There had to be more, something missing, something bigger. Something Alexander said during their confrontation finally clicked.

You have yet to fully realize what is at stake.

He turned to Alexander. "What do you know?"

Alexander looked indifferent.

"Tell me or you're out."

Alexander chuckled, but acquiesced. "You need to think bigger, King. Imagine the world laid out before you. You can mold it. It can be anything you want—a chessboard, a simulation, an escape. Given time and intelligence, it can be anything you want it to be."

King felt his back tense up. For the first time he was hearing exactly how Alexander viewed the world.

"Now imagine you're an impatient man not accustomed to the concept of eternity. A thousand years to remake the world is nine hundred ninety-nine years too many."

"You're saying he wants to remake the world?" Knight asked, sounding doubtful. "The whole world?"

Alexander met him with a hard stare. "Were I a less patient man, I would do the same."

The room fell silent as everyone in it reconsidered their alliances.

"But how?" Davidson asked, not understanding what Alexander implied. "Replace political figures with copies? Maybe just change the personalities of key people? How could he change the world?"

"You're still thinking small," Alexander said. "Up until twenty years ago it wouldn't have been possible. There is no fixed rule with the mother tongue. It is the unique sounds of the language that affects the changes to reality. Not the speaker."

"He's right," Davidson said. "A recording of the language would work just as well."

"Or a broadcast," King said, the full picture slamming home. With modern technology and the ancient tongue the world really could be remade, and in far less time than seven days. "He's going to remake the world."

The beep that came from the computer was quiet, but grabbed

everyone's attention like it was an atom bomb. Davidson spun toward the computer screen. Alexander stood over his shoulder, looking at the results.

"Amazing," Davidson whispered.

"What is it?" King asked.

"There are traces of human DNA in the clay," Alexander replied.

"Have you compared it to Ridley's profile?" Knight asked.

"Hold on," Davidson said, fingers working the keys. "If it's a match, it shouldn't take lo—"

The results appeared on the screen, showing two sets of DNA markers. They were identical. "They're the same," Davidson said, stunned. "I was right. This clay wasn't just an animated form resembling Richard Ridley, it *was* Richard Ridley."

He turned to Alexander, and then to King. "He was alive."

The silence that filled the room was broken by the ring of King's cell phone. The ID read Lewis Aleman. King answered the phone. "What have you got, Lew?"

"Last piece of the puzzle I hope," Aleman replied, his response delayed by a second. "I've been running the chemical composition of the clay recovered from El Mirador through our system. And, well, I found a match." He quickly followed with, "But it doesn't make sense."

"Just tell me where it's from," King said.

"Camp Alpha."

The name's familiarity struck King instantly. It was the title of the U.S. military base established in the ruins of Babylon that had been rebuilt by Saddam Hussein. A large number of servicemen were stationed there, including a regiment of marines. Babylon made sense, being the origin of the Tower of Babel story, but it was also the last place anyone would think to look. "You're sure?"

"Yup. It's straight from the Euphrates River, and I can peg it to Camp Alpha because of the unique contaminants it contains, courtesy of the U.S. of A."

Queen saw the bewildered look on King's face. "What did he find?"

"The clay is from Camp Alpha."

"Babylon," Davidson said.

Knight shook his head. "But how is he—"

"The tower," Alexander said. "He's found the Tower of Babel. He's not at Camp Alpha. He's *under* it."

A sudden boom of metal coupled with the implosion of the warehouse's metal roof made them forget all about the discovery. Large sheets of steel broke free and fell at them like giant playing cards. Honed by years of action, the instincts of the people in the room saved their lives. All but one of them managed to leap away as the giant blades fell from above.

A slender sheet of metal fluttered high above Davidson for a moment, held aloft by its surface area. But Davidson, whose reaction was to flinch away and raise his hands, remained in the same position as the metal sheet tilted to one side and slid down like a guillotine. It sliced off his hand at the forearm. He opened his mouth to scream, but the sheet then struck between his shoulder and neck, shaving off a side of ribs and penetrating down to his gut. The weight of the giant metal playing card pulled him over. King saw the man, nearly cleaved in half. Davidson was dead.

"This way!" Alexander shouted, leading the team out the back as a very large, unseen attacker pounded through the roof and made short work of the lab beneath.

They exited through the back door into an alleyway where a very out of place black Mercedes waited for them. A moment later, the back wall of the warehouse fell in. King looked back to see a golem, constructed from a mishmash of metal from the warehouse, a car, and chunks of pavement, rise up, ready to strike the building once more. "In!" he shouted, opening the Mercedes's back door. The team piled in and Alexander had them screeching down the alley in moments. The golem, as big as it was, would never catch them.

Alexander stopped the car at the end of the alley and looked back. The golem was trying to force its way through the tangled ruins of the warehouse. He took a phone out of his pocket and dialed a number. He looked back again. A moment later the golem disappeared in a ball of fire that consumed the entire warehouse, destroying everything inside—the samples, lab equipment, and Davidson.

As they drove away, King took a moment to mourn the death of Davidson, who had lost his life for something that wasn't his problem. Then he focused on the nagging question that entered his mind the moment the attack had begun: How did he find us?

The answer came quickly. He turned to Alexander. "Check your pockets. Your phone. Everything. One of us is being tracked."

Alexander pulled the car over. Despite the strange scene of two men patting themselves down by the side of the road, no one paid them any attention. All eyes were on the rising column of smoke.

King had searched most of his body when he realized that the only article of clothing he had yet to change since his search for Fiona had begun was his cargo pants. He'd checked the pockets first, but neglected the cargo pockets lower on his leg. He could feel the aberration as he reached for it. He took hold of the small object and pulled it from his pocket. It was the size and shape of a Tylenol capsule.

Alexander saw him holding it. "Destroy it."

King took it in both hands and snapped it in half. The fragile electronics within fell to the road.

They entered the car again without a word shared. King sat with his arms crossed. He now knew how Ridley managed to stay one step ahead of him and Alexander while the others were able to catch him with his guard down. He knew why they'd been attacked so quickly at the university and in the warehouse. But there was one question nagging at him: Who had put the tracking device in his pocket, and when?

SIXTY-FIVE
Babylon, Iraq

AS THE HUMMER door closed with a metallic clunk, King shook a storm of sand from his hair. Upon exiting the aircraft they had been greeted by a wall of airborn sand. It coated their clothing, filled their hair, and crunched between their teeth. Had the Republican Guard been as numerous and relentless, an invasion of Iraq would never have been possible. Luckily for the team, which now consisted of King, Queen, Knight, Bishop, and Alexander, the sand was only an annoyance.

The heat was the real enemy. Though dry, the temperature was unbearable in the afternoon sun. Moisture was wicked away from the body as soon as it was sweat. The team carried water bottles with them, drinking constantly to keep dehydration at bay. They felt their journey was nearing an end, which meant a confrontation loomed on the horizon, and each one of them would need their strength.

The trip to Iraq had been quick and comfortable aboard Alexander's Gulfstream jet. Getting clearance to land had been easy, thanks to Deep Blue, and the Hummer waiting for them was fully gassed and holding their requested supplies. Energy bars and water were consumed en route. Desert camouflage uniforms were provided so they could move about Babylon without raising too much attention. And a cache of weapons, including five XM25 assault rifles. The XM25s weren't scheduled for active-duty usage until 2012, but they'd been tested successfully in Iraq and Afghanistan since 2009. They were the future in handheld warfare, able to shoot both standard rounds and 25mm rounds that could explode after a specific distance determined by the weapon's laser site. Hiding in a ditch or behind a wall offered no protection when up against the XM25's smart rounds, which King hoped would also provide the punch necessary for fending off any stone golems.

Two hours after touching down, King pulled onto the road leading toward Camp Alpha's checkpoint gate. He'd waited long enough to broach this topic, but it could no longer be avoided. If Alexander tagged along with the team, he needed a call sign so anonymity could be retained. "You're call sign will be Pawn for the duration of this mission," King said to Alexander, who immediately burst out laughing.

"It's the call sign every temporary team member gets," Bishop said.

"It's the irony I find amusing," Alexander said. "I'm not opposed to the title. Pawn it is."

They passed a local bazaar full of brightly colored trinkets perfect for U.S. soldiers wanting to send home exotic gifts. The man behind the table gave them a smile and salute as they passed. Palm trees lined the road on both sides, obscuring the view of ancient ruins off to the right.

Ignoring the sites, King pulled up to the Camp Alpha checkpoint. He flashed the ID that had been provided for him.

Corporal Tyler, a young, crew-cut soldier with a southern drawl and matching cowboy swagger, approached from the gatehouse. He looked at the ID then at the passengers in the car, noting the odd mix of Korean, Arab, Caucasian, and Greek passengers. "Mind if I check this out?" he asked, taking King's ID

"Go right ahead," King said.

Tyler walked back into the gatehouse and closed the door behind him. His skinny partner, Corporal Stevens, waited for him inside. He took the ID and looked at it.

"USGS, my ass," Stevens said. "We're supposed to believe *those* guys are geologists?"

Tyler worked a laptop, typing in King's phony information. "You don't buy it?"

"No way, man. Look at them."

Both soldiers looked out the brown-tinged windows and saw King and Queen watching them from the Hummer. Tyler's stomach tensed with intimidation.

"Geez," Tyler whispered.

"You see, they're way too badass," Stevens said. "Twenty bucks says they're Rangers or Delta."

The results of Tyler's search appeared on screen. "Well, according to the database, they're from the USGS. They check out and have clearance."

"You gonna ask them?" Stevens said. "Twenty bucks, man."

After activating the gate, Tyler grunted, took the ID, and headed back out to the Hummer. "You're all set, sir." As he handed the ID back to King, Tyler noticed Queen's window was now rolled down.

"You have twenty bucks?" she asked, holding out her hand.

Tyler looked dumbfounded, but still being intimidated, reached into his pants pocket and took out a twenty-dollar bill. Queen snagged it and handed the money to King. "He bet me you wouldn't have the guts to ask if we were Delta. And since I have no money on me and you lost me that bet, you're paying."

Tyler was stunned and it showed on his face.

"We can read lips," Queen said as King began to pull through the open gate. She flashed a smile. "Everyone at the USGS can. Now go pay your friend."

Tyler walked back to the gatehouse and sat down on the single step. Stevens stood next to him, equally dumbfounded. "That was awesome."

Tyler gave a nod. "Yup."

KING PULLED THE Hummer through and slowed as he approached a bend in the road. The Ishtar Gate stood before them. The original Ishtar Gate had been one of the seven ancient wonders of the world before being replaced by the Great Lighthouse at Alexandria. The original gate stood forty-seven feet tall, was constructed of blue bricks, and held over sixty yellow and white mosaic lions and dragons. Its central arch was the eighth gate into Babylon's inner city.

As King looked at Saddam's smaller replica and pondered its history, he realized they had been driving over the buried ruins of Babylon for some time. The area they had to search was expansive, but hopefully not without some clues. Past the Ishtar Gate, King pulled the Hummer into a dirt parking lot full of military vehicles. He parked in front of the amphitheater where the U.S. military had first set up shop.

They were quickly greeted by General Raymond Fowler, who had been briefed by General Keasling. They were to have free access to the ruins in and around the base, access to any equipment they requested, and, should they ask for it, the help of every enlisted man on base. The general had protested the orders until he found out they came directly from President Duncan.

King exited the Hummer and squinted as the hot sandy Iraqi air assaulted him again. He gave Fowler a quick salute and shook his hand. Seeing the man's skepticism, King said, "Sorry for the intrusion, General. We'll try to be out of your hair as soon as possible."

The general forced a smile, which turned a scar on his cheek into an upside-down question mark, and hung on to King's hand. "That's kind of you, son. But I'd like to know if you all are going to stir up a hornet's nest in my base."

"Sir?"

"I know who you are. I know that you were a part of what happened back at Bragg. I need to know if I should expect something similar here."

King took no offense at the general's forceful tone and the strong grip he maintained. "We hope not, sir. But . . . it might be best to keep your men on alert. We're not sure what we're going to find"—King looked at the sandy ruins—"out there."

Fowler let go of King's hand. "Appreciate the candor. Will you need armed escorts?"

King shook his head, no. "We need to draw as little attention to ourselves as possible. Best if no one gives us any special attention."

"Understood," Fowler said. "What *can* I do for you?"

"Just keep the ruins clear while we're out there."

"Are you looking for something in particular? We've been stationed here since 2003 and know every nook and cranny of the ruins."

"What we're after is most likely *beneath* the ruins."

Fowler looked out at the ruins with suspicion in his eyes. Then he recalled something. "An archaeological team had been studying the ruins before we arrived. They were part of Saddam's effort to rebuild Babylon and were searching for the more famous monuments, like the Hanging Gardens."

King tried to show no reaction. If they had been searching for the Hanging Gardens it's possible they had also been searching for Babel. "That may be helpful. Knight, Bishop, why don't you check it out? We'll start in the ruins. General, do you know if the archaeologists working here are still around?"

"Two of the lead archaeologists are dead," Fowler said. "One is missing. But much of the support staff is still here in Baghdad. I'll see who I can track down."

King gave a nod of thanks. He headed for the back of the Hummer, opened the trunk, and handed XM25s to Bishop and Knight. "Keep your ears and eyes open. If you find something that points us in a direction, let me know."

"You got it, boss," Knight said before turning to the general. "After you."

Fowler gave the weapons a long look before he turned and walked away. "This way."

As Fowler led Knight and Bishop away, King turned back to the open Hummer and took out the most important piece of equipment they had with them. With the war in Afghanistan requiring better cave detecting equipment, the military had been borrowing technology from NASA's Mars program. The result were handheld Quantum Well Infrared Photodetectors (QWIPs), which could see through the desert sand and collect thermal data. The resulting images were called thermograms. They showed the difference in temperature between desert sand or bedrock and the open space of a cave, or in this case, the open chamber of a buried tower. Since the user wore the device on the left hand—sensor in the palm facedown, images displayed on the forearm-mounted LCD display— King and his team could also carry their weapons without a problem.

Armed with the most high-tech handheld weapons and technology the military had, King, Queen, and Alexander set off for the ruins of Babylon.

SIXTY-SIX
Babylon, Iraq

KING TOOK A drink from the twenty-ounce bottle he'd been nursing for the past two hours. He knew he needed to get more liquid soon, but with Fiona's insulin deadline long since up, he had to stretch the water as far as possible. And right now, that meant walking a grid over a very large area of desert. He had a second bottle with him meant for Fiona if he managed to find her. But if the day went long, he'd have no choice but to start on the second bottle.

To anyone watching he would look like a delirious soldier with a penchant for checking the time as he kept his eyes on the LCD display on his arm. He had come across several air pockets but no actual caves, and certainly no ziggurat remains. While Queen and Alexander searched the maze of ruins in Babylon proper, King had pursued a different path. Between the bank of the Euphrates River and the exposed Babylonian ruins stood one of many palaces built by Saddam Hussein. A spiraling road rounded the tall mound it stood on. Built from brown stone, it was utilitarian save for the thick arches that surrounded the building and gave it a genuine Babylonian feel. Much of the symmetrical hill was clearly man-made, but Saddam was known for building atop Babylonian ruins with no regard for what lay beneath. And when it came to his palaces, he had no trouble burying the past. What King wanted to know was how much of the hill existed before Saddam added to it. To find out, he'd push the QWIP to its limits.

As he walked up the side of the hill, he activated his throat mic. "Find anything yet, Bishop?"

Bishop's voice returned. "Not a thing, but that's not because there isn't anything here, it's because there's too much."

"We're drowning in old maps and notebooks," Knight said.

King had hoped intel would expedite the search, but it seemed finding anything useful in the archaeological archives was as much a needle in a haystack as finding a temple underground with thermal imaging. As he crossed the spiraling road and headed up the hillside, King watched the thermal imager. It showed solid earth all the way through.

As the monotony of the image continued, he looked ahead. Brush and the occasional palm tree covered the hillside. He adjusted his path to avoid a tree and then looked to the west, over the Euphrates. From this high vantage point he could see the desert stretching out in all directions. It was massive—like a tan ocean speckled with floating ruins and carved by modern roads. Fiona was somewhere out there.

As his patience began to fade, King noticed a hill on the other side of the river. Small ruins sat at its base. He toggled his mic again. "Bishop, did Babylon expand to the other side of the Euphrates?"

"Hold on . . ." King could hear rustling paper and Knight's voice in the background. "Yeah. Looks like a good portion of it did."

"That's all I needed to know." King broke contact and gave up on his current search. He turned and made for the bottom of the hill, where a U.S. military boat launch had been built. Three black patrol boats were tied to the docks, each with a mounted machine gun.

As King approached the dock, a lone soldier stomped out a cigarette and blew the smoke from the side of his mouth. "You one of them USGS fellas I'm supposed to assist if asked?"

"How'd you know?" King said.

"Been watching you walk back and forth with your head turned toward the ground for an hour now. Only two types of people do that. The clinically depressed and people in love with dirt. You ain't depressed are you?"

King grinned. "Not yet."

"You spend too much time out here and I promise you will be." He gave a smile that revealed a set of nicotine-stained teeth. "Name's Bowers. What can I do you for?"

"I need a ferryman," King said.

"Going to the other side of the Euphrat is like crossing the River Styx," Bowers said.

"How's that?"

"Ain't nobody over there to save you. You'll be on your own."

"Not quite," King said with a grin. "You're going to wait for me."

Bowers stepped aboard the nearest boat. "Well shit, this will be the most I've done in weeks."

King boarded the boat and they cast off. They crossed the river quickly, beaching the craft on the sandy bank. As King stepped out of the boat and onto shore, Bowers took note of the XM25. His mouth opened a little. "Geologist, my ass. What the hell are you looking for?"

"Just be ready for anything," King said with a glance at the machine gun. "Anything."

"You got it," Bowers said and began loading the machine gun. "How will I know what to shoot?"

King looked back as he hiked up the sand toward the ruins and the small hill beyond. "Odds are it won't be human."

THE DIM LIGHT in the barracks-turned-storage shed was hardly enough to see by, so Bishop had propped open the door allowing the sun to light the room. Unfortunately, it also allowed gritty sand to swirl inside with every gust of hot wind. They did their best to ignore the air quality and focus on combing through boxes of archaeological data.

And there was enough to keep them occupied for days. Knight spent his time going over maps. Though he couldn't read a word of Arabic, he could clearly see that there were no ancient ziggurats drawn on any maps. Bishop combed through the notebooks, skimming each entry for keywords. Thus far he'd found nothing.

Bishop and Knight were so intent on their work that neither noticed the men who entered the barracks until they closed the door. Knight turned as their light was cut in half. With his hand now on his rifle, Knight focused on the door where an Iraqi man dressed in brown pants and a white button-down shirt stood. General Fowler stood behind him.

"We tracked down one of the men involved in the pre-2003 excavations. He might be able to help make sense of all this," Fowler said, motioning to the stacks of boxes. "Let me know when you're finished with him and we'll send an escort. Now if you'll excuse me, my attention is needed elsewhere."

Fowler left quickly, leaving a nervous-looking Iraqi standing in the middle of the room.

"What's your name?" Knight asked.

"Rahim, sir. My English not so good."

Without standing or turning around to greet the newcomer, Bishop said, in perfect Arabic, "You were a part of the Babylonian excavations, Rahim?"

Rahim replied in Arabic. "I was an assistant to one of the archaeologists. I was here for three years."

"Do you know of the Tower of Babel?" Bishop asked.

"We searched for it for years," the man said, growing excited.

"And?"

"It's not here."

Bishop stopped paging through the journal in his hands. He closed it, stood, and turned around. Rahim stumbled back away from Bishop, his eyes fearful. The military hardness of Bishop combined with his muscles and shaved head no doubt brought back memories of times when men like Bishop were to be feared.

"You're Iraqi?" Rahim asked.

"I was born in Iran," Bishop said.

This only deepened Rahim's fear.

Bishop showed a relaxed smile. "But I was raised in America. You have nothing to fear from me."

Rahim's fear eased a little, but he didn't take his eyes off Bishop for very long.

The conversation was interrupted by King's voice in their ears. Rahim looked at them like they were insane as Bishop and Knight stopped everything and listened. Then Bishop turned to him. "You said the tower isn't here?"

Rahim nodded. "We scoured the whole site with ground-penetrating radar. We found many exciting sites, but no ziggurats large enough to fit the profile of the Tower of Babel. But some of the team believed the tower lay elsewhere, outside of Babylon."

"What is beneath the mound on the opposite side of the river?" Bishop asked.

The man's head snapped up, his face excited. "We never got a chance to dig, but the archaeologists suspected it was the Hanging Gardens."

"The Hanging Gardens," Bishop said to Knight in English.

Knight relayed the information. "King, a man from the original dig is here. He's saying that the Tower of Babel isn't here, and that the site you're checking out might be—"

A burst of static cut him off.

"King. King? Do you copy?" Knight looked at Bishop. The only reason King wouldn't reply was if he couldn't.

"Rahim, we need you to show us where this mound is," Bishop said.

* * *

A HALF MILE away on the opposite side of the Euphrates River, atop a mound of sand, the only trace of King's presence was a divot in the earth. With each passing moment, the wind filled the hole with fresh sand. Less than a minute after King was sucked into the earth, no trace of him remained—except for his XM25 assault rifle.

SIXTY-SEVEN
Severodvinsk, Russia

THE CITY OF Severodvinsk was not what Rook expected, not this far north. In some ways it reminded him of Portsmouth, New Hampshire—built on the coast, home to a submarine yard, featuring an old fishing culture still eking out a living—but Portsmouth's population was closer to thirty thousand. Severodvinsk supported a population of nearly two hundred thousand.

Not that he minded the crowded streets. It made hiding in the open that much easier. Being a major naval hub, the city was full of military men, some in uniform, more in plainclothes. Despite wanting a stiff drink, Rook avoided the pubs and stuck to coffee shops, all the while searching for the one man who might be able to help him: Maksim Dashkov.

After leaving Galya's cabin, he had hiked five miles before making it to a main route. Heading north, he caught a ride with a truck driver with a shipment destined for the sub yard. He'd been dropped off in the center of town an hour ago.

The coffee shop bell jangled as Rook entered. He smiled at the heavyset woman behind the counter and ordered a coffee. Black. He paid with money taken from Galya's cabin and headed for a table. Halfway to the table, as though an afterthought, he asked, "Do you have a phone directory I could borrow?"

The woman nodded, bent down behind the counter, and reemerged with a directory.

Rook reached for it with a smile. "Thanks."

But when he tried to take it from the woman, she held on tight. "One hundred fifty."

One hundred fifty rubles was just a little over five dollars U.S., but it was still a lot for using the phone book. When Rook gave her a questioning look, she added, "Times are hard. People drink more vodka than coffee."

Rook paid her and smiled. "I should have got cream and sugar."

"Those are extra, too," the woman said as he sat down with the phone directory. Thirty seconds later he had a phone number and address for Maksim Dashkov.

Rook stood to leave, but saw three men in uniform standing outside the shop. It was doubtful he'd be recognized, but on the off chance he was, he was in no condition to fight his way past two hundred thousand Russians.

He gave the woman at the counter his most winning smile and said, "How much for a phone call?"

The woman picked up the phone and placed it on the counter. "Five more."

Rook gave her the last of his money, picked up the phone, and dialed. It was answered on the third ring by a man with a rough voice.

"Maksim Dashkov?" Rook said.

Suspicion filled the man's voice. "Yes, who is this?"

"A friend of Galya's."

"Galya," the man said in a whisper. "I haven't heard from her in two years. How is she?"

Rook wasn't sure how the man would respond, but he deserved the truth. "She's dead."

"Dead? How?"

"I can't tell you that now," Rook said, looking out the window at the three sailors. "But her dying wish was for you to help me."

There was a pause on the other end. Then the man spoke. "Where are you?"

SIXTY-EIGHT
Babylon, Iraq

THE LAST THING King remembered was looking down at his feet and seeing them disappear beneath the sand. He dropped his weapon as he reached out for some nearby brush, but was unable to reach it. Then he was in the earth, swallowed down and shat out. After falling ten feet, he struck his head on something solid and lost consciousness.

He awoke with a throbbing pain on the side of his head and a scratching thirst in his throat. Other than the colors dancing in his vision, he could see nothing. The pain grew worse when he remembered the last words he'd heard from Knight.

The Tower of Babel isn't here.

If this isn't the tower, King thought, *then where am I?*

In the darkness he found his small Maglite flashlight and turned it on, keeping its beam close to the stone floor. In the dim light he touched his hand to the raw spot of his head. He felt a sharp sting as the salt from his hand made contact with the wound. But there was very little blood on his hand, which meant the wound wasn't bad.

He turned the flashlight on the wall and found a solid brown surface. Columns built into the stone rose from floor to ceiling every few feet, but appeared more decorative than supportive as they were hewn from the stone that made the wall. King aimed his flashlight up at the ceiling. It, too, was solid brown stone, but there was a sand- and stone-filled gap above him. More sand surrounded his body on the floor.

Standing over the weak spot, King had provided just enough pressure to loosen the sand. He'd been sucked down into the tunnel before it sealed above him again.

He stood with the flashlight in hand and looked for his rifle. Not seeing it, he remembered its fate. *Damnit,* he thought, and then drew his Sig Sauer handgun.

Leading with the light and gun, King walked down the tunnel. He wanted, more than anything, to find a way out and continue the search for Fiona, but what if Knight had been wrong? What if this was the Tower of Babel? He had to be sure.

He slowed as his flashlight revealed a large opening on the left side of the tunnel. He stopped at the corner and listened. He heard nothing, but the air smelled of stone, and something else.

Something fresh.

Something dead.

He chanced a glance with his flashlight and found a large open chamber. A clamshell staircase descended into a large atrium. A dried up tile pool sat at the center of the space. Large stone boxes descended on both sides of the staircase, filled with ancient soil. It was clear to King that they once held large plants or trees, and as he looked around the space, he tried to imagine it in its former glory. Flowers and trees surrounded the atrium. Water flowed from the lion's head, into the pool. Sun shown down from above, warming the stone.

He looked up at the stone ceiling. It was smooth and unnatural. Then he realized this whole space should be full of sand. The desert had claimed the structure long ago, but someone had hollowed out the insides and fortified the ceiling somehow.

Not someone, King thought, *Ridley.*

He took the stairs to the atrium floor, which held a mural of a naked, bearded man; his arms wrapped around two bulls standing on their hind legs, whose faces and beards matched the man's. Several marble statues stood around the outer perimeter of the space. They were tall and straight, hands clasped together beneath rigid beards. Their oversized eyes were inlaid with deep blue lapis lazuli.

Staring into those blue eyes, King felt a chill. Someone was in the room with him. Watching him. He could feel it. He scanned every corner, lit every shadow, but saw no one. His senses told him he was alone, but something else, perhaps a sixth sense, shouted otherwise.

Three arched doorways led out of the atrium, one to the left, one to the right, and one straight ahead. Each was girded by ancient carvings depicting goats, lions, giant eagles with outstretched wings, and large lizards. After a quick check of the three exits, King hurried through the center tunnel, eager to leave the atrium and its sinister feel behind. The central branch led to a second staircase that descended deeper into the buried structure.

As he reached the bottom of the long staircase, King came to a large mural. It was faded horribly, but he could make out a glowing building covered with arches, staircases, and hanging plants and trees. Then he recognized the central atrium as the one he'd passed through. He took a deep breath through his nose as he realized he was standing inside the Hanging Gardens of Babylon.

That same sniff also detected a foul odor. It smelled similarly to what he'd caught traces of in the atrium, but was much stronger. King rounded the corner in the next chamber slowly. The room was circular, surrounded by columns and tall statues similar to those in the atrium.

Detecting no movement or sound within the room, King moved inside. At the center of the room were several wooden tables. They looked old, but far from ancient. The dirty floor was covered in scuff marks. A glint of something shiny caught his attention. He squatted down and picked the object up.

Broken glass.

Modern glass.

Then he saw more. Food wrappers. Discarded water bottles. A pile of discarded tea. *Definitely Ridley.* The man loved fresh tea. King knelt by the tea. It looked wet, but a quick touch revealed it was a dry and flaky mass. King kicked the tea, breaking it open and felt the core. Bone dry. Ridley had been gone for some time.

"Damnit," King whispered.

A larger piece of paper caught his attention. It looked like it had fallen out of a notebook and slid beneath one of the tables, perhaps forgotten in a rush to leave. He picked it up and turned it over. The page had hand-written notes. King recognized Ridley's handwriting. At the top of the page was written, *WHO IS HE???*

Below that was a series of quick chicken scratch notes. He was able to pick out a word here and there: *ancient, god, historical figures, human (?), lost, the bell, dimension, Hercules(?).*

King paused. Ridley was trying to identify Alexander. With the name Hercules on this page, he seemed to be doing a fairly good job. Part of King wished more was revealed on the page, and another part didn't want the answers. King folded the piece of paper and placed it in his pocket. After someone deciphered Ridley's handwriting he might glean more from the page.

He stood and looked down at the tabletop. What he saw twisted his stomach and locked his feet to the ground. Part of him was thrilled because it meant he was on the right track. But the shattered remains of Fiona's insulin pump also filled him with dread. When did it break? If it happened days ago she could already be close to death. How did it break? The thing looked smashed. If she had been wearing it when this happened, she could be seriously injured *and* hyperglycemic. King picked up the fractured device and squeezed it, turning his knuckles white. He was so close.

An echoed sound rolled into the chamber. Distant and organic. A high-pitched whine. Had something heard him? And if so, what was it? The sound came again. King strained to hear it clearly.

It sounded like a girl.

Hoping Fiona had been left behind, or had escaped, King pocketed the ruined pump and headed for the tunnel at the opposite side of the chamber. The hallway sloped downward. The walls held murals and carvings, but none captured his attention. He kept his light and weapon aimed forward and moved as quickly as he could without making noise.

As he reached the bottom of the tunnel where it opened up into a larger space, a second cry sounded. This one was very close and decidedly not human. King tensed and covered his flashlight with his fingers to dim the beam. He peeked around the corner.

It took all his strength to not react.

A body lay on the floor, bloody and torn apart.

Standing around it were several large sandfish. Their tails snapped back and forth as they fought for position around the body. Intent on their meal, none of them noticed him. He rolled back into the tunnel. Ridley had gone, but he'd left behind some pets.

And a snack for them.

Needing to know if the body was Fiona's, King rolled out again and peered toward the scene, trying his best to make out features in the low light. He got his answer when one of the large sandfish nipped at the smallest. It leaped away, revealing the victim's head.

It was another sandfish.

With no other food around, they were cannibalizing each other.

But King's relief was quickly replaced by dread. When the small lizard jumped away, it gave the sandfish on the other side a clear view of King. It stared at him indifferently, chewing on a chunk of flesh. Then, without any show of emotion, it charged.

As it tore over its brothers and sisters, the sandfish took their attention away from their meal. They turned and saw King as well. Seeing a fresh source of food, the pack discarded their slain brother and joined the charge. Nine eight-foot-long sandfish, each with razor-sharp teeth, the ability to taste the air and swim through sand, were now hunting King. Only the smallest of the group remained behind, enjoying an unusually easy meal.

As the wall of running lizards approached, King's mind rifled through his choices. With three grenades on hand, he could drop a few and run. But without knowing how well supported these ruins were he risked bringing them all down on his head. He could try shooting each of the monsters in the head—he had enough rounds—but had no idea if a bullet to the brain could stop them. In the end, his instincts formed a simple three-word plan for him.

Run, run, run!

The upward sloping tunnel made King's acceleration much slower than he would have preferred. If the sandfish pack hadn't snapped and fought for position as they gave chase, King wouldn't have made it ten feet.

They entered the tunnel behind him like a wave of flesh, roiling up onto the wall before settling back to the tunnel floor. As they ran, their clawed feet arched wide, occasionally slashing their neighbor's side or limbs. But the pain and smell of blood in the air only added to their frenzy.

King glanced back and again considered using a grenade. He might be buried alive with them. As they gained, he decided that being crushed to death was preferable to being devoured. Once he was out of the tight confines of the tunnel, he would toss one of his three grenades. That is, if he made it out of the tunnel.

With the nearest sandfish nearly upon him, King took aim with his pistol and fired four shots. Three out of four struck the beast. It collapsed in a heap, stumbling those behind it and allowing King to gain some much needed distance. As he neared the tunnel exit, King pulled the pin on his grenade and dropped it, letting it roll down the tunnel floor.

King exited the tunnel, stepped to the side, and covered his ears. The explosion blasted from the mouth of the tunnel like a cannon. Grenade, stone, and flesh confetti shot out.

As the dust settled, King turned his light down the tunnel and saw that the ceiling had caved in, filling the void with sand. Before he turned away, King saw the sand move. It shook from within. A small avalanche rolled down the side. And then, as though squeezed out of a pore, one of the sandfish slid out of the wall of sand and continued its pursuit undeterred. Three more quickly followed.

King overturned tables as he ran toward the next set of steps, hoping they would slow the monsters. He eyed the circle of statues, expecting them to reach out for him as well. But they remained immobile. As he started up the stairs he heard the tables shatter beneath the weight of his pursuers.

With his light and eyes forward, King couldn't see the sandfish behind him, but he could hear their claws clacking against the stone steps.

The stairwell opened up to the atrium and he realized he had no plan of escape, only a one-way chase. As he entered the atrium, movement to his right caught his attention. He dove forward and crouched into a roll.

A moment later the nearest sandfish leaped from the tunnel, its jaws open, ready to engulf King's head. But the beast never made it. What looked like a long serrated spear stabbed the lizard through its head and pinned it to the floor. The sandfish twitched madly for a moment and then lay still.

What the fuck? King thought. He followed the spear up expecting to see someone standing above him, but the weapon's source blended into the stone wall. A second lizard, fueled by bloodlust exited the tunnel. With a quickness King didn't think possible, a second spear shot through the sandfish's skull. Again, the spear appeared to have come from a living wall. For a moment King thought he might be witnessing some kind of golem.

Then it moved and he saw the awful truth. The creature was speckled brown, perfectly camouflaged for the brown stone found throughout the region. Standing still, it had been all but invisible against the wall.

This was the presence he had detected before: a ten-foot-long, nearly eight-foot-tall praying mantis—a desert mantis to be exact.

It turned its triangle head toward him. The tilt of the head looked freakish, rotating almost a full three hundred degrees. Its two oval eyes, impossible to escape, honed in on him. He could feel the thing analyzing him. Its head twitched to alternating angles. Then its gaze rolled back toward the tunnel. The remaining two sandfish had arrived, and they were still hungry.

As the mantis flung one of the impaled sandfish away, a second oversized lizard clamped down on its leg. But the giant insect showed no reaction. It simply shook off the impaled lizard, took aim, and pierced the skull of the newcomer while it was still clamped down on its foreleg.

The fourth sandfish had eyes only for King. It charged beneath the praying mantis, intent on capturing its prize even while the massive insect turned its brethren into shish kabob. But it wasn't the only one with eyes on King. It was swatted to the side by a second mantis. The sandfish toppled and rolled, smashing into a far wall. The impact seemed to knock some sense into the lizard. It righted itself and took off running down one of the side tunnels.

The mantis swiveled its head toward King. He could see the tension in its dangerous forelimbs building for a strike. The strike of a mantis was one of the quickest, most violent acts in the natural world. Quicker than the human eye could perceive, the limbs could snap out and ensnare pray between its femur and tibia, both of which were lined with needle-sharp spikes. To a human, those small spikes are normally an insignificant threat. Right now, the smallest were three-inch-long blades. The longest matched King's seven-inch KA-BAR knife. If just one of those arms caught him, he'd be pierced upward of twenty times, perhaps even lopped in two. He had no intention of letting that happen.

Not wanting to miss, King took aim at the creature's chest and fired a single round. It made no sound, but took a step back. Its limbs twitched for a moment. Its head spun around, back and forth, as though looking for the source of its pain. Not finding anything and having fully regained its composure, it turned its head back to King.

But he was already up and running.

Its head snapped up and quickly caught sight of him.

He jumped into the central pool and ran across to the other side. He snuck a glance over his shoulder and saw the mantis giving a kind of slow-motion pursuit. The giant insect rocked back and forth with each step, as though tentative. He also noticed the second mantis had left the dead lizards and had joined in the dancelike pursuit.

King wondered if this was really the fastest an oversized mantis could move. Then decided against it. What they were doing couldn't even be considered pursuit. They knew something he didn't. He found out exactly what that was when he turned around. Standing above him on the staircase was a third mantis, its forelimbs hunched up high as though in prayer.

King made a preemptive dive to the side. Had he waited for the mantis to attack, he wouldn't have even registered its strike until his body had been turned into a pincushion. Even with his fast action he didn't fully escape the attack. The strike hit the rubber of his boot and nearly snapped his leg from the impact. It threw off his jump as well. He landed in a heap on the stairs, striking an elbow and knee hard.

But he didn't let the pain slow him. The mantis was already retracting its forelimbs for a second strike. King took aim, this time for the head, and fired off three rounds. Each found its mark, entering the insect's bulbous right eye and passing through the head. But the first two missed the tiny brain. Even with one eye destroyed and two holes in its head, all its vital functions remained intact. If not for the third round, which pierced the small brain, the creature would have continued happily. With its control center destroyed, the mantis twitched madly, falling down the stairs.

Once the danger of being struck by one of the shaking limbs passed, King wasted no time launching himself back up the stairs. This time, the two remaining mantises gave chase in earnest. He could hear the rapid-fire clicking of their limbs on the stone floor, and a barely perceivable squeaking, like mice.

Are they communicating? King wondered, but pushed the thought from his mind and focused on escape. The only spot he knew was close to the surface was where he fell in. But climbing back into the sand and out of the ruins would be impossible.

Unless I open it up. As his plan began to come together, he looked down and saw two snapping sets of beaklike mandibles rising up behind him. Both mantises had quickly closed the distance and were poised to strike. He jumped up, narrowly avoiding a dual amputation. The loud crack of mantis forelimbs on stone stairs sounded like gunshots. When he came down he wasted no time and jumped again, this time out and away from the insects.

King entered the long tunnel and broke into a sprint, keeping his eyes on the ceiling, looking for the crack that sucked him in and deposited him in this hellhole.

He saw it ahead.

After holstering his weapon, he took out a second grenade and prepared to pull the pin. His timing would have to be precise, and his luck monumental.

Twenty feet from the fissure, he pulled the pin.

As he passed beneath the crack, he leaped up as high as he could, shoved his fist into a sandy hole in the rock filled gap and deposited the grenade inside. After landing he ran for another thirty feet and then stopped.

He turned around and raised his light. The tunnel behind him was alive with movement. The mantises were still giving chase, though more slowly as they had to actually duck to fit into this tunnel. If the two mantises passed the fissure before the grenade detonated . . .

But they didn't.

The grenade exploded with a deafening boom. King fell to one knee, dropping his flashlight and clasping his hands to his ears. He opened his eyes to see a cloud of dust and sand swirling in the tunnel. But it was the brightness that held his attention. It was like looking through a blizzard, but he could see a portion of the far ceiling had fallen in at an angle, spilling its sand into the tunnel. It formed a convenient exit ramp.

Then sand began to fall from his side of the tunnel. The ceiling shifted. The roof over his head was coming down as well and if it didn't crush him outright, it would trap him on this side of the tunnel.

He ran for the exit.

The tunnel ceiling tilted under the weight of the earth it held, dumping a curtain of sand that blocked out the sun. King dove through the wall of falling sand and landed in sunlight.

The tunnel ceiling collapsed behind him, dropping down at an angle and spilling its sand around his legs. After kicking free from the sand, King crawled up the rise and caught his breath at the top. Sitting atop the hill he could see the base across the river. There were no running troops. No action at all. His battle beneath the sands had gone undetected.

Then the sand within the newly form pit shifted. A mound rose up and shifted toward him. A second followed.

The mantises had found a way through.

King stood and ran, headed downhill toward the river.

"Bowers! Start the engine!"

He saw Bowers stand up, his head appearing over the sand like a groundhog. He gaped at what he saw: King running down the hill with two giant insects emerging from the sand behind him. The cigarette in the man's mouth fell free as one of the mantises swiveled its head in his direction, locking its hungry eyes on him.

SIXTY-NINE
Location Unknown

FIONA'S JOINTS THROBBED as she pulled herself off the floor. In fact, her whole body had begun to ache. But she heard voices again and needed to know what was happening. She was the next guinea pig in line and wanted to be prepared for whatever might come.

The deep voice returned. As did the wet voice. And a whimpering. Whoever they were experimenting on this time was not as strong-willed as the last. She could hear belt buckles being cinched tight, which brought the occasional high-pitched squeal, but not a word or protest.

"Cainan, are we recording?" the deep voice asked.

"Not yet, Alpha," replied a new voice that sounded nearly identical to the first. Was he talking to himself? Or were there really two people? Alpha, the man with the deep voice who had been there all along, and Cainan, whose voice was so similar. Then there was the one with the wet voice. He had yet to speak, but always seemed to be at Alpha's side.

"Recording," Cainan said.

There was a shifting of light in front of the tunnel as someone walked past. Fiona strained to see, but her view was blocked by the narrow hallway.

There was no warning from Alpha, he simply launched into the strange language, speaking slowly, carefully enunciating. "Arzu Turan. Vish tracidor vim calee. Filash vor der wash. Vilad forsh."

No one spoke or moved for ten seconds. During that time, Fiona repeated the words in her head, over and over, committing them to memory.

Then someone asked, "Did it work?"

"Remove the tape," Alpha said.

The woman's mouth was taped shut, Fiona thought. *That's why she hadn't complained.*

There was a sharp tear, but still no complaint from the woman.

"How are you feeling?" Alpha asked.

"Blessed," the woman replied, her voice as heavily accented as the man killed earlier. If they were capturing locals, then she was being held someplace in the Middle East.

"Blessed?" Alpha said, his voice tinged with humor "How so?"

"To be in your presence."

"And who am I?"

"The Lord God."

Fiona couldn't see the man, but she knew he must be smiling.

"I am."

"My God, it worked," said a farther-off voice that didn't belong to Alpha or Cainan. How many of them were there?

"Was there ever any doubt?" Alpha replied. "Play back the recording."

After a moment, a tinny version of Alpha's voice repeated the phrase. "Arzu Turan. Vish tracidor vim calee. Filash vor der wash. Vilad forsh."

Fiona followed along, making sure she had the phrase memorized correctly, but her train of thought was interrupted by a shrill scream, followed by a stream of curses in a language she couldn't understand. Whatever had been done to the woman had been undone when the phrase was repeated.

The woman's screams became frantic and high-pitched, her voice angry and then desperate. A gunshot blasted, echoing in the tunnels.

Fiona fell back, clutching her ears.

The woman was dead. Silence followed.

Fiona fought against her tears, picked up a stone, and crawled to the side wall of her cell. As her emotions sapped the last of her energy, she began scratching at the wall with the stone.

SEVENTY
Babylon, Iraq

BACK IN THE open air, King was more in his element, but the oversized mantises showed no signs of being slowed by the sand. They not only skittered quickly over it, but they now moved in silence.

The loose sand of the desert shifted beneath King with every step, slowing him. But his course was straight and his legs fast. The river lay ahead, and the small black boat that would carry him across—if Bowers got his shit together and started it.

As though he'd seen the annoyance on King's face, Bowers turned the key on the boat and it started with a roar. But he'd failed to notice that half the craft was still beached.

"Throw it in reverse," King shouted. "Get it off the beach!"

Bowers responded quickly, putting the boat in reverse and slowly giving it gas. As the propeller blades dug into the river water faster and faster it became clear that it wasn't going to be enough to get the craft in the water.

As Bowers stood to get out of the boat, King leaped over a mound of sand separating river from desert. He landed behind Bowers.

"I'll push!" he shouted before throwing his weight into the front of the boat. King's shove and the still churning propeller launched the boat into the river. King jumped onto the front of the boat, swung himself around the mounted machine gun, and stood behind it. Already looking for targets, he wrapped his finger around the trigger of the belt-fed M240 machine gun.

"Just keep it in reverse," King said. They would reach the far side of the river a little slower, but moving in reverse would allow him to use the mantises for target practice.

As the insects emerged over the rise at the river's edge, King opened fire. The rounds fired like bursts of thunder, perking up the ears of soldiers all around Camp Alpha. While gunfire wasn't uncommon in the surrounding territories, it was relatively unheard of on base.

When the first round struck, a burst of guts shot out of the mantis's side, but it moved quickly, darting backward and down. King strafed to the side, striking the insect only once more before it and its partner disappeared from sight.

They reached the base-side dock a moment later. But Bowers didn't stop. He plowed the boat into the shoreline. The engine grinded as it chewed up sand. Neither man felt concern for the craft. They left it beached, jumping onto the shore and pounding up the incline that led to the base.

They paused ten feet from the water, looking back at the far shore.

"What the fuck were those things?" Bowers asked, his chest heaving more from adrenaline than actual physical exertion.

"Exactly what they looked like," King said. "Giant mantises."

"Okay. Seriously. Giant mantises?" Bowers shook his head, confused and excited.

King nodded as he scanned the far shore. "I think we're in the clear."

Bowers laughed. King turned to find him running up the hill toward base despite no sign of the mantises. "Bad news, buddy," he said. "Mantises can fly."

A string of curses filled King's mind as a buzzing sound rolled over the river. The mantises shot up over the Euphrates and honed in on his position, barreling toward him like kamikaze pilots.

King's mind raced for solutions. To their right were the main facilities of the base. Lots of buildings to get lost in. Lots of guns to fight back. And Bishop and Knight were somewhere in that direction. But the soldiers there had no experience dealing with this kind of freakish problem and there would likely be a lot of casualties, from the mandibles of the mantises and from panicked friendly fire. *No good,* King thought.

He needed Chess Team support, minus the regular soldiers.

The ruins.

Queen and Alexander were there, both armed with XM25s. The maze-like ruins would provide ample hiding spots and bottlenecks to make a stand. Of course, the brown stone would also make perfect camouflage for the mantises. But there was no choice. And no time.

"Stay with me," King said.

"You don't have to worry about that," Bowers said, his voice shaking. "I'm sticking to you like a tick on a collie's dick."

Despite the circumstances, King grinned. Bowers's colorful language reminded him of Rook. As they ran across the road and started up the hill that led past Saddam's Babylon palace, King glanced back.

Mantises didn't attack from the air, so the pair had to land and give chase. Given their slow and clumsy landing, King guessed these two had never landed, let alone flown before. The skill was instinctual though, and they would soon be cruising over the sand once again.

Bowers looked back as he ran up the hillside. The mantises were already gaining on them. "Oh damn. Oh damn!"

Not watching his step, Bowers tripped over some brush. He fell forward, striking his face hard on the loose soil, getting a mouthful of gritty dirt in the process. King took him by the shoulder, yanked him up, and shoved him forward.

"Move soldier!" King shouted. "I will not stop to pick you up again!"

Bowers charged up the hill. The mental spanking was exactly what he needed to keep his mind off the giant monsters trying to eat them alive. But King's mind remained on both running and the mantises, because unlike Bowers, if *he* didn't also figure out how to kill the monsters, they would *both* be dead.

SEVENTY-ONE

BEFORE KING EVER exited the sandy tomb, Knight and Bishop followed Rahim toward the river, walking at a quick pace. Knight had a pair of binoculars out and ready. When they cleared the base, Rahim pointed to a mound across the river. "Over there. Just above those ruins."

Knight raised the binoculars to his eyes and looked. "He's not there." He scanned the area, eventually reaching the river. "Hold on. There's a soldier in a patrol boat. Looks like he's waiting for someone. But he's calm."

They headed closer, skirting the river.

As they walked, more than a few soldiers stopped to give them odd looks. None of them had ever been seen on base before. Two of them were of Arab descent, one in plainclothes and one of them was Korean. Knight did his best to offer reassuring smiles. He knew they looked like a mini Axis of Evil to the men posted here.

Knight's honed senses suddenly picked up on a subtle pressure wave. He stopped and looked around. No one else had detected it, not even Bishop. Binoculars raised, he looked across the river again. A puff of sand rose up into the air above the mound. Then King appeared from within, unarmed and running. He could see him shouting at the man in the boat. Then something rose out of the sand behind King.

He could see two large creatures with spindly limbs, but as they climbed onto the sand, their brown color blended perfectly and hid them from view.

"What the . . ." He lowered the binoculars and spun around. They'd passed a security tower on their way to the river. The men inside would have a sniper rifle.

"Head for the river," he said to Bishop, handing him the binoculars.

Bishop took a quick look through the binoculars, located King's position, and took off running. Knight ran in the opposite direction, leaving a stunned Rahim standing alone in the middle of the road.

Knight reached the security tower and threw himself onto the ladder. He landed on the fourth rung up and then climbed it as deftly as a monkey. At the top, he launched himself over the sandbag wall and landed hard on the other side. The two soldiers sitting inside the small, windowed room atop the tower flinched and drew their weapons.

When Knight raised his hands, showing himself to be unarmed, one of the men said, "We could have killed you!"

The other, who was less concerned with Knight's safety, said, "Who are you and what the hell are you doing up here?"

"I need your sniper rifle," Knight said, looking at the weapon propped up in the corner next to the grumpy soldier. It was a standard-issue rifle with a day scope. It would be accurate, but its bolt action would slow him down as each round had to be chambered by hand.

The grumpy soldier scoffed. "No fucking way."

"Do me a favor and take a look across the river," Knight said. "Through the scope."

Curiosity got the best of the grumpy soldier. He squinted at Knight as he picked up the weapon and pulled up the scope flaps. He set the weapon down on the railing and scanned the opposite shore. A moment later he stepped back quickly, standing tall. His skin, tanned from the Iraqi sun, went white.

"Right now your heart is pounding in your chest," Knight said. "Your breathing is faster than a machine gun. You're scared shitless, probably shaking, and couldn't hit a target from ten feet. So you're going to let me use this weapon and save those men."

Rapid machine-gun fire broke out in the distance. Both men tensed. Knight moved. He reached in front of the stunned soldier and took his weapon. Neither man protested. Instead, they stood behind Knight and watched. In the distance, a security boat was backing across the river, a man on the machine gun firing at the far side.

Knight chambered a round and took aim. Through the powerful scope he watched the boat slam into the far shore. Then they were running up the hill toward the palace. But the giant creatures he'd seen before had disappeared.

Where did they go?

He got his answer a moment later as two massive insects—mantises—took to the sky, flew over the river, and landed behind King. He took aim and fired at the lead creature. The bullet crossed the half-mile distance and overshot the creature. He turned an annoyed glance on the grumpy soldier. "When was the last time this weapon was calibrated?"

The man offered a guilty shrug.

"Sonofabitch," Knight grumbled as he chambered a second round and took aim again. The mantises were already charging up the hill, concealed by brush, trees, and perfect desert coloring. He could see them moving within, but didn't want to waste rounds only to shoot something nonvital.

He scanned up the hill and saw King pause. "Don't stop," Knight said. "Don't stop!"

The lead insect cleared the brush at the top of the hill and lunged into the air, its two forelimbs ready to strike. Knight held his breath as King turned around positioning his face right in front of the outstretching limbs.

AS KING AND Bowers reached the top of the hill, King stopped and told Bowers to head for the ruins. It was a straight shot, downhill. *Bowers should have no trouble making it,* King thought, *unless he falls again.*

He turned around to see how close the mantises were and found two dagger-lined limbs opening up to embrace him. With a violent, bloody death only a few inches and a fraction of a second away, King did the only thing he could: closed his eyes.

The sound didn't register until after the event took place, but King heard a close, wet sucking sound followed by a distant thunderclap as a single round was fired.

King was struck hard and knocked to the ground, but his head was still intact and the attack did not continue. He scrambled up and found a headless mantis at his feet. King saw gore sprayed across the palace wall and traced an imaginary bullet trajectory back across the base to where a security tower stood.

King knew of only one man who could hit a moving target from that distance.

Knight.

A glint of light from the tower flashed a message in rapid-fire Morse code: run.

King obeyed as the brush near the top of the hill shook with the approach of the remaining mantis. His feet carried him swiftly down the hill. So swift, in fact, that he caught up to Bowers and maintained a healthy distance from the mantis. He could hear the distant sniper rifle shots being fired by Knight, but had no idea if he was hitting his target. So when they reached the bottom of the hill, which ended at a football field–sized stretch of desert sand, King gave Bowers a shove and urged him to move faster.

As they crossed the sand, King looked back and saw the mantis exit the protection of the hillside brush. A round immediately struck one side and burst out the other. The mantis staggered, but then took flight, following an erratic flight path that was impossible to predict.

As they approached the edge of the ruins, King said, "Head for the back. There are two people inside that can help. Just keep moving until you find them."

Bowers looked at King, his eyes wide with fear. "Why are you telling me all of this? Tick on dick, remember?"

"Because we're splitting up," King shouted.

The ruins loomed before them. Though he could only see the arched entrance and the halls that led to the left and right behind it, King knew the ruins were a labyrinth of open halls, chambers, and atriums. "I'll get you over that first wall," he said to Bowers. "Then you're on your own."

Bowers gave a grateful nod.

Then they were at the dull brown wall. It stood eight feet tall. King clasped his hands together. Bowers stepped onto King's hands and working together, they launched him up and over the wall. "Good luck, man," Bowers said after landing.

But King had no time to reply. The flying mantis descended toward him. Adapting to its prey, this mantis was going to attack from the air! But it didn't attack. Instead, as the hum of its clear wings grew intense, the insect rose up and over the eight-foot wall.

"No!" King shouted. "Bowers, run!"

But it was too late. As the giant predator descended on the other side of the wall, Bowers let out a scream. The shrill sound turned to a wet gargle. Silence followed, then the sound of something tearing, followed by more silence. King had seen the mantis in action and knew what happened. Bowers had been impaled, pinned to the ground, and then left. The mantis was still on the hunt.

King ran to the left, entering the maze. Before he reached the first turn, he heard the telltale clack of the mantis walking on stone, but he couldn't tell where it was coming from.

King tore around the corner, weaving his way through the chaotic ruins. An opening in the wall to his right opened up into a courtyard. Bowers lay in the center of the space, his eyes glossy, his body surrounded by a pool of dark red blood. King pushed forward and spilled from a hallway into what had once been a kitchen. He leaped over the three stone stairs that descended into the room and then over the three-foot foundation to exit on the other side.

As he ran past an open doorway, he caught sight of an aberration in the wall. Then he was struck in the side and sent sailing. He slammed into a wall, tearing ancient bricks away as he attempted to stop his descent. But the wall was old and weak. He toppled over, landing on his back.

Loud clicks filled the air as the agitated insect wiggle-walked into the hallway. King pushed away, sliding on his back. But there wasn't far to go. The hall ended at a ten-foot-tall dead end just a few feet behind him. He got to his feet, hoping to dodge the mantis's strike, and then? He had no idea.

A loud whistle caught his attention. Looking beyond the mantis, he saw Queen, XM25 aimed straight for the mantis's back. But the high-caliber rounds would pierce the mantis and strike him as well. "Down!" she shouted.

King hit the deck hard.

The mantis struck.

The roar of automatic gunfire filled the air.

Pain lanced through King's body, but being impaled by a score of daggers didn't hurt as much as King thought it would. He looked up to find a bullet-ridden mantis standing above him. Its back was arched back in death. The spikes lining its forearm had merely grazed his leg, opening a shallow cut. King dodged to the side as the massive insect toppled over. He fell forward as he ducked the flailing limbs of the dead mantis. He landed hard and rolled onto his back. With the beast immobilized, he lay still, breathing hard. Anger coursed through him.

"You okay?" Queen asked, looking down at him.

"It killed Bowers," he said. "He was a good man."

A gloved hand reached down to help King up. "Good men die every day," Alexander said.

King ignored his outstretched hand and took Queen's instead. She pulled him fast. He turned to Alexander. "Not on my watch."

Bishop arrived a moment later, KA-BAR knife drawn and ready to use. Seeing the dead insect, he sheathed the knife. "What is it?"

"A breadcrumb," King replied. "They were here." He pulled the ruined insulin pump from his pant pocket. "*She* was here."

And with all the mantises now dead, he turned his attention to the problem still at hand. "Did I hear Knight correctly? The tower isn't here?"

Bishop shook his head. "It's not."

"Shit," King muttered, rolling his neck as it tensed. If they didn't find Fiona and soon . . .

Bishop's strong hand on his shoulder stopped his rising anger. "But I think we have someone who can point us in the right direction."

SEVENTY-TWO

RAHIM RIFFLED THROUGH a stack of paper, looking for a map he keenly remembered but had no idea if it still existed. The four large, serious men and one woman standing behind him, arms crossed, faces grim, fueled his urgent search.

They had found him right where they left him, standing by the river. When he heard the gunfire begin he ducked down and hid at the side of the road. Not knowing what the conflict was about or who it was between, he wanted to look as innocent and nonthreatening as possible. So he waited.

But when they did find him, all of the politeness and patience was gone. They needed an answer to a single question and they wanted it now. There was no threat included with the question, but Rahim could feel the tension from the one they called King.

He searched a new box and opened a journal. Recognizing the handwriting of the man he'd assisted for three years gave him some relief. He was on the right track. "I think this is the right box," he said.

King sat down next to him and spoke in Arabic. "I don't understand. Most people believe the Tower of Babel is here in Babylon, that it might even be the reason for the city's name. Why would someone think it was in Turkey?"

As he flipped through the stack of pages inside the box, Rahim said, "Photos. From NASA. They showed evidence of a large, ancient construction project. But where you'd expect to see exactly what was built, there was only a mountain. Furthermore, a reinterpretation of ancient texts also lends credibility to the theory. The Targum Yonathan, an Aramaic version of the biblical accounts, states that the tower was in the 'land of Shinar,' which is now the Pontus region of Turkey, near the Black Sea."

King turned to Knight. Check in with Deep Blue. See if we can get satellite imagery for the Pontus region of Turkey."

"Will do," Knight said before exiting.

"Furthermore, many academics believe that this region is also the birthplace of most modern languages. Texts and verbal traditions can be traced back to Pontus." Rahim saw a folded map marked in red pen. He recognized it and yanked it out of the box. He smiled wide as he unfolded it. "Here it is!"

He laid the map out. It was a modern map of Turkey, but had been written on in Arabic and a small location—a mountain—had been circled in red. Next to it was Arabic text: برجبابل, which translated as Tower of Babel.

"This is a mountain," King said. "There are no sands to bury a ziggurat. Wouldn't there be some evidence of it on the surface?"

Rahim pointed out the mountain's rounded, flat top. "At some point in the distant past this mountain was a volcano. It's possible the tower was buried, or destroyed, in an eruption."

"Buried beneath a pyroclastic flow," King said. "Like Pompeii."

"Exactly," Rahim said.

"Is it possible Ridley figured all this out?" King asked, looking at Alexander.

"When he determined that the Tower of Babel was not here, assuming this theory was published, he would pursue it," Alexander replied.

"Has the theory been published?" King asked Rahim in Arabic.

"It's not widely known," the man said, "but I do believe it has been published several times since our search here ended." He became nervous and fidgeted with his hands.

King noticed. "What is it?"

"You said a name," the nervous Iraqi said. "Ridley."

King, Queen, Bishop, and Alexander tensed. "Yes," King said.

"The man who funded our search here. His name was Richard Ridley."

King nearly fell over. Ridley had been searching for Babel before he was even on their radar, before the mess with Hydra. And after all his searching, he'd found what he was looking for. "How deeply was he involved?"

"He would visit once, maybe twice a year. One time he came with Saddam himself. But that ended in 2003, when"—he motioned at the mass of boxes around him, but seemed to imply the base as a whole—"all this happened."

"And what about the Hanging Gardens?" King asked. "Did he know about them?"

Rahim shook his head. "The site was discovered just before the war. I don't believe he ever knew what we believed was buried there."

Which is why he looked for the tower there, too, King thought. *But when he didn't find it, he set up shop temporarily and then moved on.*

"And he wouldn't have been told about the site in Turkey?" King asked.

"It was just a theory some of the archaeologists held and had nothing to do with the dig here," Rahim said.

King nodded. It all made sense.

Light filled the room as Knight returned. "We'll have a satellite over the area in twenty minutes and we're cleared for a drop in Turkey. The *Crescent* is en route. We can be on the ground inside of three hours."

"Thank you, Rahim. We'll send someone to pick you up," King said as he took the map and headed for the door. The others left ahead of him as Knight held the door.

Knight stopped King at the door. "Something's going on back home. Deep Blue didn't sound like himself."

"How'd he sound?" King asked.

"Distracted."

King knew about the media blitzkrieg back home and wondered how Duncan would handle it. If his distraction was noticeable on the phone, then he must be close to a solution. The man could handle just about anything thrown at him. He'd come up with a solution. He just hoped the solution would be permanent. The team needed Deep Blue. He ran the show for a reason. He couldn't help wondering how things would have worked out if Duncan had been on board as Deep Blue. Rook might not be M.I.A.

The dead Delta operators might still be alive. And Fiona might already be back in his arms.

But there was no time to think about Duncan. He'd figure out the problem without his help. Fiona, on the other hand, needed King, and needed him now. He stepped past Knight and headed for the waiting Hummer.

SEVENTY-THREE
Location Unknown

THE BACK WALL of the cell was cold and filled Fiona with a chill that pocked her skin with goose bumps. Despite the cold, she did not move. She didn't have the energy and the cool stone helped reduce her rising body temperature. The hyperglycemia, now unchecked, exaggerated the effects of the second threat to her life—dehydration.

Her throat stung to the point where every swallow was agony. As there was no saliva in her mouth to swallow, she tried her hardest to avoid the natural reflex. Her lips were swollen and cracking. Her dry skin felt like old fabric, and the itch was maddening. But most disturbing to Fiona were the changes going on inside her body.

Her heart occasionally palpitated. She pictured it struggling to pump sludge through her body. Her breath seemed to never fully appease her body's need for oxygen. She figured her drying lungs couldn't absorb as much. And her stomach . . . Despite being empty she felt a rising urge to vomit. She expected she would only dry heave, but dreaded the pain it would bring her contracting throat and cracked lips.

She closed her eyes, fought off a wave of nausea, and focused on what she'd learned in the hours since the woman had been shot. There were now four men in the space beyond her cell. Alpha, Adam, Cainan, and Mahaleel. Based on their conversations, it was Cainan who had brought her here. And it was Adam's wet voice she'd heard earlier speaking in uncanny unison with Alpha.

They had discussions about genetics, of which she only understood bits and pieces. They spoke of ancient languages and the power they contained. The powers of creation. The future world remade.

She had listened to Alpha instruct the others on how to use the ancient tongue. She heard countless phrases, and tried to remember what she was hearing, but it wasn't possible. So she focused on the one she thought would be most useful, the one spoken casually by all when the services of the conjured stone monsters were no longer needed.

But her body was failing and unless she could call forth a spring from the stone, she would soon die. But that was just as well. If she were dead they couldn't experiment on her. They couldn't control her. They couldn't have her kill her father. Death was preferable, so she laid back, closed her eyes, and accepted it.

Darkness closed in around her vision. A faint ringing grew louder, then faded. She felt each beat of her heart, slowing. In the absolute darkness that followed, she heard a voice.

The voice of the devil.

Calling her back.

The words came as a whisper, pulling her from unconsciousness, from death. Her eyes opened. A large bald man knelt above her, his lips moving. She couldn't read his lips, but knew he must be speaking the ancient language she'd heard before because her body was responding to it. She felt herself growing stronger. The pain eased. Her thoughts cleared.

And then a canteen of water was offered.

She took it and drank. At first the cool liquid stung her throat, but it was unnaturally absorbed into her body. With the canteen drained, Fiona stood to her feet feeling fully replenished. She had been on the brink of death, but Alpha had pulled her back.

He'd saved her.

"Praise be to Alpha," she said, then knelt at his feet.

SEVENTY-FOUR
Washington, D.C.

FOR THE FIRST time in a very long time, Duncan felt at peace. Some people experienced this feeling after quitting a stressful job, or breaking up with an overbearing partner. In every case the emotion experienced is the same: freedom.

"I can't believe we did this," Boucher said, staring at the flat-screen TV. The pair had holed up in the situation room because they couldn't be seen together. Not now. Not for a very long time. To the rest of the world they were political enemies.

After watching Marrs call the press conference, Boucher had snuck back to the White House to watch the fireworks start.

Duncan looked at his CIA chief. "We did what needed to be done. It will all work out for the best."

There was no arguing that. Duncan had thought of everything. And the world would be better off for it.

The last part of the plan required no paperwork. No signatures. No trail.

Black ops were like that sometimes.

And the Chess Team would become the blackest of all black ops. Their operating budget would be lessened, but still substantial and one hundred percent under the table. They would lose their all-access pass to military support, but they could operate with total anonymity and freedom. No red tape. No political repercussions. They would retain a flight crew from the Nightstalkers, two stealth Blackhawks, the *Crescent*, and a handpicked staff of scientists, weapons experts, and intelligence operatives. The former Manifold Alpha facility hidden beneath a mountain in New Hampshire's White Mountain region would become their base of operations.

And no one, not even the future president of the United States, would know they existed. Outside of the expanded Chess Team, just Boucher and Keasling would know the truth.

Only one task remained unfinished. Duncan needed to assume his role as Deep Blue, permanently, and step down from his position as commander in chief. And for that to happen, Marrs had to fulfill his end of the deal.

Boucher switched on the wall-mounted TV and sat down on one of the couches. The press conference was just getting under way. The crowds from the recent rallies were all there cheering. And at first they were as fervent as ever. Even more so when Marrs launched into his claims. But when he offered his proof in the form of authentic documents and the future testimony of Dominick Boucher, the crowd fell silent. The reality of Duncan failing so miserably set in hard and took the wind out of their sails. Even Marrs looked sad.

"He doesn't deserve it," Boucher said. "He's a sham. You know that, right?"

Duncan nodded. "But he served a purpose, albeit unknowingly."

"A pawn?"

Duncan smiled. "Exactly."

SEVENTY-FIVE
Severodvinsk, Russia

THE DOCKS WERE quiet. For that, Rook was thankful. His host seemed far less excited. Burdened by the weight of his sister's death, Maksim Dashkov was not in a cooperative mood. The old, red-nosed fisherman was built like the great Siberian brown bear, but he had a heart similar to his sister's. He had openly wept for her in front of Rook, and had asked about the state of her cabin, how she survived the winters, and if she was happy. He expressed regret over having not seen her since the death of her husband, and told of hard winters and small hauls.

The pair stood on the old wooden fisherman's dock. The sub yard sat about a mile away. Rook could see a docked Borei class submarine, probably rotating crews and getting resupplied. A patrol boat with a large mounted machine gun cruised back and forth, ever watchful.

Dashkov breathed into his hands. "Hard times have forced me to take on less than noble jobs in the past. And I assume that's why Galya sent you to me." He made a point of looking back at the security boat. Rook had been watching it a little too keenly.

"I'd like to avoid conflicts if possible, yes."

"As would I," Dashkov said. "Which is why I cannot do what you ask."

Rook had explained, without going into detail, that he needed a quick and quiet trip out of Russia, destination Norway.

Rook frowned. "Why not?"

The large man sighed. "My ship has already been chartered."

Rook knew he was asking a lot. It was clear that Dashkov and much of the city were hurting for money. He could promise to have money sent, but that's all it was, a promise. Without money up front he was asking for a free ride.

Dashkov turned away and looked out at the gray ocean. "You seem like a good man, I'm sorry."

"Put me to work, then," Rook said. "Pass me off as a member of the crew."

"I can't afford a crew."

"Does your charter know this?"

"No, but—"

Rook stood in front of Dashkov. "What are you afraid of?"

Dashkov took out a cigarette and lit it, sucking in the tobacco smoke and letting it out slowly. "These men, they are not like you. They are not good people."

There was more to it than that. Rook waited.

"Sometimes I see things and look the other way. Understand?"

Rook did understand. The Chess Team had to do the same on occasion to serve the greater good. Deals with drug dealers, warlords, and gunrunners weren't uncommon when fighting a greater enemy. "Then I will look the other way, too."

After another long drag, Dashkov shook his head. "I'm sorry. I can't." He started to walk away.

Rook took his arm and spun him around. His patience was gone. If it took the blunt truth to make this man help him, so be it. "Hey," he said, his voice full of mirth. Rook pulled up his shirt revealing a swath of bandages with red polka dots of blood staining them. He pulled up the bandages revealing a splash of bruised skin and several small holes sewed up with thread. "Your sister saved my life."

Dashkov leaned in and looked at the wounds. "She used thread?"

"She did the best she could with what she had."

"She always did." Dashkov looked moved, but not convinced.

"I haven't told you how she died."

Dashkov lost his taste for tobacco and flicked the cigarette into the ocean. "I haven't asked."

"She died protecting me. Took the bullet meant for me and four more on top of it." Rook made sure the man's eyes were trained on his. "Her last wish in this life is that you would help me."

After a deep sigh, the old fisherman asked, "Who shot her?"

It was Rook's turn to glance at the patrol boat. Dashkov understood and gave a nod. "I will drop you off at the first port in Norway. It is not a place I would spend any time, but it is the best I can do. You will act as my first mate and will feign illness. Understood?"

"Don't worry," Rook said. "I can follow orders."

Dashkov squinted at him. "I'm sure."

An hour later Dashkov and Rook boarded his fishing boat, the *Songbird*. As he led Rook belowdecks, Dashkov whispered a reminder. "Remember. Do not react to what you see. Do not speak to these men. I am simply introducing you so that they are not caught off guard by your presence. If these men do not like the way you sneeze they are liable to throw us both overboard."

Rook nodded, steeling himself for the worst—a shipment of weapons, drugs, or other contraband. But when they entered the cargo hold where the two passengers and their package spent most of their time, Rook was decidedly unprepared for what he saw. His eyes arced around the space, taking everything in. Then he turned his eyes to the floor, careful to not meet the harsh stares of the two men.

As Dashkov explained who Rook was and what he would be doing, Rook thought about the two men. They had the distinct look of old KGB agents—thick skin; cold, deep-set eyes; and battle scars to boot. They were killers for certain. But it was the third person in the room who had fully captured his attention. The woman, perhaps in her early thirties, sat bound and gagged in a metal chair. A gash over her eye dripped blood over her face. The wound was straight and thin, delivered by a razor blade.

As the two men grunted in acknowledgment of Dashkov's explanation, Rook chanced a look up. The woman caught his eyes. She silently pleaded with him for help, but he glanced away quickly. In that moment when their eyes met, there was a flicker of recognition, but he couldn't place it. Something about her was familiar, yet he knew he'd never seen her before in his life.

He followed Dashkov to the deck and then to the pilot house. He wanted to apologize to the man in advance, but stayed quiet. Speaking his mind would only upset him and Rook needed to maintain the status quo until they were far out to sea.

Once they were on the high seas, they were at the mercy of Mother Nature. Anything could happen.

Anything.

It was normally impossible to predict what that might be, but Rook knew exactly what was going to happen. Dashkov be damned, he could not look the other way.

Not this time.

SEVENTY-SIX
Pontus, Turkey

WITH NO TIME to prebreath for a HALO jump during the short flight from Iraq to Turkey, the team would attempt a new kind of drop. The *Crescent*, flying at thirty thousand feet, would descend rapidly. Its stealth technology made it practically invisible to radar and other detection methods, but to the naked eye, the black croissant-shaped plane was easy to spot. So its insertion into Turkey's airspace needed to be done quickly. Upon reaching five thousand feet, the *Crescent* would pull up, beginning a strenuous downward arc before going vertical again and dumping the team from its backside three thousand feet from the surface.

King, Queen, Knight, Bishop, and Alexander sat at the rear of the jet's cargo hold, waiting for the drop to begin. Each was dressed in black special ops gear with night vision goggles, XM-25 assault rifles, an assortment of grenades, and blocks of C4—enough to bring down the mountain, which King was prepared to do in order to stop Ridley and save Fiona.

Knight left his seat and squatted in front of the others. He held an eight-by-ten touch-screen tablet. "Latest satellite imagery confirms our target."

The screen showed a bird's-eye view of a mountain range.

"This was taken a month ago." Knight placed a thumb and index finger over a portion of the screen and opened them. The image zoomed in on a slope. Rising up the slope was a pale zigzag pattern. "The lines you see cutting across the mountain are switchback trails. But what we're interested in is over here." Knight zoomed in on an area above the switchbacks. The featureless dark stone appeared insignificant.

"Here's the most recent image, taken ten minutes ago." Knight tapped an icon in the upper left corner of the screen. The image updated, revealing the same image with different lighting and a shadow of a cloud toward the bottom. But the change in the dark stone was what interested them. Evidence of serious digging could be seen in the light-colored debris spread out in a fan shape.

King followed the trail back to the mountain wall. There was no entrance, just a wall of stone. "They sealed the mountain closed behind them."

"We'll never get through that without announcing our presence," Queen said.

"That's what I thought, too," Knight said. "So I had them take thermal shots. Take a look." He switched the image again. This time, the topographical photo switched to shades of light blue.

"What are we looking for?" Bishop asked.

"Cool spots," Knight said. "There are three of them." He pointed to three purple spots on the image. "Here, here, and here."

"Vents," Alexander said.

"Why are they purple?" King asked. "The ambient temperature underground is fifty-five degrees. The temperature in the mountains of Turkey in the early summer are what?"

"Weather report said sixty-five," Queen said.

"So the vents should have appeared as dark blue spots. Not purple." King placed his fingers on the tablet and zoomed in on one of the purple vents. "So what is heating up the inside of this mountain?"

"Descent beginning in two minutes," the pilot's voice said over the intercom. "Better strap in and get ready for a ride."

"At any rate," Knight said, "those vents are our way in." He shut down the tablet and placed it in a wall-mounted locker. He took his seat and strapped in as the pilot gave a one-minute warning.

Their seats had been relocated from the side of the cargo bay and bolted in its center facing the doors. When the *Crescent* reached its vertical position, the team would unbuckle one at a time and fall out into the open air.

"Here we go, folks," the pilot said.

The *Crescent* dipped forward quickly. There was no moment of weightlessness that people experienced with airplane zero G simulations. Instead, intense pressure pushed against their chests as the *Crescent* quickly reached its top speed of Mach 2, and then surpassed it. With gravity helping the plane's return to earth, it reached Mach 2.5 and covered the distance in ten seconds.

But the real g-force struck when the *Crescent* began its ascent. As the plane leveled out and continued pulling up, the seat belt straps pulled tight, crushing the air from their lungs.

As the pressure reached its apex, when each and every member of the team was seeing colors dancing in their vision, the row of seats tilted forward. King knew what it meant. The fresh bolts were coming loose. He tried to speak, but the pressure was still too great.

The *Crescent* continued its ascent, heading toward a vertical position. As it reached the seventy percent mark, the pressure lessened and King shouted an order into his throat mic. "Open the bay doors now!"

"We're not yet at a vertical position sir, the draft could throw us off," the pilot said.

The bolts gave again, tilting the group forward. If they tore free, the team would be flung against the back doors at incredible speed. King had no doubt only Bishop and Alexander would survive the impact.

"The chairs are about to break loose!" King shouted. "Open the doors now!"

The red light above the door immediately turned green and a loud grinding filled the cabin. The doors opened quickly. Wind pounded over them. If not for the goggles over their eyes, seeing would have been impossible.

King felt a slow tilting of the chair as the bolts slid from the floor. Gravity, wind, and g-forces were working against them. With the bay doors open halfway King could see the Turkish mountains shrinking away beneath them.

"Fifteen seconds," the pilot said.

But they didn't have fifteen seconds. The chairs were about to break loose, and with the doors now open sixty percent, there was barely enough room to fit. "Duck your head and pull in your legs," King shouted to the team.

The bolts gave way all at once. As the team fell, they followed King's orders, ducking their heads and bringing their knees up to their chests. Forty-five hundred feet above the earth, the Chess Team shot out from the back of the *Crescent* still strapped into a row of chairs like a bunch of teenagers at a carnival death drop.

SEVENTY-SEVEN
Babel

PUSHED AND PULLED by high winds, the row of seats spun madly as it carried the team toward the rocky mountain slope below. They had just seconds to separate and deploy their parachutes. King, who was sitting in the middle of the five man team, shouted his orders.

"Bishop, Alexander, go!"

Both men heard him clearly in their ears. They unbuckled from their seats and rolled away. Seconds later they pulled their chutes and the bench rocketed past them.

Only seconds remained.

"Queen, Knight, go!"

Both were ready, pushing from their seats and pulling their chutes once far enough away. They shot above the bench, and King. With only fifteen hundred feet left, King unbuckled from the bench and shoved off it with his feet. He yanked his cord. As his fall slowed with a sudden yank from his opening chute, he watched the bench finish its fall. It smashed on the mountainside. An explosion of small parts burst from the bench as it folded in over itself.

King cringed. He had no idea what kind of surveillance or security the site had, but they had undoubtedly just announced their skyward approach. He readied himself for an attack, but none came. In fact, the barren mountainside was as quiet and empty as it had been before. The only difference was that it was now rushing toward him.

King bent his knees as he struck, and rolled with the impact. But he was headed downslope and the cool air descending the mountain caught his parachute, dragging him down the steep grade. He spun himself around and planted his boots on the ground. He shot to his feet and dug in, grabbing the lines of his parachute and reeling them in. With the billowing fabric under control, he quickly bunched it up, found a crag in the rocks, and stuffed it in.

He turned back to find the others above him, hiding their chutes as well. With the vent a hundred yards above them, he started up the hill at a run. The others joined him and stopped when they reached the vent.

It was a three-foot hole in the earth, concealed by brush. It descended into darkness, but a tiny speck of light could be seen at the bottom.

"Depth?" King asked.

Knight aimed a laser range finder down the hole. "Two hundred feet."

"Measure out one-ninety and throw it in," King said to Bishop, who was uncoiling a large spool of titanium cable.

Bishop lowered the cable into the hole, watching as the spool's digital readout scrolled toward two hundred feet. He stopped the cable at one hundred ninety and placed the spool on the ground. Using what looked like a miniature staple gun, he fired five titanium staples into the mountainside. Their long barbed tips could support three hundred pounds each. But Bishop didn't want to risk their lives on what the staples were *supposed* to do. He fired five more and stepped back. "Good to go."

King clipped a stop descender onto the line. Its squeeze trigger would allow him to slow his descent by loosening his grip. The counterintuitive function of the device was hard to get used to, but once mastered, it worked without flaw. Of course, that was when rappelling down a cliff face feetfirst. King was descending a vertical stone pipe—head first. He wrapped his feet around the line to keep himself from flipping over and slid into the tunnel. Hidden from the light of day, he reached up and pulled his night vision goggles over his eyes.

The tunnel shot straight down as far as he could see. With wiggle room on either side and a clear shot down, King squeezed his stop descender and plummeted down the hole. The others followed, one by one, spacing out their drops every twenty seconds.

The air grew warmer as King dropped down the pit. And the light ahead grew brighter; so much so that he had to reach up and remove his night vision goggles. Something was down there, he just hoped he wouldn't find himself dangling above a pit of lava, or a firing squad.

As King approached the bottom of the hole he eased up on his grip and began slowing. The yellow tip of the line's end was thirty feet below. If he didn't stop by the time he reached it, he'd fall to the floor below.

Before he expected, King was out of the vent, dangling over a large orb-shaped room. He quickly scanned the space for danger; finding none, he zipped down the line to the stone floor. The others followed him quickly, leaving their descenders clipped to the dangling line. Should anyone find it, their presence would be detected. But they weren't planning on remaining covert for much longer.

As King approached the room's only exit and a tall hallway beyond, he saw the light source ahead and paused. A sphere of light, the size of a small plum, floated eight feet above the floor. There was no bulb that he could see and no line dropping down to the light.

Alexander joined him. "This is very bad."

They entered the room slowly, unable to take their eyes off the light. King motioned to Bishop and Knight. "Take point." As the pair moved to the far end of the hallway, King stopped beneath the light. He held his bare hand up to it. The heat was searing up close, but dissipated quickly. He shook his head in amazement. This small sphere was lighting and heating several large rooms beneath a mountain.

Queen crouched next to him and picked up a handful of sand from the hallway floor.

"What are you doing?" King whispered as she stood.

"When you got close to it, your hair stood on end," she replied.

"A static charge?"

Queen answered by throwing the sand to the side of sphere. The sand farthest from the light fell away. The sand closest fell into the light, sucked in by an invisible force. And the sand in between floated as though in orbit around a star. "Not static. Gravity."

For the small object to have gravity, it would have to be incredibly dense. "They're miniature suns," he said.

"*Very* bad," Alexander repeated before heading past the sun. "Scientists at the National Ignition Facility are trying to achieve a sunlike fusion reaction using lasers that would supply infinite energy, but this . . . this goes beyond any science known to me."

"And I don't see any lasers," Queen said.

They all knew the implications. Ridley had unlocked the secrets to not just immortality, animating stone, and imbuing clay with life, or a close approximation of it, but he'd also unlocked the secret to creating light—not in a Thomas Edison sense, but in a real creator of all existence sense. Something beyond their comprehension.

King looked at his high-tech XM-25. Its exploding rounds seemed crude compared to the tiny sun behind them. Could he really stop a man who had made himself a god? He looked at Alexander, who had manipulated history so that the world believed he, the mighty Hercules, was a half-human half-god myth. But now Ridley had, in fact, achieved such a thing.

Alexander met King's eyes. "He's still human."

Realizing they'd been thinking the same thing, King asked, "How do we kill him?"

"We can't kill him," Alexander said. "But we can silence him."

"How?"

"Take off his head. Burn the flesh."

"Like the Hydra."

A raised hand from the front of the hall silenced the hushed conversation. Knight pointed through the tunnel exit, then to his ear. They heard somebody. King met them at the end of the tunnel and stopped to listen. The deep baritone voice was impossible to mistake.

They'd found Richard Ridley.

A second voice, identical to the first, replied.

They'd found *several* Richard Ridleys.

SEVENTY-EIGHT

KING LED THE team toward the voice, moving slowly and silently. He stopped at a tunnel that branched away and turned back to the others. He pointed to Queen, Bishop, and Knight. "See where this goes. Keep your eyes open for Fiona."

Queen hesitated, but then nodded. She didn't want to miss taking out

Ridley, but King was right. Their best chance of finding Fiona was splitting up. Each member of the team carried an insulin shot. It didn't matter which one of them found her first. As long as *someone* found her.

Queen led Bishop and Knight down the side tunnel, their path lit by equally spaced mini-suns.

King and Alexander resumed their approach toward the hallway's end, toward the voices. The exit was narrow and provided plenty of wall on either side for the two men to hide behind. They stood flat against the brown stone and peeked into the chamber beyond.

The space was vast and separated into two rings. The outer hall wrapped around the room. Its walls were covered in stone murals and blocks of cuneiform. The floor was nearly smooth, constructed from massive stone blocks fit tightly together. Several tall statues, arms raised high, separated the outer hall from an inner chamber. They appeared to be supporting the roof, but King suspected they were decorative.

He eyed the closest statue. Its style was clearly Sumerian—rigid posture, straight limbs, curved joints. All were masculine in build but wore what looked like shin-length skirts. Stiff-looking rolls of hair stretched down just below the shoulder line. King had no doubt that if he could see the face it would have the same oversized, oval, blue lapis lazuli eyes he'd seen beneath the sands of Babylon.

He motioned to Alexander and then to the two nearest statues. Alexander responded by taking a quick peek into the room and then dashing across the twenty-foot distance to one of the statues. He stopped behind it, throwing himself against its backside without making a sound.

King noticed how easy it was for Alexander to move with stealth. How many times had he snuck up on an enemy? How many wars had he taken part in? *Better yet,* King thought, *how many wars has he started?*

Alexander peeked around the statue briefly and then waved King in.

King covered the distance to a second statue quickly and stopped behind it. Its legs, hewn out of a solid chunk of marble, easily hid his crouching form. He leaned around the statue's base and looked into the center of the chamber.

He didn't notice the stepped ceiling or the faces of the eight other statues wrapping around the room. He paid no attention to the tables stationed over a dark brown stain on the stone floor, or the lab equipment and specimen cages they held. He only saw Richard Ridley.

Two of him.

They stood to either side of a third man, whose body and head were concealed by a hooded cloak. But he appeared disfigured somehow, like a hunchback. The three men were speaking with hushed voices, impossible to discern. In fact, King wasn't certain what language they were speaking.

Then it hit him, they're speaking the mother tongue!

But were they having a conversation or doing something more nefarious?

King's question was answered by a puff of grit that fell from above. He saw it fall slowly past his face and land on his arm. He turned his head up, tracing the fallen dirt's path back up.

Two football-sized blue eyes, twisted with rage, stared back at him. The statue's head had turned around! Its puglike nose was pulled up to reveal a snarling mash of sharp teeth. Though clearly Sumerian, the statues were not designed to look human. Not fully human at least.

Before he could move or shout a warning to Alexander, the statue sprang to life, wrapping its large arms around his ribs in a crushing bear hug. He marveled at the speed and silence with which the golem moved. It seemed Ridley was perfecting the art. Then the pain struck as his body was pinned in a stone embrace. His weapon and gear pushed against his body, making struggling painful and escape impossible. He pummeled the golem a few times, but his efforts were fruitless. It couldn't feel pain. *Hell*, King thought, *it probably can't feel anything.*

He was lifted off the ground and turned around. Twenty feet away, Alexander was being treated similarly, though his arms were pinned to his sides while King's remained free. But he continued to fight against his bonds. The injuries Alexander received were healing as quickly as he inflicted them on himself, but even he was unable to break free.

The two Richard Ridleys and the hooded man faced the pair.

Ridley's voice filled the chamber, "Welcome, King," but neither of the Ridleys had spoken.

The man in the middle is also Ridley, King thought. *Ridley 1.0. But what's wrong with his body?*

"And our unknown adversary I presume?" Ridley said.

King saw the cloaked figure's hood turn toward Alexander as he spoke, confirming his suspicion that he was also Ridley.

"We have much in common, you and I," Ridley said. "Though you seem to lack my ambition."

Alexander remained silent, his arms shaking as he tried to pull them free of the golem's grasp.

"Or is it that you just lack the brains? After all, you were born into a world that was flat. You would have had no concept of the world as a whole. I respect what you've done, the lives you've lived. But you have been small-minded for thousands of years. Of course, you didn't have the mother tongue. It was gone before your time. Even if you could speak the language, the lack of technology would have created logistical problems. How could you reach a planet full of people?

"Happily, that's no longer a problem." Ridley reached into his pocket and pulled out a flash drive. "Fifteen seconds of audio to change the world. When I'm done there will be one language again. One god. The human race will be united under me for all time."

Ridley turned back to the table, opened a laptop, and plugged in the flash drive. King followed the cable leading out of the laptop. It hung down to the floor. From there, the cable stretched out between two of the statues and ended at a row of blinking servers. He hadn't noticed them before, hidden in the darkness. Several more cables came out of the servers, many descending into the stone floor, and just as many rising up through the ceiling.

"You're connected to the whole world?" King asked.

As the computer booted, Ridley turned around. "It's a simple matter really, though not possible without the help of my Russian friends. How is Rook, by the way? Did he run into any trouble in Siberia?"

King remained stoic. Rook's fate was something he couldn't worry about right now.

Ridley smiled when King didn't take the bait. "The Russians have given me access to land lines, cell towers, and satellites around the world. Their hackers have arranged for a thirty-second, all-access pass to the rest of the world's communications. Of course, the Russians believe my goal is to hack into and collapse the U.S. financial market, but they won't complain when they learn the truth. No one will ever complain again."

Ridley tapped his head. "Because the real hack, that's up here. In the human mind. Did you know that there was a time in human history when the human race was docile? Call it the subservient gene or naïveté gene. Whatever you like. We were loyal, loved unconditionally, and lacked cunning. Like biped cows. We had free will to choose whether or not we would, say, eat an apple or a grape, but knew nothing of good and evil. And then, something flipped the switch." He snapped his finger. "And we changed. We became killers, consumed with greed, lust, and envy. The original speaker of the mother tongue made us this way. I'm going to fix things."

"So you're flipping the switch back?" King asked. "Is that it? You're going to save the world?"

With a nod, Ridley said, "That's exactly what I'm doing. The human race will know peace again. There will be no war. No hate. No fear. We will be innocent once again. I'm simply modifying the language, redirecting humanity's adoration from the original speaker of the language—to me." Ridley stretched his arms out. "'And God will wipe away every tear from their eyes; there shall be no more death, nor sorrow, nor crying. There shall be no more pain, for the former things have passed away.' You see? It's all been prophesied."

Ridley smiled. "But you're still wondering how? Oh ye of little faith. Some things are beyond human comprehension, King. The origin of the universe. The emergence of life on our planet. The same science that developed the theory of evolution and the big bang theory tells us both are statistically impossible. Yet here we are. The universe exists. The human race has evolved. And it all came to be . . . because of a language. Whether it's the language of God, an alien tongue, or the tones of the universe, I don't know. I don't yet understand its origin, but I *do* understand its power."

"Like a child with a loaded weapon," King said.

Ridley considered King's statement for a moment, his expression darkening. "Do you understand how a nuclear sub works? Stealth technology? The Aegis combat system? Could you even tell me how to smelt the metal your weapons are made from?"

In fact, King could answer most of those questions, but the stone giant's grip around his chest had begun to tighten. Were Ridley's mood and the golem's actions tied together? If Ridley grew angry enough would the golem respond by killing him? "Point taken," King said, fighting to hide his pain.

A smile returned to Ridley's face and the grip on King loosened. But then he said, "You should be glad you're here, King. This is one of the few places on the planet that is protected from the change. But I'll take care of you personally. You and your little girl."

King's insides ached with rage, but he didn't fight his bonds. Buying time for the others to act was his primary goal. If he had to remain behind while they blew the place to kingdom come and made off with Fiona, he would do so willingly. The words of his father came back to him. *There is no greater love than a father who is willing to lay down his life for his children.* If it came to that, he would. And with that, King realized how truly attached he'd become to Fiona.

Damnit, he thought, *I love the kid.*

King saw the laptop was fully booted and some new software was loading up. Hoping to keep Ridley's attention off the laptop, King asked, "What happened to you, Ridley?" King asked. "After you jumped out of the helicopter."

The hooded Ridley turned toward King.

"I lost an arm," Ridley replied. "Nearly my head."

"And I was born."

The second voice came from the cloaked Ridley, but sounded different. Had Ridley's injuries wrecked his voice? Were his regenerative abilities not as refined as Alexander's?

"The injection I gave myself just minutes before our brief meeting had not been perfected." He chuckled. "When I jumped from the helicopter I had no idea if I would survive or not. But I did. I had received the regenerative gene of the Hydra, but there was one other gene that had yet to be culled. I discovered its effects when I looked in the rearview mirror of the car that carried me to freedom."

King noticed that Alexander had stopped struggling and started listening.

"It was this side effect that spurred my continued research into the mother tongue. For years, long before we met, I searched the past for clues to long-forgotten powers—which, as you know, led me to the ancient remains of the Hydra. Ancient maps, runes, texts, hieroglyphs—I collected and studied the world's history and came to a stunning conclusion: the Tower of Babel story is *real*. I don't yet fully understand the mechanics of *how* mankind's language fractured, only that it did. In the past two years I have pieced together several key phrases of the lost language that allow me to alter and reshape the physical world as well as the thoughts and emotions of the people in it. Not to mention I now have the key to ridding myself of this unfortunate disfigurement."

"Be kind," said the higher pitched, wet voice.

"Apologies, Adam. You will always be my first son."

Adam. The name struck a chord with King. Ridley had been naming his golem clones after the bloodline from Adam to King David. Was this Adam the first of his lifelike golems?

"I hoped to separate myself from him—from Adam. Thankfully," Ridley said, holding up a stone tablet, "the final piece of the puzzle arrived from Stonehenge."

King could see a series of Egyptian-like runes covering one side of the bluestone tablet. He could probably spend his whole life on the task and never decipher what it said. Ridley, on the other hand, had apparently done so already. "One of Merlin's greatest hits?"

Ridley grinned. "I'm afraid Merlin can't take credit for the words recorded here. He simply recorded the words taught to him in Egypt. And it's just one of the many ancient efforts to preserve the ancient language in stone—the only medium that can reliably last the test of time."

"El Mirador," King said, realizing that Ridley had been collecting bits and pieces of the spoken *and* written language.

"One of many sites that contained written samples of the mother tongue," Ridley said. "Your primitive friends in Vietnam, though unable to read the words carved on the walls, added to my knowledge as well. And with the words gleaned from Merlin's fragment, Adam and I can rejoin the world above as whole individuals." Ridley affectionately rubbed a hand over the tablet before placing it down on the table behind him. "And you are just in time to witness our separation." The cloaked Ridley stepped forward, raising his arms out to the side. "Show yourself, Adam."

King gaped as a third arm reached up over Ridley's head and took hold of the hood. The fingers, thin and bent, wrapped around the fabric and then pulled back quickly.

Ridley stood before them, bare-chested and pale, his bald head shining under the light of a halo of mini-suns. The third arm reached up and over his torso, gripping his chest tightly. A head followed it, rising up behind his shoulder. The face was Ridley's, though slightly disfigured.

"Thank you, King," Adam said. "Without you I would have never been born."

SEVENTY-NINE

QUEEN WAITED BY the entrance to a small room, keeping watch while Bishop and Knight checked out what was inside. She was bothered by the lack of security. In the past, Ridley had surrounded himself with the high-tech security force known as Gen-Y. They had ultimately failed him, so it was understandable that they were no longer in his employ, but if he had reason to be paranoid about security before, he had twice as many reasons now.

Yet the hallways were empty.

Which meant Ridley had no need for security, had lost his marbles, or had plenty of security that they had yet to discover; she hoped it was the second, but suspected it was a combination of the first and last. Maybe all three.

Knight and Bishop exited the room. "Looks like it used to be an armory. Lots of old blades buried beneath a layer of fibrous dust. Probably ancient wood."

"Doesn't look like anyone's been in there recently," Bishop said.

"Probably not since this place was built," Knight added.

Queen moved on in silence, her thoughts on the mission, but also with Rook. *He should be here now,* she thought. But he was either dead and not returning, or alive and in trouble. *Of course,* she thought, *he could be alive and choosing to stay away.* But if that were true . . . She forced the thought from her mind and turned her full attention to the entryway ahead. She could hear a scratching sound. She detected a foul combination of odors next.

She paused and breathed through her nose.

Piss and shit.

With her XM25 pressed firmly against her shoulder, Queen entered the chamber and froze. Large cages filled the room, lining every wall and stacked three high. She quickly noted the stenciled labels on the front of each cage, written in Russian. And beneath the labels, a Manifold

Genetics logo, also in Russian. "Look," she said, pointing to one of the logos. "These cages were either here before we took Manifold down—"

"Or the company is still active," Knight finished.

"In Russia," Queen said. They had witnessed the destruction of Manifold Gamma and Beta. And they had captured the Manifold lab in New Hampshire known as Alpha. But with plenty more letters in the Greek alphabet remaining, who's to say there weren't as many Manifold facilities left?

Before Queen attempted to read the labels, she noticed the cages were not empty. The cages held a variety of twisted forms. Many on the lower level were indiscernible as any living creature on Earth, with limbs where heads should be, hoofed feet mixed with human hands and scaled faces. Many appeared dead, but their bodies rose and fell with each breath, despite not having any visible mouth or nose.

Those in the middle cages were hale, but fearful, shifting to the back of the cage. These were oversized lizards and predatory birds. They were covered in feces from the animals on the cages above—dirty and pitiful. Despite their size, they seemed to be as docile and fearful of humans as their smaller, wild, counterparts.

Perhaps these were wild animals before they were experimented on, Queen thought. Then she saw the top row.

Sitting still and watching her were several mammoth, stubby-tailed gray cats. Larger than Siberean tigers, the giant cats had black-tipped ears with long tufts of fur pointing up from them. Their yellow feline eyes seemed to never blink. Their sandy gray coats were covered in oblong spots, but the fur beneath their chins and bellies was white, though stained with blood.

Someone had been feeding them. She saw the remains of a human hand in one of the cages. Someone had been feeding them people.

What stood out most were the long saberlike teeth that protruded down over their lower jaw, and the two-inch-long retractable claws the cats flexed in and out.

"Are they saber-tooth tigers?" Queen asked.

"Lynx," Bishop said. "They're native to these mountains."

"If these are lynx," Knight said, "then someone's had a genetic field day with them."

"Richard Ridley's calling card," Queen said before moving through the wide path between the cages, keeping her eyes on the large cats that simply watched her move past. "Let's get out of this fucked-up menagerie and find Fiona."

The U-shaped room exited into another hallway. The three moved into the hall quickly, eager to leave the giant predators behind. As they approached the end, Ridley's deep voice returned.

They crept forward and then heard a second voice, this one unmistakable.

King.

Queen motioned for Knight and Bishop to remain behind and crept up to the tunnel exit. She peered into the chamber beyond and saw five people. Two men who appeared to be Richard Ridley, or golem duplicates, and a cloaked man stood with their backs to her. King and Alexander were on the far side of the space, held several feet off the floor, clutched in the arms of two giant living statues. She quickly noted eight more statues around the chamber and slid back into the hallway.

Walking silently, she passed by a dark slit in the wall. Something about it made her pause. She leaned in close, trying to see through the darkness. Two hands shot out at her, reaching for her face. She jumped back and aimed her weapon.

But the hands meant no harm. They were outstretched. Desperate. And they belonged to a thirteen-year-old girl. Fiona!

Queen rushed up to the wall and took hold of her hands. She gave them a squeeze of reassurance. Neither spoke, knowing it might draw attention. After a moment, Queen stepped back. She took out a water bottle and insulin shot, handing them both to Fiona through the crack. She didn't need to tell her what they were for. She would know. Queen held up an index finger and mouthed the words "Be right back."

Fiona turned one of her thumbs up and pulled her hands, along with the water and shot, back inside the cell.

Queen returned to Bishop and Knight, who had seen what happened, but stayed by their post. "We need to get in there now."

"How do we do that without attracting attention?" Knight asked.

"We give them something else to worry about," Queen said, and then headed back toward the menagerie. "Just get through that wall and take her topside."

"When should we blow it?" Knight asked.

Queen looked back over her shoulder. "When the screaming starts."

EIGHTY

KING WAS SPEECHLESS. He felt a combination of revulsion and pity: revulsion at what Ridley had become—he was more devil than god—and pity for the sickly looking version of him clinging to him like a child refusing to wean from its mother.

"How did you escape Stonehenge?" one of the two golem Ridleys asked.

That one's Mahaleel, King thought, but didn't say a word. His eyes were still focused on Adam's, like a predatory bird.

A hint of fear filled Adam's eyes. The real Richard Ridley had faced King before and did so again now as fearless as any immortal being should be. But Adam . . . he was something different.

"You have defiled the past," Alexander said.

King wasn't sure if Alexander really wanted to make a point or if he had seen the subtle motion of King's right arm. Either way, King was thankful for the distraction.

Ridley and Adam guffawed in unison. The conjoined duo walked toward him, leaving Cainan and Mahaleel behind. They stopped short and squinted at Alexander. "Shall we compare who has defiled what? Hmm? I'm sure King would love to hear. I know more about you than you think, Hercules."

"You know nothing," Alexander said. "I will be your undoing."

"Funny, I was just thinking the same thing about you."

Alexander flexed against the stone arms that held him tight. And though he was not able to break free, he did succeed in pushing the golem's arms away from him. The Herculean feat of strength was enough to fully captivate the attention of all four Ridleys and gave King the opportunity to strike.

As King unclipped the Sig Sauer handgun strapped to his thigh he considered his four targets. The two clay golems in the form of Ridley may fall to a bullet, but he wasn't positive they could be killed. The original Ridley had as little to fear from firearms as Alexander or Bishop. Shooting him would just be a waste of time.

But Adam. The fear in his eyes had planted a seed in King's mind. As it grew, he remembered the Hydra. Only its central head was truly immortal. Its body could be cleaved away and would die. As could its other heads. Could Adam be killed? With only two of Hydra's genes in Ridley's body, would his regenerative abilities extend to Adam?

There was only one way to find out.

As King pulled the weapon from its holster, Adam glanced in his direction. He immediately saw the handgun rising in his direction. His eyes spread wide. His mouth twisted in fear, revealing bent teeth. The abject terror expressed in Adam's face answered all of King's questions a second before he found his aim.

Then he pulled the trigger.

QUEEN ENTERED THE menagerie with her arm over her nose and her weapon lowered. She walked through, taking stock of the giant cats, whose heads followed her path through the room, rotating mechanically. She stopped at the center of the room, looking back and forth at the cats. Not one of them moved.

She turned to one of the lower cages that held a motionless, ghastly body. She took out her KA-BAR knife and stabbed it into the flesh. The body convulsed, but stopped moving again after she withdrew the blade. A fresh gush of blood followed the knife out of the body.

Three of the cats immediately stood and began pacing in their large cages.

Those are the ones, Queen thought, and then moved to the closest cage. The cage doors were held shut by simple sliding pin locks. She pulled the first pin, but didn't open the door. Instead she moved to the next two cages and pulled their locking pins as well. Then she moved to the exit leading away from Bishop and Knight, back the way they'd come.

"Here kitty, kitty," she said when none of them moved for the doors.

The largest of the three reached out and swatted at the door. It flinched back when it swung wide open. But it quickly recovered and slowly approached the open door. The other cats saw what happened and nudged their unlocked cage doors as well.

Queen said, "Come on kitty, don't be a pussy."

When the largest of the three looked at her, she ran, not waiting to see if the cats would take the bait. With the scent of blood in the air and a fast-moving prey running away, she knew their feline instincts would take over.

USING HIS SLENDER arm, Knight reached through the thin slot in the wall of Fiona's cell and placed several small directional charges. The charges packed a punch despite their size, but would direct most of their energy into the hallway, rather than into the cell. Still, he did not envy Fiona's proximity to the explosion. Her ears would most likely be injured and it was possible she might catch some shrapnel, too. But he could think of no other way to quickly open the wall.

He looked at Bishop, who was crouched by the tunnel exit, watching King and Alexander speak to Ridley. He had no idea what Bishop was seeing, but the man looked disturbed.

Knight finished squishing the last bit of C4 into a crag in the wall. He quickly placed four remote-triggered blasting caps into the claylike explosives and switched on the receivers. With the C4 now "hot," a simple push of a button would blow the wall and give them access to Fiona.

Knight crawled to Bishop and tapped his foot.

Bishop looked back. Knight gave a thumbs-up and motioned back down the hall with his head. They met in front of Fiona's cell. Her dirty face looked back at them through the space in the wall.

"What are you doing?" she asked.

"Go curl up in the back corner," Knight said. "Close your eyes, cover your ears, and open your mouth. It will help."

"Is this going to hurt?"

Knight hated saying it, but he wouldn't lie to the girl. "A bit."

"Then wait," she whispered. "Let me try something first."

"Fiona, there isn't ti—"

But she had stepped back into the darkness. He could hear her soft voice saying something, but didn't understand the words. *Fiona's using the mother tongue!* Knight thought, wondering how it was possible.

The walls slowly parted, forming a door.

Both men wasted no time entering. Fiona fell back against the back wall looking weak. They rushed to her, bracing her with their hands.

"That was something else, kid," Knight said.

"How did you learn the language?" Bishop asked.

"I'm a good spy," she said, smiling wide.

Knight noticed how healthy Fiona looked. Other than being dirty, she looked as fit as she had at Bragg. Did Ridley take care of her? If so, what was the point? He looked around the cell, searching for evidence that Fiona had been well cared for—water bottles, food remnants, anything. But the only thing he saw was the water bottle and insulin shot Queen had given her. The water was gone, but the shot had not been used.

What the . . . Knight picked up the syringe and held it up for Bishop to see. Bishop turned to where Fiona had been standing. "Fiona, why didn't you—"

But Fiona was gone.

Both men turned toward the exit and found the walls closing in. Fiona stood on the other side, smiling at them, holding Bishop's KA-BAR knife. They dashed for the exit, but it was too late. They were sealed inside. Even the long slit that had been there closed over with six inches of solid stone.

A moment later, they heard a muffled gunshot.

EIGHTY-ONE

MOVING AT FIFTEEN hundred feet per second, the single round fired by King covered the distance between the handgun and Adam before the weapon's report registered in anyone's ears. The bullet whizzed beneath Ridley's chin, grazing his flesh and opening a wound, before piercing Adam's forehead and punching out the back of his skull. The sound of the single shot reached the group just as Adam's brain exploded in a cloud of blood and flesh. Ridley spun with the impact, seeing the brain matter splatter on the floor at his feet.

Adam's grip on Ridley's chest loosened, and then let go. The one-armed, quarter of a body slid back and dangled limply from Ridley's back.

"Adam!" Ridley shouted in shock. "Adam! No!"

Mahaleel and Cainan rushed forward to help. Mahaleel held Adam's limp weight. Cainan helped Ridley lean back against the table.

"He's not healing," Mahaleel said. "He's dead."

What happened next was completely unexpected and derailed every plan King had come up with. Fiona walked into the room, hands behind her back. She looked healthy, strong, and totally unafraid.

Ridley turned toward her.

"Fiona, run!" King shouted.

But she didn't. She walked halfway between King and Ridley and stopped.

"What are you doing?" King asked.

Fiona looked over her shoulder toward Ridley.

King's stomach twisted. Something was very wrong.

Ridley's smile looked like a wolf bearing its teeth. "You may have killed Adam, but I've still got my Eve. The first of her kind."

"What are you—"

"Kill him, Eve."

Fiona stepped toward King. She wore a slight smile. "Yes, Father," she said and then pulled the seven-inch blade out from behind her back. Her little bare feet padded against the hard floor. Her black pajamas were dirty and full of holes. Her straight black hair hung loose around her shoulders. But her eyes were wrong. They were devoid of emotion and still, as though in shock.

He looked at the gun in his hand. He could shoot her and save himself, but it would destroy him. He'd rather die than kill her.

"Fiona, stop!" was all King could shout before she plunged the knife into his chest.

KNIGHT CRACKED A glow stick. It lit the small space in bright green light. They quickly scanned the space. To the right of the outside wall Knight saw some letters scratched into the stone. Had they not been near the back of the room, they would have missed it. He knelt down and held the light up to the wall and read the text.

SAVE ME
Arzu Turan. Vish tracidor vim calee. Filash vor der wash.
Vilad forsh.

"What do you make of this?" Knight asked.

"It must be some portion of the ancient language," Bishop replied. "Something she thought could help."

"Something that could return her to herself."

Bishop tilted his head in agreement. The girl had certainly not been herself. "We need to get out of here."

Knight opened his hand revealing the transmitter. "The charges are probably embedded in the wall, but they should still work."

Bishop took out a small camera with a digital display and snapped a photo of the text. "Do it," he said, taking a step back. But something made him pause. Something about the writing on the wall.

Knight stood waiting against the back wall. "What's wrong?"

"Arzu Turan," he said. "It's a name. Turkish. Probably common for women in this area." He looked at Knight. "I don't think its part of the mother tongue."

"So we leave it out?"

"Replace it," Bishop said. "With Fiona Lane."

Knight understood what Bishop was getting at. If Fiona had overheard the phrase directed at someone else, she might not have recognized the first part as a name. And if it was a name, Arzu Turan may have been the poor soul on the receiving end of whatever these words did. It seemed Fiona had been, too, or at least she believed she would be when she scratched the words into the wall.

Bishop took a step back. "Okay, now blow it."

AS QUEEN RAN down the hallway, past the ancient armory, she glanced over her shoulder. The first of the big cats bounded into the hall behind her. The other two were close behind. Their muscles flexed with each leap forward. Their eyes focused on her, locked on target.

My God, they're fast, Queen thought. *Too damn fast!*

As she rounded the first of two corners that would take her back to the hallway where they'd left King and Alexander the cats had cut the distance between them in half. Queen knew she could shoot and kill all three animals if she had to, but to achieve maximum chaos, she needed them alive. So instead of shooting the beasts, she willed her limbs to move faster and prayed for a miracle.

She rounded the final corner, running as fast as she could. She could hear the giant lynx behind her, the soft pads of their feet thumping against the hard stone floor. With a final burst of speed, she lunged through the door and into the open chamber beyond.

* * *

FIONA HAD AIMED for his heart, but King had shifted his body to the side. The knife had come to rest between two ribs to the right of his heart and lungs. It hurt like a bastard, but had missed anything vital.

"You son of a bitch!" King shouted.

Ridley began to reply, but his voice was cut short by an explosion behind him. A cloud of dust and stone burst from a hallway at the side of the chamber.

Disoriented by the explosion, but not down, Mahaleel and Cainan began speaking the mother tongue, their words barely audible to King across the room, but the effect of their words became quickly apparent as the remaining eight statues began moving.

But then a new voice filled the room, loud and booming. It was Bishop, and like Mahaleel and Cainan, he was speaking the ancient language as well. "Fiona Lane. Vish tracidor vim calee. Filash vor der wash. Vilad forsh."

Ridley shook his head, recovering from the explosion. "Kill him!" he shouted at Fiona.

But the girl didn't move. King looked down at her and noticed a change in her eyes. She was looking up at him, first at the knife buried in his chest, which she still gripped with one hand, and then to King's eyes. Her lips quivered. She had returned. But with the return came a weakening. He saw her pale. Dark rings formed around her eyes.

"Kill him, now!"

Fiona looked back at the knife and whispered, "Sorry."

He was about to tell her it was okay, it wasn't her fault. But then he saw her hand grip the knife. She wasn't apologizing for what she'd done. She was apologizing for what she was *about* to do. And King knew exactly what that would be. While they hadn't let her fire a weapon at the range, they had shown her how to throw a knife. And she was good.

With the last of her energy, Fiona yanked the blade from King's chest, whirled around and sent it flying.

The blade buried itself into Ridley's thigh, sending him to the floor.

Fiona fell as well, her body curling up into a fetal position.

Using the distraction, King took aim to fire at Cainan, but a sudden pressure flexed his ribs where Fiona had stabbed him. The golem holding him tightened its grip. He shouted in pain, fighting against blacking out.

Alexander was being treated similarly, but as he fought the golem's grasp with his formidable physical strength and invulnerability, he looked more angry than in pain.

A blur of movement shot between the two men and entered the center stage.

Queen.

She ran straight past Fiona and launched herself into the air, diving over Ridley. King wondered why she would do that and got his answer a second later as three giant cats pounced into the room and dove on the nearest moving objects—two at golems and one at Ridley himself.

AFTER SHOUTING THE strange sentence Fiona had scrawled on her cell wall, reading the words from the small display screen on his camera, Bishop waited until he saw Fiona freed from control. Then he turned and ran back to the cell. Knight struggled to his feet. The impact had pounded his body, but unlike Bishop, he needed time to recover.

Despite the pain, Knight's mind was still on task. "Did it work?" he asked.

Bishop steadied Knight. "Whatever was done to her has been undone."

"Good," Knight said, standing on his own and lifting his weapon. "Let's get into this fight."

With his XM25 at the ready, Bishop moved toward the large chamber, now shaking with the sounds of battle, both human and feline. As he stepped into the space, followed by Knight, he was greeted by a giant stone golem with a lion's face.

Knight turned to backtrack, but a second golem with the face of a jackal, hunched in the hallway, pounded toward them.

"Back in the cell!" Bishop shouted.

Knight saw Bishop drop a live grenade at the lion-headed golem's feet and dove for the cell.

AS DARKNESS BEGAN to consume his vision King watched one of the big cats tackle a golem to the floor. A second cat was batted to the side, sliding across the floor and stopping at the far wall where it lay motionless. The third cat's leap through the air caught Ridley's attention. He looked up in horror.

But the cat never made it.

King fell to the floor, the pressure on his chest gone. He sucked in a deep breath and watched as the golem that had dropped him snagged the cat in midflight. The cat flailed and scratched with its large claws. Chunks of marble flew from the golem's body, but it did little good.

As the golem with the cat turned away from Ridley, King had to duck beneath its flailing hind legs. The cat fought for freedom. The sudden motion filled his oxygen-deprived vision with spots, forcing him to catch his breath.

Ridley was on the floor, just twenty feet away. Fiona lay between them.

With his face twisted with anguish and rage, Ridley quickly pulled the knife from his leg and rattled off a string of foreign words.

As his vision and head cleared, King watched Adam's body slide away and separate from Ridley's. The body was half a man, his small chest full of disfigured ribs, his torso tapering off to a twist of flesh like a tied-off balloon. King doubted the half-formed Ridley duplicate could have survived the separation even without the bullet hole in his skull.

But Ridley didn't see it that way.

"King!" Ridley's voice was a bestial roar.

The two men locked eyes.

"Kill him!" Ridley shouted, now staring beyond King.

The impact came quick, knocking King across the room. Only the padding provided by the giant cat's thick fur and his instinct to roll as he landed saved his life. He got back to his feet and immediately dove back down as the now-dead cat turned club sailed over him.

QUEEN ROLLED UPON landing and quickly gained her feet. The lab table next to her exploded into the air, smashed by a hawk-headed golem. As lab equipment rained down around her and the golem raised an arm to strike her, she took aim with the XM25, let the laser sight determine her target's distance, and pulled the trigger. Explosive rounds burst from the weapon, striking and exploding against the golem's marble head. Its blue eyes shattered. Its face disintegrated.

But still, it came for her, finishing the swing it began.

Queen ducked the arm that would have removed her head, but lost her weapon as it was struck and destroyed.

With a quick glance, she looked to the hallway where she hoped to see Bishop and Knight, but saw only another golem. Then the ground at its feet exploded, blowing off its leg and sending a cloud of shrapnel in her direction.

*   *   *

KNIGHT SHOOK HIS head, fighting against the ringing in his ears, and stood up. Dust fell from his head. He waved it away, coughing and turned to Bishop. "Good-bye perfect hearing, hello tinnitus."

The hallway swirled with dust, reducing visibility to only a few feet. There was no way to know what was out there, but they had no choice. They entered the hall, which was now full of dust. The golem blocking their exit lay in pieces, motionless. The second golem, however, emerged from the dust like a specter, still seeking them out.

The pair ran for the large chamber, having no idea what to expect. What they found was their worst-case scenario made real.

King was pinned against the back wall of the room, a golem charging toward him using one of the large cats as a club. Two more cats lay dead on the floor. Alexander was still clutched tight in the arms of a golem, whose continually crushing arms were now wearing down the ancient man. Queen lay on the floor, not far away, blood covering her face where a large stone fragment tossed by Bishop's grenade had struck her. She was down, but still conscious.

And the Ridleys, all three of them, stood at the center of the room, speaking the ancient language like conductors, orchestrating the actions of the nine remaining golems.

A new golem, whose face looked more like a demon than any living thing, turned toward Bishop.

Unless something drastic happened, there would be no escape for any of them. Knowing he couldn't kill Ridley with the weapon in his hand, Bishop dropped it and ran into the chamber. With killing Ridley impossible he hoped to distract the man enough to dull his control on the golems, or at the very least, turn their attention to him alone, giving the others a chance to escape.

As he leaped past Queen, she saw his hand reach into his shirt and pull out the crystal hidden beneath—the crystal that kept him from becoming an unstoppable killing machine. "Bishop, don't!" she shouted.

But it was too late. He'd already yanked the crystal loose and tossed it to her. A moment later, his raging wail turned all eyes on him.

Ridley's eyes widened as he instantly recognized the mania in Bishop's face as the curse he had created. Bishop, now a regen, charged straight for his maker.

EIGHTY-TWO

CAINAN, SEEING BISHOP running toward Ridley, but not fully compre-hending the rage in his eyes, moved to defend his creator. Being a golem, he felt no pain. Being modeled after Ridley, his size was formidable. But against a regen Bishop, he didn't stand a chance.

Bishop struck the clay-man like a vampire linebacker. His hands dug into Cainan's shoulders while his jaws clamped down on the man's throat, tearing out a chunk where the man's jugular should have been. With a mouthful of flesh turning to clay in his mouth, Bishop reached down and swiped a hand across Cainan's belly. It spilled open, dropping organs that turned to clay as they fell.

As Cainan's body began to lose its form, Bishop swiped into it again, tearing it in half. It fell to the floor as two large clumps of wet clay.

Bishop's eyes locked on the man's duplicate, staring at him with wide eyes. He lunged.

The man ran.

Raking his hands down Mahaleel's back, Bishop tore large chunks of flesh turned clay. The Ridley golem staggered forward and fell. Bishop took the man's leg in his hands and bit into it. The flesh turned to clay in his mouth.

Spitting the clay out, Bishop roared and turned on the third, and last Ridley. Fueled with bloodlust and anger toward the form of Ridley, he charged. Arms outstretched. Fingers bent like hooks. Drooling jaws open wide. He would tear Ridley apart, eating his flesh until his stomach burst. Then he would heal and continue his meal until Ridley's body had been consumed. But Ridley's flesh would regenerate as quickly as Bishop ate it and the two would continue in the vicious cycle indefinitely.

Fear gripped Ridley as he realized this potential outcome, but it was replaced by confidence. He had the knowledge to stop it.

As Bishop dove for his throat, Ridley shouted a string of words similar to those he had used to purge Adam from his body. It felt strange to be shouting words of healing at an attacking enemy, but it would stop the attack. Not only would Bishop's mind and moral compass return, but he'd no longer have his regenerative abilities. The man would be killable.

The effect was immediate.

Bishop's legs failed him and he fell to the floor before reaching Ridley. He shook his head and pushed himself up. He held his clay-covered hands up before his eyes. The taste of the stuff filled his mouth. Bishop looked at Ridley. "You . . . you cured me?"

Ridley grinned. "Just in time, it would seem."

A brute force struck Bishop from the side and sent him sprawling to the floor.

WITH RIDLEY'S LIFE in jeopardy, all the golems in the room had turned their attention to him. The first thing King saw was Knight, sneaking out of the side tunnel. He made a dash to the center of the room, moving fast, staying low, and drawing as little attention to himself as possible. He scooped up Fiona, saw her condition, and quickly produced the insulin shot he carried. He stabbed the needle into her leg and depressed the plunger. But there was no time to see if it would return the girl to them.

The two soldiers locked eyes.

"Get her out of here," King said.

Knight gave a quick nod and ran back the way he'd come.

Seeing Fiona's limp body in Knight's arms, filled him with an anger he'd never experienced before. It gripped his body and trained his mind on the man responsible for his girl's condition.

Ridley!

King acted quickly. He'd seen the way Bishop's grenade had worked on the golem and left one of his own behind as he made his escape.

The booming explosion from his grenade threw him forward. He landed between Queen, who was just getting back to her feet, and Bishop's weapon. He rolled to Bishop's weapon, picked it up, and fired a barrage at the golem still holding Alexander. The golem stumbled back as several rounds struck its arms.

Just as many rounds struck Alexander. He shouted in pain as his body was torn apart.

"What are you doing?" Queen shouted.

But King didn't answer. As the golem regained its balance Alexander had already healed from the wounds and pushed against the weakened arms. They shattered and exploded out.

Alexander—Hercules—was free.

And pissed.

He launched himself on the golem that had been holding him and tackled it to the ground, pummeling it with his fists, which were bloodied with each strike, but healed in time to strike again.

Queen's headless golem arrived, raising its arms to strike her down. She ducked down as King raised the XM25 and fired into the stone giant's midsection.

In the chaos, King saw the opportunity to create a clear path for the team to escape with Fiona.

There is no greater love than a father who is willing to lay down his life for his children.

He shouted to Queen over the barrage of bullets. "Get Bishop! Cover Knight and Fiona!"

Queen nodded and dove past the headless golem. As two more of the stone giants headed for her, she reached Bishop and yanked him up. He was conscious, but injured.

Injured.

"Snap out of it, big man," Queen shouted at him. "It's time to bug out!"

Bishop carried some of his weight, allowing Queen to help him toward the exit where Knight stood with Fiona over one shoulder and his XM25 in his hand. He raised the weapon, holding it with one arm, and fired.

The round zinged past Queen and struck the golem behind her. The impact slowed the golem, but came far from stopping it. And with Fiona over his shoulder, Knight could only fire one round at a time. Even a three-round burst might throw off his aim enough that he'd hit his teammates.

As Queen and Bishop reached him, they all rushed into the tunnel that led down at a steep grade. A golem filled the space behind them and squeezed itself into the tunnel. On its hands and knees, the fit was tight, but the golem paid the scraping of its marble body on the stone walls no heed. It pursued them relentlessly down the tunnel, toward the exit—

—an exit that Queen only now remembered had been sealed with a solid wall of stone.

THE HEADLESS GOLEM'S midsection gave in to the barrage of exploding rounds and cracked. The top-heavy torso fell away and smashed on the floor. King saw Queen, Bishop, Knight, and Fiona disappear into the exit tunnel, but one of the golems shoved itself in behind them and gave chase. He took aim at the second golem about to enter the tunnel and fired off a few rounds.

The golem turned toward him and stood.

"Duck!" came Alexander's voice.

King listened and felt a breeze rush by his head. A marble arm swished past and struck the wall next to him. He turned to rejoin Alexander, but found the large-bodied man flying through the air toward him. In his moment of distraction—saving King's life—the golem beneath Alexander had struck him hard.

The two warriors stood as the remaining six golems walled them in against the curved wall of the chamber. Behind them was a carving depicting five crude winged figures in the sky above a ziggurat that had to be Babel before it was buried beneath a pyroclastic flow.

Ridley stepped past the outer rings of golems. He looked at King and Alexander, knowing neither man posed a threat. His eyes trailed from the two men to the large carving behind them. Slowly, his countenance morphed from confidence to anger. He stepped back without a word and walked to the laptop that had somehow made it through the battle unscathed.

With a finger hovering over the keyboard's Enter key, Ridley turned to King. "Not every prophesy comes true, King."

What's he talking about? King thought. Alexander's hand on his shoulder turned him around. The big man pointed to the stone carving behind them. King looked at the image with a new perspective. It depicted a prophecy. Five angels descending over Babel. But were they angels or men? Were they wings . . . or parachutes? As King's eyes widened, a *click* whirled him around.

Ridley pushed the button.

The golems closed in.

EIGHTY-THREE

AS THE BULK of the golem pursuing them blocked the light from below, Queen couldn't determine the length of the tunnel. But she could see the hulking shape of the golem as he ground its way toward them.

With Bishop's weight supported by one of her arms, she yanked her night vision goggles from her neck with her free hand and placed them against her eyes. Looking down past Knight, who descended the incline with Fiona over one shoulder, she saw the end of the road seventy-five feet ahead.

If the golem caught them there they would all be pounded into oblivion.

She ran through their options.

C4 would take too long to rig.

A grenade in the tight confines of the tunnel might shred them.

Her eyes locked on Knight's weapon again. *It might work,* she thought, and said, "Knight, give me your XM."

Knight paused and shrugged his weapon from his shoulder and handed it back to Queen.

She nodded to Bishop. "Can you handle both of them?"

"You know I can," Knight said, and then took Bishop's weight off of her with a grunt.

Free of Bishop's bulk, Queen ran ahead, raised the XM25 to her shoulder, and pulled the trigger. The end of the tunnel lit up as it was struck by a ceaseless barrages of exploding rounds. A sound like thunder rolled down the tunnel. Queen ran forward, finger on the trigger, hoping to punch through the wall before she ran out of ammunition.

"I'LL GET THEIR attention," King said to Alexander. "You try to get Rid—"

But Alexander had his own ideas. He popped the cap from a small vial of black liquid and raised it to his lips. King recognized it as the adrenaline-boosting drink Alexander had taken back in Rome.

"Give me some," King said.

Alexander paused. "It could kill you."

"They're definitely going to kill me."

Alexander poured the liquid under his tongue and then quickly handed the bottle to King. There were a few drops left. Wasting no time, King shook the remaining drops under his tongue.

At first he felt nothing.

Then his heart beat hard, like a punch to his chest.

Then again.

And again.

It was like a monster had been unleashed beneath his rib cage. He felt his blood flow through his body, pulsing with energy. As the pressure grew stronger, a hot stinging covered his skin. The tiny blood vessels in his body were bursting.

Then the effect struck his mind.

He'd taken LSD once as a teenager. The mind-altering drug had nothing on this stuff. King viewed the world as though in slow motion, but not because things were moving slowly, his mind simply processed and reacted more quickly to his sensory input. And the energy flowing through his body gave him the ability to respond just as quickly.

The pain from his many wounds, including the deep stab wound, faded away, allowing him to react without pause.

And it saved his life as the nearest golem dove for him. King leaped in the air, and took hold of the top of the carving, pulling himself out of harm's way. Now above the golem he fired his weapon into its back, pulverizing a hole straight through. When the XM25 ran out of ammunition, King tossed it to the side.

Alexander barreled into the golem nearest him, striking it with a force King could never achieve. While he'd only had a few drops of Alexander's adrenaline booster, Alexander had taken almost the whole vial. Combined with his ability to heal, he was nearly as strong as the golems, and he was twice as fast. As the golem stumbled backward into a second, Alexander jumped back and looked for a weapon. He found it in the shattered remains of the golem King had blasted apart. He picked up the broken marble arm, wielding it like a club, and smiled.

Seeing him with the club, King recalled a statue he'd seen in Florence, Italy, depicting Hercules battling Caccus the Centaur. The sculptor had captured his likeness so accurately that King now wondered if Alexander had commissioned the sculpture himself.

A lizard-headed golem launched toward King. He reacted without thinking, diving toward the golem.

He sailed over its shoulder, wrapping an arm around its head as he passed. Holding on to the golem's head, he swung around, planting his feet on its back. With his hands gripping the lizard-headed golem beneath its chin, King used his whole body to yank the monster's head back. It bent back and reached its arms up, trying to grab hold of him. But the movement combined with King on its back threw off its center of gravity.

As the golem fell back, King pushed off hard with his feet.

Too hard.

The elixir that had boosted his speed and strength had not made his body more durable. He had jumped farther than he could have ever done before, but at the sacrifice of one of his ankles, which shattered from the intense pressure.

Distracted by the sharp pain shooting up his leg, King slammed into the body of a devil-headed golem and fell at its feet. In his dazed state he barely registered the giant foot rising up above him, but it seemed that with his mind in hyperdrive, that small perception was all he needed to react. He rolled away just as the giant foot slammed into the stone floor.

QUEEN CONTINUED HER charge toward the sealed exit. She had no idea if anyone had fallen behind, or if the golem had caught them. She was focused solely on the task of punching through the wall. But with the shaft now full of dusty debris, she couldn't see the wall, just the bright explosions from her XM25 rounds.

Then a light cut through the dust like a lighthouse beacon. She aimed at the small fissure and unloaded. The light grew larger with each exploding round until a large portion of the wall fell away, big enough for them to fit through.

Queen stopped by the hole and looked back. Knight was right behind her, still holding Fiona. Bishop followed him, walking on his own now, but looked beaten and tired. But the golem was there, too, still forcing its way up the tight passage. She waved Knight through, and then Bishop. She followed them into the bright light of day.

Knight kept moving, somehow knowing that the chase was far from over. Bishop fell to one knee, gripping his chest.

"Can't breathe," he said.

"Hang on," Queen said. She wrapped her arms under Bishop's armpits and dragged him down the mountainside. A few seconds later, the remainder of the tunnel's stone seal exploded out. It rained down around them like hail.

When it cleared, a fifteen-foot marble giant stood above them. It looked even more fearsome in the light of day.

"Let me go," Bishop said as Queen continued to drag his body, which was nearly twice the size of her own. "You can make it without me."

Queen never got a chance to tell Bishop to shut the fuck up. The golem took two steps toward them, cutting the distance between them in half.

And then it stopped.

Slowly, it turned its head back toward the tunnel like it saw something within, or sensed something wrong. *What's happening in there?* Queen thought, as she continued to run backward.

Knight shouted into his throat mic. "This is Knight. We have Pipsqueak. Requesting immediate evac!"

With a UH-100S Stealth Blackhawk transport helicopter flown by a pilot from the Nightstalkers circling nearby, Queen knew they would make it. But as she looked back at the black tunnel, she wondered about King. Would the team lose its leader? Would Fiona lose her father?

THE GOLEM BENT down for him, its stone fingers separating and reaching out. A blur of marble crashed down on the arm, shattering it. For a moment, King thought the golems were attacking each other, but then Alexander flashed into view, slamming his body into the golem. He was covered in his own blood, but as he turned to King and reached out his hand, he appeared unharmed.

As King stood on his one good foot, he felt a painful throb in his chest. He grit his teeth and pitched forward. *Alexander was right,* he thought. *That stuff is killing me.*

But then he saw Ridley retreating toward the back of the chamber. Seeing King and Alexander holding their own against the stone giants must have sapped his confidence. If they lost him he might escape into the very earth itself.

But there was something else he needed to do before hunting down Ridley. King drew a throwing knife and took aim at the laptop, which showed a spinning blue circle at its center. Hoping the computer was still in the process of transmitting the audio file that would change the human race into a giant Ridley cult, he took aim. He knew hitting the screen wouldn't necessarily stop the computer from working. And piercing the base from this angle was impossible. So he aimed for the only critical weak spot he could think of and let the knife fly.

The blade flew through the air, spinning rapidly. It passed over its target, but as the blade spun up, its razor sharp edge hit home and easily sliced through the network cable. The line to the outside world was cut.

King turned away from the computer to find three golems closing in. Beyond them, Ridley was making his getaway. King turned to Alexander and shouted, "Throw me!"

King pointed to Ridley and Alexander immediately understood. He took King by the back of his bulletproof vest and his belt, spun quickly, and with a loud grunt, threw King into the air.

King soared above the golems, out of their reach as he arced over the center of the chamber. He passed over one of the glowing orbs, feeling its heat on his body. Looking down he saw a large, dark brown stain on the floor. He recognized it as the blood of some ancient man who had died here. And then he was falling, dropping like a cannon ball aimed at Ridley's back. King drew the only weapon he had left, his seven-inch KA-BAR knife.

He heard Alexander's voice in his mind.

Take off his head. Burn the flesh.

King pulled his arm back, ready to strike.

Pain gripped his chest again. He fought it, refusing to curl up, eyes focused on the back of Ridley's neck.

Their bodies struck hard as King fell. A blur of motion. A tangle of limbs.

King hit the floor with a loud crack and rolled like a rag doll. He slid to a stop with his legs over Ridley's motionless torso.

Alexander saw the collision and held his breath.

It seemed the golems did as well. Their attack stopped.

And then Alexander saw why. Richard Ridley's head rolled into view, severed from his body by King's blade. A pool of blood so dark it almost looked black spilled from the headless body.

Alexander rushed past the dumbstruck golems and ignored King's body. He took Ridley's head in his hands and looked at the face. His eyes twitched madly. His mouth opened and closed, trying to suck in air like a fish out of water. Though his mind was overwhelmed with the pain of suddenly missing its body, Ridley was alive. And as the first tendrils of skin expanded from the neck, Alexander knew he would regenerate if given enough time and liquid.

He stood and ran to one of the small orbs still lighting the room and held the head up to it. Flesh crackled and popped as the super hot light cooked Ridley's exposed neck. As Alexander took the head down to inspect his handiwork, the air filled with the smell of broiled flesh and the sound of a whispering voice.

Alexander spun, looking for the source. King was still lying limp on the floor. Ridley had no lungs to force air past his voice box. The golems remained motionless. Then he saw him, lying on the floor with his back gouged out. One of the clay golems made in Ridley's image spoke a final string of words and then grinned.

A violent shaking sent Alexander to the floor. The whole mountain churned violently. As he regained his footing, he looked up and saw the small orb above him shrinking. But it wasn't dimming, it was growing brighter. The implications struck him quickly.

The tiny stars were growing dense, reducing in size as their gravity intensified. The energy inside them would magnify until each one went supernova.

EIGHTY-FOUR

QUEEN STUMBLED AND fell back. Bishop landed hard on top of her. The mountain shook beneath them. As she pulled herself free from Bishop's body she felt less sure of their escape. With the Blackhawk still several minutes out, they were sitting ducks on a barren mountainside. Ridley had obviously set something large in motion, and that was never a good thing.

There was no time to wonder, though. The mountain above the tunnel entrance began to crumble, sending large boulders tumbling toward them. She hefted Bishop back up and continued pulling him down the mountain.

A large boulder bounced over the tunnel entrance and headed for the golem. It did nothing to avoid the impact and shattered into pieces when it struck. The boulder broke as well, sending a shower of grit down the mountainside.

Within the cloud of debris, Queen saw something that gave her equal parts hope and dread. Alexander ran out of the tunnel looking as strong as ever. But he held King's limp body over one shoulder and a thick satchel over the other. They had made it out, but at what cost? King's lifeless arms dangled.

As Alexander gained on her, he waved for her to move faster and shouted, "The whole mountain's going to explode!" Then he had an arm under Bishop and hoisted the man up, continuing to run down the mountainside with both men over his shoulders.

Queen, despite being free to run at full speed found keeping up with Alexander a challenge. Even with five hundred pounds of Delta operators in his arms, he ran without slowing.

A deep, resonating rumble filled the air. The small stones on the mountainside bounced like manic jumping beans. As they reached the bottom slope, a wave of pressure knocked them off their feet. But the force had not pushed them from behind, it had been sucked past them—*toward* the mountain.

They all looked back as the mountain collapsed in on itself.

Alexander squinted. It was not the result he had expected.

"It imploded," Knight said.

"Why?" Alexander wondered aloud.

A grinding movement deep within the ruined mountainside answered his question. It stood slowly, as though awakening from an ancient sleep. Standing more than one hundred feet tall, the golem, as featureless as it was immense, stepped out of the crater and turned its flat face toward them. It was a mix of old mountain, hardened pyroclastic flow, and the ruins of Babel.

When it took its first step, its stumplike foot dented the solid stone mountainside.

"It's super dense," Alexander said.

"What?" Queen said. "How?"

"The small stars. They were collapsing when I left. I thought they would go supernova, but instead their gravity drew the stone in, compressing it."

"Ridley did this?" Knight asked.

"One of his duplicates."

"Where is Ridley?" Queen asked.

"Headless," Alexander said, then met Queen's doubt-filled eyes. "He's inside. Buried." He turned to Knight. "Forever."

The mountainside shook as the giant stepped toward them. With its gait covering twenty-five feet, it would only take the golem a moment to reach them.

Knight tried to stand, but the violently shaking earth stumbled him.

Escape was impossible.

Knight tightened his grip on Fiona and felt her move. *Not now,* he thought, *don't wake up now.*

But a sharp crack launched her upright.

She looked up at the source of the sound through squinted eyes. The stealth Blackhawk was circling the giant, peppering it with a stream of bullets from its side-mounted minigun. The barrage glowed like an orange laser beam thanks to the bright tracer rounds. But the thousands of rounds striking the giant did nothing more than scratch its face. The golem swung its arm out, forcing the copter to bank away.

Fiona looked up at Knight and saw his worried eyes looking back at her. She looked to the side and saw Queen on the ground beside Bishop, whose face was twisted in pain. She saw Alexander next and then King, laying on the ground, his eyes closed.

She tried standing up, but Knight stood and held her tight. "I'm taking her. Going for the Blackhawk."

But Fiona fought against him, thrashing and shouting, "No!" Her voice was raspy, but clear.

She broke free of his grasp and hobbled to King's side. Her vision faded for a moment as she fell over his body. She pressed herself into him, head on his chest. With her eyes closed she ignored the voice of Knight pleading with her, the boom of the golem's footsteps, and the chop of the Blackhawk.

And she heard the one thing she needed to hear—King's heartbeat.

She stood on wobbly legs and turned toward the giant golem. Her dark hair billowed in the wind. The team watched in amazement as this thirteen-year-old girl stepped *toward* the golem.

The golem turned its head toward her, stomping forward. It would reach her in five more steps.

In a voice as loud as she could muster, Fiona shouted, "Tisioh fesh met!"

The golem reacted immediately.

Its knees buckled and fell apart.

Its arms fell away and crashed to the ground.

And its torso and head fell forward, crashing to the sloped mountainside and sliding to the bottom where their super dense weight buried them into the soft soil of the valley—just fifteen feet from where Fiona stood.

Fiona collapsed, falling on top of King's chest. She clutched him as she lost consciousness, listening to the sound of his heartbeat and the chop of the approaching Blackhawk.

EIGHTY-FIVE
Barents Sea

COLD AIR WHIPPED against Rook's face, frosting moisture onto his blond beard. But he remained at the bow of the ship, gloved hands on the rail. They had been at sea for three days and he had endured the presence of the *Songbird*'s two passengers—and the whimpered cries of their prisoner—long enough. With their voyage to Norway nearly at an end, it was time to act. On his way to the deck, he'd stared down one of the men and then laughed at him. Mocking him.

The man showed no reaction, other than watching Rook leave. But the insult wouldn't go unanswered. Not by these two. Rook knew he could have simply shot the men. He still had his Desert Eagle. But he wanted the confrontation to look unprovoked. He wasn't sure how Dashkov would react if Rook killed them outright. But if it was self-defense . . .

A moment later, Rook heard the cabin door open. Two sets of footsteps walked casually across the deck. The killers were confident. Relaxed.

Rook held up a pack of cigarettes he'd borrowed from Dashkov. "Smoke?"

"Not today," one of the men said.

Their footsteps grew closer. Too close to shoot. *These guys really are old school*, Rook thought. He guessed the plan. Stab him in the back.

Maybe whisper some parting words. And then shove him overboard. They'd probably done it before.

So when the nearest man paused to aim his strike, Rook spun. The thrust blade passed by his abdomen and beneath his arm. Rook took the attackers forearm, pulled him closer, wrapped his free hand around the man's neck, and hurled him overboard.

The second man roared with anger and charged. Though he was probably a good fighter in his day, the man was slow and couldn't match Rook's reach. Rook's fist slammed head on into the man's nose. The man stumbled back, ignoring the gouts of blood pouring from his ruined face, and drew a pistol.

But once again, Rook was too quick. He kicked the weapon from the man's hand and elbowed him in the chest. The man stumbled back and landed against the rail. Wasting no time, Rook took the man by his feet and flipped him, ass over teakettle, into the freezing arctic waters.

A third set of footsteps approached from behind. Rook turned.

Dashkov flicked his lighter and held it out to Rook.

"I don't smoke," Rook said, handing the pack of cigarettes to the man.

Rook could read the man's questioning glance and pointed to the pack. Dashkov looked at the cigarettes and found a small mirror fragment taped to it. When Rook held the pack up, he'd got a peek at both men.

Dashkov shook his head with a laugh. "What took you so long?"

"You don't mind?"

"I'm not a bad man, Stanislav." He smiled. "And they paid up front."

"And if someone comes looking for them?"

"I'll tell the truth, that I dropped them off and haven't seen them since."

Both men laughed at this.

"I think their plan was to disappear anyway," Dashkov said. "Along with the girl."

"How long until we reach our stop?"

"Two hours."

Rook smiled and headed for the cabin door. "I'll go cut her loose and give her the good news."

ROOK STOOD AT the rail once again, the newly freed woman by his side. She had wavy black hair cut to her shoulders. Her body was feminine and in great shape. Her dark brown eyes shown with intelligence and despite the wounds inflicted to her face, she was still quite striking, not to mention familiar. But he couldn't place what was familiar about her and didn't dwell on it.

She had offered a quiet "Thank you" after being freed, but hadn't said a word since. When she saw land ahead, she turned to Rook and again said, "Thank you."

"Do you need any help once we land?" Rook asked.

For a moment he thought she wouldn't reply, but then she spoke. "I'll be fine."

She spoke with a confidence that convinced Rook she would be. "Sorry," he said.

She turned to him, confused. "For what?"

"Not freeing you sooner."

She shrugged. "These things happen."

There it was again. The familiarity. Something in the casual shrug. Or was it the indifference to being bound and tortured?

She noted his attention. "What?"

"I feel like we've met before," he said.

After looking him up and down, she said, "No."

He wasn't convinced. "What's your name?"

"Asya," she said. "Asya Machtcenko."

Nope. Didn't ring a bell.

He turned back to the rail, looking at a small Norwegian village in the distance. The collection of small buildings looked like they couldn't support a population of more than a thousand. There was a single line of electrical wires leading into the town and only two roads. A long pier stretching out into the ocean held ten fishing boats.

Dashkov rested his elbows on the rail to Rook's right. "You don't want to go there. Let me take you a bit further. To civilization."

"Why?" Rook asked as he glanced down at the flask in Dashkov's hand. "Is it a dry town?"

The man didn't laugh. "It is a cursed place."

Rook turned to him. "Cursed by what?"

"Wolves," he said. "Even out here you will hear them howl at night."

"Wolves aren't so bad," Rook said. As a native of New Hampshire, he had a long love affair with the outdoors, and the idea of living among wolves, no matter how afraid people were of them, appealed to him.

"You wouldn't say that if you heard them," Dashkov said. "I have never felt such fear."

"Superstitions," Asya said with a shake of her head. She wasn't buying it either.

"If it's so bad, why does anyone live there at all?" Rook asked.

Dashkov shrugged. "I have not stopped to ask. No one does."

"Then it's safe to say not many people visit?"

The fisherman frowned and nodded begrudgingly. He could see Rook making up his mind. He placed a hand on Rook's shoulder. "Please, Stanislav. I will not come back for you here."

Rook looked at the shoreline, frigid and barren. The town appeared empty, though a few lights glowed in windows. The place was quiet, and despite Dashkov's tales of frightful wolves, peaceful.

"*No one* will come for you," Dashkov added.

Rook looked back at his new friend. "That's the idea."

Dashkov looked beyond Rook and met the eyes of Asya. She nodded. The village was the perfect starting point for both of them. He pocketed his flask and headed back to the pilothouse. "I would look the other way one last time, Stanislav. For you. For Galya."

Rook tilted his head in thanks. "That's all I ask."

EIGHTY-SIX
Washington, D.C.

THE FIFTH-FLOOR WINDOW provided a view of the oval courtyard in front of the Walter Reed Army Medical Center. Queen stared out the window, arms crossed over her chest. Dressed in jeans and an army green T-shirt, she looked like any other concerned family member of someone in the armed services, with one blazing exception. The red star-and-skull brand on her forehead glowed in the late-day sun.

Knight sat in a chair next to her, feet up on the hospital bed next to him. He, too, was dressed casually, as casual as he dressed, in a black button-down shirt and black slacks. He looked down to his chest where Fiona's head rested. It had been five days since the events in Turkey, and Fiona had been cleared to leave her room that morning. After four days on an IV, eating nonstop and receiving her glucose-balancing insulin, she had made a full recovery. She'd spent the day with Knight and Queen keeping vigil over Bishop and King, who were not recovering as quickly. In desperation, she had tried to remember the healing words Ridley had used, but could not remember the phrase. In fact, all traces of the language had been destroyed. The speakers of all the languages on earth that contained fragments of the mother tongue were dead, except for Fiona. All of the physical evidence Ridley collected had been condensed and destroyed within the super-dense golem's body. Even Bishop's camera, which held an image of the phrase Fiona scrawled on the wall had been destroyed in the battle. Nothing remained. The mother tongue had been buried deeper than ever before.

Losing hope, Fiona had spent the majority of the morning crying over King before falling asleep on Knight.

Bishop had several broken ribs, one of which had punctured a lung, a fractured collarbone, and more than a few bruised organs. After a round of surgeries he'd been wrapped up tight and placed in a bed. But he was expected to leave within the week.

King, on the other hand, would not be recovering soon. If ever. The prognosis was grim. No one knew exactly what had happened to him—Alexander had disappeared shortly after their hurried departure from Turkey and returned to Iraq—but his symptoms were varied and extreme. His heart appeared scarred. Many of his veins had burst, leading to intense internal bleeding throughout his body, and in his brain. The resulting coma, according to the doctors, might be permanent, especially with the physical damage to his body being irreparable. On top of that, he had a shattered ankle, which was now bound in a liquid cast, and a four-inch-deep stab wound.

Fiona wished she had no memory of what she'd done while under Ridley's control, but she remembered it all. Trapping Knight and Bishop. Stabbing King. But the worst memory was that of adoring Ridley. She remembered the joy of hearing his voice, of following his orders. Stabbing King at that moment was the happiest moment of her life. Until Bishop undid the spell. As her mind returned to her, all the bliss faded away, replaced by seething hate. She was dealing with the emotion now, seeking guidance from Queen and Knight, but also seeing a therapist.

Given the clandestine nature of their mission, family and friends hadn't been notified of their return until that morning. Rook's family was hit hard as they learned he was officially missing in action. As were George Pierce and Sara Fogg when they learned of King's condition. Sara was still stuck in Africa, but would be returning in a few days. Pierce had hopped on the first available flight and would be arriving shortly. But the people everyone thought would be most eager to hear word of King, his parents, had not yet been reached. They'd been tried at their hotel room and at their home with no luck.

Queen, Bishop, and Knight had waited in silence for the next shoe to drop. Only they and a few other people in the administration knew it was coming, but they understood why it had to be done. With new strange and violent enemies cropping up around the world, Deep Blue and the Chess Team needed to respond without encumbrance, without public attention. And there was only one way to achieve that goal. It would be the greatest sacrifice of Duncan's life, but to truly protect the people who had elected him to office, it was the best course of action.

Bishop picked up the remote from his bed and unmuted the TV mounted on the corner of the room. The voice of the reporter speaking on screen was excited. "We're just moments away from President Duncan's impromptu address to the nation. There has been a lot of speculation about what he'll say. Since Senator Marrs revealed evidence that the president knew about the impending attacks on the Siletz Reservation and Fort Bragg and not only failed to act, but refused to act, he has remained silent behind the walls of the White House, giving no indication about his intentions. As the investigation proceeds, streamlined by CIA director Dominick Boucher's full disclosure, the president's options may be limited and out of his hands. Many expect him to fight the charges, but Boucher himself has asked for the president to step down."

"This is bullshit," Queen said.

"He's doing the right thing," Knight said.

"This is how it has to be," Bishop said. "He understands that."

Queen crossed her arms over her chest. "Doesn't mean I have to like it."

The reporter held his hand to his ear. "Okay, the president is taking the stage. We now go live to the White House."

The image cut to an empty podium. Duncan took the stage looking very serious, but well. His posture was straight. This wasn't a defeat for him, it was a transition. To something new. Possibly something better. He

paused before the microphone, looked over the gathered sea of reporters, and spoke in a clear voice. "As the president of the United States, I
swore to protect this nation from all enemies. In this endeavor, I have
failed. I have made mistakes that are unforgivable." He paused and faced
the camera. "Some have said the president of this country is the leader of
the free world. I would disagree with that. I represent the people of this
country and as such it is you who are the leaders of the free world. And
you need someone who represents you . . . better than I have."

He paused again. "As of nine o'clock this morning I have resigned as
the President of the United States—" A loud murmur became a torrent of
shouted questions as the press corps could no longer contain themselves. Duncan raised his voice over the din. "Vice President Chambers
is now the president and he will answer your questions."

With that, Duncan stepped down. The white-haired former vice president shook his hand and then took the stage.

Bishop shut the TV off.

In the silence that followed, Bishop, Queen, and Knight immediately
became aware of a presence in the room. They turned to find George
Pierce standing over King's unconscious form—holding an empty syringe.

Queen stormed toward him. "What the hell are you doing!"

Pierce held his hands up defensively, still holding the syringe. "Trying to help."

Queen snatched the syringe from his hand. "What was in this?"

"You won't understand."

"Try me."

"An . . . an apple seed. Crushed. Liquefied."

She whipped the syringe into a nearby trash can. It shattered inside.
"You injected King with an *apple seed*?"

"From the Garden of the Hesperides. But I'm not really even sure they
are apple seeds."

The name of the garden sounded familiar to Queen, but she continued her death stare at Pierce. She knew the man would never intention-
ally hurt King. They were like brothers. But desperate people sometimes
make deadly mistakes.

"I got them from Alexander."

Queen's temper flared. "Alexander!"

Pierce took a step back and found Queen more intimidating than a
golem. "I stole it. In Rome. From Alexander's gallery."

Queen knew the story, how they found Alexander beneath the ruins of the Roman Forum. She took a deep breath and eased back. "Did you test it?"

"I only had enough to—"

"Can you two be quiet, please?" Fiona stood behind Queen rubbing her eyes. Knight stood behind her, urging Queen to calm down with his hands.

Queen shook her head and stepped back. "Sorry, kid."

Fiona stepped to King's bed and climbed up into it. Laying next to King, her wiry body dressed in pink sweatpants and a Powerpuff Girls T-shirt, Fiona looked more fragile than ever. But they all knew she was strong. She had proven that when she had faced down a one-hundred-foot-tall golem and saved all their lives.

"Remember, he can hear what we're saying," Fiona said. She turned to King's face and said, "I love you, Dad." She snuggled into him and felt a hand on her back, squeezing her tight.

She opened her eyes slowly as the realization of whose hand was holding her set in. George Pierce stood on the other side of the bed, his face smiling, his eyes wet. Then King's other arm reached up and wrapped around her. She buried her face into his chest with a sob.

King was alive.

Her father was alive.

King opened his eyes. He saw Pierce first and grinned. "I heard what you said. Alexander won't be happy if he finds out."

Pierce shrugged. "What's he gonna do?"

King surveyed the room, seeing Knight and Queen. Then he looked over at Bishop and eyed his mass of bandages. "No more regeneration?"

"No more regen," Bishop said with a smile. "It's gone."

"And Rook?" King asked, looking at Queen.

"No word," she said with a frown.

As he ran his fingers through Fiona's hair, he asked her, "You're okay?"

She just squeezed him in response.

"The docs gave her a clean bill of health this morning," Knight said.

King's eyes drifted around the room again, looking beyond the group. "Where are my parents? Do they know?"

"We haven't been able to reach them," Knight said.

As egocentric as it was, King knew his parents would be waiting by the phone for news. His mother always did when she knew he was deployed.

And with them knowing exactly what he was up against and who he was fighting for, she would have—

A burst of panic made King feel queasy. He sat up straight. "Do I have any clothes?"

Fiona grinned. "I made them bring some. Just in case." She pointed to the dresser across from the bed. On top sat his signature jeans and black Elvis T-shirt. He began to get out of bed.

"What are you doing?" Queen asked. "You just came out of a coma."

King stood, steady, tall, and healthy. "Whatever he gave me has me back to normal. A little better than normal, actually, and I need to leave."

King lifted his leg and unbuckled the liquid cast. After it fell to the floor, he wiggled his ankle. The apple seed was like a single dose of regeneration. He stood and bounced his weight on his legs. Never better.

"Where are you going?" Pierce asked.

"It's likely there are other Ridley golems out there. If they know about my parents—"

He didn't have to finish. Queen stepped out of his way. "I'm coming."

"Me, too," Knight said.

King turned to Pierce as he took his clothes to the bathroom. He motioned to Fiona and then to Bishop. "Keep an eye on them."

Thirty seconds later, King was dressed, leaving the hospital and a string of stunned doctors and nurses behind him.

Twenty minutes later, Knight pulled his car into the parking lot of the hotel in which King's parents had been hidden away. He pulled into a space and turned off the car. "They're in two-twenty."

Knight and Queen took out their sidearms and chambered rounds. "Have an extra?" King asked.

"Glove compartment."

King opened it and found a Sig Sauer.

They exited the car and vaulted up the stairs to the second floor. King quickly led the way to room two-twenty. He paused outside the door, letting Knight and Queen take positions on the other side, just in case.

King knocked.

No answer.

He knocked again. Harder. Followed by, "Mom. Dad. It's Jack."

He tried the doorknob and found it locked.

"I'll do it," Queen whispered. She stood across from the door and slammed it with her foot. Wood shattered from the powerful blow and the door swung inward.

King moved in. Weapon raised. Prepared for anything.

Except what he found.

There were two queen-sized beds in the room. On each lay a blood-soaked human body.

King launched forward and flipped over the nearest body, dead for days. But the man was not one of his parents. Nor was the other body. Both men held weapons. And both had been shot through the head. King remembered the story his mother had told him, about shooting the man who had come for them. It now seemed all the more believable.

But the fact that these men were dead didn't supply any hope. There was no way to know how many assailants there had been. And his parents were gone, perhaps dead, dying, or on the run.

King and Queen checked the bodies for identification, Knight searched the bathroom.

As Queen rifled through the dead man's pockets, she spotted a necklace poking out from under one of the beds. She picked it up and looked if over—a silver chain and cross. The cross design was simple and held a small black stone in the middle.

King saw it dangling. His eyes widened as he reached out for the necklace.

She handed it to him. "Recognize it?"

"Yeah," King said. "It was Julie's."

As he looked the necklace over, memories of it around his sister's neck came back to him. It had been a gift from their father. After she died in the plane crash, his mother wore it. Every day. He'd never seen her take it off. But here it was, on the floor.

King unclipped the chain, wrapped it around his neck, and refastened it. With the necklace hidden beneath his shirt, he turned to Queen. "Call it in."

Queen nodded, switched on her cell, and left the room.

"King," Knight called from the bathroom. "Check this out."

The bathroom looked normal until Knight stepped to the side, revealing the sink. A board had been placed atop the basin, serving as a workspace. The makeshift countertop held several small electronic components, spools of impossibly thin wires, miniature microchips, a magnifying glass, soldering tools, and pill-sized capsules. Knight picked up one of the completed devices and handed it to King.

A mixture of confusion, anger, and sadness filled King as he looked at the tiny device that perfectly matched the tracking device he'd found hidden in his pocket. His chest ached as the memory of his last good-bye with his parents returned. His mother's firm embrace. The slow slide of her hand against his side as they separated.

His mother had bugged him.

Betrayed him.

"What do you think?" Knight asked.

It pained him to say it, but he couldn't deny the evidence. "My parents are still Russian spies, and they almost got us killed."

As his mind raced to put together any missing pieces, anything he'd missed, something else nagged at him. Some other unanswered question. Then he remembered. Turning to Knight, he asked, "What happened to Ridley?"

EPILOGUE
Somewhere

THE TEN-FOOT-SQUARE CELL was empty, save for a single chair and its occupant, a prisoner, and his interrogator. The man in the chair was gagged—jaw spread wide holding a red ball gag. He was strapped to the chair around the chest and waist. There was no need to bind his arms and legs because he had neither.

His interrogator walked around him in lazy circles. "This can end whenever you want it to."

The man's shouted reply was muffled and distorted, but the tone was defiant.

The interrogator chuckled and jabbed a finger into the open wound where the man's shoulder should have been.

The man wailed in horrible pain as the interrogator twisted his finger deeper into the flesh until it struck the man's rib cage.

"Whenever you want it to end . . ."

A sucking pop filled the air as the finger was quickly extracted from the meat.

The man screamed again.

"You're probably wondering how this is possible?"

The man made no reply other than his heavy breathing.

"The Hydra can't regenerate without a sufficient supply of water, which it can leach from the air itself on a humid day. You were given enough water for your torso to regenerate, but without more, you will remain a quadruple amputee. The pain you're feeling is your dry cells screaming out for fluid. You can't even bleed. As you've probably noticed, the air in this cell is not only hot, but also very dry. Your wounds will remain open indefinitely. Your bones will not heal. Your mind will not rest. The pain will never dull."

The interrogator crouched before the legless torso, looking at the fragment of femur protruding from the man's partially formed thigh. He grasped the bone with two fingers and wiggled it.

The prisoner's breathing sped up.

"You *will* tell me everything about the language of God."

The interrogator quickly slid his finger inside the bone, pushing hard, compressing the marrow.

A fit of spasms shook the prisoner. His voice became a high-pitched shriek. But when the finger was removed, his face twisted with rage. He shouted a string of muffled curses.

The interrogator simply smiled and stood. He leaned forward, placing his hands on the arms of the chair. He looked the prisoner in the eyes. "Perhaps you haven't fully grasped the situation, Mr. Ridley. I am *not* who you believe me to be. I am not who your enemies believe me to be. And I can do this until the end of time, can you?"